D0499988

THE STORY OF LEX AND LIVIA

TIME OF THE TWINS

KENDALL & KYLIE JENNER
and
ELIZABETH KILLMOND-ROMAN
& KATHERINE KILLMOND

Regan Arts.
NEW YORK

Regan Arts.
65 Bleecker Street
New York, NY 10012

First Regan Arts hardcover edition, November 2016

Library of Congress Control Number: 2016954997

ISBN 978-1-68245-007-9

Cover design by Louise Mertens and Richard Ljoenes

Printed in the United States of America

10 9 8 7 6 5 4 3 2 1

This book is dedicated to our fans.

You are always there for us.

We love you!

PROLOGUE

The group of twenty men and women sit around a large table, squeezed tightly together, in a room barely large enough to accommodate them. The ceiling is low, like all rooms in this underground world, where space is limited. The air has quickly become warm and stifling.

Atros stands in front of the assembled group, his lean figure composed to appear relaxed, his fingers loosely interlaced. He has handpicked these twenty people, the most powerful of their society, the elite. He must make them his allies. Though he has only reached the midpoint of his life, and most of them are older, he is not intimidated. He must convince them his plan is the only way for them to keep the power and prestige they have. This should not be difficult. People with power never want to lose it. They always want more. That is the way of greed and ego. Atros knows this well. He is a man who knows how to persuade, to dominate, and to control those around him.

In his commanding voice, Atros says, "I have called you all here for one reason, our future. My exploratory team of scientists and engineers on the surface has made great strides in a short time. Though the atmosphere above is still hostile, they have erected a dome under which they have safely lived for weeks. It is my dream, my vision, that we will build a great city under a dome. I have engineers working on plans to expand the dome to accommodate the city we will build. They assure me it is possible."

An older, distinguished man at the table interrupts, "So your twin brother, Andru, was right. We can live above the ground."

Atros locks his keen eyes on the man and replies, "My brother's idea of living aboveground was limited. He thought only of breaking through to the surface, not what to do after. He would have pushed for freedom over control. He would have stood in the way of progress. That is not the path to greatness. He was an obstacle, and I did what was necessary to ensure that the future would move forward in the right way."

The man continues, "But he was right. Maybe he didn't have to die in order for your vision to be fulfilled. It was most unpleasant. Brother killing brother."

Atros raises his hand to stop him and looks around the room at the group menacingly. "In Andru's vision of the future, everyone would live aboveground. We all agreed Andru's altruistic ideas were unrealistic and would undermine the structure we have worked so hard to build. We decided he had to be stopped. You all knew what that meant. I did what had to be done. Everyone in this room was complicit." He pauses, his eyes scanning the faces around the table. "With the resources held by those in this room, we can design and build a city worthy of us. In time, more can move aboveground, but it must be slow and controlled. Resources will still be limited. As we expand the dome and build the city, we will bring up those who work for us and support our way of life."

A woman, very pale, with almost translucent blue eyes from a lifetime without sun, asks, "How long will we have to live under this dome? I'm sure I do not speak just for myself when I say that although this dome sounds better than being trapped underground, to have to live under anything is not appealing. Will the outside world ever be safe?"

Atros passionately explains, "Madam, the dome will give us control. It will be the key, so we are never again at the mercy of the Earth and its whims. I envision a world where anything is possible for generations to come. We will be the creators of the food, air, and energy. Under the dome there is potential for estates and grand structures of beauty like our ancestors before us had. With our guidance, the mistakes of our forefathers will never be repeated."

A man similar in age to Atros corrects him, "It was not just the Earth that drove mankind underground after the Great Catastrophe. The mistakes of man were many."

Atros replies, "That is why I have chosen you to be the founding members of the new High Council. So weak, single-minded men and women will never again be able to destroy what we will create. There will be a system and structure, and our families will be the royal bloodlines of our new city, making sure generation after generation prospers under the dome. It is time to build up. My brother broke the surface, but I will bend it to my will, and anyone who stands in my way will meet the same fate he did. I will not allow anyone to stop the birth of this new world, which will be called Indra."

1

Lex & *Livia Cosmo*

Livia holds Lex's hand tightly in hers, both of them wearing packs on their backs as they head down the tunnel toward the bright light. Livia looks at Lex, just a quick glance. *I can't believe I'm escaping from Indra with my sister. My twin! We are going to meet our mother in the Outlands. Yesterday I didn't even know Lex existed and I thought my mother was dead.* She reaches out to sense how Lex is feeling. *I have always been able to know what people are feeling, but my gift is particularly strong with Lex. She is quite tense, understandable since we are running from the Population Control Forces.*

"Are you all right?" Livia asks Lex.

"Yeah. I'm fine," says Lex. "Can we not hold hands?"

"I thought we should, since we are sisters." Livia releases Lex's hand.

"Well, since we just met yesterday and I wanted to kill you, I don't think I'm ready for all this sister stuff just yet."

"Understood," says Livia. "I just wanted to make sure you're okay. We've been through a lot since we found each other."

"I'm great. I don't need you fretting over me. No one ever has before. Just keep to yourself and walk, less talking." *Livia's worried about me? She shouldn't be. She can just do her weird sensing thing on me and know I am fine. She's the one who was living her pampered and sheltered life up on Helix, her floating island. Livia Cosmo, an airgirl, the Cosmo Airess. I made it out of the Orphanage and was a cadet at the Academy. This isn't hard at all.*

Kane walks next to Lex, his arm draped across her shoulder, leaning on her for support. His short, blond hair is dirty and matted, his hazel eyes occasionally fluttering open as he shuffles forward.

Lex tightens her arm around his waist and says, "The one we should be worried about is Kane."

"I am worried about him," says Livia, looking at Kane. "The boosters he got in the Rebel Base helped, but he is still so weak."

"Weak?" groans Kane, his voice hoarse. "I was tortured for days in High Security Detainment before you rescued me. I think I'm doing pretty good."

"Yeah," says Lex. "You're doing great. You ready for me to let go?"

"Maybe not just yet," says Kane, his eyes closing.

"That's what I thought," says Lex.

"I can help too," offers Livia.

"No need, Airess," says Lex.

Livia faces forward, her pace unwavering as she strides toward the light ahead. *I wish I could help with Kane, but Lex is so possessive of him. I understand they have known each other much longer than he and I have, but they are only friends. Kane and I are something more. The night I met him at my Emergence Ball, we had an immediate connection. I could sense that he had feelings for me and that I could trust him. That was the beginning, and now everything has changed. In one day, I have traveled down through every level of Indra all the way to Rock Bottom. The only thing I knew about Rock Bottom before today was from the first chapter of* The Book of Indra.

Excerpted from The Book of Indra, *Chapter I: "Indra: The Origin of Our Great City"*

THE CREATION OF INDRA

Centuries ago, in order for what was left of humanity to survive the Great Catastrophe, innovative and ingenious men dug deep under the surface of the Earth and created a world protected from all that was destroyed above. For generation upon generation, our ancestors lived buried beneath the Earth, able to sustain themselves, but they did not thrive. Again, humanity was in jeopardy. With unflinching courage, brave and persistent men reclaimed the surface. They built the first dome and forged the City of Indra. Today, under the guidance of the Independent High Council, our great city is more spectacular than those founders could have imagined. That was the beginning of Indra as we, her proud citizens, know it today.

The birthplace of Indra, now known as Rock Bottom, has since disintegrated. Infested with mutants, Rock Bottom is a testament to what could have become of humanity if our vigilant founders had not forged a new life for us.

Livia looks ahead of the group and studies the stark silhouette of Zavier blocking part of the glaring light. *I wonder if Lex, with her gift of exceptional vision, can see past Zavier. He is from Rock Bottom. In* The Book of Indra, *they made Rock Bottom sound like it was nothing but mutants, but that isn't true. He is clearly not a mutant, but he is a rebel. In Rock Bottom, I saw how the people live sealed off from the Hub above. It is no wonder the rebels are from Rock Bottom. They fight for the people who live off nothing but the discards of the upper levels.*

Lex adjusts Kane's arm on her shoulder. *This feels just like the patrol simulations Kane and I did at the Academy, except this time he's injured. In those simulations we hunted rebels. But now we're with a rebel.* Lex looks up at Zavier in the front of the group. *He's not much more than a black shape, but I can see he is carrying both his pack and Kane's. On his large frame, it doesn't seem to be much effort.*

Zavier turns around and walks backward for a few paces. Lex is the only one who can see the blaster slung across his chest and his bright blue eyes behind his shaggy hair and scruffy beard.

Zavier yells, "Pick up the pace back there. Do I need to carry all the packs?" He turns back around.

"Just keep going," snaps Lex. "We'll keep up." *He is so arrogant. I don't trust him. I can't believe I'm following this rebel, but with the Population Control Forces hunting us, I have no choice. Now I'm a deserter from the PCF, down here with a rebel. Just being with a rebel my life would be forfeit under The Rebel Penalty.*

Excerpted from The Book of Indra, *Chapter VIII: "Indra: Protecting Our Great Society"*

THE THREAT FROM BENEATH:
THE POPULATION CONTROL FORCES ARMY
PROTECTING INDRA FROM DISSIDENTS

Indra is a perfectly coordinated and finely balanced system. There are those who wish to threaten the stability of the great City of Indra. The disruption of the harmonious operation of the City of Indra cannot to be tolerated. Any group or individual who cause a disruption in the functioning of the city, either by word or action, is considered a rebel and is an enemy of Indra. The lives of those engaged in rebel activities are subject to immediate forfeit as outlined by the Independent High Council Decree VII, The Rebel Penalty.

Most rebel activity can be traced to Rock Bottom. The Special Operations Unit of the Population Control Forces are tasked with patrolling Rock Bottom to eliminate all rebel activity and prevent mutants from coming up into Indra. Citizens of Indra are prohibited from attempting to access Rock Bottom. Any citizen of Indra found in Rock Bottom will be considered a rebel and subject to The Rebel Penalty.

Any citizen who has knowledge of rebel activity must report it to the Population Control Forces. A citizen who does not report rebel activity will be considered a rebel collaborator and subject to The Rebel Penalty.

All citizens' memories are fed directly into the Archives via the Archive access chip. These memories are Indra's primary surveillance system and are under constant review. This is for the safety of Indra and all of its citizens.

Lex looks directly into the light, willing her eyes to see more. *We've left Rock Bottom. This tunnel will take us to the Outlands. I hope this tunnel is as secret as the rebels think, and the Population Control Forces can't follow us. In these black silitex jumpsuits, we look like PCF troops. Ironic, I was a PCF officer and now I'm a fugitive impersonating one. I bet the uniforms were stolen from the PCF years ago. They are a good idea, though. The jumpsuits will regulate our temperature and prevent us from getting dehydrated in the tunnel.*

Livia adjusts her pack. *This is heavy, but I can handle it. I'm in good shape from years of zinger training. I am surprised I was able to convince my guardians I should be allowed to practice sword fighting. It is such an indelicate pastime, not an activity for a Proper Indrithian Young Lady. But I've abandoned my family's island of Helix. I'm going to meet my mother in the Outlands. She was alive all this time, and I never knew. Why did she leave me alone on Helix? Why did she leave my sister in the Orphanage? I don't know what will come next. It should scare me, but it is actually thrilling.*

Lex's ears are alert to the sound of the distant battle. Though it must be a mile above them, Lex can hear the blaster fire as PCF troops rampage through Rock Bottom. *People must be dying to help us escape. It's my fault the PCF are in Rock Bottom. They came down here looking for Livia, Kane, and me. They must have heard that we were here from Lieutenant Hauser. I can't believe he was down here and found me. I should have shot him when I had the chance.*

From behind the light, someone yells, "It's them! Kill the light!"

The light cuts out and Lex's eyes adjust quickly to the drastic change. She can see that the bright light they have been walking toward is a floodlight, a giant man standing next to it. There is another huge man just behind him. Both men are standing behind a low barricade, heavily armed with multiple blasters strapped all over their bodies and wearing mismatched pieces of silitex armor. Behind them is a wall of earth. It looks like they have reached the end of the tunnel, a dead end. Lex grabs her blaster.

"What is this, Zavier? Where are we?" Lex demands.

Livia draws her zinger. Kane lifts his head, but just barely. Lex adjusts Kane so he is standing a little straighter. Zavier is the only one who doesn't seem alarmed by what's happening.

"Put your weapons down," says Zavier. "This is the final weapons station. The farthest point of the Rebel Base."

"We call it Ass End," says the man who killed the floodlight.

Lex grips her blaster tighter. "Why didn't you warn us? I could have killed one of them!"

"I doubt it," says Zavier, unimpressed. "They were behind the barricade and you were a bit slow. Meet Deacon and Sid. They knew it was us coming down here, or we would be dead. Usually they blast first and ask who you are never."

"Lex is right," says Livia. "You should have warned us. She could have easily gotten off a shot before you explained."

"Well, no one got shot. So that's good," says Deacon, the man who turned off the floodlight. Reluctantly, Lex and Livia put their weapons away.

Zavier steps up to Deacon and clasps his hand. "Good to see you, Zavier. Been a while. All that noise we hear 'cause of these two?" he asks, gesturing to Lex and Livia. "Are these two really The Twins?"

"This is them," answers Zavier.

"Well I'll be core-low," says Deacon. "Didn't think I'd ever meet a set of twins. Never seen any in Rock Bottom, and twins have always been against the law in Indra."

"Amazing," says Sid, studying Lex and Livia. "They don't look exactly alike, but they're definitely twins, right?"

Livia shifts uncomfortably as Sid stares at her face. *He is right. Lex and I are not exactly identical, though we do look incredibly similar. We are both tall and slim with brown eyes and dark hair, but I am slightly taller and not as muscular. Perhaps because we have had very different lives. The one thing that is unmistakably identical about us is the tiny neon green mark we each bear in the iris of our right eye.*

"Definitely twins," says Zavier. "They're Delphia's girls."

"Really?" asks Deacon astonished.

"Yep," says Zavier.

"Done catching up?" Lex's tone is harsh. "We need to get going!"

"A little bit of bite," says Deacon, smiling at Lex. "I like this one." Lex sighs and Deacon's eyes move to Kane slumped against Lex. "Who's this guy? He's not lookin' so good. You really think he can make it?"

"We don't need a medical assessment," snaps Lex. "We need to keep moving." Lex can hear Kane's ragged breathing. *He is in bad shape. The boosters they gave him before we left helped, but he is still so weak. Please be all right, Kane. I need you to be all right.*

"Yes, sir," says Deacon, giving Lex a crisp nod. "No more chitchat."

"Come on through," says Sid. He leads the group behind the barricade and along the back wall to an opening. They enter into a vast, dimly lit room packed with racks of old weapons, boxes of energy cells, and grenades. A worktable in the center of the room is piled with pieces of disassembled weapons in various stages of repair. Deacon follows and stands in the door, where he can keep an eye on the front approach to the weapons station.

Lex looks around and asks, "Are there real weapons in another room, or is this it?"

"This is our main stockpile," says Sid defensively. "Scavenged from all over. I spend most of my time getting these old relics working." He picks up a device from one of the shelves that fits in his palm and hands it to Zavier. "Here, take some of these stunners. Made 'em myself." It is a small ball of wires with a round button at the top. "Push the trigger button hard and throw it. You'll have five seconds before it sends out a nasty shock wave. Handy for mutants."

"Sounds good." Zavier takes a few off the shelf and loads them in his pack.

"No. It sounds terrible, actually," corrects Sid. "The mutants hate it. Cover your ears after you throw it."

Deacon adds, "Martine and her new guy were the last team through. They're still at the Outpost."

Zavier shrugs. "Thanks for the heads-up."

"They said they cleaned out two mutant nests, so it shouldn't be that bad, but still keep your eyes open."

"Got it," says Zavier. "Let's go."

Sid leads the group to the far end of the room. The back wall is lined with shelves stacked with outdated and grimy weapons. Sid reaches behind a set of shelves and pulls a catch. A portion of the wall swings forward, revealing the hidden entrance to the tunnel.

"In you go," says Sid. "Tell Martine I miss her."

"Tell her yourself when she comes back through," says Zavier dismissively.

The group rushes through with Zavier in the lead, followed by Lex supporting Kane. Livia is the last to go through and reflects, *I am leaving Indra, my home. But I can't turn back. I must move forward.*

Sid stands in the opening. "As soon as I close this door behind you, we're gonna blast the tunnel section you just came through that leads into Ass End so the PCF don't discover this entrance. With PCF scouring Rock Bottom for our base, and now you ladies too, it's the only way to be sure the tunnel to the Outlands will stay secret. Once the PCF are out of Rock Bottom, we'll clear the cave-in. It'll take several days and a lot of manpower to open it up again, but it's the safe move. All right, go. Good trip." Sid pushes the wall back into place.

2

The small amount of light that was coming in through the open entrance is now gone. The tunnel is pitch-dark. The air is still and stagnant. Quickly, Lex's eyes adjust. She can see that the tunnel stretches out in front of them. The ceiling is low with a dirt floor, rough and uneven, covered in rocks. At inconsistent intervals, there are metal supports that line the wall and ceiling.

"Get your beamers on," orders Zavier, as he pulls a small, black cylinder from his pack. He switches it on and a bright shaft of light cuts through the dark tunnel. Zavier pushes a button on the side of his beamer, and the shaft of light transforms into a soft-edged globe that floats just in front of the beamer. The globe of light moves up from the beamer as Zavier makes an adjustment. "Set your beamers to hover two feet up. It's better to set the light to follow overhead so we can see the whole tunnel." He attaches the beamer to his jumpsuit's shoulder mount. The single sphere of glowing light projected from the beamer floats over Zavier's shoulder. With experienced movements from her Academy training, Lex pulls her beamer from one of the side pouches of her pack, flips it on, adjusts the light, and mounts it to her shoulder while Livia fumbles with her pack to find hers.

"You need some help, Livia?" Lex asks with a smirk, and pulls a beamer from Kane's pack.

"No," says Livia. "I'm perfectly capable of finding my beamer."

"Sure," says Lex with a shrug as she attaches Kane's beamer to his shoulder mount.

Finally, Livia pulls a beamer out of her pack, flips it on, makes the adjustment, and mounts it to her shoulder. Even when all four have their beamers on, the light is meager in the long, dark tunnel.

"Let's get moving," says Zavier.

With Zavier in the lead, the group begins to move forward. Livia is behind Zavier. Lex follows, supporting Kane. After just a few minutes, there is a huge explosion. The ground shakes, Lex loses her hold on Kane, and he is knocked to the ground.

"That was the guys blowing the tunnel," says Zavier. "No way back now."

Lex crouches down to help Kane up and puts her mouth close to Kane's ear. She says quietly, "All you have to do is walk. You can do this. You survived being tortured, don't give up now."

"You'd kill me if I did," says Kane.

Lex smiles. "I might."

Livia crouches down on Kane's other side and helps Lex get Kane to his feet.

Zavier watches the girls help Kane and says, "I hope your boy can pull it together. I'm not going to carry him, or either of you. Are we ready?"

Zavier turns and walks off into the tunnel. Kane walks with Lex and Livia on either side.

"How far are we going?" asks Lex.

"The first leg is twenty miles," explains Zavier. "It won't be easy. It grades up the whole way. Some parts are pretty steep. Plus, it's rough. Lots of rocks from old cave-ins. That'll get us to the Last Outpost. It will take the whole day and into the night. We won't sleep till we get to the Outpost, but we'll rest when we get there. It's a small station run by rebels. It marks the edge of the footprint of the dome of Indra."

"I hate to be indelicate," says Livia, "but if we are going to be in this tunnel for hours upon hours, how do we relieve ourselves?"

"Leave it to the Airess to be worried about that," says Zavier, smiling. "If you can't hold it till the Outpost, you can hang back for a little privacy. But really we should stick together 'cause there are mutants, and you do not want to be alone if they show up. Even worse, with your pants down. Between here and the Last Outpost is the most dangerous stretch for coming across mutant nests and traps. There aren't really any mutants past the Outpost."

"In the Academy," says Lex, "they made it seem like everyone in Rock Bottom was a mutant."

"Our main training simulation was called Mutants of Rock Bottom," says Kane.

"We were required to log ten hours a week in the MRB sim," says Lex.

"They were training you to kill, not to think," says Zavier. "Easier to kill people if you think everyone in Rock Bottom is less than human."

Livia's brow furrows, and she asks, "Are mutants not human?"

"For centuries, Indra dumped its toxic waste down into Rock Bottom. It's done a lot of damage. There are a lot of people in Rock Bottom with genetic defects, but the mutants are a different thing. Mutants are very dangerous, genetically really far gone, not really human anymore. Mutants are unpredictable and desperate but still intelligent enough to work together. They're vicious. They'll take everything you have, kill you, and eat you. They are mostly in Core Low, below Rock Bottom, and out here in the tunnels."

Livia is shocked. "Eat people?"

"Absolutely!" says Zavier.

"In the Academy no one ever talked about Core Low," says Lex. "I didn't realize it was a place. I thought it was just an insult."

"It's an insult because it's a place," says Zavier. "It's the lowest, the worst of the worst."

"Well, let's not run into any," says Lex. "How do they get into this tunnel?"

"They live all throughout the old pipes system. Some of those pipes connect up with this tunnel. The mutants are savage and will kill for the kind of supplies and equipment we carry. They set booby traps to catch groups passing through. We need to be ready to fight at any time."

"I should be in the lead," Lex challenges Zavier. "I can see in the dark, way beyond the light of our beamers."

"You've never even been down here," argues Zavier. "I was a tunnel runner. I've guided rebels to the Last Outpost too many times to count. I know you hate for anyone but you to be in charge, but too bad. You need to check your ego. Just back off."

Zavier charges ahead, leaving a gap between himself and the rest of the group.

Lex says to Livia, "I could kill him. He's such an ass."

"I hope he's as competent as he thinks he is," says Livia.

"He's been through here before," says Kane. "I think we have to trust him."

"Well, I don't," says Lex.

After walking for an hour, the group starts to pass through a section with loose, uneven rocks covering the ground. Zavier is still in the lead, though he seems to have slowed, his steps more hesitant.

"Do you need me to be in front?" asks Lex.

"No, I got this," says Zavier. Just then, he stumbles over a trip wire that knocks down a huge pile of scrap metal. The loud crash reverberates in the tunnel. For a moment they are all frozen.

Zavier pulls out a blaster and yells, "The mutants won't be far. Get ready."

Lex pulls out a blaster. Livia draws her zinger. Kane pulls out a blaster, but he is visibly unsteady. Lex and Livia stand on either side of Kane, ready to defend him. Before they are in the light of the beamers, Lex can see a group of revolting mutants coming down the tunnel.

Lex yells, "There are three of them!"

Zavier takes out one of Sid's stunners. "Cover your ears!" he shouts as he presses the trigger and throws it down the tunnel toward the mutants.

Lex hesitates for a moment but nothing happens. "How long before it goes off?"

"Sid said five seconds!" yells Zavier.

The mutants hurtle toward the group. Their jerky movements make it hard to tell where each hideous arm or leg belongs.

Lex shouts, "It didn't work!"

"I know!" yells Zavier and mutters, "Stupid Sid!"

The first mutant crashes into Zavier, knocking him to the ground. Its long and powerful arms claw at his silitex. His jumpsuit is torn open and his arm is gashed and bleeding.

Lex takes only a heartbeat to assess the situation. *The mutants are splitting up. One's got Zavier. He's in trouble. Guess who's coming to his rescue?* She aims her blaster at the mutant attacking Zavier and fires. The shot hits the mutant in the head and it goes down. Without a moment of hesitation, Lex pivots and aims her blaster at the second raw, red, scaly mutant, which is coming straight at her. She fires, hitting the mutant in the neck, and it falls forward, pinning her legs under its dead weight.

The last mutant barrels off the wall, headed for Livia, who is standing guard next to Kane. It is larger than the others, with thick legs and huge rolls of fat that lead straight into a wide head riddled with disgusting, oozing growths. Livia swings her zinger up and across, hitting the mutant's side and deflecting it backward. Barely disturbed by Livia's strike, it pivots back at Kane. Livia pushes Kane down. *This mutant has chosen the quickest path to death. I will not hesitate like before. I will not let Kane be touched.* She jumps over Kane and brings the blade up through the mutant's chest. The mutant falls dead in front of Livia.

Though it barely lasted two breaths, the attack leaves the group winded and shocked. The tunnel is quiet.

Lex yells, "I need help getting this stinking pile off me."

Livia rushes to Lex, and together they roll the huge mutant off Lex, and she gets to her feet.

"Thanks," says Lex. "I'm glad you are so good with that zinger."

"I've learned not to hesitate," says Livia.

"I bet that mutant wishes you had."

Zavier slowly rolls to his knees, positions his one good arm underneath him, and pushes himself up. He is shaky, standing with his back against the tunnel wall. Lex walks over to Zavier. The silitex on his upper arm where the mutant struck him is ripped and wet with blood.

"How bad is it?" Lex asks. "Can you walk, or am I gonna have to carry you?"

Zavier looks at his arm. "I'm good. It's nothing." He raises his arm, then freezes, breathing in sharply. "No, it's bad."

Lex punches Zavier in his good arm. "What is wrong with you? You almost got us killed!"

"Take it easy. We're all alive."

Lex pulls off her belt and ties it around Zavier's arm as a tourniquet to stop his wound from bleeding. "I don't care what you think. I'm now in the lead with you. At least I will be able to spot a blasted trip wire."

"Fine," Zavier reluctantly agrees, lurching forward into a walk. "Try to keep up."

"You're unbelievable!" Lex goes to help Livia get Kane to his feet. "You all right, Kane?"

"Yeah. Thanks to your sister."

"She's good with her zinger."

Lex runs off to catch up with Zavier. He is ahead of the group but not by much. Livia and Kane follow, his footsteps slow, barely picking up his feet. Livia can feel his distress. "You are going to be all right."

"I'm a burden. I'm slowing us down. I couldn't even defend myself back there. You saved my life."

"You would have done the same for me."

Kane sighs. "Yes, I would have, but the point is I didn't. I couldn't."

"You just need to get through this part of the tunnel. Zavier said we can rest at the Outpost. Don't worry about defending anyone. Just walk." Livia takes Kane's hand and they walk together. Kane's hand is warm in Livia's. *He is weak but so strong too. I feel he is fighting to carry on. He will make it. He has to.*

Livia and Kane walk a few paces behind Lex and Zavier. Livia asks,

"Zavier, how long has the tunnel been here? Did the rebels dig it?"

"Most of the tunnels have been here since before Indra was aboveground."

"What do you mean most of the tunnels?" asks Lex. "I thought this was the only tunnel."

"No. There are lots of tunnels. There are at least three tunnels out of the city, but this one leads to your mother in the Outlands. The first tunnels were dug when everyone was underground. They tunneled up and created the City of Indra, but they also tunneled across and out. There are many tunnels that run under Indra. Some include parts of the old pipe system that brought surface air and water underground to be filtered. The tunnels leading up from Rock Bottom into Indra were blocked or destroyed. The rebels have reopened as many as they can but still have to keep them concealed so they don't get shut down again. Indra doesn't want any of us Rock Bottom scum popping out of tunnels into their beautiful, clean city."

"Are you sure?" asks Livia. "There is nothing about tunnels in *The Book of Indra*."

Zavier waves his hand dismissively. "*The Book of Indra* is all propaganda."

Lex raises her eyebrows with a smirk. "Propaganda? That's a big word."

Zavier smiles. "Impressed? That's what happens when you are around Roscoe too much."

An image of Roscoe flashes in Lex's mind, of him as a tall, lean man in a PCF uniform. *He brought his group of rebels to the High Council Building dressed as PCF when we were rescuing Kane. We were pinned down. If it wasn't for Roscoe and his men, Livia, Kane, and I might not have gotten out of there. We met him just a day ago, but Livia says we can trust him. I trust him only because he and his rebels helped us save Kane.*

Livia thinks back to Roscoe in his library, his threadbare Islander clothes under a PCF uniform. *Roscoe was an Islander, and now he is the leader of the rebels. How did that happen? He knew our parents. They entrusted him with the Archive memories he showed us. Wonderful, heartbreaking memories of their life together and our birth. I sensed we could trust him. It is because of him that we are on this journey to meet our mother.*

"Since he came down from the Islands and became the leader of the rebels, Roscoe has had his own way of doing things," Zavier continues. "He made me read a lot of those books he's collected in his library. Now, I sometimes use big words. My point is, *The Book of Indra* is what the Council wants you to believe."

"Have you read *The Book of Indra*?" asks Livia. "Have you ever seen a copy?"

"Nope. I wish I had a copy of *The Book of Indra*. It would be great for wiping my ass."

"There's no need to be vulgar," says Livia. "What makes you such an authority?"

"I'm not. But Roscoe is. I didn't even know the book existed till he told me about it. How it's required reading. Makes sense, though. If you're in charge, you make everyone learn your rule book. You get to write your own version of history and tell everyone that's the truth. Roscoe told me about the pledge of Indra too."

"It's called the Indrithian Citizen's Pledge," says Lex.

"I heard everyone in Indra has to recite it every day," says Zavier.

"Well, not every day," says Livia, "but Life Guide certainly had me recite it at the start of lessons."

"Yeah, we said it every day at the Academy," says Lex.

"How does it go?" asks Zavier.

Lex and Livia recite together:

> We the Citizens of Indra,
> Revere the Founders,
> Protect the dome, and
> Respect the Independent High Council.
> We praise the Founders for creating the great City of Indra.

> We praise the dome for protecting us from
> the deadly world outside.
> We praise the Independent High Council for
> their guidance and wisdom.
> We praise Indra.

"That is serious propaganda," says Zavier.

"If *The Book of Indra* isn't true, what is?" asks Livia.

"In Rock Bottom we have the Tellings. They are stories that have been passed down generation to generation. They change a little from family to family but not much. Older people tell them to the younger people to keep our history alive. Some people repeat them every night."

Livia asks, "How many are there?"

Zavier thinks for a moment. "I know eight or nine. Some people know more. Some people less. So I don't know how many there are really. There is no official list. They are not written down anywhere. Well, except by Roscoe. He has been writing them down. He wants to keep a record. Not like we could make a book of Tellings anyway. Even if there was a way to print it, most people in Rock Bottom can only read the bare minimum, signs and stuff. And if the PCF found someone with a book like that, a book that basically says the Council is a bunch of liars . . ."

"That would not be good," says Kane.

Zavier nods. "Yep. No one wants more trouble. So the Tellings are just spoken. No record. Less danger."

"Can you recite one of the Tellings for us?" asks Livia.

Zavier shrugs. "Sure. What do you want to hear? I know 'The Beginning,' 'The Tunnels,' 'The Heel of Indra,' 'The Rebels.' . . . Oh, I know which one to do. 'The Telling of the Time of the Twins.'"

Kane smirks and says, "That's a lot of t's."

Lex is astonished. "There's one about twins? About us?"

"Don't get excited," says Zavier. "It's not really about you. It's the twin lore. Everyone knows that one." Zavier clears his throat and begins to recite in a rhythm different from his normal way of speaking:

THE TELLING OF
THE TIME OF THE TWINS

When all were trapped below in darkness
The twins broke through to the light
The life of one brother was sacrificed
Indra was forged in his blood
But all were not free
Indra would crush the bones below it
The Time of the Twins will come again
With these twins there will be no rivalry
When the twin saviors come of age
They will bring freedom to Indra and all its people
On their backs the bottom shall rise up
And Indra shall fall
They will lead all to live in the light

"The twin lore started way back, before Indra was built," explains Zavier. "Supposedly, the beginning lines of the Telling are about these twin brothers, Andru and Atros. The story is that they were the ones who dug up toward the surface so people could live aboveground again. But the brothers disagreed on what the future should be, so Atros killed his brother Andru and founded Indra the way he wanted."

"That's brutal," says Livia. "I was taught that Atros led us out of Rock Bottom, but I've never heard of Andru, or that Atros had a twin."

"Not in *The Book of Indra*, 'cause that's a part of the story they don't want you to know," says Zavier. "That's the version of the Telling I learned growing up, but there is a version that says, 'A set of twins in their seventeenth year will be discovered and bring freedom to Indra and all its people.' Whichever version people know, you guys being twins, and seventeen, most of Rock Bottom will think the Telling is coming true. That can be powerful if we use it right."

Lex interjects, "Use it? You mean use *us*?"

"Look," says Zavier, "I don't believe in prophecies or the Telling coming true, but if just hearing that a set of twins has come can light a fire under the people of Rock Bottom to join the rebels, then I'm all for calling you the Twin Saviors. You two are important. Or could be, anyway."

"This is stupid," says Lex. "I don't think the Telling could possibly be about us."

"It might not matter whether you believe," says Livia.

Zavier adds, "Just the fact that you exist could be a self-fulfilling prophecy, and that could be useful."

The group walks quietly. Livia's thoughts race. *It is so strange to think that this twin lore has been passed on by generations and I never heard of it. And now we are a set of twins in the middle of this revolution. If being a twin is a powerful tool, I will use it, but I won't be just a pawn. If I can do something useful in this rebellion, I will.*

Finally, Livia says to Lex, "We could be The Twins that fulfill the Prophecy. That is amazing."

"Maybe," says Lex. "We'll see."

3

After walking silently for several hours they hear a muffled, crackly voice coming from Zavier's pack, "Zavier, this is Roscoe. Respond."

Zavier stops and puts his hand up to tell the others to stop. They impatiently stand and watch as Zavier fumbles with his pack, then pulls out a communications device. The rectangular holocomm has a flickering keypad and looks like it has been patched together from pieces of older components. It is banged up, covered in scratches and dents. It easily fits in Zavier's large hand. He presses a few keys and a blue projection of a man's face flickers to life, hovering just above the holocomm.

Lex studies the projection, and though it is small, the image is clear. Roscoe is quite close to the holocomm on his end, and she can see the wrinkles at the corners of his eyes and a wall of books just behind him. *It's Roscoe, from his library in Rock Bottom. When we left, they were under siege by the PCF. At least we know Roscoe survived.*

Roscoe says, his voice louder and less muffled, "Zavier, this is Rosc—"

The projection abruptly cuts off with a flicker and a loud burst of static. Zavier inspects the unit. He jiggles a few wires, gives it a hard smack, and pushes a button on the flickering keypad. The projection of Roscoe pops back up.

"It's Z. Go," says Zavier.

Roscoe smiles. "Good to see you, Zavier. I'm sure you are anxious for a status report on Rock Bottom. After you all left, we were able to throw the PCF troops off the trail of both the Rebel Base and the girls. PCF didn't find the base, and the tunnel entrance is secure."

"Is everyone okay?" asks Zavier.

"There was a lot of fighting and confusion. We lost some good people, but it could have been worse. How's the tunnel?"

"We're moving. But slowly. We will be lucky if we get to the Outpost today."

"Any trouble?" asks Roscoe.

"I tripped a mutant trap. We had to fight off a nasty group of three."

"Keep Lex up front," says Roscoe. "She's got good eyes."

Lex smiles at Zavier with an "I told you so" look.

Zavier grudgingly nods and answers, "Yes, sir. I'm aware."

Roscoe tells them that in their supplies they have parts and equipment to repair the communications setup at the Outlanders' colony, which has been down for more than a month.

After Zavier signs off with Roscoe, Kane points to the holocomm and asks, "What junk pile did you pull that from? I can't believe it works."

"Sorry, we don't get the latest gear down in Rock Bottom," Zavier says, irritated. "In the upper levels, if it's not new and pretty, you just throw it away. We have to take what we can find and make it work. This may look like scrap, but it's heavily encoded so the PCF and the Council can't monitor us."

"Sorry. I didn't mean to offend you," says Kane. "It's impressive."

"It is," says Zavier as he puts the holocomm back in his pack. They start walking, and Zavier says, "When we get to the Outpost, we'll have to remove Livia's chip."

"What?" Livia's eyes go wide. "Why? When you removed Lex's chip, Roscoe said my chip didn't need to be taken out."

"We checked your chip and it is only operating at 20 percent. At that level, it can't be used to track you and it's not connected to the Archives, but it still has to come out. It was more that we didn't have time to deal with it in Rock Bottom. Lex's had to come out immediately or the PCF would have found us. If we weren't leaving Indra, your chip could stay in, but the chip is a lot more than a locator. It records everything to the Archives and dampens your emotions. It's also a perimeter control device. If you pass more than two miles beyond the footprint of the dome, the chip will self-destruct. It melts and fries your brain. You won't die, but your mind will be gone. On the surface, you could go maybe a mile past the irradiated zone. That's it. Down here, the Outpost is the marker for the edge of the dome."

"I can't believe the chips have this perimeter control function," says Livia. "It is barbaric!"

"You shouldn't be surprised," say Zavier. "Indra tells everyone the dome is for their protection, but really it is a cage."

Excerpted from The Book of Indra, *Chapter VI: "Indra: The Dome Is Life"*

THE DOME

The dome is for the protection of all of Indra. The irradiated world outside the dome of Indra is uninhabitable. The Independent High Council constantly monitors the world outside in the hope that one day it may be possible to live outside the dome. A time in the distant future, when the toxic air has cleared. A time when the unstable atmosphere, with its extremes in temperature, of boiling hot to below freezing in a day, has calmed and regulated. Until the day the world outside is once again suitable for habitation, the Independent High Council considers the protection and preservation of the dome one of its primary responsibilities.

THE DOME RESTRICTIONS AND PENALTIES

Under no circumstances and for no reason should any citizen attempt to travel outside the dome of Indra. Any attempt to breach the dome is a crime against Indra. Any unauthorized person attempting to breach the dome will be immediately detained, will lose all rights of citizenship, and will be put on indefinite Shadow Status.

Any actions that cause damage to the dome, regardless of intent, are a crime against Indra. Any person who damages the dome will be immediately detained, will lose all rights of citizenship, and will be put on indefinite Shadow Status. Shadowed citizens are rendered voiceless and sentenced to wander the Archives for the remainder of their lives.

THE DOME GATES

There are four egress gates in the dome that are strictly controlled by the Population Control Forces. No unauthorized citizen should attempt to access these gates. The Population Control Forces are able to exit the dome through these gates only under strict conditions in order to inspect the perimeter of the dome and ensure its integrity.

It is every citizen's obligation to protect the dome, for the dome protects every citizen.

"You can't safely go any farther than the Outpost," says Zavier. "We would have removed your chip in Rock Bottom, but with the PCF attacking, there was no time. I can't believe the citizens of Indra believe the Archive access chip in their wrist is their only connection to the Archives. Of course Indra has put chips in their brains. How else could they record your memories?"

"Indra has been quite successful in keeping the Archives and how they work secret from its people," says Livia. "I'm ashamed to admit I never really gave it much thought before. I just accepted that Indra was doing whatever it needed to do to protect us. I never thought so much of it was a lie."

"Propaganda," says Zavier with a smirk.

"Getting my chip pulled out was not fun," says Lex. She teases, "Now it's your turn to get a metal skewer stuck in your brain."

Livia is quite distressed. "Who is going to perform the procedure?"

"I was going to do it, but now with my slashed arm, I think the chief will have to," says Zavier.

"Who's the chief?"

"He's in charge at the Outpost. He's the one who taught me how to do the procedure."

"What is the Last Outpost like? Will it be sanitary?"

"Not exactly, Airess. I'm sure life floating in the air high up on your island was always sanitary. Things are not exactly like that down here. We'll do the best we can to meet your high standards."

Lex chimes in, "Livia don't be so uppity. Zavier took my chip out, and clearly it worked out fine."

"That remains to be seen," says Livia.

"What does that mean?" snaps Lex.

"Who knows what the long-term effect of having your chip removed will be?"

"Enough," barks Zavier. "It has to be done. Or you can always return to your island. Oh, wait. You can't."

Kane reassures Livia, "I'll be with you."

"Wait a minute," says Lex, indignant. "I'll be with her. She's my sister. Plus, I've already been through it."

"In case you forgot," says Kane, "so have I. They took my chip out at the High Security Detainment before you rescued me. I was awake and they weren't concerned with my comfort, and I'm pretty sure they weren't going to put it back in."

"You think they were going to leave you without a chip?" asks Lex. "That doesn't make sense."

"It does if they planned to kill me."

"I can't imagine they were planning on killing you," says Lex, alarmed. *They were going to kill him? I could have lost Kane. Who would order that? Not the PCF. The Council? Why would the Council want him dead?*

"My mission to kill Livia had to come from high up. Higher than the PCF. After the mission I was going to basically disappear. When I got arrested by the PCF, they had no record of my mission. I was on my own. I was probably just hours away from being killed or put on Shadow Status. I think I was just lucky you two rescued me when you did. If I had been there much longer, I don't think I would be alive."

With relief in her voice, Livia says, "I'm so glad we got there when we did. I could see it was bad, but it never occurred to me they would kill you." *He is already so important to me and he could have died.*

Lex breaks in, "Regardless, I can stay with Livia when she has her chip taken out."

"As much as I appreciate all this attention," says Livia, "to settle this debate, I've decided you both can be there."

"Thank goodness that is all worked out," says Zavier sarcastically. "I was so concerned about who would hold the Airess's hand. So, now that that's decided, let's pick up the pace or we'll never get there."

The ground becomes wet and they start to smell a terrible odor.

Zavier says, "Enjoy the smell? This is a gift from the city above. We get to slosh through their body waste."

"This is disgusting," says Livia, horrified.

"Yep," says Zavier.

"It's pretty close to the smell of a hundred dirty diapers crammed into a broken refuse chute at the Orphanage," says Lex.

Livia gags slightly. "That is revolting."

"It was," says Lex.

"Looks like we only have to deal with it for a hundred feet or so," says Zavier. "I've been through here when it's much worse. Just watch your step," he cautions. "The ground is slimy and slick. You really don't want to fall in this."

"This is from Indra?" asks Livia, her face pinched in a horrible grimace. "I thought the city had clean waste disposal."

Zavier laughs. "The city has always dumped its garbage in Rock Bottom. Sewage is no different. As long as it goes down, they don't care where it goes, or if it leaks."

They move forward slowly. Kane walks close to Livia. He is unsteady and begins to lean heavily on her. Together they have a hard time navigating the slick ground. Kane slips and starts to fall. He is taking Livia down with him when Zavier reaches back and grabs the front of Kane's jumpsuit, lifting him up before he hits the ground. Without Kane's weight pulling her down, Livia regains her balance.

"Thank you," says Livia. "That was superior timing."

Kane adds, "Yeah, thanks," as Zavier lowers him back to his feet.

Zavier lets go of Kane. "That's the last time. Don't expect me to save you again. If any of us get hurt and can't walk, break something, twist something, that'll be it. We can't turn back, and I'm not dragging any of you to the Outpost."

"What a gentleman," says Lex.

"Just facts," says Zavier. "If you're down, you'll stay down. Till a mutant finds you, then you're dead."

"You won't have to," says Kane. "I'll make it."

"You sure about that?" Zavier asks as he adjusts Kane's pack. "I don't know what Roscoe was thinking, forcing me to bring you."

"We get it," says Lex. "You're the biggest, strongest tunnel runner expert ever."

Zavier smirks. "I'm happy we understand each other."

"Enough!" yells Livia, irritated. "Can we just continue?"

As they walk, Zavier looks down. "Well, the ground is almost dry. At least we're through the worst of the sludge. Now, since I am the tunnel expert," he shoots Lex a smile, "you should know that once we leave the Outpost, we'll be in the tunnel for about three more days. I've never been farther than the Outpost, but I hear that part will be very hard."

Lex interrupts, "Wait. I thought you said you had led rebels out of Indra?"

"I never said all the way to the Outlands."

"Great! So you have no idea what you are doing."

"I know more than you!"

Livia says calmly, "Lex, let Zavier finish what he was saying. Everything doesn't have to be an argument."

Zavier glares at Lex. "Thank you, Livia. As I was saying, after the Outpost, it will take us three days to reach the exit to the Outlands. There should be less danger of mutant attacks, but they are still possible, especially after we killed three of them. They might send more after us. So we'll need to be ready for anything and keep watch at night, sleeping in shifts. It will be very difficult with limited supplies, only what each one of us can carry. We'll all have to pull our own weight," he says, looking directly at Kane.

"If you are worried about me, don't be," says Kane. "I can handle it."

Zavier is clearly skeptical. "Are you sure?"

Feeling the tension building, Livia asks Zavier, "So how many people have left Indra and made it to the Outlands?"

"It started slowly about twenty years ago," says Zavier. "I think there were only about ten people who had left Indra when your mother went out after you two were born."

Livia realizes, *I always thought the Islands were as far as I would ever go. I could not have imagined leaving Indra. To think, my mother was the first Islander to leave, and now I'm following in her footsteps. Traveling along the same tunnel she did gives me an odd sense of pride.*

Zavier continues, "Roscoe says that back in those days, small groups of five or six would make the trip out, maybe three groups a year. Then about five years ago, the rebels made it easier to get through the tunnel, and more and more started making the trip. The groups were still small, but there has been a group moving through the tunnel almost every month for the past five years."

Lex asks, "Who's leaving Indra?"

"In the beginning it was only people from Rock Bottom. Now there are more people from the Hub and Middler level of Indra. That is more complicated 'cause all the Uppers have chips. Not a problem for us in Rock Bottom. No chips. At least that's one thing we don't have to worry about. The people of Rock Bottom are the most motivated to try and live outside Indra, but still it's a hard decision and a difficult journey to make."

"So does that mean there are around five hundred people in the Outlands?" asks Kane.

"Yeah, genius, that's some quick math. There are almost five hundred people, give or take, with some deaths and births over the years. But we don't really get anyone from the upper levels of Indra. I think your mom was one of the first and last from the Islands who wanted to leave. Most people living life up in the Islands have all the advantages, such a decadent and luxurious life. They don't want to leave or see anything change."

Livia stops him. "I don't know about all Islanders, but I felt Helix was a prison. Both the island and my life had very clear borders."

Zavier holds up his hand. "Whoa. Were you ever hungry or cold? Or afraid that there would be a PCF raid any minute and you'd be killed for no reason?"

"No, but I had no real freedom. I had just been presented at my Emergence Ball and was about to be paired with a Proper Indrithian Young Man to cohabitate, someone I would have barely known. But my ball turned out to be a fiasco. Marius, my guardian on Helix, would have been lucky to have bartered me off to anyone after that scandal. And that would have been my life."

Zavier is indignant. "You can't possibly think I can feel sympathy for you. How bad could that have been? You might have moved to a different beautiful island. Most Islanders don't care that their way of life is made possible by the oppression of the people of all the lower levels."

Kane interrupts, "Back off, Zavier! Livia is not exactly a typical Islander."

Lex looks at Kane. "Also, don't forget that Kane was trying to kill Livia."

"Thanks for the reminder, Lex," says Kane coldly.

"He didn't go through with it, which almost got him killed," says Livia defensively.

Lex rolls her eyes and sighs. *Is this how it is going to be with the two of them? Always together and me on the outside? How am I the odd one out? Kane is my best friend, and Livia is my sister. If anything, Livia and I should be a team or me and Kane.* "Don't be so defensive. I get it, almost dying together bonded you two for life." Lex stalks ahead, and Zavier follows her.

Livia and Kane trail behind. Kane is visibly wincing with each step. Livia asks, "Did the mutants hurt you?"

"No, I don't think so, but honestly at this point everything still hurts from the special treatment I got in High Security Detainment. But I'll make it."

"I know you will, and hopefully when we get to the Outpost, they will have something to help with the pain."

"I'm counting on it," Kane says with a smile that quickly fades to a grimace.

"Does it upset you that Lex seems angry at us?"

"Well, I'm not surprised she is angry," Kane says with a shrug. "It's her primary reaction to everything, particularly if she feels threatened. As long as I've known Lex, she has always acted as if she doesn't need anybody, but that isn't true. Lex doesn't want to be alone any more than you or I do. At the Academy, she was reluctant to make friends. I was the only one she ever got close to. I'm her only friend. Now you show up and seem to be getting between us."

"I'm not trying to get in between you two," Livia argues. "I know you're friends, but we have our own feelings for each other, and she is clearly not happy about that."

"And what exactly are our feelings for each other?" asks Kane, raising his eyebrows.

Livia shyly responds, "I was so hopeless that day of my Emergence Ball. I truly believed I was doomed to a life on another island with some Proper Young Man for whom I felt nothing. After all the years of

Etiquette Training, my Tutor made me feel that was my destiny, that I didn't have any choice."

"Did it really feel like your future was so bleak? From what little I know of your parents, they seemed in love and they had met at Delphia's Emergence Ball. Maybe you would have met someone like that too."

"I very much doubt it. I was on display as the Cosmo Airess. I was nothing more than a legendary name and a prestigious island. I'm sure many of the Proper Indrithian Young Men would have offered to cohabitate with me, having nothing to do with who I am as a person. No real relationship was going to come out of that. Then it was your turn at the Courting Dance, and I felt something. In that moment, I hoped maybe the outcome could be different. But then you disappeared."

"Until I found you in Veda's stable and tried to kill you."

"Yes, that was unfortunate," says Livia with a small grin.

"That's a nice way of putting it."

"I was very well trained by my Etiquette Tutor on the List of Acceptable Topics on which Proper Young Men and Women of Indra are allowed to converse, and murder is not one of them."

"Well, I have never been proper, so it's okay, and I think we should discuss it. I want you to know, the minute I spoke to you at the ball, I knew I could not complete my mission."

"But you still came to find me and did pass the pill that was meant to kill me into my mouth," says Livia, with a hint of confusion in her voice.

"I came to find you because I was intrigued by you. I had already decided not to go through with my mission. I was not going to pass the pill to you, but then you kissed me. I must have bit down on the pill and it started to dissolve in my mouth before I accidentally passed it to you. I never meant for it to get that far. But I didn't anticipate an Airess being so aggressive."

"It's not like you pushed me off right away."

Kane laughs. "Why would I? I wanted to kiss you. I just wasn't about to act on it."

"Well," Livia shrugs, "you did seem to enjoy it before we both almost died."

"Almost dying was very distracting," says Kane with a smile that lifts just one side of his mouth.

"*Distracting*? Not exactly the word I thought would describe my first kiss."

"Maybe *surprising* is better. That's why I lost control of the pill and passed it to you. The next time we kiss, I won't be in danger of killing us both."

"So there will be a next time?" Livia asks playfully.

"Yes," says Kane matter-of-factly.

The tunnel changes again as the path narrows, and rocky outcroppings hang from the ceiling all the way down to the floor, each obstacle hundreds of tons of sharp rock. They are forced to squeeze in between them, scraping their packs and silitex.

Ahead of Livia and Kane, Lex and Zavier walk without talking. Lex stares down the tunnel. *I can't believe neither Livia nor Kane has tried to catch up with me. It has been at least an hour. It's like they have forgotten all about me. I will not just let Livia take Kane away from me.*

Lex breaks the silence. "You said you were a tunnel runner. There doesn't seem to be much room to run," she says as she squeezes through a tight spot. "So what do runners do?"

"Well, we don't run. We are the lifeline for the people stationed at the Outpost, and we help people leaving Indra. Sometimes we took people through the tunnel who were escaping Rock Bottom, making sure they didn't have to fight off mutants by themselves. We also brought in supplies for the Outpost. There are a few teams. Always at least two. I had a partner I worked with for a couple years."

"Why did you stop?"

"I got more involved with Roscoe and had to stop being a runner. Listen, I know I haven't been past the Last Outpost, but I have heard a lot about it. This part of the tunnel is tough, but the rest will be worse. Kane is really slowing us down. He is barely going to make it to the Outpost. I won't drag him all the way to the Outlands."

"You won't have to," Lex bites back. "He is tough. He will make it."

"Look, it's three days uphill. The two nights, someone always has to be on watch. We'll have to sleep in shifts and split the watch, so there won't be much rest. I'm serious. Kane is really not up for this. He is just too weak. I wanted to leave him in Rock Bottom, but Roscoe insisted we bring him, but it's like pulling a bag of rocks behind us. We should leave him at the Outpost."

Lex snaps, "We should leave you at the Outpost."

4

Hours later, Livia walks slowly with Kane a few paces behind Lex and Zavier. Livia watches Zavier's feet. *Is it my imagination or is he slowing down? We've been walking for hours and we're all exhausted, even our relentless leader. Is he getting ready to stop? Maybe take a break? We all need it.* Abruptly, Zavier stops.

Lex asks, "What is it? What's wrong?"

"Nothing. We're here. Finally. That's the longest it's ever taken me to get to the Outpost. It's practically morning already." Zavier pulls out his holocomm.

Lex looks around. "I can't see anything. It doesn't look any different."

Zavier is smug. "That's the point."

Livia and Kane catch up to Lex and Zavier. Livia asks, "What's going on? Why have we stopped?"

"This is the entrance to the Outpost," says Zavier. Then he says into his comm, "We're outside. It's all clear."

"Really?" asked Kane, looking around. "Are you sure?"

"Yes!" snaps Zavier. "It's camouflaged so the mutants can't find it."

"Well, it's amazing," says Kane. "I'm surprised anyone can find it."

Zavier speaks into the comm again, his tone more aggressive. "We are outside. It is all clear. Do you copy?" They all wait. There is no response.

"Actually," says Livia, "I can feel that there are several people nearby."

Zavier shouts into the comm, "Hey, wake up! We're outside. It's all clear."

There is a long pause. Finally, an image flickers on above the holocomm. A bald man, with his eyes barely open, says in a groggy voice, "Copy."

Zavier crams the comm back in his pack. There is a loud scraping noise and a section of the tunnel wall slides open. A huge bald man stands just inside the once-hidden doorway. He is holding himself up, propped against the opening. He is nearly as wide as the entrance. Zavier scowls at him as he yawns.

"Sorry to wake you, Ike," says Zavier. "You gonna let us in?"

"Yeah, yeah. Come in," says Ike, rubbing his eyes. He moves to the side, ushering them in, revealing a second huge man whose long, unkempt hair hangs in tangles, with more long hair covering his face and shirtless upper body.

"Oh, my!" says Livia, alarmed, and looks away.

"Wow!" says Lex. "For a second, I thought you were a mutant."

As Zavier steps through the entrance, he says to the second man, "Hey, Murray, where's your shirt?"

Murray moves farther back into the corridor of the Last Outpost to make room. "Oh, sorry!"

"Nobody but Ike wants to see that. Can't you two keep your hands off each other for five minutes?" asks Zavier with a chuckle.

"Yes, when we're working. We weren't doing anything, we fell asleep." Murray reaches down and picks up what looks like a grubby rag off the floor and pulls it over his head. "I was resting my head on it. I get hot."

"Hot? I'm sure," says Zavier with a smirk. "I guess we're lucky you didn't take your pants off."

"Sorry, man," says Ike with a smile. "We tried to stay awake."

Livia looks at Ike and Murray as she and Lex help Kane move forward. *So these two are a couple. I had heard of this, men in the company of men, but this is the first time I've ever met such a couple. Certainly it would never be an Indra-approved cohabitation.*

"That was a slow trip," says Murray, adjusting his shirt and smoothing down his wild hair.

"Yeah," grumbles Zavier. "I've been held up mostly by this one." He points to Kane as Lex and Livia help him through the entrance.

Ike comments, "He looks half dead."

"That is pretty accurate," says Zavier.

Kane mumbles, "I'm not quite dead. I can still hear."

"He needs to rest," says Lex. "And maybe some boosters."

"Sure, we'll get him some help," says Murray.

Once the group is inside, Zavier helps Ike and Murray heave the door closed.

Ike notices Zavier's arm is injured. "What happened to you?"

"We had to fight off a group of three mutants. It was my fault. I missed a trap."

Murray ribs Zavier. "You're out of practice. That's what happens when you've been out of the tunnels for too long. You get rusty. Glad you're not dead. So are you going to introduce us?"

Irritated, Zavier indicates to each of the girls and Kane, "Lex, Livia, and Kane. Meet Ike and Murray. Tunnel runners."

Murray says, "Lex and Livia. The Twins." Awkwardly, he starts to bow, his long hair almost touching the ground.

"Oh no, please," says Livia, embarrassed. "Stand up."

"Yeah, stand up," says Lex. "We're not special. We're not on the High Council. You don't need to kiss our boots."

Ike grabs Murray's shirt and pulls him back up straight, saying under his breath, "What are you doing?"

Murray defends himself, "They are the Twins. *The Twins*. What are we supposed to do?"

"Nothing," says Ike. "Just go tell the chief they made it." Murray hustles off down a narrow corridor.

Ike leads the group through the Last Outpost, where the walls and floor are much smoother than those in the tunnel. "Come on. Let's get you all back to the mess. It's the biggest room we got." The narrow corridor forces them into a single file line. It is dark and very tight with a low ceiling requiring them to duck their heads a bit. Lex walks directly behind Ike, followed by Kane, then Livia, with Zavier at the end. Ike adds, "Everybody's been waiting up to meet you guys."

Zavier says to Ike from the back of the line, "Not everybody."

"We were awake most of the time," Ike says defensively.

Lex shakes her head. *So these are the people we're relying on, and they can't even stay awake. Sure I'll be your Twin Savior, right after you get up from your nap!*

"Originally, the Outpost was just a section of huge old pipe that survived," Ike explains as they move through the corridor, tunnels branching off to either side. "People would be traveling through the tunnel, they would reach the pipe, and it was a good place to rest. As people tried to escape Indra, they would hole up here to sleep or heal, then continue on and never be heard from again. That was before we had any reliable communications. The problem was that it was still vulnerable to mutant attacks, so a bypass tunnel was dug and the section of pipe was concealed. Now it's a way station that marks the end of the tunnel's danger zone. A lot of equipment and procedures have been figured out here to make it more likely to reach the Outlands. But from here people are on their own, support and safety left behind."

Ike turns down a side tunnel, taking them past what appears to be salvaged transporter doors mounted in the side of the dirt wall. He continues, "Now, it's a maze of tunnels and small rooms dug out of the earth. All built up around the old pipe. That pipe has been turned into the mess. It's really the only common area."

Livia looks around skeptically. *Well, I assume he doesn't mean a banquet hall. I have no idea what to expect anymore, but I know Governess would not have allowed me anywhere near any of this.*

Zavier comments with a grin, "You're quite the tour guide, Ike."

Ike shrugs. "I'm a little nervous."

Finally, they reach the mess. It is a huge room, its walls made out of a giant concrete pipe, twenty feet across. Murray stands at the far end of a large table in the center of the room where three people are sitting.

As they enter, Ike announces, “Here they are!”

A stout old woman with short hair gone white with age looks up and exclaims, “Zavier! There you are!” She gets up from the table and with surprising speed comes over to Zavier and wraps him in a hug. “Oh, it’s good to see you. I’ve missed you.”

Zavier winces as she puts pressure on his injured arm, but still he cracks a smile. “Hi, Roya. Good to see you too.” He looks noticeably uncomfortable. “Okay, you can let go now.”

“When I’m done!” After a few more seconds, Roya finally lets him out of her fierce hug and kisses him on the cheek. “Now I’m done!” Zavier wipes his cheek.

“Oh, blast! What happened to your arm?”

“Mutants. It’s not too bad.”

A tall, broad man a good deal younger than Roya walks over from the table. “We will get you fixed up, Zavier.” He looks at the girls. “So these must be Lex and Livia. Welcome to the Last Outpost. I’m Chief Benton. This is Roya, our cook, and at the table is Virgil.” The last person at the table, a skinny man with short gray hair, jumps up and comes over to the group. “He is in charge of comms.”

Virgil says, “Good to see you, Zavier.”

Roya addresses the room. “You girls look good, but this one,” she indicates Kane, “let’s get him in a chair. Murray. Virgil.” Murray and Virgil jump to Kane’s side and help him over to the table and onto a chair.

A young man and woman enter the mess. Livia quickly looks them over. *Who are these two? She is tall and attractive in a strong, no-nonsense way. And him, with that full beard, he looks rough but still good-looking. He is not as tall as Zavier but looks like he may be stronger. They’re maybe a few years older than Lex and me. Zavier’s age. I sense that these two are a couple. Are they tunnel runners?*

Roya says, “Martine, Berk, meet our guests, Lex, Livia, and Kane. Now, Zavier and Martine, I know you’re exes, but I don’t want any fighting. Be nice.”

"You don't have to worry about me," says Martine with a shrug.

"I'll be on my best behavior," says Zavier. "Just for you, Roya." Martine gives Zavier an icy look while Berk seems to be preoccupied with looking at Lex and Livia.

The chief says, "As you can see, Roya keeps everyone in line. She's the self-appointed second-in-command."

Roya, ignoring the jab, continues, "So look at The Twins. Real twins." The room is quiet while Roya and the others study the girls.

Livia looks at everyone staring at her and Lex. She reaches out to sense them. *I can feel that they mean us no harm, but this is quite unnerving. We are twins, but their reaction is so extreme. What do they expect from us?*

Lex scans the mess. *I'm in a room with seven rebels. Most of them staring at me. I feel like I should pull out my blaster and kill all of them. That is my old life. My old enemies. I must find a way to trust them, or at least suppress the urge to kill them.*

The chief is the only one who is not mesmerized by the presence of Lex and Livia. "All right, everyone. Stop gawking. Let's get to work. Zavier's arm needs attention. Roya and Ike, deal with that." Roya leads Zavier over to a side table, where she clears off a few pots and knives, and then grabs a medical bag from a cabinet underneath.

She orders, "Ike, bring me a chair." Ike grabs a chair from the table and brings it over.

"I'll go contact Roscoe," volunteers Virgil. "Let him know that they made it," he says, and scurries out of the mess.

"This young man," says the chief, "Kane, is it? He needs boosters and fluids. Martine and Berk, take Kane to one of the empty rooms and take care of him." Martine and Berk make their way over to Kane and help him up. "And it's my understanding that Livia has to have her chip removed."

"Yes," says Zavier. "We didn't have time to take it out back at base. You'll have to do it, Chief. I can't with this arm."

Kane, who is being led out of the mess by Martine and Berk, protests, "Wait! I want to stay with Livia while you take her chip out."

"Oh, I see," says the chief with a small chuckle. "Let him go." Martine and Berk let go of Kane. He takes one step and crumples to the ground. "I thought so," says the chief.

Livia rushes to Kane's side. He says, "I want to stay with you." Martine and Berk help Kane get to his feet.

"You don't need to," Livia says, putting her hand on his shoulder. "You need to take care of yourself. I will be fine. Lex will be with me."

Kane says pathetically, "But I promised I would be with you."

Lex interrupts, "I can take care of my sister. Kane, you need to rest if you want to continue with us the rest of the way."

Zavier mumbles under his breath, "Good idea, but he still might not make it." Lex shoots Zavier a warning glance.

"I'm sorry," says Kane, defeated. "I'll be stronger tomorrow."

"I know you will be," says Livia. "Go with them." Martine and Berk hold Kane up, one under each of his arms, as they walk out of the mess.

Livia watches silently as Kane is taken out of the room.

Lex walks over to Livia and says, "He will be all right. He needs to get his strength back."

"I know," agrees Livia. "He's been pushing himself so hard."

Lex nods. *I'm almost glad Kane was too weak to stay with Livia for the procedure. I feel possessive of her. Why? Really, I barely know her. I've known Kane longer. It didn't even cross my mind that I should leave her and go with him. Is it because she is my sister? Could that bond already be strong? I can see that they are already close in a way that Kane and I never were. I'm not ready to share her or lose him. I don't want it to always be the two of them with me on the outside. I hate that I'm jealous.*

"Okay, Livia," says the chief, "let's get that chip out of your head."

Roya finishes stitching up Zavier's arm. "I can help," Zavier says as he walks over and stands next to the chief. "I just can't do the extraction."

"Where are we doing this?" asks Lex.

"Best place is right here in the mess," says the chief. "It's got the best light."

Livia objects, "But don't you take your meals here? It doesn't seem sanitary."

The chief smiles at Zavier. "She really does sound like an Islander." He turns to Livia. "Yes, Airess, we eat here. But it's better than the latrine." Livia shudders. "I was joking. The light in the latrine is very poor," he continues with a smile. "All the other rooms are quite small. We'll put you up on the table. Roya, will you wipe it down for Livia? Ike, go get the machine."

Ike rushes off and Roya begins to clear off the long dining table made from several old metal beams.

Roya observes, "I hadn't noticed how rusty it's gotten. Murray, go find something to put under Livia's head."

Murray thinks for a moment. "I might have an old rag somewhere."

Livia grimaces. *An old rag? Was he joking? I don't like this. I don't like any of this. But I have to do it. Maybe it's not as bad as I think.*

"When was the last time you did this?" asks Livia.

"I haven't done it in a while," says the chief. "Most people coming through from the upper levels have already had their chip removed by the time they get here. And of course, people from Rock Bottom don't have a chip."

Zavier admits, "When I took Lex's chip out, it was a bit touch-and-go. I thought I was going to fry her brain trying to get that thing out."

"Yeah, that has happened to me. It's not pretty. I haven't pulled one out in at least a year."

"This is causing me to seriously doubt your abilities," says Livia, forcing her voice to stay calm. "Perhaps it would be better if you both stop talking."

"Here we go," Ike yells as he rushes in pushing a small wheeled cart with a metal machine on top.

The machine has several dials and a long, metal spike attached to one side. The chief detaches a paddle from the top of the machine and flips the switches under the dials. The machine grinds to life, the dials glowing with yellow numbers. Roya hands Zavier a wet cloth.

"Sterilize her right ear," she says to Zavier.

"Yep. Always the right ear," he says as he runs a wet cloth all around Livia's ear.

Lex starts to explain to Livia, "At first it's more uncomfortable than painful, and then the noise frequencies will almost drive you mad. Just when you think you can't take it anymore, it will be over."

Livia says quietly to Lex, "Don't leave my side."

Lex reassures her, "I promise I won't."

Livia's thoughts race. *I must do this. It will be fine. And Lex is here to help me through it. I wanted to be there when her chip was removed. It bothered me that I wasn't. I'm glad she is here.*

Murray walks in carrying what appears to be a grubby bundle of cloth. "I got something for you to put under your head."

Livia sees what Murray has brought in with him and forces herself not to grimace. She quickly says, "Oh, I think I will be fine. Thank you, though."

Murray shrugs and throws the rumpled cloth in the corner.

"Livia, up you go," says the chief. He and Murray help Livia up on to the table. "Everything is ready. It's time to scan for the chip. Lay back."

Livia does, and reaches out her hand for Lex.

Lex whispers in her ear, "Don't worry, I'll kill them if they mess you up."

Livia lets out a small laugh. "I'm sure you will."

"We heard that," says Zavier.

"Good," says Lex. "I meant it."

The chief scans Livia, waving a humming metal paddle over her head.

"Oh, this is going to be tough," says the chief, his eyes narrowed. "Your chip is hard to detect. The transmission is so low. I can see why they didn't rush to take it out in Rock Bottom. It definitely can't be used to locate you."

Lex keeps her voice calm, but she is concerned. "Can you still get it out?"

"Yeah, it will just be harder to pinpoint it. We have to go slow and

be very careful. The transmission doesn't turn down on its own. It's been deliberately turned down. Someone with great skill adjusted your chip. It's unusual but not unheard of. Your chip's signal is low like those of well-placed rebel spies in Indra who need to hide their activities. The spies in Indra can't remove their chips. That'd be a red flag. They need to have some signal, but they do not want everything they do feeding back to the Archives."

Zavier adds, "I've never met a rebel spy. Roscoe knows who they are, of course."

Lex snaps, "Should you really be talking right now? Maybe just focus on getting my sister's chip out."

"Fair point," says the chief. He continues to scan Livia with the humming paddle and calibrate the machine in silence, turning dials and pushing buttons on a keypad.

Livia closes her eyes. *Lex is so fierce. She is protecting me. This is what sisters do for each other.*

Finally, the chief says, "Okay, Livia, first I have to drive in the spike and make contact with your chip. Then it will take three ultra high-pitched sonic waves to disable it. The frequencies are beyond the range of hearing, but in your mind they will seem incredibly loud. After the first frequency wave, you won't be able to talk. It interrupts the speech center of your brain. After that first frequency, you will be able to hear us, but you will have to use hand gestures to communicate with us. Inserting the spike is the most painful part. Should only take five minutes. You can take it. You're strong."

With surprising calm, Livia says, "I appreciate your confidence. I will also appreciate your speed."

The chief nods. He puts the paddle back on the top of the machine and detaches the metal spike from the side, a long red cable stretching out behind it. Livia eyes the metal spike as the chief moves it toward her ear.

Lex smiles encouragingly, though Livia is squeezing her hand very tightly. *Yeah, five minutes of torture, but she can take it. She is strong! I mean, I did pass out, but that's probably for the best. Wait, I'm holding my breath, I*

have to breathe! I don't want her to know how worried I am. I have to calm down! Exhale.

"I've got the chip's location," says the chief. "Now for the final push with the spike to connect to it. This will hurt."

Livia tenses as the pain overwhelms her. It is excruciating. It's over after a moment, though it felt like it was much longer.

The chief smiles. "Great job, here's the first frequency."

The sound pierces Livia's thoughts. *It's so loud! It is in my head. I can't see! Everything is black. There is only this noise. It is too much! Too intense. Is this killing me?*

As the sound dissipates. Livia takes a deep breath. *Thank goodness it's ending. My vision is returning to normal, but I can't move or say anything. That was only a few seconds, but it seemed so much longer. An eternity. There are two more frequencies. How can I bear this? I can't stop it, so I must endure it.*

Lex grips her hand. "That's it, Livia, just move your hand in mine to let us know you're all right."

Livia focuses her mind. *I can do this. All I have to do is just move my hand. Everything is so heavy, but I can do this!* Livia squeezes Lex's hand.

Lex beams, "I felt it! You're doing so good, Livia!"

The chief braces himself and nods at Lex. "Now here's the second frequency."

Lex moves closer, ready to hold Livia down if she has to. *I remember this. It was like my body wanted to tear itself to pieces. I'll make sure she makes it through this.*

The frequency starts. Livia's thoughts race. *This is not as bad as the first one. I thought it was going to get harder, but this is less intense. Just a loud rushing in my ears. Almost not disturbing at all.* The frequency passes. *Is it over already? That wasn't nearly as long as the first one. Only one more frequency. I feel stronger. I am almost through this.* Livia raises her other hand and motions for them to continue.

"Oh, I guess you're all right then," says the chief. "It must be the reduced transmission on your chip, a lower power setting, that is making it easier to disable. I haven't seen that before. Last one, third frequency."

As the third frequency enters Livia's mind, she is calm. *This is nothing more than a whisper. Almost like my hearing being cleared out and being restored to normal. I can feel my body coming back to me. I think it is over. I can move.* She releases Lex's hand.

The chief slowly retracts the spike, and the small chip is attached to the end. Finally the chief says, "All right, we got it. You okay, Airess?"

Livia weakly responds, "I am, but that was most unpleasant."

"Unpleasant," Lex repeats, raising her eyebrows. "Well, her brain seems to be all right."

Livia, with characteristic poise, says, "Thank you, Chief. And Zavier. That was not as bad as I feared."

The chief gives her a small smile. "Not bad at all."

Livia says to Lex, "Thank you."

Lex smiles and shakes her hand. "I think the blood is coming back into my hand."

The chief orders, "Ike, Murray, take her to a room to rest." They rush over, and Ike gingerly picks up Livia and carries her out of the room.

5

In a small, dim room, Livia lies on a sleeper. When she opens her eyes, she sees Kane sitting in a chair next to her while Lex stands close to the open doorway.

"How are you feeling?" he asks.

"I feel all right. It wasn't that bad." She looks closely at Kane's face. *He is looking a little better. He has more color. His eyes are more alert.* "How are you? You are looking better."

"They gave me fluids and a bunch of boosters," he says. "I don't know what they were exactly, but I feel much better."

"I'm so glad, but you should rest. You don't need to be here with me."

Kane takes Livia's hand. "I'm not leaving you."

Lex shifts awkwardly. *I'm so out of place. They are so ridiculous. How can they be so serious about each other so soon? They just met. I could never be so mushy. Kane was never like this with me. They are something different.*

Lex says briskly, "Looks like Kane's got you. I'll be around if you need me," and heads out the door.

When Lex is gone, Livia says to Kane, "I could tell Lex was uncomfortable. It must be hard for her to see us getting so close."

"I'm not sure what we can do about that," says Kane. "I can't help how I feel about you."

"I can sense how you feel about me," says Livia.

"Can you?" Kane asks with a smile. He pushes her hair back from her face. "I'm definitely not trying to hide it."

"I don't think you could even if you wanted to. I felt it the night we met at my Emergence Ball, that you were attracted to me, but also that you wanted to protect me."

"Yes, I wanted to protect you. It just all went wrong."

"I know it was an accident. You weren't really trying to kill me. I knew then and I know now that you would never hurt me."

"Never, but I don't want to hurt Lex either. What Lex and I had . . ." He corrects himself, "What we *have* is not the same. We're friends. I would protect her with my life, and I know she would do the same for me. I don't want to hurt her, but what we have is something special. Something deep and strong. I feel like I've known you all my life. When I watched you from the rig—"

Livia interrupts, "Let's not talk about how you spied on me for months."

"Well, it was more like weeks," Kane corrects.

"Still, it is disconcerting to think about you watching me. I can't remember what I did. What you saw me do when I thought I was alone."

"Nothing embarrassing. Mostly I saw you riding your horse, the wind in your hair. You looked so free."

"Oh, Veda," Livia says, distressed. "She is the only living horse in all of Indra. My father created her for my mother. She rode her every day like I did. I'm worried about her. I don't know what will become of her without me there."

Kane puts his hand on Livia's cheek. "I'm sorry. I wish there was something I could do."

"There is nothing that can be done. It breaks my heart to think of her being alone. It sounds foolish, but she was my only friend." *Kane cares about me. This is real. I can tell him anything. I can feel the warmth of his hand on my face. It is so comforting. Just his touch is making my heart pound.*

Kane traces Livia's eyebrow with his fingertip and smiles. "You are so beautiful. I don't want this to sound stupid, but I am your friend."

"It doesn't. I never let myself even dream that I would find someone that I would have true feelings for. It never seemed to be an option."

Kane's hands stay on her face. "It's not a dream. I'm right here." He leans over to Livia and kisses her. It is sweet and tender.

This is a man I could love. He is more than I ever thought I would have. I can be myself with him. I can let go. I don't have to hold back. Livia winces. "Wait . . ."

Kane pulls away. "Are you okay? Is it your head?"

"I'm not sure. I just got dizzy, but it wasn't painful. My head . . . I was just spinning. I think it was you."

"I'll take that as a good thing, then."

"You should." She pulls Kane closer and they begin kissing again.

After a moment, Kane slows the kiss. "We need to rest. I don't want to stop, but we should. Someday soon there will be nothing holding us back."

"I'm looking forward to it," says Livia with a wicked smile.

"Me too." Kane kisses her on the forehead.

Through the dark halls of the Outpost, Lex makes her way back to the mess, where she finds Zavier with the crew. The chief sits sedately at the table with Virgil while Roya is hunched over a work counter pouring brown liquid into cups. Zavier leans against the edge of the table watching Ike and Murray, who are standing in the middle of the mess arguing loudly.

"You almost made the ladies faint when we opened the door!" yells Ike. "I've begged you! You've got to cut your hair. Trim it at least. Your face, your chest, everywhere!"

Murray smiles. "Never! I like the low-maintenance approach. Out here, who cares anyways?"

"I do!" yells Ike. "We all do!"

Martine and Berk are huddled in a corner looking over a piece of equipment, ignoring the ruckus.

"You're starting to look like some kind of mutant with fur," adds Virgil.

"You kinda smell like one too!" says Zavier, chuckling.

Murray laughs. "Virg, what do you know about mutants? When was the last time you were anywhere near one? You haven't been out of the Outpost for years!"

"Well, I know they are scary and gross, and that's you, friend."

Zavier laughs and pulls his shirt off. "This is what it should look like. Not that mess you've got going."

"Hi, Lex," says Roya. "Let me get you a cup."

"What is it?" asks Lex.

Roya winks. "It tastes better if you don't know what's in it."

"It's a chemical concoction that Roya makes out of mysterious ingredients," says Virgil. "Try it, it's not half bad."

"No thanks," says Lex.

Zavier takes a swig from his cup. "It won't kill you to loosen up." He takes a cup from Roya and brings it over to Lex.

"Are you joking?" asks Lex, her anger rising. "Tomorrow we set out on what you have said is going to be an exhausting climb. We should all be resting up. Instead, you're getting blasted."

Zavier smiles. "Just blowing off steam. I deserve it."

"Deserve it? For what?" challenges Lex.

"For getting you all here."

"I seem to remember you were the one that almost got us killed. I can't believe you are supposed to be our guide. You're so irresponsible. Just a self-important ass. You make me sick." Lex pushes Zavier and he stumbles and spills the full cup he brought over for Lex on both of them, the brown liquid soaking into the bandage wrapped around his arm.

"Oh! Sorry," says Zavier.

"You idiot!" yells Lex.

Roya steps in. "All right, you two! Out! Leave the cups and go." She takes the cups from Zavier. He is a bit unsteady on his feet as he moves toward the door, brushing the mystery drink off his bare chest. "Lex has a point, you both should get some sleep." With a wave of her hand, Roya ushers Lex and Zavier out of the mess.

Lex and Zavier make their way down the corridor. Zavier trails one hand on the wall to steady himself.

"You really are a mess," says Lex. "You don't need to come with us tomorrow. You should stay here. You've never even been through that part of the tunnel. Just stay here with your buddies and get fried."

"That sounds good to me, but I promised Roscoe I would get you three to the Outlands, and that's what I'm going to do, but he never said I have to be nice to you."

"I don't care what Roscoe said. We don't need you."

Zavier leans against the wall and grabs Lex's hand to stop her. "Wait. Just stop for a minute. Maybe you don't need me to come tomorrow. You're pretty capable. Even Livia is tougher than I thought. But Kane. He's still a drain."

"He's not that bad. I bet after a night's sleep he will be much better."

"Sure. Good as new," says Zavier, his words dripping with sarcasm. "Look," his tone changing to playful, "I'm going with you tomorrow. And we can share the lead. I don't have a problem with you. I like a tough girl. Actually, you're just the kind of girl I like."

Lex is incredulous. "Have you lost your mind?" *He's still holding my hand.* Zavier pulls her closer. *Is he going to try to kiss me?*

Zavier's speech is a bit slurred. "I don't have to like you to, you know, like you. You know what I mean?"

What was in that drink? He really has lost his head.

Zavier continues, "You're a pain in the ass, but you look good in that silitex." He is still holding her hand and reaches his other hand around and runs it up her back. "You're such a badass. It's so hot."

I wish he wasn't so fried. But if he wasn't, I don't think he would ever admit to feeling anything but contempt for me.

Zavier pulls Lex against him, their bodies pressed tight. *He's so tall. I never realized. His skin is so warm. I've been close to him before but not like this. He held me when we parazipped down from the High Council Building. But dropping down from the Spear I wasn't really paying attention to him. He is so solid. Strong. I can almost feel his scruffy beard. No one at the Academy or in the PCF would ever be allowed to grow one. Why do I like it? He smells, but it's good. It's making me light-headed. Even though his eyes are half closed they are staring directly at me. They are such a clear, bright blue. I don't know how to look away. I think he is going to kiss me. Do I want this? Would he want this if he wasn't wasted on Roya's mystery drink?*

Zavier leans in and kisses Lex. Lex lets him and even gives in to the kiss for a moment. *Zavier is kissing me. Gruff, grouchy Zavier. I can't believe this is happening.*

The kiss starts slow but quickly grows in intensity. *This kiss is not like my only other kiss. The one time Kane kissed me, before he left the Academy. That was more like a good-bye. This feels so different. Do I like Zavier?*

Zavier buries one hand in Lex's hair, his other hand starts sliding down her back. *Is his hand moving to my butt? Okay. This has gone too far.*

Lex pushes Zavier away. "That's enough."

Zavier stands a few steps away from Lex with his hands held up. "Okay. Okay. You don't need to get mad. No harm done. Now we know that you want me. Why don't you come back to my room and we can see where this goes?" Zavier takes a step toward Lex, and she kicks him in the gut. He crumples to the floor.

Zavier groans and says, "I guess that's a no?"

"Unbelievable! You're an idiot," Lex says as she walks off down the corridor, leaving him on the floor. *Did he really think I was just going to go off to his room with him? Too much, too fast. He could barely stand up. Even before I kicked him. I thought he hated me. I thought I hated him. Now I'm not so sure.*

Lex makes her way back to Livia's room, where she finds both Livia and Kane asleep. Kane is still in the chair by Livia's sleeper, his head resting on its edge. They are holding hands. *I shouldn't be surprised. I guess they are together now. I can't stay in here. Maybe I should take Zavier up on his offer. At least I wouldn't be alone. Wait. Since when have I worried about being alone? I've been alone all my life. It's made me strong. There must be an empty room somewhere.*

Lex heads down the corridor. She turns a corner, and Martine is walking toward her.

Martine asks, "You shouldn't be wandering around."

"I'm not wandering," says Lex, irritated. "I'm looking for somewhere to sleep."

"I thought you would be with Zavier."

"Why would you think that?"

Martine smiles. "Aren't you two together?"

Lex is indignant. "No!"

"Oh. Okay," says Martine with a shrug. "It's just, he is obviously attracted to you."

Lex thinks, *It wasn't obvious to me until he kissed me.*

"What made you think that? He's always rude and dismissive."

"That's Zavier," says Martine. "He doesn't want to want anyone. He's really good at pushing people away. A little advice, you should really steer clear. Deep down he's never going to let anybody get close to him. He's no good for anyone."

"I am not interested in Zavier. Not in the least."

"Good. He's all fire in the beginning, but he burns out."

Lex nods. "Thanks for the warning."

"I know where you can sleep. Come on."

Martine walks down the corridor and Lex follows. *She seems nice. I can't believe she just warned me off Zavier. I wonder what their story is. He must have hurt her. I'm sure she's right about him. He is not someone I should get involved with. Why did he kiss me? It was so much easier just to hate him before that.*

They make a few twists and turns, then Martine stops at a door and opens it. She reaches in and flips a switch by the door and a weak light flickers on. It is a small room much like the one Livia and Kane are in, with a sleeper against the wall. "Here you go. I hope you get good rest. From what I hear, you'll need it."

Lex walks into the room. "Thanks." Martine nods and walks away.

Lex shuts the door, flips off the light, and walks to the sleeper in the dark. She can still see, even though there is no light in the room. She lies down. *I'm alone. This is how it will be. Livia and Kane together and me somewhere else. I have been alone. I don't need anyone. I certainly don't need Zavier. I hope he is still on the floor.* Lex smiles as she closes her eyes. *Poor Zavier. He's going to wish he never let his feelings slip out.*

6

In the morning, Lex, Livia, and Kane are in the mess loading up their packs and weapons, prepping to head out with the help of Ike, Murray, Roya, and Chief Benton.

Roya hands Kane some supplies to put in his pack. "You are looking much better, Kane. I'm sorry to see you go. I was kind of hoping you would have to stay here for a while. I like it when handsome men come to visit me."

"Sorry to disappoint you," Kane says with a grin. "I'm still a bit weak, but the expert medical attention and rest have really helped."

Zavier walks in, his face shadowed and his pace slow.

Murray takes one look at him and says, "Oh, man! You look like you been dragged through Core Low by a couple of mutants. Roya's mix was too strong for you. You're getting weak, friend. Weak."

Zavier is uncharacteristically quiet. He grabs his pack and starts loading up.

Lex smiles to herself. *That's right, Zavier. He must be feeling the effects of Roya's drink and the kick to the gut. He must be embarrassed too. He can't even look at me. Unless he doesn't remember. I hope he remembers. He kissed me, the big idiot.* Lex ignores Zavier and puts on her pack and weapons.

The chief brings out a crate of equipment, "You'll all have to wear these breathing devices to help you adjust to the air outside of Indra."

"Why?" asks Lex. "What is wrong with the air outside of Indra?"

The chief explains while pulling four small, hard plastic cases from the crate. "Nothing. It's the air inside Indra that's the problem. The air has been manipulated by the Council with an additive, a vascular dilator that makes it impossible to breathe regular air." The chief pops open one of the cases, revealing a small rectangular unit with a slender, clear tube attached. "Originally, it was added to the air so people could breathe the thin, oxygen-poor air. Now the air pumped in from outside is oxygen rich. The additive is no longer necessary, but the Council still puts it into the air system." The chief looks over the unit and hands it to Livia.

"Why would the Council continue to use the additive?" asks Livia.

"It's just another way the Council is controlling everyone," says Zavier. "They tell everyone they can't leave Indra because the air outside is toxic." While the chief hands one of the cases to him, Zavier continues, "Really, it's the air inside Indra that is poisoned."

The chief nods at Zavier and says, "If the additive is not present in the air, your blood vessels constrict and your lungs collapse. Beyond the Outpost, the amount of additive is minimal. Basically, you will suffocate." He holds up a device and extends the clear tube. "You clip this tube to your nose and the unit will pump additive into your airway to mix with the pure air as you breathe." He hands it to Lex.

He holds up the fourth unit and points to a dial on the side. "This is where you adjust the regulator on the device so the amount of additive is slowly reduced so you can adjust to pure air."

Kane asks, "How long will it take to get off the additive?"

"It takes several days, but it depends on the amount in your system," says the chief. "The higher you lived in Indra, the more dependent you'll be. Livia, our island Airess, will have the most in her system, and Zavier, from Rock Bottom, will have the least."

"Why do I have the most?" asks Livia.

"Indra has always provided the higher society with what they believe is the best of everything, including the air," says the chief. "By the time you get to Rock Bottom the additive has been greatly diluted. Like everything else in Rock Bottom, where they get nothing but the dregs, the air is the worst. Only in this case, it's a good thing. The device will wean you off the additive, so you don't go through withdrawals. It's extremely painful. You'd get disoriented and could have convulsions. We don't want that."

Lex interjects, "That sounds fun. Let's not do that."

"It's difficult to secure the additive," the chief explains. "That is one of the reasons it is so hard to escape Indra. We are only able to help a few people a month get out of Rock Bottom. Before we knew about the additive, people would travel through the tunnel to get out of Indra, and when they got past the Outpost, they would start to get sick and die. Eventually they figured out that if they went really slowly, they wouldn't get too sick. Before the breathing device, it would take almost a month to get to the Outlands. The supplies alone for a trip that long were a huge problem."

Virgil comes into the mess holding four canisters. "Got the additive, Chief." Virgil hands them each a canister.

"You slide it in on the side," says the chief.

Virgil helps Livia put the canister into the regulator. There is a click as it fits into place. Lex, Kane, and Zavier follow Virgil's example.

Virgil says, "Then clip the unit to your belt." Virgil helps Livia clip the unit to her belt. The others do the same. Virgil holds up the tube, which has a metal clip on the end. "Clip this on your nose, then tuck the tube behind your ear."

"So, Livia," says the chief, "you should set your dial to ten. You can go down one click a day. That should be slow enough. Kane and Lex, try dropping two clicks a day. You can do one midday and another at night. You'll just have to see if you feel any side effects. You may have to slow down. Zavier, you should be good at two clicks a day, maybe three."

They put on their packs and weapons. Kane is wearing a pack that is about half the size of Zavier's.

"Last thing," says Roya. "You all got to write on the wall." She hands Lex a sharp knife.

"What do we write?" Lex asks.

"Whatever you want," says Roya.

Lex, Livia, and Kane walk up to the wall, looking at it closely for the first time. The walls of the mess are marked by hundreds and hundreds of names and messages carved over and across each other, some to loved ones who may or may not follow:

bye Mum n Dad
see you soon Calvin

Others have left scathing good-byes to Indra:

BLAST you Indra
Go to core-low PCF
Council are mutants

Lex reads a carved message that looks very old:

RB is Death - Outlands are life - I must live

Lex runs her fingers over the carving. *They must have felt so desperate to leave. To risk their lives to be free. I hope this person made it.*

Next to Lex, Livia holds hands with Kane as they read messages. Livia says to Kane, "Look at this one." She points to a message on the wall:

lost child - lost life - I go in hope

"It's heartbreaking," says Livia, with a tear running down her cheek. Kane brushes it away.

Roya walks to the wall and points out one of the carvings. "Here, come look at this. This is what your mother wrote when she came through. That was before my time."

Lex and Livia come over to look at the spot on the wall. It reads:

I am Delphia. I belong to no one.

"Very her, from what I understand," says Roya.

Livia runs her finger over Delphia's message. *My mother. Delphia came through here. She stood right here. Maybe before there was much of an Outpost at all. What an amazing woman. I wonder how long it took her group to get to the Outlands. Much longer than it will take us.*

Lex ponders, *"I belong to no one?" Who was she talking about? Father? Us?*

Next to Delphia's is a carving that reads:

Freedom lies in being bold - Roscoe

"Roscoe has been to the Outlands?" asks Lex.

"Yes," says Roya. "He's come through a few times, but we haven't seen him in years."

"Roscoe didn't tell us that he'd been to the Outlands," says Livia.

"He's good at keeping secrets, and so am I," says Roya. "Now, let's get this moving. Sign the wall."

Lex puts the knife to the wall and carves:

I am Lex. You can't stop me.

Lex hands the knife to Livia. Livia thinks for a moment and then carves:

For all those who went before
and all those who come after,
I wish you freedom and happiness.

It takes her a long time.

"You're not writing *The Book of Indra*!" says Lex, exasperated. Livia hands the knife to Kane.

Kane carves:

I will make it

Lex reads Kane's carving and smiles at him. "I have no doubt."

Zavier carves:

Outlands here I come - Z

Then he says, "All right, let's go." He walks out of the mess and everyone follows.

The group weaves through the small, twisting corridors of the Outpost and finally reaches the door. Martine and Berk are there waiting.

Berk reports, "There's been no activity. It's clear to go."

Martine says, "Good to meet you all. I hope you have a safe trip."

"Be careful," says the chief. "Things are always changing in the tunnel."

"Yes, sir," says Zavier.

Roya gives Zavier a big hug. "And since this time you are going to the Outlands. . . ." She kisses him on the lips with a big smacking noise. Zavier smiles.

"She does that to all the men who come through," says Ike with a wide grin.

Roya smiles at Kane. "You too, handsome. It's a tradition."

Kane smiles. "Well, if it's a tradition."

Roya walks over to Kane and kisses him on the lips. "Okay, now get going."

Murray and Berk heave the door open. Zavier is the first through the door. As he passes, he says to Murray, "You could stand a haircut and a shave."

Murray chuckles, "So could you, friend." He slaps Zavier on the back of his huge pack.

Kane is next through the door, followed by Lex and Livia. As they pass Murray, he says, "Sorry about the no shirt thing yesterday, ladies."

Livia smiles at Murray. "I didn't mind." She kisses him on his beard-covered cheek. Murray beams as Lex and Livia pass through the door.

The chief yells, "Get those breathers turned on!" They all reach down and turn on the breathing devices and clip the tubes to their noses. With an effort, Berk and Murray push the door closed.

7

Zavier is in the lead, closely followed by Kane, with Lex and Livia walking together behind them. The ground is covered in loose rocks and dirt. Quickly, the tunnel becomes very steep and the climb is difficult. Kane's breathing is loud and labored.

"Make sure your breathing unit is set to the highest level," Zavier says to Kane. "That should help."

Kane checks the dial on his unit and adjusts it. "Thanks."

Livia asks Lex, "Can you believe we are going to meet our mother? What do you think she will be like?"

"I have no idea. She seems complicated. In those old Archive memories Roscoe showed us, she was a beautiful Islander, happy and fun. But she was fierce when she got pregnant and left Indra. She's been living in the Outlands for seventeen years. I really can't imagine what she will be like."

"I know," says Livia. "She is surprising. She was a privileged Islander. She gave that up for us."

"Yes, for us," agrees Lex. "But she was protecting herself as well."

"That is what Islanders do," says Zavier. "They protect themselves. They are selfish and blind."

"Livia and I are both from the Islands and we're not selfish or blind," argues Kane.

"And what about our mother?" challenges Lex. "She was an Islander and gave it up."

"Also, Roscoe was an Islander," adds Livia. "Now he leads the rebels."

"As leader, his knowledge of all the levels of Indra has been useful," says Zavier. "He's from the Islands, but he knows all about the Middler level and the Hub. Things we would never have known. He even brought us one of our most important benefactors. But Roscoe will never really understand what it means to be trapped in Rock Bottom. He is an Islander at heart. Still, he is different from all of you."

"Why?" asks Livia.

"Because he chose freely to leave his island life and become a rebel," says Zavier with contempt. "You, Kane, and your mother didn't really have a choice, did you?"

"I had a choice," says Livia with defiance. "I could have told the PCF that Lex forced me to go with her. She suggested I abandon her. But I wanted answers, and they were not to be found trapped on Helix."

"Still," says Zavier, "you didn't just decide one day to leave your island and join the rebels."

"Actually, I jumped off Helix Island onto a rig with Lex, and I have not looked back."

"You jumped onto that rig because the PCF were about to blast us off your island," says Lex, "but, you did jump. That took guts. It was pretty strato."

As they walk, the tunnel gradually becomes more narrow.

"This part is unstable," says Zavier. "The last group through reported collapses and slides."

They climb over piles of rubble from past rock slides. In one section the tunnel is so steep, they have to climb on their hands and knees over a huge pile of loose rocks. With no firm ground beneath them, progress is slow. Every move sends rocks tumbling down the hill as they try to move up, their feet sinking deep into the rubble. In the front of the group, Zavier slips and starts to slide down the hill, crashing into Kane, his boot hitting Kane in the chin as they all tumble to the bottom of the hill.

Zavier says to Kane, "Um, sorry about that. You all right?"

"Yeah. I think I ate some dirt. You know, I was expecting you to kick me in the face sooner or later, I just thought it would be on purpose."

Zavier smiles. "Maybe we should spread out a bit more."

"I think that's a good idea," says Kane, rubbing his chin.

Past the piles of loose rock, the tunnel flattens out.

Lex asks Zavier, "Why did Roscoe choose you to lead us to the Outlands if you have never been beyond the Outpost?"

"Roscoe is the only one I know who has been to the Outlands and come back to Rock Bottom. He gave me this assignment, and you don't question his decisions."

"Sounds like when you get your Final Placement at the Academy," says Lex. "Why didn't Roscoe come with us?"

"He stayed back to make sure that the rebellion is on track, get the word out that The Time of the Twins is coming."

"The Time of the Twins is coming?" Lex asks, raising her eyebrows. "I'm not part of your rebellion."

"So you're not a rebel," says Livia. "You certainly are not with the PCF anymore. What are you, then?"

"I'd guess a fugitive," says Kane. "I'm sure the PCF would consider us enemy number one. They would blast us on sight."

"How did this happen?" asks Lex angrily. "I never wanted to be a rebel. I was trained to kill them!"

"Yeah, I know," says Zavier. "But you don't know anything about the rebels."

Lex says without hesitation, "They hate all of Indra and want to destroy it!"

"That's a PCF answer," says Zavier. "You've seen enough now, I thought you'd understand. The rebels exist because Indra oppresses the people of Rock Bottom. The Independent High Council has set up a system that gives all the advantages to the people of the Islands and everyone else is exploited to support their way of life. The rebels are fighting for freedom and fairness. I became a rebel because my father was a rebel. He was the one who convinced Roscoe to join the rebels."

"How did your father even know Roscoe?" asks Lex.

"Roscoe came to Rock Bottom looking for a place to hide your mother," says Zavier. "It must have been just after they discovered she was going to have twins."

"From what we saw in our parents' Archive memories," adds Livia, "I don't think it would have been that difficult to turn Roscoe into a rebel. He seemed devastated by what happened to our parents and the choices they were forced to make."

"No," says Zavier, shaking his head. "It was hard for Roscoe to turn his back on Indra and become a rebel. He was sympathetic to the rebels' cause, but he had a good life. He was from a powerful island family, and Indra treated him very well. But my father was very persuasive. He and Roscoe became good friends."

"Where is your father?" asks Lex.

"He's dead," says Zavier coldly.

"I'm so sorry," says Livia, compassion in her tone. "What happened?"

"He was murdered in a PCF raid a few years ago. That's why I became a rebel."

Lex asks, "If your father was a rebel, weren't you one already?"

"No. My father was a rebel, but that didn't automatically make me one."

"I assumed you were always a rebel," says Livia. "You seem well suited to it."

"You don't know anything about me!" yells Zavier. "Such an Airess thing to say!"

Kane jumps in. "Hey! Take it easy, Zavier!"

"I apologize for making that assumption," says Livia. "I did not intend to offend you."

Zavier takes a breath and explains, "I had other ideas for how I could help Rock Bottom free itself from the oppression of Indra. Roscoe and his books were making that happen. I wanted to start to teach the children of Rock Bottom, and my father supported that cause."

"You wanted to be a teacher?" asks Lex, shocked. "In Rock Bottom?"

"Why are you so surprised?" challenges Zavier. "Is it that I am more than just a rebel or that Rock Bottom could be more than a toilet for Indra?"

"No, I just couldn't imagine you working with kids. Patience doesn't seem to be one of your virtues."

"That wasn't always true. But when my father was killed by the PCF, I felt I had to take more of an active role. I felt teaching kids wasn't enough. I wanted to help protect them. I became a rebel, and I started as a runner. Roscoe was disappointed. He argued that education was the key to freedom. But he respected my choice."

"But you had a choice," says Livia.

"It never felt like I did," says Zavier. "It seemed most of my life was decided for me."

"Then we have that in common," says Livia.

Lex stops suddenly. "Wait. What is that noise?"

Zavier keeps walking. "I don't hear anything."

A moment later the ground begins to shake and chunks of rock start to fall off the tunnel wall all around them.

Zavier yells, "It's a cave-in! Back up!"

Rocks and dirt come crashing down on all sides. Everyone scrambles to get out of the way.

"Get down!" yells Kane, grabbing Lex's hand and pulling her back.

A huge boulder falls through the roof of the tunnel, forcing Lex and Kane back the way they came.

"Move!" yells Zavier, pulling Livia forward as an avalanche of dirt and rocks pours in around the boulder, filling the tunnel opening, splitting the groups apart. Lex and Kane are on one side of a wall of rubble and the imposing boulder, with Livia and Zavier on the other.

8

A thick dust cloud hangs in the air.

Zavier yells out, "Livia? Where are you? Are you hurt?"

Livia answers, "Surprisingly, no. Are you?" As the debris settles, she reaches out to find Zavier and grabs his shoulder.

"No, I'm okay too."

"Good. But now what do we do? Lex and Kane are on the other side."

Zavier begins to inspect the cave-in. "Okay, good. This side is not as impacted or blocked by the rock. It could have killed us. I hope they are all right."

Livia takes a moment. She closes her eyes and lets herself feel for Lex and Kane. *Though there is a wall between us, I can feel them. Almost see them in a way, not with my eyes but with my mind. Lex is stronger, more clear than Kane, but I sense them on the other side. Alive and uninjured. I am so relieved. We must get to them.* "I feel they are unharmed. But how do we get to them?"

"Relax, Airess, we are prepared for this. This isn't the first cave-in, and it won't be the last. We're not dead, and that's all that matters. Now it's just work." He goes into his pack and pulls out a small, collapsible shovel. He snaps the handle into place and holds it up. "Your pack will have one too." He begins to dig.

Relieved, Livia finds the shovel in her pack and immediately starts to dig next to Zavier.

On the other side of the cave-in, the dust has settled and Lex is helping Kane to his feet.

"You all right?"

"Yeah," says Kane, brushing dirt off his face. "Nothing broken. You think they're all right?"

Lex pauses and listens. "It is faint, but I can hear a scraping noise. They must be digging. They are okay." Lex pulls off her pack and puts it on the ground. "You rest. I'll dig."

"No, I can help." He pulls off his pack and sets it on the ground.

"All right, if you're up for it."

Lex rummages through her pack looking for something to dig with. She pulls out a collapsible shovel. She unfolds it and locks the two pieces into place. Kane goes through his pack and finds his shovel. They start to dig.

Kane stops and asks, "Wait. Where should we dig, so we meet up with them?"

Lex pauses and listens again. She moves to the other side of the rock.

"I can hear them. They are right here, on the other side." They begin to shovel.

On Livia and Zavier's side of the cave-in, they are digging exactly across from Lex and Kane but have made very little progress. It is clear that digging out is going to take a long time.

Livia asks, "Are you nervous about going to the Outlands?"

"Why would I be nervous?"

"Because it is the unknown, someplace you have never been."

"I guess, but *nervous* wouldn't be the word I would use. I'm charged up to finally see them. The way Roscoe has described them over the years, I've always wanted to go out. But I never thought I'd get the chance to or be put in command of a mission to the Outlands."

"In command," she says with a small laugh. "Don't let Lex hear you say that."

"She seems to have a real problem with authority. Only reason Lex survived the Orphanage is 'cause my sister Samantha was looking out for her. Lex would have bottomed out if Samantha hadn't been there."

He must know Samantha saved my life, thinks Livia. *But he doesn't know how I feel about it. I have to tell him.* Livia says timidly, "You know Samantha saved my life too."

"I know."

"I froze in Rock Bottom when a mutant aimed its harpoon directly at me. All the years of zinger training left me and I couldn't move. It would have killed me if Samantha hadn't shoved me out of the way."

"I know."

"I'm so sorry she died. I tried to save her, but it was too late."

"I know." Zavier doesn't look at Livia and keeps digging.

Livia can sense Zavier's reluctance to discuss Samantha, but she pushes on. "She was so important to Lex. And I can only just start to imagine what she meant to you, since I just discovered my own sister. How did Samantha end up in the Orphanage?"

Zavier takes a deep breath. "We had the same father but different mothers. Her mother was high on boosters all the time and my father wasn't around. He was very involved with the rebels. In Rock Bottom, kids often only have one person looking after them, and sometimes they don't even have that."

"That sounds terrible."

"Well, we don't have cohabitation laws or Emergence Balls that pair us off, and there is no EX2 pill to control births. People just have kids whenever and with whoever. My father was with a lot of other women, but Samantha and I were his only kids. The PCF took her one day in a raid and put her in the Orphanage in the Hub."

"The PCF can do that?" Livia asks, shocked. "Just take the children from Rock Bottom?"

"Airgirl, you don't think Indra would leave perfectly capable workers in Rock Bottom? If they need people, they take them. Best to grab them when they're little. If you take them young enough, they'll never remember where they came from, the families they were taken from, and what Rock Bottom was really like. They will accept what they are told. That

Rock Bottom is a scary place full of mutants who will eat you, so stay in line and don't bottom out and be a good slave for Indra."

"That is horrible. I had no idea. How old was she when she was taken?"

"She was maybe two years old. Back then, kids were taken all the time. It started happening less and less over the last few years. I guess they didn't need as many kids. When Samantha was taken, I didn't even know she existed. My dad and Roscoe decided to leave her in the Orphanage. They had people working in the Orphanage who were looking out for her. I guess my dad figured she would be safer there than in Rock Bottom with her mom. A few years after Samantha was snatched, her mom took some nasty boosters and died, so maybe she was safer there. Still, I could have gotten her out and brought her home to Rock Bottom, but no one listened to me then. When she was a little older, they used her as a spy."

"But it was good she was there when Lex arrived."

Zavier says sarcastically, "Yeah, I guess it all worked out for Lex's benefit."

"I didn't mean it like that. I meant that they had each other."

"I know what you meant."

"From the very short time I knew her and what Lex told me, she was very smart, strong, and sweet. I will deeply regret my moment of hesitation that took her life for the rest of mine."

"I know you will."

Livia continues digging. *I had to tell him how sorry I am. How bad I feel. I hope he does understand. I am responsible for taking away someone he loved. That will be hard to forgive. I can't even forgive myself. How could I expect him to forgive me? Maybe in time. At least I told him.*

On the other side of the cave-in, Lex digs with unrelenting intensity. Kane digs, but with much less force.

Lex asks, "Do you want to take a break? You can rest."

"No, I'm okay. I can keep digging."

"Are you strong enough for this trip? It is still a long way. You could go back to the Outpost. Rest up and come later."

"No. I can feel my strength coming back, and I don't want to leave you and Livia."

Lex doesn't look at Kane. *We are alone. I have to ask him.* She focuses on the dirt in front of her and says, "So you and Livia? You two are really together already? That seems fast."

Kane smiles. "I know it is fast, but we're a good fit. Maybe it's because we're both from the Islands, we relate to each other. When I was watching her, I was intrigued. She was different than I thought she would be, more interesting."

"Why? Because she was prancing around on her horse and practicing with her zinger?"

"Exactly. I'm not sure what I thought she would be doing, but it wasn't that. Most Islanders live very sedate lives. Their children are groomed to follow in their parents' shadows. Obviously, Livia was being raised by people other than her parents, but I still thought she would be living the rigidly controlled life of a Proper Indrithian Young Lady. Which would certainly not include riding a horse all over the island and training to do combat with a zinger."

"So she is different, like you?"

"Yes. My upbringing was not traditional either. When I was young, before I was taken to the Academy, it was just me and my father on our island. My mother died when I was very young. I have no memories of her, and my father mostly wanted to be alone. We had almost no staff on the island, which is not typical. I spent my time working with my Life Guide, but I was allowed to do my sound painting and sculpting. My father actually encouraged it, maybe because he wanted me out of his way. Then, when I met Livia face-to-face at her Emergence Ball, I could tell she wasn't like other Islanders. She was going through the motions. Everything looked proper, but there was something behind her eyes. Something defiant. Livia and I are from the Islands, but we are not really Islanders."

"How did you get the assignment to kill her?"

Kane shrugs. "I never knew anything more than my mission. The officers who gave me my orders weren't standard PCF or Special Ops. They were some special unit. I think I got the assignment because they knew I was island-born and would know what to do at an Emergence Ball. They promised me I would be released from service and I could return to my family's island if I completed the mission."

"I didn't realize you wanted out of the PCF so bad. I thought we were in it together."

"We were in it together at the Academy, but I'm sure the PCF would have split us up with our Final Placements. They knew we were friends. There's no way they would have given us the same placement. Plus, I wasn't allowed to talk about the mission. It's not like I asked to be released from the PCF. It was part of the assignment. In the end, I couldn't go through with it."

"Really?" asks Lex sarcastically. "I'm surprised. She's so annoying and uppity. I definitely could have killed her before I knew she was my sister." They both laugh. Lex continues, "We're gonna have to figure out who sent that order. That's a huge piece of this puzzle. Who wanted Livia dead and why?"

"I know. That's why I want to help protect both of you."

"Both of us?" teases Lex. "You seem to be pretty focused on Livia. But I get it. You two seem to fit. If you want to get all cozy with her, you have my permission."

"I didn't know I needed it."

Lex laughs. "You don't. You can do whatever you want, but if she hurts you, I don't care if she is my sister, I'll blast her."

After almost an hour of relentless digging, Lex is covered in dirt and Kane's face is slick with sweat. He is out of breath, though he is not digging as fast as she is.

Lex yells, "I can see a light breaking through from the other side!" She tosses her shovel to the side and scoops the dirt away with her hands.

"I see you!" yells Livia.

"Keep digging," yells Lex as she pushes away piles of dirt and rocks to clear an opening. With Livia and Zavier digging frantically, the opening quickly becomes big enough for Lex and Kane to crawl through, pulling their packs behind them.

"Lex!" yells Livia. She rushes to Lex and hugs her with such ferocity that Lex can hardly breathe.

"Okay," Lex laughs. "I'm all right." *My sister is insane! She might kill me with this hug. Still, I am relieved too. I did worry about her, no denying that.* "We're both all right."

Livia releases Lex from the hug. "I could feel you," says Livia. "I knew you were all right."

"Yeah," says Lex. "I could hear you digging on the other side."

Livia hugs Kane. *I am so grateful they are both safe. I would do anything to protect them. I've never felt responsible for anyone before, but now I feel I must take care of these two.*

"Okay, reunion's over," says Zavier. "Let's get away from this area. It's too unstable."

They pack up and Zavier leads them deeper into the tunnel.

9

Gradually, there are less loose rocks on the ground. The rock walls and ceiling are becoming more solid with fewer cracks. The tunnel is striated with colors, showing different layers of rock and earth. They continue to climb for another hour, though they are all lagging and sore.

When the walls are solid all the way around them, Zavier stops. "We should eat something, then get some rest." They all pull off their packs and sit down. "Food first. Roya put rations in our packs."

They begin to dig out their rations, compressed brown bars and a thick gray liquid in a small pouch.

Lex smells the bar and grimaces. "These look delicious."

While loudly chewing, Kane says, "Not bad. Better than some of the rations we had at the Academy. What's it made of?"

Zavier takes a bite of his bar and says, "Not sure. Synth-plant based, that's all I know. It's Roya's secret recipe, and she won't tell anyone. I actually don't want to know. Her ingredients can be very creative."

Livia swallows a bite and says, "They are good and quite filling."

Lex takes a gulp of the thick liquid and spits it out. "But this stuff is gross."

"Don't waste it!" Zavier barks.

"It's like sludge!" Lex shoots back.

"It is highly concentrated for a reason. It will keep you hydrated for a long time, and it's not like we have freshwater down here. You shouldn't be so quick to throw something away before you fully understand it."

"All right, no need to jump down my throat," says Lex. She then takes a large swig, slightly gags but swallows, and forces a smile directly at Zavier.

Zavier ignores her, finishes his bar, and gulps down the last of the gray liquid in his pouch. "We need to sleep in shifts," he says. "Though I doubt any mutants will get out this far, there's always got to be someone on watch, just to be safe." He looks at Livia and Kane, who have finished their rations and are holding hands. "You two can take the second shift. Sorry I can't offer you a private room."

"That would be lovely, but I could sleep anywhere at this point," says Livia.

Livia and Kane lie down together and are quickly asleep. Lex and Zavier sit leaning back on their packs, propped against the tunnel wall. Lex looks at Kane and Livia, his arms wrapped around her. Livia's face is resting on Kane's chest. *That doesn't look comfortable. They're so tangled together. It's sweet, though, I guess. I'm happy they have each other, but a part of me is jealous. I don't want to be, but I am.*

Lex turns to Zavier. "So what's with you and Martine? She didn't seem happy to see you. She warned me about you. Said you were no good," Lex says with a smirk. "It ended badly, I'm guessing?"

"Why do you care?" A small grin crosses his face. "You liked our little moment in the Outpost?"

"I thought I was pretty clear. Should I have kicked you harder? I'm just asking 'cause she told me to stay away from you."

"It didn't end badly. It just ended. We were tunnel runners together for a while. About a year, I guess. That was before I get more involved with Roscoe and the operations side of things. I sort of became Roscoe's right-hand man, and I had to choose. I couldn't keep doing the runs with her and work with Roscoe. He needed me in Rock Bottom."

"And you chose Roscoe."

"Yeah, I stopped doing runs and we were over. So what about you? You left a long string of broken hearts at the Academy? Got somebody wondering where you are?"

She turns away from him and snaps, "I'm not talking to you about this."

Zavier grins. "You and Kane ever?"

How dare he! He knows he's making me uncomfortable, and he loves it. He's trying to get a reaction out of me, but what? Anger? Why would he want that? I don't want to talk about Kane with him. This is private. I don't want to think about me and Kane. Any thoughts I had about Kane and me are over, in the past. "We were never like that." She turns her back to him.

Zavier is smug. "If you say so."

They sit in silence for the rest of their shift. When it is Livia and Kane's turn to sit on watch, Lex and Zavier make their way to opposite sides of the tunnel, sleeping as far away from each other as possible.

Livia and Kane sit close together. She waves her hand, indicating the distance between Zavier and Lex. "If they were any farther apart, Zavier would be headed back to the Outpost."

"I'm sure Zavier would be happy if I went back to the Outpost."

"I don't care about what would make Zavier happy," says Livia, moving closer to him.

Kane smiles. "Neither do I." After a pause, he says, "When we were separated by the cave-in, I was telling Lex about my life on our family's island, Viridans. It was untraditional, not really proper. My mom died when I was young—"

Livia interrupts, "Oh, no. I'm so sorry. That must have been awful."

"I was very young, I don't remember her at all. And my father was not really around. Well, I mean, he was on the island, but I rarely saw him. I was more or less raised by my Life Guide and Cook, the woman who ran the kitchen. They were the only staff on the island. It was very lonely. When I was watching you, I saw that loneliness in you."

He is so perceptive and kind. How could I help but fall in love with him?

"You are right," says Livia. "I was incredibly lonely. There were many people on Helix, but nevertheless I was very isolated. I had Governess. She was very kind when I was young, but as I got older she was under pressure to be more proper and was forced to pull away. That was difficult for both of us. I had a Life Guide. He was an adequate teacher, though not challenging. I had my guardians, Marius and Waslo. They were cohabitants, a very odd match, though. Marius was with me most days, kind and interesting but still distant. I was not her child, after all. Waslo was awful, condescending and rude. I can usually sense what people are feeling, but with him I couldn't. I think that made him seem worse, because I never knew how he was feeling."

"Have you always been able to sense people? How does it work?"

"When I was a child, I didn't know it was anything special. I sort of knew what people were thinking or feeling. Not exactly, but an impression. I didn't tell anyone about it, and as I got older, I realized it was not something everyone could do. Then I made sure to keep it secret. I've noticed since the chief took my chip out, it is stronger."

"Why do you think you couldn't sense anything about Waslo?"

"I don't know. No matter how hard I tried, I couldn't feel anything from him. I didn't know that much about him or Marius. Taking care of me was a job, I know that. I was fond of my Master, but we only focused on zinger training and nothing more. Truly, my horse, Veda, was my closest friend. I always felt like we could communicate. There was something special between us. Riding her was the only joy in my life."

"I felt that way about sound painting, it was the only thing that made me happy. I think my father was unhappy when I was recruited into the Academy, but also relieved that he wouldn't have to deal with me. I hated the Academy. Lex was the only good thing about it. She made it bearable."

"I'm glad you two had each other. Were you two friends right away?"

"It developed over years. I liked her right away, but she took her time deciding if she wanted to let anyone in. She pretty much hated everyone at the Academy. In some ways she is made of steel."

"She is. She is so strong, but a little part of her has melted."

"I don't think I would have made it through the Academy without her. I might have tried to escape and gotten myself killed. She is my best friend. You are something different. When I watched you I knew we were alike. Somehow the same." He trails his finger down her cheek. "When I finally met you, I think I was already in love with you."

Livia smiles, "When I met you at the ball, I felt a connection, and now, though I have only known you for a few days, already I feel so close to you. It feels sudden and yet not, like I have known you much, much longer." Livia kisses Kane. It is tender and quick. When she pulls back, she studies his face. *The bruises are fading, but I can sense that he needs more rest.* "It's calm and quiet, I will sense if anyone is coming. You should sleep."

"Maybe just for a little while." Kane reluctantly rests his head on her leg.

Livia runs her fingers through his hair as he falls asleep. *Even dirty and beat-up, he is beautiful. I can feel I'm falling in love with him.*

10

Lex is the first one to wake. She sees Livia sitting up, diligently keeping watch, while Kane is sleeping draped over her leg.

"Just like Kane," Lex says snidely. "Getting someone else to do his work. Reminds me of him at the Academy."

Livia frowns. "I doubt very highly he would have avoided his responsibilities."

Lex smirks. "Believe me, his charm went a long way. It seems to be working on you."

Livia ignores her comment. Lex and Livia go quiet as Kane and Zavier stir awake. Kane lifts his head and smiles, first at Livia and then at Lex.

Lex asks Kane, "Good shift on watch?"

"I wasn't really asleep," says Kane.

"Sure," Lex says with a nod. "Just getting the low-angle view."

Zavier stretches and rakes his fingers through his hair. With a yawn, he says, "It's gonna be another long day."

"Can't wait," says Lex.

Everyone packs their gear.

"We lost some time yesterday, so let's make sure to move fast," says Zavier, and heads off.

Lex and Livia look at Kane, who nods. "I'm actually feeling pretty good. But let's not let Zavier get too far ahead. I don't want to be playing catch-up with him all day."

"I'll keep him in check," Lex says. "Make sure to go down a click or two on your breathing units and then see how you feel. I'll go remind our fearless leader." Lex hurries after Zavier.

Livia puts her hand on Kane's shoulder. "Perhaps we should start walking before you make any adjustments to your device, just for good measure. I don't want you collapsing on me."

Kane's lip curls up in a smile. "Well, we don't want that."

He reaches for Livia's hand and they start walking. They settle into a good pace. Livia is letting him lead. *He really does seem to feel stronger. His stride looks better and his breathing is easy. I'm pleased he is recovering so quickly.*

After a few minutes, Livia says, "I suppose we can adjust our breathing units. If it ends up being too much, we can always change back."

Kane nods and adjusts the regulator on his breathing device one click as they continue walking. His breathing remains consistent.

Lex practically has to run to catch up with Zavier, who is walking at a quick pace. "Are you part of this group or not? We should stick together."

"Well, I can't go much slower than this," says Zavier, not reducing his speed. "Don't worry, I'll make sure poor Kane doesn't get left behind."

"This is a group!" says Lex, furious. "We're all going to the Outlands together. However long that takes."

"Well, it's taking forever," says Zavier under his breath.

Lex ignores him. "And have you adjusted your breathing unit? I had to tell Livia and Kane."

Zavier seems surprised and annoyed. "I didn't think I needed to remind everyone. If you're feeling good, I'd think you'd adjust your unit. I'm not a babysitter, and I don't need one either."

"Great leadership," says Lex. "Now, slow down so they can catch up."

They go silent as Zavier slows his pace, letting Livia and Kane get closer. The tunnel opens into a vast cavern, hot with steam seeping up from wide, deep cracks in the floor and walls. The steam is billowing up, reaching farther and farther up the sides, never seeming to end. It has formed into clouds, making a hazy ceiling in the far, far distance. The walls have been worn smooth from all the moisture, and there are droplets everywhere. The water makes a faint noise when it falls onto the rocks and into pools of water that have formed on the ground.

Lex focuses on the sound of the falling water. *From the echo, those aren't just cracks, they are fissures. And it sounds like they are really deep. We're gonna need to be careful.*

Livia and Kane catch up with Lex and Zavier as they enter the humid cavern.

"Glad you could join us," says Zavier. "Ready for a steam?"

"Just walk," says Lex.

"Glad we have on silitex or the heat would be much worse," says Zavier.

They all walk together as a group. Lex catches Livia's eye and motions to Kane, who is looking at the steam leaking from one of the cracks. Livia nods and mouths, "He's good."

Lex looks down and sees Livia and Kane are holding hands and quickly looks away. *Holding hands? Like they're on a happy little stroll on her island. Ridiculous.*

"If anybody is thinking about checking out those cracks, don't," says Zavier, looking at Kane. "They're obviously dangerous."

"And we need to stay as far away from the ones in the ground as we can," says Lex. "They are more like fissures, and judging by the sound the water makes when it hits the bottom, they are really deep."

"Yeah," says Zavier. "Let's get through here quickly."

"Real smart," Lex challenges. "The ground is very wet and slippery. So it's better to be careful than quick."

"Be quiet," says Zavier. "I need to listen for threats."

"I think I got that covered," says Lex, exasperated. "Idiot." She goes around him, striking a different path through the steam.

Livia and Kane follow behind, watching as the distance between Lex and Zavier increases. Lex moves toward one side of the wide cavern while Zavier moves closer to the other.

"I don't know who to follow," says Livia. "Plus, they are starting to go faster again."

"Yeah," says Kane. "Pretty soon we won't be able to keep them both in sight."

"I don't want to get separated," says Livia, growing frustrated. "This is dangerous. Why is she doing this, just to prove a point? We know she is capable and doesn't need anyone's assistance, but her stubbornness borders on stupidity and could get us all killed. I'm going to go get Lex. Do you think you can catch up with Zavier?"

"I think so," says Kane. "I do feel a lot better. But don't be too hard on Lex when you catch up with her."

"You don't always have to defend her. She is responsible for her own decisions," says Livia, wiping moisture off her face that is dripping from her hair. "This steam is getting worse. I can only see a few feet in front of us now. Try to hurry. Don't lose Zavier."

Kane hurries ahead of her in the direction they last saw Zavier, and Livia goes off toward the far edge of the cavern, where she last saw Lex.

As she moves forward in the thick steam, suddenly, Livia can see nothing but a huge boulder right in front of her. It juts up from the ground in the middle of the cavern, cutting Kane off from her sight.

Livia yells, "Lex? Kane? Lex?" *I can't hear them, but I can sense them moving forward, and at least I know they're all right. This boulder could not have come at a worse time, when we're already separated. I'll have to get to the other side quickly. We need to be together.*

Livia hurries forward and then breaks into a run. *I can't see anything, the passageway around this boulder is so narrow and the steam is even thicker. I can't believe how stupid Lex is being. She only thinks of herself. This is all about her pride, her ego.* Finally, Livia reaches the end of the boulder and skids to a stop. She spots the hazy image of Lex through the steam, still quite far away.

Relieved, Livia yells, "Lex! Wait!"

Kane runs out from the other side of the boulder, his pace slow and breathing labored. In the thick steam, he almost passes Livia before spotting her.

He stops and crosses over to Livia. "Are you okay? That boulder blocked my view of everyone. Zavier got away from me. Where's Lex?"

"I saw her for just a moment once I got past the boulder. I yelled, but she didn't stop."

"I'll try to catch up to them and make them stop."

"Do you need to rest?" asks Livia.

"No, I'm fine." Kane starts running and disappears in the steam.

Livia begins to move forward, calling, "Lex! Lex!" *This is so infuriating.*

As the cavern narrows, the steam starts to disappear. Livia can clearly see Kane in the tunnel ahead and Lex farther beyond him. *We have to stay together! Why can't they see that? Lex and Zavier are so stubborn they'll march us right into a huge crack just to prove each other wrong.*

Kane catches up to Lex. "Slow down, killer." Lex continues at her quick pace. Kane takes deep, ragged breaths as he walks next to Lex. "Blast this additive," he says, and reaches down to adjust his regulator, turning it back up. "I'll turn it down later. I can't run and get off the additive. Lex, what are you trying to prove?"

"What do you mean?" Lex shoots back. "I've been taking it slow, waiting for the two of you to catch up to me!"

"Well, I did, and Livia is right behind me. I'm going to go stop Zavier, and once we're all back together, we're going to stick together. No more storming off."

"I didn't storm off," says Lex. "I was giving you space. I was feeling like you didn't really want me around."

Kane looks confused. "What are you talking about?"

"I saw Livia and you holding hands. Was I supposed to grab your other one, and we'd all skip through the tunnel together?"

"Just stop," says Kane, grabbing Lex's wrist, forcing her to stop walking. "You are way off. No one is trying to edge you out."

With a sharp tug, Lex pulls her wrist out of his grip. "Really?" she asks, her voice full of anger. "Because it sure feels like it."

"What is wrong with you?"

"What's right?" Lex bites back. "Our lives have been turned upside down, and I'm the only one that seems angry about it."

Kane takes a deep breath and says, "Yes, everything has changed and I'm not angry. That is true. I hated what my life in the PCF was going to be, you know that. I was willing to kill an innocent person to get out of it. And that almost got me killed. So I'm actually pretty happy with where I am right now."

Lex's eyebrows pull together, her tone incredulous. "You are? In this tunnel, running for our lives to the Outlands? I hate it! But we have no choice, now, do we? So let's all stick together like you said, and I'll plaster a smile on my face and pretend this is the best thing that ever happened to me."

"Now, that's the spirit!" Kane pats Lex on the back. "I'm going to try and catch up with Zavier." Kane smiles and breaks into a run.

Lex starts to run after Kane. *I am not waiting for Livia. She will catch up or she won't. I have had enough! Let's see what happens if somebody pushes me one more time. Just try it. I need to get out of this tunnel. Then I'm not gonna follow anyone anywhere.*

Zavier hears someone running toward him and before turning around says, "What is it? Poor Kane can't make it?"

Kane rushes past Zavier, Lex right behind him. Kane says, "Not quite." He stops and bends over, his breathing heavy, putting one hand against the tunnel wall to steady himself. Lex stops and stands next to Kane. She is not out of breath at all.

Kane turns back to Zavier, gasping. "Stop wandering ahead." Kane holds his hand up to Zavier before he can speak. "We're gonna take a break."

"Fine," says Zavier, pulling off his pack and placing it by his feet. "Looks like you need it."

Kane sits down, leaving his pack on, and leans his back against the tunnel wall. Lex sits next to him. Kane takes slow, deep breaths.

A few minutes pass before Livia runs up, her breathing steady, her face slightly flushed. "I didn't know this was a race."

"Everything's a race, Airess," says Zavier.

She throws her pack on the ground and sits down next to Kane. She puts her hand on his, their fingers instantly interlace.

"Well," says Kane, "for the rest of this trip, let's stay together."

Zavier asks with a smirk, "Should we all hold hands?"

"I don't think that will be necessary," says Livia, drawing her hand away from Kane's, clearly embarrassed and a bit irritated.

"Zavier, you can hold my hand," says Kane with a grin. "If that will help you get through this."

"You're not funny," Zavier says with a scowl.

"Let's just rest for a minute without talking," says Lex.

"Excellent idea," Zavier says as he sits on the ground and closes his eyes. No one speaks. Kane reaches out and takes Livia's hand. She catches his eye and gives him a small smile.

Lex looks away. *I don't know how much of this I can take. Are they going to start kissing while we are all sitting here? I'm glad Zavier made his little joke. I just wish it had made them stop. Zavier is a core-low idiot, but on this I agree with him. This is not the time for mushy romantic garbage.*

Livia studies how her hand fits in Kane's. *I don't care if they don't like it. Zavier clearly thinks it's a nuisance. Lex is furious, but her feelings are not going to stop me. I don't need her approval or permission.*

After a few minutes, Zavier says, "That's enough." He stands and puts his pack back on. "We need to get going. Kane, if you're still out of breath, turn up your breathing unit."

"It's already all the way back up," says Kane.

"Well, turn it back down as soon as you can," says Lex, "or you'll never get off the additive."

"And it will run out if you keep it turned all the way up," says Zavier. "There is only a limited amount in the canister. Let's go."

Everyone gets up, and they all start walking.

"I'm surprised there isn't a map of the tunnel," says Livia. "It would make it easier if we knew what to expect."

"Sure," says Zavier, "but the tunnel is always changing."

"Yes," says Livia, "so could the map."

"And there's the security issue," says Zavier. "What if a map of the tunnel ended up in the hands of the PCF? It's just safer to keep it all word of mouth. Every time someone goes through to the Outlands, we get a report on the condition of the tunnel, what they had to deal with."

Livia asks, "So did you know about the big steam cavern and the huge bolder?"

"Not in detail," says Zavier, "but I had some idea of what was coming. I knew the cavern was huge but narrows back down, and there was only one way out. It doesn't branch off with other tunnels."

"Still, we should have stayed together," says Livia. "What if someone had gotten hurt while we were separated?"

"Well, no one did," says Zavier with a shrug.

"So, what's next?" asks Lex.

"I know there is a muddy area coming that smells like sulfur," says Zavier.

"What is sulfur?" asks Kane.

"No idea, but I guess it smells bad," says Zavier. "That's why it is hardly worth talking about. What am I supposed to say? Hey, everybody, there's going to be some smelly, weird mud ahead, but I don't know where or when."

"Still," says Livia, "it is better to know something about what is ahead of us, even if it is not particularly detailed."

"Well, now you know as much as I know," says Zavier.

After a stretch in silence, Zavier says, "The boulder up ahead, left side looks better to pass on."

"Definitely not," says Lex. "Right side." She heads toward the right side of the rock and slips between it and the wall of the tunnel.

Zavier hesitates before following Lex, muttering, "Blasted stubborn PCF cadet telling me what to do." He reaches the boulder and stops. "This rock has more give than her," and kicks the boulder. He turns and glares at Livia and Kane. "After you," he waves his hand, indicating they should go ahead. "It's probably good if I'm not too close to Lex. Far enough so I can't get my hands around her throat."

"Perhaps that is best," says Livia as she passes. Kane passes without a word. Zavier kicks the boulder again and then follows.

Livia is relieved. *At least we're staying together. They may not like it, but it is safer.*

They continue, the endless dark tunnel stretching before them. Lex notices a smell beginning to grow. *That is horrible, and it's getting stronger. Different than the sewage before. I'm so lucky with my "gift" I get to smell this before everyone else.*

"Can anyone else smell that?" asks Lex.

"A little bit," says Zavier. "But it's not that bad."

Lex laughs. "Well, get ready. It's disgusting."

11

Soon the others start to register the stench. Livia's eyes go wide and she puts her hand over her nose. Kane grimaces. Lex smiles. *There we go. Now they know what I'm talking about. And it just keeps growing. My eyes are already watering. What is it? I can't see anything yet!*

"This is torture," says Kane, burying his nose in his arm. "It's stinging my nose when I breathe."

"Stop complaining," says Zavier. "Just keep going. It must end at some point. Probably another crack."

The ground starts to get softer and wet.

Looking down, Lex says, "The surface looks almost the same as the sewage we passed through before, but this is a lot of water and dirt."

Pinching her nose tightly, Livia says, "This smell is unbearable."

Zavier smirks. "So sorry everything isn't perfectly controlled to your liking, like it was on your island, Airess."

Livia scowls. "I would not like to imagine its source."

"Well, it's not coming from me," says Zavier. With his next step, Zavier's foot disappears into the ground. He groans, "So this must be the mud I was talking about." Pulling out his foot releases an intense wave of the stench. "And that's what smells. So now we know sulfur smells really, really bad."

"Yeah, thanks for that," says Lex. "Watch where you place your feet."

Zavier barks, "That's what I'm doing!"

"Well, I can see a drier path to follow," says Lex.

Zavier laughs. "Oh, really? You can tell how deep mud is by looking at it? Not a chance."

Livia snaps, "Stop it, Zavier. Just follow Lex. Maybe we will get past this easier."

Zavier grumbles but follows Lex as she weaves a path. Soon Lex is having to stop and test different areas, often having no choice but to sink into inches of mud.

Lex stops again, dry heaving at the stench. "I need a second. Every way looks bad, and this blasted smell just keeps getting worse."

"I have some extra cloth," says Kane, and slips his pack around to the front so he can pull it open without putting it down on the muddy ground. "Let's try covering our noses." He pulls out a rag from his pack, tears it into strips, and hands them out.

"Great idea," says Livia, wrapping the rag around her nose and knotting it behind her head. "Thank you."

Lex, Kane, and Zavier tie pieces of rag over their noses. Lex says, "Well, I still want to vomit, but I guess it's better. I'm gonna try jumping over this section. It looks a bit better a couple feet out."

Zavier folds his arms. "Sure. We'll just wait to follow your perfect path."

As Lex takes one step forward, her foot immediately sinks straight down.

"Blast!" yells Lex as she falls forward, her leg sinking in past her knee, her other leg bent and sinking into the mud knee first.

"Hold on!" yells Zavier as he frantically grabs at Lex, trying to catch onto her arm or pack. He catches her elbow and jerks her upward. Lex leans back and her whole body falls backward onto Zavier, covering him in mud and splattering Livia and Kane. Lex rolls off Zavier and they all scramble back. Now they are all covered in the foul-smelling mud.

"You practically tore my arms out of the sockets," complains Lex, standing up and rotating her shoulders.

Zavier stands. "I think what you meant to say was 'Thank you,'" he says with a smile on his mud-splattered face. "I'm glad you were in the lead."

Lex tries to wipe some of the mud off, but it is useless. "You're such an ass."

"I thought I was your hero," says Zavier.

"Never," says Lex.

"Enough bickering," says Livia. "Does anyone have any ideas how we can get through this?"

Lex and Zavier turn away from each other and scan the cave for some sign of dry ground.

"Maybe we should tie a rope between us," suggests Kane. "Just in case we hit another deep pocket."

"Not a bad idea," says Zavier. "We do that when we are climbing up steep or broken pipes from Rock Bottom. It's a lot easier to pull someone up if there's a rope around their waist."

Lex yells, "Why didn't either of you mention that idea before?"

Zavier shrugs. "Because I certainly did not want to be tied to all of you."

Kane interrupts. "Lex, what do you see? Is there a good way forward?"

Reluctantly, Lex tears her attention from Zavier and looks around. After a moment, she says, "Nothing looks good, but it looks better closer to the wall on that side."

"But first the rope," says Livia.

Zavier is gruff. "Fine."

Zavier gets the rope out of his pack and ties a loop around each of their waists. First around Lex, then himself, coiling a long section of slack between them. Then he ties loops around Livia and Kane on the end. Zavier hands Kane the rest of the coiled rope.

"Last one gets to carry the tail end," says Zavier. Kane nods.

"Just one big, happy family," says Zavier. He moves to the front of the line and looks back at Lex. "Which way, leader? I propose . . ." Zavier points toward the right side of the tunnel.

Lex studies the floor of the tunnel for a moment before putting out one foot in that direction to test the depth. She takes a step and her foot sinks but slowly, only up to her ankle.

"Seems good," says Lex. "Zavier, keep that rope tight."

Zavier nods and coils the slack between them so the rope is taught. Lex takes a few more steps. Progress is slow, Lex sinking into the mud up to her calf with each step, and it sucking at her boots before she can get them free. Zavier follows slowly, focusing on keeping the rope to Lex tight before moving forward. Livia and Kane plod behind. With each step the smell gets worse and the mud gradually moves up past Lex's knees, slowing her progress.

"If this gets any deeper or thicker," says Lex, "we won't be able to move."

Zavier's eyes are red and tearing up. "Does this ever end?"

"This better be as bad as it gets," says Lex.

The mud creeps up a couple more inches, almost to her hips. Lex is barely able to wade forward.

"After this," says Livia, "I'm not sure I'll ever be able to properly smell anything again."

Lex sighs, "Would you stop. We are all smelling it and your nasal future is the least of my concerns right now. I do not want to die drowning in this crap."

"Come on," jokes Kane, "this is what I always imagined Paradise Island would be. Haven't you heard of the rejuvenating mud baths? They smell terrible, but they're great for your skin."

Livia laughs, then starts to cough and gag. "No jokes. Laughing makes it worse."

"I think it's starting to get better," says Lex. As they move forward, the ground beneath the mud becomes uneven. After a few rises and falls, it levels out and the height of the mud stays at their thighs.

They all start to move quicker, and soon the mud is only up to their knees.

"It is starting to look good in the distance," says Lex. "But still a ways to go."

Zavier struggles to move faster. "Good, I can't stand it. I gotta get out of this." The rope behind Zavier, connecting him to Livia, is becoming taut as he moves closer to Lex.

Livia yells, "Zavier, slow down. I can't keep up with you. The rope is pulling me forward."

Zavier pulls the knot around his waist loose and slips the rope over his head. Kane yells, "Zavier, what are you doing?"

"It's been stable for a while," Zavier yells back. "I gotta get away from this smell."

Out of the rope, Zavier catches up to Lex and tosses her the coil of slack. He passes around her.

"I wouldn't do that," says Lex. "It still looks liquid and soft in places. There might be a few deep spots ahead."

"It looks fine to me," says Zavier.

"You know what, you're right," says Lex, sarcastically. "Just do whatever you want."

Zavier continues forward slowly, but he's still caught off guard when his feet start sinking quickly.

"Little help here!" says Zavier.

"You know what would be great?" says Lex as she slogs closer. "If you were still tied in and we could just pull you out."

The mud already up to his hips, Zavier says, "Just throw me the rope," as he continues to sink. Lex throws him the coil of rope. Zavier catches it and quickly gets a good grip with both hands. Lex and Livia move back and get tension on the rope. Zavier stops sinking with the mud up to his waist.

"Now, hold on," says Lex. "Kane, get up here in between us. Livia, let's move closer together so Kane can grab both sides of the rope. We will all pull and back up together."

"Great plan," says Zavier. "But hurry before I sink. I can't feel anything solid beneath my feet."

Kane trudges up and positions himself in between Lex and Livia. He grabs the rope, one hand on the rope connecting Lex to Zavier and the other on the rope running from Livia to Zavier.

"Just stay still," says Lex. "We'll save you."

"You've been waiting to say that," says Zavier, and Lex smirks. "Try not to enjoy this so much."

"I'll try," says Lex.

"All right, come on!" says Zavier. "The rope is cutting into my hands."

"Everybody pull," says Lex. Slowly they pull and start to move back. Zavier is pulled forward, his chest dragged through the mud. He holds tight to the rope and arches his neck back to avoid the mud.

"Blast, this is disgusting!" says Zavier. He starts to scramble. "Oh, I feel the ground!" He lurches forward, and the tension on the rope is released. Livia, Kane, and Lex fall back into the mud. Zavier fumbles forward, landing on top of Lex.

Kane says, "That worked well enough." He gets to his feet and helps Livia up.

"I would have preferred not falling into the mud," says Livia. "You gonna be all right, big boy?" Lex asks as Zavier gets to his feet.

He offers her a hand. "Just get us out of here." Lex takes it and he pulls her up. "I'm going crazy."

"I'm trying," says Lex.

She assesses the path forward and starts to guide the group again. Walking a little faster, it is just a couple minutes before they are back on almost dry ground.

Lex stops, exhausted. "We're through, and it looks like a steady incline with no obstacles for a while. We should stop and rest for a minute, maybe put this rope away."

Zavier gags. "No, keep going."

"I agree," says Livia. "Let's keep moving. The smell is still quite strong. I'd like to put some distance between us and this foul mud."

"Fine," says Lex. "Zavier, just give me some space, so I'm not right next to your horrible smell."

"You know you're all covered in the stuff too," says Zavier.

"Less than you," says Lex, and starts walking. Zavier walks next to her with Livia, and Kane follows close behind. After a moment, Lex says to Zavier, "You're not tied in. Maybe you should be at the back."

Zavier smirks. "You sure you want to be that far away from me?"

"Farther would be better," grumbles Lex.

Kane adjusts the cloth over his nose and asks, "In the reports about the tunnel, did anyone ever say anything about what comes after the mud? Are things going to get better or worse?"

"I have heard there is water somewhere past the mud, but not always," says Zavier. "I think it depends on the time of year for some reason. If there is, we might be able to clean off this mud. That would be better, but there's no way to be sure. All we can do is keep moving."

12

It has been a long and challenging day. Livia can sense that Kane needs to stop. *Kane is exhausted. He needs to rest. But I don't want to point that out to Zavier. He is already so hard on Kane. Zavier might leave him behind.* She says, "I think it's time to rest for the night."

"We should push on for a few more hours," says Zavier, not slowing.

"No," says Livia, her voice hard. "I need to stop and eat something."

"Is this too much for you?" asks Lex. "I guess you didn't get this much exercise on Helix, just circling it again and again and again on Veda."

"That is correct," Livia concedes. "Zavier, if this area is safe, can we all please stop? Unless you think we are close to somewhere we can rinse off this putrid mud."

"Rinse off?" Zavier softens. "That's a nice idea. If we haven't come across the water by now, there probably isn't any. All right, Airess, let's stop."

Kane basically collapses and looks at Livia with obvious relief. She sits next to him while Lex and Zavier sit far apart, with Kane and Livia between them. They all take off their packs, pull out rations, and start to eat.

Zavier takes a drink of the gray liquid and says, "I think Kane and I should take the first watch tonight."

Protectively, Livia says, "I'll take Kane's place."

"Fine, suit yourself," says Zavier. "But he has to take the second shift. We all need rest."

"I'll do the second shift," Kane says defensively. "I'm not trying to avoid my part."

"Could have fooled me," says Zavier. "Feels like we've almost carried you the whole way."

"What?" Kane pulls himself up in an aggressive stance. "You try doing this after being almost tortured to death. I bet you couldn't have made it past the Last Outpost."

"I'm not going to fight you," Zavier says, mocking him. "That would be too easy and the end of you, so just sit down."

"Don't tell me what to do," says Kane, challenging. "Come on!"

Lex jumps up. "Can you handle two of us?"

Zavier stands and taunts Lex, "Yeah, I can handle Kane, who's barely standing, and a *girl.*"

Lex charges at him.

Livia stands up and grabs Lex, holding her back. "Enough. Stop. We cannot fight."

"Let me go," says Lex. "He is such a core-low piece of waste."

"What did you call me?" Zavier puts his fists up.

"You heard me!" Lex says, trying to wriggle away from Livia. "I've never hit a girl, but you are barely one, so . . ." Zavier lunges at Lex. Livia is pinned between Lex and Zavier as they flail at each other.

Livia yells, "Lex! Zavier! Stop!"

"Both of you stop!" shouts Kane. "Livia, get out of there!" He takes the rope that still joins him to Livia and gives it a hard yank, causing Livia to fall and taking the others with her to the ground.

Livia jumps up, whips out her zinger, and cuts the rope that joins them. She points the zinger at Lex and Zavier and coldly warns, "Stay down or I swear I will hurt you."

"You wouldn't," says Lex.

"I would!" yells Livia. "I have had enough. Move away from each other. Now!"

"I would do what she says," says Kane.

"I am," says Zavier as he moves a few feet away and sits down with his back to them, facing up the tunnel to start his shift of night watch.

"Fine. But you and your zinger don't scare me," snaps Lex, her voice sharp with anger. With her jaw clenched, she lies down, rolls over, and stares at the tunnel wall. *Zavier was going to hit me. Core-low piece of waste. If I catch Zavier sleeping, I might just strangle him. I doubt anyone would miss him.*

Livia orders, "No more talking or moving until it's time to change guard."

Lex forces her eyes closed. *And Livia with that stupid zinger. She thinks she is better than all of us. Spoiled Airess. I don't need or want her help. I can fight my own battles, like I have my whole life. I hate that I have to rely on anyone. How will I ever get any rest tonight? Is it even night? I hate this tunnel!*

Livia lowers her zinger and walks over to Kane. He is standing, still holding the cut end of the rope with a shocked expression on his face. "Wow, you were kind of scary, but in a really impressive way."

Livia begins to shake, her increased adrenaline from the confrontation combined with the fatigue from the long hard day hitting her all at once. Kane puts his arms around her. *He has a calming effect on me, but this is all too much. I need to be alone right now.*

"Thank you for trying to help," says Livia, pulling back from him.

"I didn't know what else to do," says Kane, shaking his head. "They looked like they were going to tear each other apart, and you were right in the middle."

"Yes, again, thank you. But now I need a little time alone. That was so intense. I'm used to being by myself and now all this." She motions with her arms wide. "Lex, Zavier, the tunnel, everything. Even you. It is sometimes too much." She slumps down to the ground. "I'm on watch. You get some rest."

"All right, if that's what you need." Kane walks a few steps away, lies down with his head on his pack, and closes his eyes.

Livia looks at Lex and can sense her anger. *She's so mad it's keeping her awake. Serves her right. She's such a hothead. I know from the battle we had on Helix the day we met that she is strong and well trained, but how could she think she would have a chance against Zavier? He's huge compared to her. And Zavier wasn't going to fight Kane. Lex escalated the whole situation. It was so reckless. I am afraid Lex's impulsiveness will cost us all dearly one day.*

13

Livia jerks awake. *I was asleep! I'm on watch! I can't believe I fell asleep! Is everything all right?* Livia is immediately alert and looks around. She sees the globe of light from Zavier's beamer further up the tunnel, where he is awake and still keeping watch. *Why did I wake? I feel something. Something close and getting closer. What is that?*

Livia yells to Zavier, "I can feel something, but I don't know what it is. Do you hear or see anything?"

Zavier draws his blaster and looks down the tunnel in both directions. "No. Nothing."

Livia yells, "Lex, wake up!" Both Lex and Kane stir awake and sit up.

Livia's sense of alarm is growing. "Lex, there is something coming! Do you hear it? Can you see anything? What is it?"

Zavier yells, "I still don't hear or see anything! Is it close?"

"It's coming toward us quickly, but it's not mutant or human!" Livia says, starting to panic.

"Yeah, I can hear something," says Lex. "It's like a lot of scratching or clicking noises, all very fast. It has a very high-pitched noise too. Almost a vibration."

Kane asks, "Livia, what is it?"

Livia stands and draws her zinger. "It's like a big body with tons of moving parts all thinking the same thing . . . forward." *Why did I fall asleep? This is all my fault.*

Lex yells, "I see something!" She points down the tunnel. "It looks like the floor of the tunnel is moving!"

Out of the darkness, a wave of hundreds of small, dark rodents races through the tunnel toward them, their furry bodies blending into one huge mass. They have tiny, red eyes that seem to have a film over them from lack of sunlight.

"Core-low!" yells Zavier. "What is that?" He fires his blaster into the writhing swarm coming toward them and the creatures redirect and head straight for Zavier. In an instant they are on him, crawling up his legs. He bats them away with his arms, but there are so many that the few he is able to get off make no difference.

"They're biting me!" Zavier screams as the rodents claw their way up his legs to his waist and chest. Kane and Lex rush toward Zavier to help.

"Get these blasted rodents off me!" yells Zavier. "I'm gonna be eaten alive!"

"We're trying!" yells Lex as she and Kane kick and swat at the savage creatures, but this only seems to make it worse.

Stunned, Livia can only watch as the three are engulfed by the horde of small creatures. *What can I do? All their fighting is making the rodents more frantic and aggressive. I can sense these creatures. It is fear. All they are feeling is fear and panic. None of the rodents have come near me. Why are they leaving me alone but attacking them? What am I doing differently?*

Lex yells, "Livia, come help us!"

"No!" shouts Livia. "It won't help. All of you stop. Stop fighting them and don't move!"

Lex screams, "Are you crazy? They are attacking us!"

"No!" yells Livia. "They are defending themselves. They are panicked and scared. If you stop attacking them, they will stop attacking you. Get into a ball and cover your faces. Trust me."

Zavier yells, "You better be right or we're dead."

"I'm right!" yells Livia. "Do it."

Reluctantly, Zavier, Lex, and Kane stop moving and drop completely down to the ground. The rodents continue to overrun them but stop biting.

Livia commands, "Be very still." *The animals have calmed. I sense the change in them. They are not panicked. Now they just need to leave. Come on, little creatures, leave. Like before, forward. Forward. Forward. Forward. Can you hear me little ones? Forward. Forward. Forward.*

The rodents begin to crawl off Zavier, Lex, and Kane. They start to run off down the tunnel.

"They are going!" yells Livia, elated. *There you go, ugly, little creatures, forward. Am I controlling them? Or are they just leaving?* Livia focuses her thoughts, willing the rodents to move on. *Forward. Forward. Forward.*

The floor of the tunnel is covered by the rodents scurrying away. The last few run across Zavier's back and jump off his head before scampering down the tunnel. Livia watches the rodents disappearing into the dark when a slightly larger fur-covered animal runs past them.

"Whoa!" says Lex, getting to her feet. "What was that?"

"I don't know," says Livia. "Maybe that was what they were running from in the first place."

"Can you sense if any more are coming?" asks Lex.

"I don't sense anything else."

"That was one of the most creepy experiences of my entire life!" says Lex with a shudder.

Kane stands, walks to Livia, and hugs her.

"I thought I was going to be eaten alive," says Zavier as he stands. He turns to Lex. "How bad are the bites?"

"It looks like a hundred needles poked you," says Lex. "Do I have a lot?"

He smirks and says, "Not really. Maybe they liked how I tasted better."

"Please." Lex turns to Livia and asks accusingly, "Livia, you were on watch. How did this happen? Did you fall asleep?"

"Don't start, Lex," Kane says, jumping to Livia's defense. "She couldn't have done anything to stop the attack, so what does it matter?"

"I was talking to Livia," says Lex. "And it does matter if she can't be trusted to stay awake on watch." Lex says to Livia, "I asked you, did you fall asleep?"

Livia turns away from Kane to face Lex directly and, with remorse in her voice, answers, "I did. I am deeply sorry. I failed."

"You sure did," says Lex with satisfaction. "You could have gotten us killed, so I hope you enjoyed your nap! I can't believe you couldn't stay awake for a few hours."

"Enough!" barks Zavier. "She did save us. And those things were coming down the tunnel whether Livia was awake or not."

"You are defending her now?" Lex asks, shocked. "I can't believe it. Everyone is always on her side."

"I'm not on anyone's side," says Zavier. "So knock it off."

Livia buries her face in Kane's shoulder and softly cries.

"You're going to cry?" says Lex, infuriated. "Kane, why are you comforting her? We are the ones who were attacked, and it was because of her!"

"She's upset," says Kane as he continues to hold Livia.

Lex lets out a loud groan. "Livia, you wouldn't have survived one day in the Orphanage much less the Academy. You are so weak!"

"Come on, Lex," says Kane. "That's not fair."

"You know what else isn't fair?" asks Lex. "She doesn't have one bite on her. Why?"

Livia picks her head up from Kane's shoulder, wipes her eyes, and explains through her sniffling, "I sensed the creatures meant us no harm. They were afraid of us."

"They seemed pretty fierce," interrupts Zavier. "I thought I was about to have one of the most embarrassing rebel deaths of all time."

Kane laughs, releasing some of the tension.

Livia continues, "Zavier, when you shot at them with your blaster, they went into defense mode. Like any living thing would, they were fighting for their survival. You threatened them, so they attacked. That is why I had you drop to the ground, so you all were in a more submissive position."

Lex is impatient. "That still doesn't explain why they left you alone."

Livia answers with rising irritation, "I was about to tell you."

"Well, then do it already," says Lex.

Livia yells, "I am!" She lets out a long sigh. "I wasn't a threat. That's all."

"Yeah, but they left," says Lex.

"Because you had all stopped threatening them," says Livia.

"Still," says Kane, "it was sort of sudden how quickly they started leaving."

"Well," says Livia, "I could sense they had calmed, and I just kept thinking, *Forward,* over and over. That is what I first sensed from them before they attacked. I wasn't sure it would do anything, but I did try to send them the thought, and they started to go."

"Are you saying you controlled them?" asks Lex, incredulous.

"No, not controlled them," says Livia. "I don't think so. But I don't know. Maybe. I willed them to leave, and they did. But maybe they would have anyway."

Everyone is stunned into silence for a few moments.

"Did you know you could control living things?" asks Kane.

"No," says Livia. "And I don't know that I did."

"They sure left in a hurry," says Zavier. "So maybe you did send them away."

Lex says, "You better not try any of that mind control on me. Stay out of my head."

"With pleasure!" Livia bites back.

"Well," says Zavier, "I don't see any of us going back to sleep after that. We should just get moving."

Kane nods. "That is a great idea."

They gather their gear and start to walk.

Zavier breaks the silence, "Did anyone else notice those little monsters seemed to eat most of that mud crap off our suits? Also, I think it stopped them from getting through the silitex and nibbling the rest of our bodies."

"So that is one positive from this otherwise truly miserable day," says Lex.

"Once again, I apologize," says Livia. "I will try never to let you all down again. And if it helps, I still have all that horrible mud on me."

Lex says with a grin, "Actually, it does, Airess."

14

After several hours of negotiating the dark, winding passages of the tunnel, the incline steadily increasing, few words have passed between them.

Livia looks at Zavier, who is slightly slumped but trudges on. *I'm so tired, but I can sense Zavier is consumed with grim determination. He is forcing himself to keep going even though he is exhausted. He was the only one awake when I should have been awake too. I should not have had any sleep. I will not ask to stop. I will make it out of this tunnel and show my strength. This is a test, and I will pass.*

Livia asks, "Zavier, do you have any idea how much longer?"

"No, but we have to be getting closer. Based on the days, we should be out by today at some point."

Livia nods. *That is welcome news. I am so relieved, and I can sense the relief Lex and Kane are feeling. This should be our last day in the tunnel. I don't think we could endure another.*

"At some point today?" questions Lex. "That's vague. I say we pick up the pace and make sure we're out today." Lex starts to run, racing ahead of the group. "See if you all can keep up with me." *I don't care if they collapse once we get to the Outlands.*

Zavier is the only one who acknowledges Lex's challenge and picks up his pace to a halfhearted trot.

Lex rounds a bend, abruptly stops, and lets out a loud gasp.

"Lex! What is it?" yells Zavier as he breaks into a run to catch up to her. "What's wrong?"

Lex stands still, looking straight up. She points, and Zavier looks up. Livia and Kane, a little farther back, panic and run to catch up with Lex and Zavier, who stand mesmerized looking up at the tunnel ceiling.

"That is the most beautiful thing I have ever seen," says Lex. "It's like a million lights in the sky, but we're underground. They're moving slightly. What is it?"

"I heard about this from people who have gone through before," says Zavier, his head cocked, staring up. "They said there is a part that twinkles. They're insects or worms that glow."

"Worms that glow?" asks Livia, amazed. "What is a worm?"

Zavier chuckles. "It's a kind of bug, Airess."

"Well, it's quite remarkable," says Livia, staring up at the ceiling. "I would love to know how they do that."

"Yuck!" says Kane, ducking his head. "I think one of them just relieved itself on me."

"Ugh!" chokes Zavier. "I just got hit by some."

"All right," Lex snarls at the group, "let's get through here before we are covered in mud, rat spit, and worm waste from head to toe." Lex strides off, and the rest follow.

After walking for more than an hour, Lex says, "I hear water. It's somewhere up ahead and it's getting louder."

"Really?" says Zavier excitedly. "Let's go." He starts to run.

"So *now* we're running," says Lex irritated, and starts after Zavier.

"I don't see why we need to run," says Livia.

"Maybe we will be able to wash off the rest of this mud," says Kane.

Livia looks down at her mud-covered PCF jumpsuit and smiles. "I suppose that is a good reason."

Zavier yells, "I hear it. It must be just ahead."

Moments later, Lex and Zavier come up on a wide ravine filled with flowing water that cuts across the tunnel. Lex quickly assesses, *There is no way around the water. It is too wide.*

"It's too far to jump over," says Lex.

"If we can't go around it," says Zavier, crouching down, "we'll have to go through it." He gets as close to the water as he can. "It's crystal clear." He runs his hand through the water. "And cold." With both hands, he scoops up some water and splashes it on his face, washing mud off his neck and out of his hair and beard.

Lex crouches down, scoops up water, and washes off her face as Livia and Kane catch up to them.

"It doesn't look that deep," says Lex, studying the water.

"I'll check," says Kane, pulling off his pack. He runs forward and jumps into the water with a loud splash, yelling, "Woohoo!"

"Kane!" screams Livia. "Your breathing device!"

Kane stands up in the water, which reaches up to his waist, and checks his nose clip, "Oops! Yeah, it's still on. That would have been bad."

"It's probably not a good idea to get them wet," says Lex, splashing water on her face.

"Too late," says Kane. "It got soaked, but it's still working." He pulls the breathing device off his belt and shakes it a little, water dripping off.

"Well, to be safe." Zavier unclips the breathing device from his belt and holds it over his head as he lowers himself into the water. "It's freezing! But worth it to get this mud off."

Kane holds his breathing device above the water with one hand and rubs mud off his jumpsuit with the other. "Lex, Livia, get in!"

Lex turns to Livia and challenges her, "You first, Airess."

"Fine, if you are scared," Livia taunts.

"I didn't say I was scared," says Lex defensively.

"All right, I'm going in," says Livia.

"Yeah, go. I'll be right behind you."

Livia nods, holds her breathing device up, and steps gingerly into the water with Lex following her in.

Zavier and Kane are splashing each other in the shallow water and it seems to be taking an aggressive turn. They see Livia and Lex enter the water and start aiming large splashes in their direction.

"Hey! Stop!" yells Lex, shielding her face.

Realizing they are not going to stop, Livia goes into attack mode, sloshing through the water toward Zavier and Kane, splashing as she advances. Kane and Zavier splash at Livia fiercely, and she quickly caves.

"You win! You win!" laughs Livia. "Truce!" Everyone stops splashing. "Remember, this isn't good for the breathing devices."

"Now you're worried about the breathing devices," says Zavier with a grin. "You didn't seem too worried a minute ago."

Lex sloshes over to the group.

"You missed all the fun," says Livia, laughing and splashing Lex.

The splash hits Lex in the face, and she is caught off guard. She loses her balance and falls backward into the water. She flails wildly and comes up sputtering and gasping, water coming out of her mouth, and croaks, "What were you doing? Trying to kill me?"

Lex pushes Livia, and she stumbles back. "I'm sorry," stammers Livia, trying to keep her balance. "I thought it would be funny."

"Funny?" yells Lex. "I could have drowned."

"How? This water is only waist deep." Livia seems to realize something. "You can't swim?"

"No, I can't," says Lex. "There wasn't any swimming at the Orphanage or the Academy."

Zavier interjects, "Well, there wasn't any swimming in Rock Bottom either, but if you just stay standing you'll be fine."

Lex glares at Zavier, who shrugs.

"I'm sorry," says Livia. "I didn't realize." *I must not forget that my life has been so different from hers. Of course she can't swim. She was scared and I didn't even notice. I should have sensed it.*

"Relax, Airess," says Zavier. "She's not dead, and now all the mud is gone."

Kane wades over to the edge of the water, where they left their packs, and climbs out. "Come on, we should get going. Everyone come over, and I will hand you your packs."

"Look who's all full of energy," says Zavier as he wades over to the edge.

"I do feel much better," says Kane, grabbing Zavier's pack and handing it over to him. "I forgot what it was like to be clean." Zavier makes his way to the other side, holding his pack and breathing device over his head. Kane hands Lex and Livia their packs and they wade across holding them over their heads like Zavier. Kane follows with his pack.

On the other side, Zavier climbs out, drops his pack, and clips his breathing device to his belt. He rakes his fingers through his wet hair.

"We can eat while we walk," he says as he pulls a food bar and a pouch of liquid out of his pack, then slings it over his back.

Lex throws her pack on the ground and pulls herself out of the water. She clips her breathing device back on her belt and pulls a food bar out of her pack. She watches Kane help Livia. First he gets himself out, then he takes Livia's pack and helps her out. *Oh, yes, the Airess needs help getting out. I almost died, but nobody helped me.*

"This silitex is strato," says Zavier, chewing and adjusting his pack. "I'm not cold at all."

When they all have their packs back on, Zavier says, "Let's move."

They walk in silence, eating their rations and drinking the gray sludge. It is not long before they come upon several strange dark cables dangling from the ceiling, some as thick as a man's finger and some as thin as fine string.

"What are they?" asks Lex.

Kane looks at them closely. "They are the roots of plants. My father grew all sorts of plants on our island as part of his work. When I was little I would help him move the plants if they got too big. We would dig them up and put them in bigger pots, or move them outside. These are definitely roots."

"We must be very close to the surface," says Zavier.

"We must be," says Kane.

They walk into an area unlike any part of the tunnel they have seen before. The floor is hard, not the soft dirt they have been walking on for days. Thick, knotted vines creep over the ceiling and walls.

"It feels like a floor, not dirt," says Zavier. "This must be from before the Great Catastrophe."

"I wonder what it was like," says Livia. "No one ever talks about it. Not what the Great Catastrophe was or what life was like before it. It's not in *The Book of Indra*. Not in any detail, anyway."

Zavier clears his throat. "I know a little something about it." And he begins to recite:

THE TELLING OF BEFORE

Before when the air was clean
Before when the Earth was green
Man lived under the sun
and moved free across the land
But mankind was hungry
He devoured all that was good
The mother of all living things showed her wrath
Many died and the air became poison
The mother banished mankind
He crawled under the shell
and hid from her fury

"What does that mean?" asks Lex.

"I think that it was good before, and man . . . people messed it up," says Zavier.

"That isn't much help," Lex challenges Zavier. "You have any actual details?"

"Well, I wasn't there, and Roscoe had only a few books that referenced it. So my apologies if I can't give you a full history lesson."

"Not sure what kind of teacher you would have made," Lex needles, "if you can't answer questions about our past."

"A good teacher needs a good student, not an arrogant brat."

"So asking questions makes someone an arrogant brat?" asks Lex abrasively.

Livia closes her eyes for a moment and sighs. *I can sense where this going.* She interrupts, "Zavier, you would have made a fine teacher, and who knows, you still might one day."

"Thank you, Livia. If so, I'll be sure to pick my students carefully."

"Don't worry," says Lex. "I have no desire to be one of your pupils. But I'm sure Livia would be perfect."

"Stop!" Livia yells. "Enough of the bickering. My Etiquette Tutor taught us that silence should be often observed and practiced. Let's try that now."

"I think I would really hate your Etiquette Tutor," says Lex.

"I did," Livia agrees.

Kane is leading the group for once as the tunnel intersects a cross section of what appears to be another tunnel. The walls of the tunnel had been getting more level and uniform, though still covered with vines, but this new part of the tunnel is perfectly straight with an even floor, walls, and ceiling. As he takes a step, the group hears something crack under his foot.

He raises his hand for the group to stop. "Wait. Let me make sure it's safe to walk on."

Kane bends down to brush the debris away, and reveals a faded, broken light blue tile floor beneath.

"What is it?" Lex asks him.

"This is actually a floor," says Kane. "It's tiled."

"The air feels different here," observes Livia.

Kane walks around inspecting the area. "Look, it drops off over here, and there is some sort of track, but wherever it went, it's now collapsed in on itself."

"There are tiles on the walls over here," Livia says as she starts to explore. "I think there are a few steps leading up a staircase too, but it all seems to be cut off now, and the tunnel just crosses through it. Was this part of their transportation network?"

Clearing his throat again, Zavier starts, "Since I see there are some students here who want to learn from my wisdom, I am happy to share."

Lex is sharp. "Please don't."

"Ignore her, Life Guide Zavier," Kane adds, egging him on.

"I will. From the many books I have been fortunate enough to read, I can tell you this is part of an old underground train system. It was called a subway." He smiles at Lex. "It would take passengers all over a city. It is a fascinating and unexpected glimpse into our past."

Lex sighs. "If the lesson is over, can we move on now?"

Zavier continues, "The one last thing I will *teach* about subways is, although underground like Rock Bottom, they were usually close to the surface."

Lex scoffs, "What does that mean?"

"Can't you feel that? It's fresh air," says Zavier.

They all turn and look forward in disbelief.

Zavier says, "You ready for the Outlands? We're here."

15

With newfound energy, the group runs up the last part of the tunnel. They burst through a curtain of vines that camouflages the tunnel opening and into the bright sunlight. They all have to shield their eyes.

Livia exclaims, "We made it! I can't see anything, but we made it!"

Lex's eyes are the first to adjust. She looks around. They are surrounded by a heavily forested area at the foot of a towering mountain range. There are tall trees and plants of all kinds. The ground is covered in small flowers and fallen leaves. She can see tiny particles of dust floating through the gleaming shafts of sunlight filtered by the leaves of the trees.

Lex's voice is quiet. "It's beautiful."

Slowly, Livia, Kane, and Zavier uncover their eyes. Livia is taking it all in. She looks up at the sky and smiles. "There is nothing in the way. That is the sky. The real sky. It is magnificent."

Kane walks over to a tree and touches it. He runs his fingers over the coarse bark. "Look at all the colors." He looks up at the sky. "I've never seen blue like that."

Zavier looks around. Despite himself, he is in awe. "This is pretty strato."

Quite suddenly, Livia's eyes flutter and she sways, rocking back, losing her balance. *There are so many! So many. Are they animals? Where are they? All around. Everywhere.*

Livia mutters, "So many. I can't . . ."

She falls to the ground. Kane and Lex rush over to her, kneeling on either side of her.

"Are you all right?" asks Kane, panic in his voice.

"I need a moment," says Livia. "Everything is alive. With my chip out, I can feel so much more."

Kane strokes her hand. "Take a deep breath."

"I'm sure it will take some getting used to," says Lex.

Lex and Kane help Livia sit up, her head starting to clear. Zavier is standing not far away, looking at the sky.

Without warning, they are attacked by a group of four people who spring from the forest, lightning fast and precise. Each pouncing on a member of the group. Lex, Livia, and Kane are knocked to the ground, and the attackers rip off their breathing devices. Zavier is attacked from behind with a savage blow to his back, and his breathing device is ripped off. Without the breathing units pumping the additive into their airways, Kane and Zavier instantly gasp for breath. Zavier falls to his knees, his attacker quickly backing out of the reach of Zavier's clawing hands. Kane falls sideways to the ground, clutching his throat.

Lex takes a deep breath and realizes, *I can breathe. I don't need the additive.* She kicks her feet out, and the attacker closest to her goes flying back. She jumps to her feet and draws her blaster.

Simultaneously, Livia breathes in and realizes, *I'm all right. I can breathe pure air.* She pulls out her zinger and swings, lashing one of the attackers across the leg. It is a nasty wound that quickly starts to soak his light-colored pant leg with blood. The attackers retreat as quickly as they attacked.

Lex is up on her feet and yells at the attackers, "Get back!" She turns to look at Kane and Livia. Kane is starting to convulse. Livia scrambles to put his breathing device back on.

Lex yells to Livia, "Help him!"

Kane is thrashing, and Livia is having a hard time getting the nose clip back on. "I'm trying! You help Zavier!"

Lex looks around for Zavier while keeping her blaster pointed in the direction of the attackers who have pulled back into the trees. Zavier is on the ground gasping, his face turning blue. Lex moves quickly to Zavier, still holding her blaster pointed at the trees. She drops to one knee, grabs the nose clip off the ground, and reattaches it. Zavier's quick, shallow breaths start to slow as he breathes in the additive. *That's better.* Lex stands and looks over at Livia. She is kneeling next to Kane and has her arm around his back, holding the nose clip in front of his mouth. He has stopped convulsing.

"He's breathing it in now," says Livia. "He'll be okay."

"Good," says Lex. *Kane almost died but he didn't. Livia saved him. Not me. She kept her head. She is strato in a fight. I'm glad she was here. She will protect him when I can't. I think she really hurt one of them. Good for her.*

Livia looks down at Kane, his breathing becoming more normal. "I'm here, Kane. I have you. You are safe. Just breathe."

Lex turns toward the trees and yells, "Who are you? What do you want?"

Someone yells back, "We want you to leave, PCF scum!"

Lex yells, "We're not PCF, you idiots! We are here to see our mother, Delphia!"

After a quiet moment, someone yells, "I'm coming out. Don't shoot."

"I can't make any promises!" yells Lex.

One of the attackers, a young man with light brown hair, not much older than Lex and Livia, comes out of the trees holding out his empty hands. "You're Lexie and Livia?"

"Yes, I'm Lex and this is Livia," says Lex. "And Kane and Zavier."

"In those silitex jumpsuits, we thought you were PCF troops, that the PCF had found the tunnel leading out of Rock Bottom."

"Well, we're not PCF."

"I can see that now. I'm Quinn. Me and my group, we're from Del's . . ." He corrects himself, "*Delphia's* colony. We were on a routine patrol and when we saw PCF troops," he corrects himself again, "what we thought were PCF troops, near the tunnel exit, we had to act fast. Communications have been down so we didn't know anyone was coming through the tunnel. I was told Delphia's daughters would be coming to the Outlands, but no one was sure when."

Lex lowers her blaster and looks at Quinn. His clothes are threadbare and shabby, a strange mix of materials in the muted colors of the forest, the weapon on his belt old and battered. *So this is an Outlander. Not very impressive.* "You almost killed my friends. Pulling off the breathing devices was a nasty move."

Quinn says, "We figured it would be a good way to incapacitate you. We've never had to do it before. The PCF stay close to the dome, so we just stay clear of them. How come it didn't work on you or your sister?"

"I don't know," says Lex. "Just lucky, I guess, or you guys would have killed all four of us."

"Look, one of our team is badly injured. We need to get him back to the colony. We have speeders. We can double up, but one of you will have to drive his. He is in bad shape. I'll take him on my speeder."

"I can drive one," says Lex.

Livia helps Kane get to his feet and reattach his nose clip. Lex offers Zavier a hand, and he takes it and stands. Quinn leads the group into the trees, where two other Outlanders kneel next to the injured fourth member of their team, all dressed in a style similar to Quinn's. They have pulled out a med kit and are injecting the injured man with boosters. They have used ripped pieces of clothing to make a tourniquet, but his leg looks bad, his pants soaked with blood.

"Pick him up," says Quinn. "We'll put him on the back of my speeder." The two Outlanders lift their injured friend and follow Quinn deeper into the trees to the four rundown-looking speeders. Quinn hops on the back of one, and his friends secure the injured Outlander behind him, belting him to Quinn so he doesn't fall over. The two Outlanders jump on their speeders.

"Follow me," says Quinn, and speeds off.

Kane gets on the back of one of the speeders and Livia gets on the other. Lex jumps on the last speeder and Zavier sits behind her.

"You ready?" Lex asks Zavier.

"Always," he says, taking a deep breath.

"Hold on tight. But don't get any ideas."

"I almost died. I only have one idea. Breathing."

The two remaining Outlanders speed off with Livia and Kane. Lex follows, Zavier's arms tight around her. They weave through trees large and small. Lex can't help noticing how beautiful it is. *It is so green. The light coming through the leaves is amazing. And this speeder is fast. Much faster than I thought it would be. It looks like it should have been retired to the scrap heap a decade ago, but it has power.*

Livia's arms are wrapped around the Outlander driving the speeder. It is going fast. The air is whipping by like a roaring wind in her ears. She looks over at Kane holding tight on the back of the other speeder. He has his eyes locked on her, and he smiles. *How can he smile after what he just went through?*

Kane mouths, "I love you."

Livia smiles and mouths back, "I love you too."

Kane yells, "Whoa!"

Livia closes her eyes and throws her head back, enjoying the ride.

16

The four speeders approach a clearing surrounded by small buildings well camouflaged in the woods. The sound of their approach brings several people out of buildings and from the nearby trees into the clearing. A tall woman with long, dark hair leads a small group of people coming out to greet the returning patrol. As the speeders enter the colony, Lex scans the faces of the people and recognizes the woman in front immediately, her high cheekbones and dark brown eyes. *It's Delphia. Our mother. She looks exactly like she did in the Archive memories Roscoe showed Livia and me. It's been seventeen years, but she looks like she is barely older than me! She hasn't aged at all. How can that be?*

Delphia watches the patrol enter the colony and sees there are two riders on each speeder. Livia sees her break into a run and sprint up to the speeders. *That is her. I can't believe it. She is really alive. She is right there. I have a mother. Lex and I have a mother. She must be excited to see us.* Delphia rushes up to Quinn's speeder and starts to unstrap the injured Outlander on the back of his speeder.

Urgently she asks, "What happened to my son?"

Livia is shocked. *Her son? That is her son?* Livia looks closely at the young Outlander, his dark hair falling over his forehead, his fine features similar to Delphia's. *Lex and I aren't her only children. Is he my brother? Oh, no. I'm the one who hurt him. She will hate me.*

As they all get off the speeders, the two other Outlanders from the patrol rush over to help Delphia and Quinn. "Jules took a swipe from a zinger by that one," says Quinn, and points to Livia.

Lex says defensively, "They attacked us. We were just defending ourselves." *This is bad. Livia hurt her son. I hope he doesn't die. This is not a good start.*

A young man breaks through the group surrounding Delphia's son, Jules. Lex looks at him and makes a quick assessment. *He is tall and strong but young. Maybe a year or two younger than me. He also looks a lot like Delphia. Dark hair, brown eyes, similar facial structure. He looks startlingly similar to Jules, though it's hard to be sure 'cause Jules is a crumpled mess and this kid is a ball of fury.*

He yells at him, "Jules!" Jules lifts his head slightly and groans. "I knew you shouldn't have been the one sent on patrol. You've never been good in combat."

Delphia barks orders at the young man. "Enzo! This is not the time or place. Take Jules to Medical immediately!"

Enzo ignores the order and glares at Lex, Livia, Kane, and Zavier, and accusingly asks, "Who did this to my brother?"

"We did attack them," says Quinn. "We thought they were a PCF patrol."

Delphia demands, "Enzo, I said take your brother now!"

With help from the two other Outlanders, Enzo angrily lifts Jules and leaves to take him to Medical.

Livia whispers to Lex, "This is not going well."

Delphia watches them leave, then turns toward the group. "Our comms have been down. We didn't know you were on your way out. We knew you were coming, we just didn't know exactly when."

Lex bristles. *This was not the reception I was anticipating. I thought she would be happy to see us.*

Lex's tone is cold. "Well, we're here now, Mother."

There is a noticeable shift in Delphia's demeanor. She says calmly, "Yes, I'm sorry. I'm Del. You are Lexie and Livia?"

Lex corrects, "Lex and Livia. This is Kane and Zavier."

Del nods. "I am pleased you made it safely."

Livia says, "I'm so sorry I hurt your son. Jules, is it? We had no idea who they were. They ripped off our breathing units. If Lex and I hadn't been able to breathe, they would have killed us."

"Mistakes were made." Del turns and strides off. "Follow me." The four fall in behind her.

Zavier says to Lex under his breath, "So I guess no hugs."

Lex is not amused and shoots back, "Shut up, Zavier!"

Quinn walks with the group, while Del strides ahead, leading them out of the clearing into the colony. They pass more buildings in the woods, structures made from pieces of plexi-clear and steel salvaged from Indra's garbage, mixed with natural pieces from the surrounding forest. They are various shapes and sizes, but each one seems to blend into the environment.

"What interesting buildings," Livia observes.

"We have to use what is thrown away, and what the Earth provides us," Quinn explains.

They see people dressed in mixtures of all the uniforms and coveralls of Indra. The colors, fabrics, and textures overlapping and combining in unique patchworks. The rigid uniforms imposed on Indra's citizens by the High Council are absent.

Two groups of small children run by playing a game, throwing a large ball back and forth.

"Kane, that kinda looked like zip ball," Lex observes.

"Yeah, minus the blood and broken bones."

"Ah, come on. Our games at the Academy were fun."

"Yeah, because you were usually the one causing the damage."

Zavier says, "Why does that not surprise me?"

A loose ball rolls over and almost causes Lex to trip. She picks it up and looks over the odd material, feeling its weight for a moment.

One of the kids yells to her, "Hey, you! Throw it over."

Lex takes the ball in both hands over her head and hurls it back to the group.

Quinn nods his head. "You could be quite good at our version of zip ball."

"I would have to get used to playing without electrified gloves," says Lex.

"I don't think it is a good idea to let Lex play with kids," says Kane. "She is a killer."

"Oh, not with the kids," says Quinn. "There are a couple teams in the colony. We play against each other every few weeks. It gets rough and bloody."

Lex smiles. "Sounds good."

"Is this where everyone lives in the Outlands?" Livia asks.

"This is the center of the colony, but most of it is spread out through the woods," explains Quinn. "There are some who live in caves, others in structures on the ground or in trees. We have lookout posts in the high trees and in higher parts of the mountain to watch for PCF, but they have never come out this far. Like I said, they stay close to the dome, but Del feels we should always be cautious. She sends groups out on daily patrols to monitor the perimeter of the colony. We've never seen PCF out here, but you guys came out of the tunnel in those uniforms. So we thought the PCF had discovered the tunnel in Rock Bottom. Sorry we almost killed you all."

"Yeah," says Zavier. "We were lucky Lex and Livia could still breathe. I'd hate to be dead right now."

They pass into an area of thick woods and follow a path uphill for a few minutes that leads to a wall of rough rocks. Ahead of them, Del slips in between two huge rocks.

When they catch up to her, she says, "This is where you will stay for now." She pulls back a heavy cloth draped across the opening of a cave that serves as a door.

She holds the cloth back as everyone files in. Quinn is the last to enter and takes hold of the cloth as Del releases it. The light from outside spills in through the opening into the small cave. It is surprisingly well furnished, with four cots and a low table surrounded by cushions.

Del's manner is curt. "You need to rest. There is water to wash up. I will have food and fresh clothes brought to you. We can talk tonight." Del leaves.

Quinn asks, "Did you bring equipment for our comms setup?"

"Yeah," says Zavier. "I've got it." He pulls off his pack, puts it down, opens it, and pulls out some gear. He hands it to Quinn.

"Thanks," says Quinn, and leaves, releasing the cloth to fall back over the mouth of the cave, plunging it into near darkness.

Everyone but Lex blinks several times as their eyes adjust, and soon notice the low, dim lights mounted on the walls.

Lex rounds on Livia. "What was that?" asks Lex. "We have brothers? That's our mother? She doesn't seem to care about us at all!"

"She has not seen us since we were three days old," says Livia. "I guess she has no attachment to us."

"I guess not," says Lex. "And did you notice she hasn't aged?"

"Yes." Livia nods. "I saw it too. I didn't notice at first, then when she was closer I could see that she looks the same as she did in the Archive memories, but that was seventeen years ago."

"What do you mean?" asks Kane. "How could she look the same?"

"I don't know," says Lex. "And she has two boys, her sons? Who is the father?"

"And they look exactly alike," adds Zavier. "Another set of twins? Maybe you two aren't that special."

"Well, there's definitely something special about us," says Lex. "We don't need the additive, and you two sure do."

Livia cuts in, "Look, we're all exhausted. I think we should listen to Delphia . . . I mean Del, and get some rest and food. We'll get our answers tonight."

"I hope so, 'cause I have a lot of questions," says Lex. She walks over to one of the cots, drops her pack on the ground, and lies down.

Zavier says, "I'm going to go look around the colony." He drops his pack by one of the cots and walks out of the cave.

Livia pulls off her pack, sets it down, and sits on one of the cushions at the table. Kane comes over and sits next to her. "I hurt her son," Livia says, distressed. "What if he dies? Even if he lives, how could she forgive that?"

Kane puts his arm around her. "You didn't know who he was. He almost killed you. There's nothing we can do but hope he pulls through."

"Is he really my brother?"

"I guess so. I mean, if he is, and Enzo too, if they are Del's sons, then they're your brothers. Half brothers at least."

"I was so looking forward to meeting her, to finally getting to know my mother, and now it's such a mess."

"You can't do anything about it right now. You'll just have to wait and see what happens. This whole situation is unbelievable. We're in the Outlands. We've left Indra. You have your sister, you've met your mother, and you have me."

"That is true. I would not have believed any of this was going to happen. I thought I was going to be stuck on Helix, and now my life is nothing I could have predicted."

Lex says from across the cave, "Will you two keep it down? I'm trying to rest."

Livia laughs. "Sorry." She looks back at Kane and whispers, "On the back of the speeder, did you say what I think you said?"

He smiles and whispers, "Yes. And so did you. I plan to say it a lot. Are you trying to take it back?"

"No."

Lex clears her throat. "Hey, remember, I have really good ears over here. I can still hear you."

"Yes, sorry," says Livia.

"I don't need to say any more," says Kane, and pulls Livia close.

17

Livia and Kane lie tangled on a cot sleeping while Lex is on hers staring at the rough rock ceiling of the cave. *I can't believe we are in the Outlands. What do I do now? I knew what my life with the PCF was going to be. I had gotten my Final Placement and I was ready to be a PCF officer. Now it is all unknown. What am I going to do out here?*

Zavier comes back into the cave, and for a moment, the room is flooded with an orange glow until the cloth door falls back into place.

He looks at Lex on her cot and sees her eyes are open. "Naptime over?" he asks in a loud voice that stirs Livia and Kane awake.

"I guess," says Lex, yawning and sitting up.

"Good," he says, and pulls back the cloth. "You don't want to miss this. Come see."

"What is it?" asks Livia, stretching.

"I have no idea," says Zavier. "It just started a few minutes ago."

Lex, Livia, and Kane join Zavier at the cave opening. The sky is streaked with bright red and orange clouds.

"Whoa," says Kane, his mouth hanging open.

"Beautiful," says Livia.

They all stand quietly watching the sky and hardly notice when Quinn walks up carrying two canvas bags.

"Enjoying the show?" asks Quinn, stopping and standing with the group. "We don't have holoshows, so this is some good Outland entertainment."

"What is it?" asks Lex. "Why is it doing that?"

"It's called sunset," says Quinn. "It happens every night. Sometimes even more beautiful than this. And it can be a lot of different colors. It's even better after a storm."

"What's a storm?" asks Zavier.

"I'll explain another time," says Quinn, and walks into the cave. He puts the bags down on the table and unloads food from one and clothing from the other.

Livia watches as the sun drops behind the mountains, the color in the sky fading to a light gray, leaving only a few deep red clouds. *The dome was either light or dark but never had color like this. The sky is so amazing. How can it change so quickly? When we arrived it was blue and white, then moments ago it was on fire with color. Now it is fading to gray.*

The last of the sunlight is fading from the sky and the forest is quickly falling into darkness. The trees beyond the cave now appear almost black.

Quinn walks up to the group. "That's the end of the show for now. You might be interested in the sunrise. Very similar, only very early," he says, smiling. "Yes, sunrises and sunsets are beautiful, but the sun is dangerous too."

"What do you mean?" asks Livia, her face tight with concern.

"Don't look directly at the sun. You'll damage your eyes. And if you're out too long in direct sunlight, it'll burn your skin. Most newcomers can only be in the full sun for a few minutes. Later tonight, you should get a good view of the moon and stars."

"Moon and stars?" asks Zavier.

"You'll see," says Quinn. "The stars will come out first, too many to count. Just little dots of light in the sky. The moon will come up later. Newcomers are always mesmerized by the sky. When I first got out here, I watched the sunset every night for months. You do get used to it eventually."

"I can't imagine getting used to seeing something so beautiful," says Kane.

"You will," replies Quinn.

"The sky through the dome never looked like this," says Livia. "Even in simulations the sky was not alive like this, changing and full of color."

"Well, there are plenty of sunsets to watch out here," says Quinn. "I left food and clothes for you. You can change and eat, then Del wants to speak to all of you. Someone will be back to get you in a little while."

"Thank you, Quinn," says Livia as he walks out of the cave and into the dark forest.

"I hope he has a beamer," says Kane. "It got dark quick."

"Let's see what Quinn brought," says Zavier, and drops the cloth over the cave entrance.

They all walk to the table and start inspecting the food and clothes Quinn left.

"So Zavier, where were you?" asks Lex picking up a piece of clothing.

"You miss me?" Zavier asks with a grin.

"No," says Lex. "I was enjoying the quiet."

"Yeah, me too," says Zavier, with a nod. "Well, while you all were having naptime, I was looking around. This colony is much bigger than I thought. The Outlands go on forever."

Livia says, "I can't wait to explore it."

Kane reminds her, "Your mother wants to meet with us first."

"Don't call her that," Lex says harshly. "She has never been a mother to me."

"Okay," Kane says calmly, "don't get worked up. Let's get changed and then eat some of this strange-looking food. Zavier and I will step outside."

Zavier narrows his brow. "Are we getting changed outside? In the dark?"

"Unless you're afraid," Kane teases.

"No," says Zavier, smiling. "I just know Lex has been waiting to get a better look at me. I wouldn't want to deprive her of the pleasure."

"I'll survive," says Lex.

"Your loss," says Zavier. He and Kane step out of the cave.

As Lex and Livia change into the Outlander clothes, Lex observes, "Looks like I have parts from the Middlers and some of the PCF uniform." She is pointing at different swatches of fabric on her clothes. "And this reminds me of what we wore in the Orphanage."

"It doesn't look bad," Livia reassures her. "It's just very interesting. Mine seems to be made from Hubbers coveralls. I like it."

From outside the cave, Kane yells, "Is it safe to come in?"

Livia yells, "Yes."

Kane pulls back the cloth, and he and Zavier reenter the cave dressed in their mismatched Outlander clothing.

Lex points to pieces of Kane and Zavier's clothes. "That is definitely Middlers and that is PCF."

"I'm just happy to be out of that silitex," adds Zavier. "It's so tight in certain areas. For me, anyway."

Lex rolls her eyes. "I don't even want to think about what you are referring to."

"Are you sure about that?" asks Zavier with a smirk.

"Very," says Lex.

As they sit down at the table to eat, Livia gags slightly. "The colors, smell, and texture of this food is so different from synth. It's sort of overwhelming."

"Because it's real," says Kane.

"Do you know what all of this is?" asks Lex. "At the Academy and the Orphanage, we only had rations."

"We had a wide variety of synth food on my island when I was a kid," says Kane. "Plus, my father grew all sorts of other stuff that was edible. I think this is a type of fruit," he says, holding up a yellow, oddly round-shaped item. He takes a bite and slightly grimaces but swallows it. "No. Not sweet enough. It must be a root vegetable."

Zavier grabs a piece and puts it in his mouth. He chews for a moment, then with a shrug says, "I've had worse."

Livia studies a bowl filled with something small and round. "These are obviously some kind of nut. But not one I've ever seen before."

Zavier takes a handful of nuts and starts to eat them all at once. Still chewing, he says, "They aren't bad."

Lex watches Zavier pop more nuts in his mouth. "You seem to be willing to eat or drink anything," she says with a frown. He smiles back at her and puts a slice of the root vegetable in his mouth.

"This white, sort of flaky stuff reminds me of synth fish," says Livia, "but there is something so different about it."

"Roscoe's talked about fish," says Zavier. "He said it swims around in the water and they catch it."

"That explains it," Livia says as she slides it away. "I can feel it was once alive."

"They eat things that were once living?" Lex asks.

"Our forefathers did before the Great Catastrophe," says Zavier. "I'm sure it's one of the only ways they have been able to survive out here."

"I'll just stick to the nuts and plants," says Livia, gingerly putting a nut in her mouth.

Lex starts to take small bites of the various foods. Kane gathers every type of food and starts to try them while Zavier stuffs everything in his mouth.

"These flavors remind me of my family island," says Kane. "My father grew a lot of different herbs that Cook would put on the food. I'd be interested to see their gardens."

"This whole place is a garden," says Zavier through his still full mouth.

"Everything I ate on Helix was tasteless compared to this food," says Livia. "This will take some getting used to."

Lex glares at Livia. "Stop your whining. We were basically starved in the Orphanage."

Livia nods and puts a small piece of vegetable in her mouth. Lex eats a little of everything.

When they are just about done eating, Enzo enters the cave. "My mother is ready to see you."

Lex says sarcastically, "Well, if Del's ready, I guess this is a good time."

"Get yourselves together, and I'll take you to her," says Enzo. He turns to exit the cave, evidently planning on waiting for them outside.

"Enzo, please wait," says Livia. He stops and turns back. "How is Jules?"

"Conscious. In pain but alive," he says curtly.

"I'm so sorry. I acted on instinct. I truly hope he will make a full recovery."

"That seems unlikely," says Enzo, his tone cold. "His leg is in bad shape."

"I feel terrible."

"You should," says Enzo as he roughly pushes his way through the cloth door, which falls closed behind him.

As the group gets up to follow Enzo, Lex turns to Livia and says in a low voice, "I wouldn't expect him to admit it wasn't really your fault. Jules got hurt 'cause they made a snap judgement when they saw us and acted too quickly. If they had taken a moment to really look at us, they would have seen we weren't PCF. They attacked, and the consequences are on them."

"All of that may be true," says Livia, almost whispering, "but I'm the one who hurt Jules. It was my zinger that cut his leg open. I feel awful about it, and the circumstances don't change that."

"I'm just saying, don't let Enzo get under your skin. Don't take all the blame."

Zavier adds, his voice loud, "And don't forget, their mistake almost killed Kane and me. I'm not going to forget what it felt like to be gasping for breath."

Livia sighs and shakes her head. "It was so frightening watching the two of you choke."

"Well," says Kane, "in the next few days we'll be off the additive altogether, and that type of attack will never be an option again."

They exit the cave and find Enzo standing by the edge of the woods, the light from the beamer in his hand floating down near the ground.

"The woods are pretty quiet," says Enzo, glaring at them. "You can whisper or yell, voices carry."

"Good to know," says Kane.

Enzo leads them through the forest, Livia and Kane walking side by side, Lex and Zavier behind them. The air is crisp and cool. Livia looks around but can see nothing in the forest beyond the light of the beamer. *I can't see anything, but I can feel people scattered in the woods. They are peaceful and content. There are animals all around us, busy with their own survival. Without my chip I am feeling so much more.* Livia reaches out and takes Kane's hand. *I could be happy here, I think.*

Zavier clears his throat to get Lex's attention, and she looks over at him. He nods at Livia and Kane and looks down at their joined hands and then back to Lex. Quietly, he says, "You can hold my hand if you are feeling left out." His face breaks into a grin.

"No, thanks," says Lex with a scowl.

Lex looks around. With her keen eyes, she can see the flickering lights of fires burning deeper in the woods. She can smell the faint wisps of smoke in the air. *There are people all through this forest. More than I thought. I like the smell of the fires. Very different from anything in Indra.*

Livia says to Kane, "I hope Del can forgive me for hurting Jules."

From behind them, Lex objects, "You don't need her forgiveness! Stop worrying about her. She doesn't seem to be worried about us. I don't care what she thinks."

"Don't be so hard on her," says Livia. "This must be a difficult situation for her too. Jules has been hurt, and she wasn't expecting us yet."

With a scowl, Lex says, "I know this isn't the warm reunion you were hoping for."

Livia nods. "No, but we are here. This is her colony, her people. Let's give her a chance."

"I just want to hear what she has to say, then we need to figure out what we should do. We're in the blasted Outlands. Our lives have been turned upside down. I need to figure out what's next."

18

Enzo leads Lex, Livia, Kane, and Zavier up a rocky hill to a cave set high above the center of the colony. Enzo pulls back the heavy cloth at the mouth of the cave, holding it back as they all walk in. The cave is a huge space lit by several small lights set into the ceiling. There is a neat cot and several stacks of books against one wall. The books look similar to those in Roscoe's library back in Rock Bottom, all different sizes and colors, the spines worn with age. Del and Quinn are sitting at a large table in the center of the cave discussing something in low voices. She looks up as the group enters.

"Please sit," she says.

Lex, Livia, Kane, and Zavier sit down around the table. Quinn gets up and leaves the cave. Enzo stands by the entrance and leans against the wall.

Livia says, her tone grave, "Del. Mother. There are no words to express how sorry I am for injuring Jules. Enzo said he is not doing well."

"No, he is not," Del says curtly. "But it could be worse. The patrol should not have acted so rashly. The four of you could be dead, and that would have been catastrophic."

Lex adds, "If Livia and I hadn't been able to breathe, we would have been."

"Yes," says Del, "you adapted very quickly to the lack of additive. I believe I know why."

"Really?" asks Lex, surprised. "Why?"

"That is just one of the many things I will explain," says Del. "I'm sure you both have questions, and I will do my best to answer them."

"I've got one," says Lex. "What are these green things in our eye? Livia and I both have them."

"I'm sorry to say I don't know," says Del.

"This is a great start," says Lex, looking at Livia.

"Just let Del tell us what she does know," says Livia.

"Yes," says Del. "I will start at the beginning. Or as near to it as I can. There is a great deal to cover."

"Yeah, there is," says Lex. "Seventeen years."

Del looks Lex in the eyes, her gaze penetrating. "Yes, seventeen years, but even more than that. This all started many years before you were born when Armand, your father, developed the EX2 pill."

"What does the EX2 pill have to do with us?" asks Livia.

Del says, "He developed EX2 for the Independent High Council primarily to prevent multiple births, twins. There were already very strict birth regulations in place, but the Council was adamant that no twins be born. After Armand created EX2, he was an Independent High Council favorite. The Council pushed him for new innovations. They wanted Armand to develop more extreme population regulators and methods of selective sterilization. He felt this was wrong and was horrified by the direction the Council wanted to take Indra. You know about the cerebral chips? You know what they do?"

"Track you and record everything you do," answers Lex.

"Yes. The chips are very dangerous and invasive. Armand, knowing he was being monitored via his chip, made it appear as if he was working diligently to achieve the goals the Council set for him. But really he was working on a way to block the chips from transmitting to the Archives, so he could limit the control the Council had over him. When he could successfully block the chips, he was able to hide his most important work from the Council, including his secret lab and his work to help me become pregnant."

Livia interjects, "Yes, we saw some of that in Archive memories. Roscoe had them."

Del nods. "Yes, Armand and I gave those memories to Roscoe. We hoped he would be able to show them to you one day. The memories Roscoe showed you were never part of the Archives."

Livia asks, "What was wrong? Were you sick?"

"Not sick, but I could not have children."

Lex looks at Enzo and says, "Well, he fixed that. You had us and Jules and Enzo."

"Yes, he did. And I will get to all of that. But let me explain how it happened. When we realized I could not have a child, Armand developed a method of genetic modification to heal me. He was hoping to strengthen my health, which had always been weak. He hoped to boost my fertility and give our child the best genetic makeup he could design. I got pregnant, and when we realized I was having twins, we knew they were in trouble. With so many people coming and going from Helix, it was common knowledge that I was pregnant, but only Armand and I knew I was carrying twins. We reached out to the rebels for help. I wanted to escape with both of you and begged Armand to leave Helix, but he wouldn't. He felt he could do more to stop the Council if he stayed. We knew it would be safer to split you up. So Armand and I decided one of you would stay on Helix with him and I would take the other to be hidden in Rock Bottom. We thought it would appear that I had left and abandoned my newborn on the island. We hoped no one would come looking for me. Just days after the two of you were born, Roscoe helped get Lex and me off the island."

Del turns to Lex and says, "Initially, Roscoe and I planned to live with you in Rock Bottom. But the Council was hearing rumors that I had given birth to twins. They wanted to find me and were relentless. If they found me with you, those rumors would be confirmed. The Council would know I had given birth to twins, and both of you would be in danger. It was imperative I put as much distance between myself and Lex as possible. The Orphanage in the Hub was the best solution."

Lex interrupts, "How could you say it was the best solution? It was a nightmare! You abandoned me."

"I'm sorry it was so difficult, but we could see no other way. No one could know you were my child. The rebels had people working in the Orphanage who would look out for you. I had to leave Rock Bottom, and the only place I could go was to the Outlands. At that time the journey to the Outlands was incredibly risky. Most people who attempted it died. Taking you with me was unthinkable. I wanted you to live, not die with me trying to escape Indra. I believed you would be safer in the Orphanage, and you were."

"It sure never felt like anyone was looking out for me in the Orphanage," says Lex.

"But you did survive," says Del.

Lex concedes, "Barely, but I did."

Del continues, "Roscoe and I both had our chips removed and made the trip through the tunnel to what is now this colony. It took two months to move through the tunnel."

"Two months!" Lex blurts out. "That trip was awful, and we did it in four days. I would have lost my mind if I was in that tunnel for two months."

Del fixes Lex with a cold gaze. "It was our only choice, so we did what had to be done."

"Right," says Lex with a shrug, and Del looks away. *Why did I say anything? Now she thinks I'm weak. I could have stayed in the tunnel for two months if I had to.*

"That must have been very difficult," says Livia.

"It was. We didn't understand about the additive back then. We only knew we had to go slow or we would die. At that time the colony was barely ten people, little more than a camp. Living together, Roscoe and I became close."

Lex interrupts, "Are you saying Roscoe is Jules and Enzo's father?"

Enzo says snidely, "At least you're paying attention."

Del says to Enzo, "There is no need for that. You and your brother didn't take it well when you found out about Lex and Livia. Everyone needs time to adjust."

Zavier stammers, "Roscoe has children? Two sons? He never said anything."

Del nods at Zavier. "I'm sure he never told anyone in Rock Bottom about Jules and Enzo, even those people he was close to." Del turns to Lex and Livia. "Roscoe and I had not planned to become involved, but we spent a lot of time together, first in Rock Bottom and then out here. When I left Helix, Armand and I knew we would most likely never see each other again."

Lex sarcastically says, "Well, then I guess it's fine."

"I'm sorry you don't approve, but that is what happened. Of course, I gave birth to Jules and Enzo out here. When they were a little over two years old, Roscoe went back to Rock Bottom to lead the rebels. He has come back out to the colony several times to see me and his sons, but he spends most of his time in Rock Bottom."

"Roscoe could have told us about the two of you," says Lex. "And about Jules and Enzo."

Del nods. "We agreed it was my responsibility to tell you."

Livia asks, "Did you ever go back with him?"

"No. I've never been back to Indra. Over the past fifteen years, the colony has slowly grown to a few hundred people. Most came from Rock Bottom, but a few from the upper levels of Indra have come out to the colony. As the years passed, I realized that Armand's genetic modifications made me different from other people. I know from Jules and Enzo that my children share these modifications to varying degrees. The first thing I noticed was that I never got sick and could heal incredibly quickly. I think that is why you girls could breathe when your devices were taken off. Your bodies were able to adapt to the sudden lack of additive."

"In the Orphanage," says Lex, "despite all the boosters they gave us, the other kids were always getting sick, but I never did. I just thought I was lucky."

"It's your immune system," says Del. "It is much stronger than that of a normal person. I believe that is why I don't really age. I heal and repair to the point that I regenerate healthy tissue. I look almost the same as I did when Armand did the modifications."

Livia asks, "Are you saying we won't age?"

"It's impossible to know how many modifications I passed on to you and how they will affect you. I have other gifts, enhanced senses and special skills. I can do things most people can't. I have heard you two have gifts as well."

"I don't have gifts," says Lex.

Livia fixes Lex with a harsh glare and says, "You do. We both do. There's no reason to deny it. I can sense people's feelings, and Lex's vision, hearing, and sense of smell are incredibly strong. We're not normal. I think I'm just starting to understand that."

"I suspect that other gifts will present in different ways, some subtle, some more obvious. What I really want to focus on is that you are twins and what that means within Rock Bottom and to the rebels."

"You mean the twin lore?" asks Livia. "Zavier told us about it."

"I told them the version of the Telling about The Twins that I grew up with," says Zavier.

"Yes, the twin lore, The Time of the Twins, but it's more than that," says Del. "You are the prophetic set of twins. You are the ones who can spark the revolution."

Enzo becomes visibly agitated and shouts, "This is a mistake! They don't have to be The Twins." He turns and storms out.

Del ignores Enzo's outburst and says, "Enzo is not happy about this. He thinks the Prophecy could be referring to him and Jules."

"He's right," says Lex with a shrug. "This Twin Prophecy isn't about us."

Del folds her hands calmly and says, "The Prophecy doesn't have to be about you. We just need people to *believe* it's about you."

Lex asks, "Why does it matter what people believe?"

"Belief can be a powerful tool," says Del. "We need people to believe so we can motivate them."

"Motivate who to do what?" Lex snaps, exasperated. "What are you talking about?"

Del takes a deep breath. "It is complicated. Roscoe has a source very close to the Council. Through that source, we have learned that the Council has a plan to eliminate Rock Bottom and Core Low once and for all."

"What do you mean?" asks Livia, shocked.

"The Council wants to kill everyone in Rock Bottom?" asks Zavier, outraged. "It's not enough that we're barely surviving, trapped below their precious city. Now they want to wipe us out?"

"Rock Bottom has been cut off from Upper Indra for years," says Del. "Yet rebels still break through. The Council has to devote resources to keeping Rock Bottom confined and separated. They have always felt that Rock Bottom and all its people are nothing more than a festering burden. Finally, the Council has devised a way to rid themselves of Rock Bottom all together. They plan to flood the lowest levels of Indra."

"How can they do that?" asks Livia. "There can't be enough water in the Aero-Crown."

"The water is not in the Aero-Crown," explains Del. "They've been building up water in a reservoir outside Indra. The Council rebuilt an old dam outside the city to the north, and water has been collecting in the reservoir behind it. The project has taken years. They connected the reservoir to the old pipes, so when there is enough water in the reservoir, they will open the floodgate valves at the dam and flood Rock Bottom and Core Low, killing tens of thousands. They hope to kill everyone below the Hub."

"That is terrible," says Livia, visibly distressed. "What can we do?"

"Wait!" says Lex. "Slow down. First, I don't know what a dam is, or a reservoir. And I don't know how you could use one of them to flood Rock Bottom. Second, you're telling me there were people working outside of Indra for years? I've never heard about anything like this. How is that possible? And you still haven't explained what us being twins has to do with any of this."

"Yes, I said it was complicated," says Del. "I'm trying to explain. First, a dam is a structure built to stop the flow of water, and a reservoir is the place where the water is collected once the dam is in place. This dam is a seven-hundred-foot structure that was built before the Great Catastrophe. It was damaged long ago, and there was no water in the reservoir. The Council repaired the dam, and the water started to build up in the reservoir. The Council has connected the reservoir to the old pipe system that goes right into Rock Bottom. When they open the valves, the water will rush out of the reservoir through the pipes into Rock Bottom and Core Low. I suspect that the reason you haven't heard anything about it is because the Council didn't want anyone to know. The Council went to great lengths to keep this project a secret. Everyone who worked on it was under strict orders not to talk about it. They were told if they did, they would be banished to the Archives. The workers were provided with breathing devices like the ones you've been using so they could work outside the dome."

"And all of this is from Roscoe's source in the Council?" asks Lex.

"Yes," says Del, "but I have seen the dam and the water in the reservoir. It is a long ride from here, but I wanted to confirm it was really happening. I have a group of my people stationed near the dam. Thanks to the communications equipment you brought with you, they report that the water levels in the reservoir have been steadily rising and there is an increase in activity at the dam. Also, we have successfully restored contact with Roscoe, but his report was not good. The situation is worse than we thought. His source confirmed that the Council's plan is imminent. The Council estimates they will have enough water to fully flood Core Low and Rock Bottom in just a few weeks."

"All right, so the Council is going to flood Rock Bottom," says Lex. "Again, what does us being twins have to do with it?"

"We will use the Twin Prophecy to motivate the people to leave Rock Bottom before they are all killed," says Del.

"How would you do that?" asks Livia.

"We reenter Indra and join forces with Roscoe's group of rebels," says Del. "We will return to Rock Bottom with you two. We will use you two, The Twins of Prophecy, to rally the people of Rock Bottom to prepare to leave."

"This is insane!" says Lex, throwing her hands up. "We just got out of Indra. Why would we go back?"

"We thought there would be more time," says Del. "But as I said, the latest reports are that this plan is moving forward sooner than we thought. It was not my intent to have you come through the tunnel just to turn around and return to Indra."

Lex shakes her head. "Why do you need us to go? Can't Roscoe and his rebels tell everyone what the Council is planning and that they need to get out?"

"The Council has been threatening those in Rock Bottom all their lives, and they have survived," says Del. "It would be impossible to convince them that this time it is different, that it is not just another PCF raid or attack where a few hundred will die. It will take something extraordinary to convince them they must leave their homes and their lives for the Outlands."

Livia asks, "Would a set of twins really mean that much to the people of Rock Bottom?"

"We think so," says Del. "We think seeing a set of twins would inspire the people of Rock Bottom. They will need a strong motivation to get out. Most people would never leave without some kind of sign. They would stay no matter what we told them was coming, but if they think it is The Time of the Twins, we think they will leave."

"Are you going to try and stop the Council from flooding Rock Bottom or just hope everyone gets out in time?" asks Zavier.

"Our main goal is to get everyone out of Rock Bottom, but we also have a plan to stop, or at least delay, the flood," says Del. "After we rally the people of Rock Bottom to leave, we will split up to tackle two operations. Lex will go with one team of rebels headed to the reservoir to stop the water at its source. Meanwhile, Livia will go with the other team to infiltrate and sabotage the main air filtration plant, where the additive is mixed into the air. We have a way to slowly decrease the additive from the air so people can breathe outside of Indra. If we cannot stop the flood, we must delay it until all the people of Rock Bottom are free from the additive and can travel safely out of the tunnels."

"Lex and I just found each other," protests Livia. "I don't want to be separated."

"And we haven't agreed to do any of this," adds Lex.

Del raises her hand. "The plan is in motion, and you two will do what needs to be done or thousands will die. This isn't a choice. This is your destiny."

Lex stands. "Our destiny? You sound insane. What makes you think you can give us orders? You have no authority over us. We don't have to do what you say."

Lex starts to storm out. Livia gets up and is following Lex when Del raises her voice and says, "We will also rescue your father."

Lex and Livia both stop just inside the mouth of the cave. Livia takes in a sharp breath, while Lex calmly fixes her eyes on Del.

"Our father is alive?" asks Lex, narrowing her eyes at Del.

"Rescue him?" Livia stammers, shaking her head. "What do you mean rescue him? Where is he?"

"Armand has been trapped in the Archives for almost sixteen years," explains Del, her tone softened.

"I thought he was dead," says Livia as she sits back at the table.

"We both thought he was dead," says Lex, crossing her arms, standing firm at the cave mouth. "In the Archives for sixteen years? Why?"

Del takes a breath. "They wanted his work. Soon after I left Helix Island with Lex, the Council secretly captured Armand and confiscated all his research. The Council announced that both Armand and I were dead." Del looks at Lex. "Please, Lex, come sit while I explain."

"Fine," says Lex, her face tight. She moves back to the table and sits next to Livia. "Go on."

"The Council forced him to work in the labs they had constructed in the High Council Building. They had genetic manipulation projects they wanted him to focus on. Projects that would make the members of the Council stronger and more powerful than all the rest of Indra, as if they weren't already. In fact, they wanted the exact type of manipulations he had successfully achieved with me, though at the time he could not have known how successful they would turn out to be. He felt these would be bad for the people of Indra. The Council spent about a year trying to get him to work on their genetic projects. They used Livia as leverage to pressure him to do what they wanted, promising that when he was successful, he could return to her on Helix. When he refused, the Council banished him to the Archives, the living death of Shadow Status, but the Council never gave up hope. According to our source close to the Council, they bring him out of the Archives every couple years to see if his will has broken and he is ready to do what they ask, but he has never given in."

"We should rescue our father first," argues Lex. "Nothing is more important."

"Absolutely," Livia agrees. "I can't believe he is alive. We must get him out of there immediately. What is the plan for rescuing him?"

Del raises her hand. "We will rescue Armand, but we must stick to the plan. Eliminating the danger for the people of the Lower Levels has to be our first priority. That is what your father would want."

Lex slams her hand on the table. "How would you know what he wants? You left him on Helix. You left him in the hands of the Council. He was probably tortured before they gave up and locked him in the Archives. Sixteen years as a shadow!"

"It is precisely because he allowed himself to be put in the Archives rather than help them that makes me so sure I know what he would want," says Del calmly. "He sacrificed his freedom to try to protect the people of Indra. He would want us to save them before we tried to rescue him. I'm sure this has been overwhelming for you, but we all have no choice. The Council has oppressed the people of Rock Bottom and Core Low for centuries. It is inhumane, and now they plan to commit this atrocity. The powers at work here are evil. I know this. It's too complicated to explain to you now. But you must trust me. They will not stop. If this attempt fails, there will be another. They won't stop until they kill everyone in the Lower Levels of Indra. It is time to rise against the Council. One of my ancestors died trying to get the people out of Rock Bottom, and I will too if I have to."

"I will help rescue my father," Lex says, "but I don't want to be a part of any of this Twin Savior trash."

"Obviously, it is your choice," says Del, her eyes locked on Lex. "I can't force you. I can only hope that you choose to do what is right. Roscoe needs the next two days to get the final pieces of the plan in place on his side. We will leave at first light in two days. You have until then to decide if you want to be part of the plan. We can do it without you, but it will be very difficult. I firmly believe that the people of Rock Bottom will not leave without a catalyst. You two standing before them as The Twins of Prophecy could save their lives. I can't make it any plainer than that." Del stands. "Good night. Rest well."

The group stands, and Zavier steps to Del. "I'm proud to be a part of this operation."

Del smiles and says, "It's good to finally meet you, Zavier. Roscoe has told me many good things about you."

"It's nice to hear someone thinks highly of me," says Zavier. He flashes Lex a wicked smile. "I was thinking, if all those people are going to be coming through the tunnel, I have some ideas that might make it an easier trip. Maybe lay down some scrap, use ropes, that sort of thing."

"Yes," says Del, with a nod. "Let's get you in contact with the rebels in Rock Bottom who have been preparing for the tunnel exodus. Quinn, take Zavier to the comms center so he can talk to Rock Bottom."

"Yes, ma'am," says Quinn.

They all head out of the cave, Quinn and Zavier heading off down a different path.

19

Lex, Livia, and Kane walk back to their cave. Lex kicks a rock as she stomps down the path. The rock goes flying into the woods.

"What is wrong with her?" she blurts out, her voice loud and hostile.

"She is very focused," Livia says, her tone calm. "She sees us as a means to an end."

"Our mother and the rebels just want to use us," snaps Lex. "This twin thing? I can't believe they think a set of twins would really make any difference."

"Well, they believe it can, and I can see how they may be right."

"We have nothing to do with this," protests Lex. "We're not rebels. We just happen to be twins."

"But I think we can help," says Livia. "I've always sensed there was something very wrong in Indra. Now I know it's corrupt. The way the Council controls people is terrible."

"We can't stop the Council," says Lex, frustrated, pulling on a branch as they pass. "We don't know who or what the Council is."

"We are not trying to stop the Council, but the flooding of Rock Bottom we can try to stop."

"Yeah," says Kane. "We can't just sit by. We have to help them."

Lex sighs. "Great, so you two are going to gang up on me now." They walk the rest of the way back to the cave in silence.

When they pull back the cloth and enter the cave, they find a dark-skinned, short man and a woman with long black hair waiting inside. Lex reaches for her blaster, but Livia quickly puts her hand on Lex's shoulder, saying, "They mean us no harm."

The woman says, "Sorry to intrude. We wanted to meet Lex."

Lex looks at the couple and says, "That's me. Why?"

"We are Vippy's parents, Corah and Otto." Smiling, Corah comes forward and hugs Lex.

Lex stands awkwardly with her arms at her side as the woman hugs her. Lex flashes on an image of tiny Vippy at the Academy, with her short black hair, wide brown eyes, and quick smile. *Vippy was a good cadet at the Academy. When Livia and I were rescuing Kane from High Security Detainment, if Vippy hadn't shown up when she did, we wouldn't have gotten out of there. It was a shock to learn Vippy was a rebel. I can see Vippy in them. Her dark skin like her father and straight black hair like her mother.*

Lex tries to pull away from the woman. "I'm sorry. How do you know who I am?"

The woman releases Lex from the hug. *Finally.*

Otto grins. "We're quite excited to meet you, Lex."

Corah can see Lex is confused, and explains, "I'm sorry. We have heard so much about you and the Academy from Vippy in her comms over the years. She thought you were very impressive."

"Thanks," says Lex, still confused. "But what are you doing here? I mean, in the Outlands? Vippy was a Hubber."

Corah nods. "Yes, we were Hubbers, but we've always been rebels. When Vippy got into the Academy, everything got more dangerous for her, and she asked us to leave our life in the Hub so we could never be used as leverage if she was caught. It took a few years to get out of the Hub without raising any suspicions. Roscoe arranged for us to get out to the Outlands and has helped us keep in touch with Vippy with the occasional holocomm. Now that she has her assignment in the High Council Building, she is one of Roscoe's best-placed spies. There is no telling what she may be able to learn that could help the rebels. Roscoe said having her assigned to the Spear could be invaluable."

"I just found out that Vippy is a rebel," says Lex. "She saved us when we were rescuing Kane from High Security Detainment."

Vippy's mother is shocked and proud. "That's my girl. Brave and strong."

"She helped us, then she had me stun her," says Lex. "Won't she be discovered for helping us? Can't someone watch her Archive memories?"

Otto waves his hand dismissively. "Vippy had a control switch implanted so she could cut her connection with the Archives. I'm sure she had you stun her to cover that she had turned her chip off."

Lex frowns. "I didn't know that was possible."

"As you can imagine, spies have to be very careful," says Corah. "If you have a chip, it is recording everything you do, but the Council doesn't have eyes on everyone all the time. You have to do something to draw their attention."

"Well, she saved our lives," says Livia. "We are very grateful she helped us. I hope she is safe."

Otto nods solemnly. "We hope so too. It was more than we hoped, to hear any news of her."

Corah takes Otto's arm. "We'll leave you," she says with a small smile. "We just wanted to meet you and wish you a warm welcome."

"Thank you," says Lex with a nod.

Corah and Otto walk out of the cave. Lex watches them go, then says to Kane, "I don't know what to think. I feel like I'm the only one who is having a problem with all of this."

Kane says, "There's a lot happening."

"Of course, I can see that the plan to flood Rock Bottom is horrible, but I don't think I can work with the rebels." Lex flops down on a cushion at the table. Kane and Livia make their way around it and sit next to each other across from Lex as she continues, "We were just in the Academy. They trained us to hate and fight the rebels. I can't just turn that off. Can you?"

"I didn't turn it off," says Kane. "I know they are rebels. I'm just not so sure that the rebels are the enemy we were taught to fight in the

Academy. That was blind hate. That doesn't work now. We know some of them. We know what they are fighting for. They have even helped us."

"I know," says Lex. "I should feel indebted to them. When we were rescuing you, if they hadn't shown up when they did, we would all be in High Security Detainment."

"Most likely we would be dead," says Kane. Livia gives a small shudder and moves a little closer to Kane. He reaches out and strokes her back.

"I'm grateful they helped us," says Lex. "And you're right. We probably wouldn't be alive if they hadn't, but they're asking us to go back into Indra with them. To fight with them. Before, when we escaped with them, we had no choice. The PCF was chasing us. Now we have a choice. We could stay out of it. I know there is no way back to the life I thought I would have in the PCF. But now, if we do this, we will be making the PCF our enemy. We may have to kill PCF officers. I don't think I can do that."

"I guess I'm not really looking at it as the PCF versus the rebels," says Kane, looking thoughtful. "I am just thinking about what is right and wrong. The rebels are fighting for freedom. I can see their position. They have a right to exist. If this flood is allowed to happen, it will kill everyone in Rock Bottom, and the rebels are the only ones who can stop it. We're talking about innocent people. You've seen for yourself what Rock Bottom is really like. It's not what the Academy led us to believe. The mutants are terrible and beyond hope, but mutants and Rock Bottom are not the same thing."

"This is a lot to ask of us," says Lex, letting out a sigh. "We would have to officially work with the rebels. Just being with a rebel is a death sentence."

"I'm sure the PCF would kill us now whether we were with the rebels or not. You did break me out of High Security Detainment."

"Right!" says Lex, her eyes wide. "If they catch us, they will absolutely kill us. We are fugitives. So why would we go back into Indra?"

"Because they need our help," says Livia. "If I can help, I'm going to.

That is my choice. You have to make your own. I would just say, when you were in the Academy and you imagined your future in the PCF, what did you think it would be? Did you think you would be helping and protecting people?"

"Yes," says Lex. "I figured I would be on patrols in Rock Bottom killing mutants. And rebels."

"Well," says Livia with a nod, "think of it this way, you planned to protect people, there are people in danger, and you can do something to help protect them. And like Kane said, at the Academy they made it seem like everyone in Rock Bottom was a horrible mutant, and that wasn't true. Killing all those people is wrong, and you can help save them. Think about it. You have a little time. But not much."

20

Lex stands at the mouth of their small cave, holding back the cloth, looking up at the moon and stars. *It is so open here. I didn't realize it, but I was trapped. Trapped in Indra. Caged by my life. This is freedom. No dome, no Indra. I can't go back.*

Zavier walks in past Lex. "Looking at the stars? Pretty strato," he says as he walks over to his cot and starts unloading gear from his pack.

From inside the cave, Livia says, "Lex, come in and lie down. You need sleep. We all do."

Lex turns and walks into the cave, letting the covering fall back over the opening. Livia is lying on a cot, covered by a thin blanket. Kane sits on the cot nearest to Livia studying a leaf. Lex goes to her cot, lies down, and pulls the thin blanket over herself.

Livia says, "I guess this is what cold feels like."

"Yep," says Zavier. "Bet you were never cold on your island. Just a little taste of how us Low folk live, Airess."

"Back off, Zavier!" snaps Lex.

"No, he's right," says Livia. "My life on Helix Island was always temperature-controlled perfection." She pulls the blanket up under her chin.

"The silitex has body temperature regulators," says Lex. "You can put your jumpsuit back on."

Livia gives a shudder. "No, I'll be fine."

Kane stands, grabs the blanket from his cot, and walks to Livia. He puts his blanket over hers, then lies down next to Livia and wraps his arms around her.

"Or that," mutters Lex.

Zavier gets up, grabs the blanket from his cot, and walks across the cave. To Lex it looks like he is walking toward her. *Is he coming over to me?*

"I'm not cold," says Lex.

Zavier smirks. "I wouldn't care if you were," and walks out of the cave.

Livia asks, "Where's he going?"

"Who cares," says Lex.

Livia lies wrapped in Kane's arms. *He makes me feel safe. I never felt safe on Helix. Not really.*

Livia whispers, "Don't ever leave me."

"Never," says Kane, and pulls her closer.

21

Lex is the first to wake. She looks over at Livia and Kane squeezed together on the cot. *That cot is far too small for the two of them. How could anyone get any sleep like that? Well, at least she was warm.* She notices Zavier's cot is empty. *He never came back. Probably found some girl. Spent the night in her cot.*

Livia opens her eyes and sees Lex is already awake. "I hope you got good rest."

"I did," says Lex. "How about you and Kane? Were you warm enough?" Kane is slowly waking up. He stretches his arms.

Kane says groggily, "Best sleep of my life."

Livia smiles and gets up from the cot. "Zavier never came back last night," she says as she walks over to the table and sits.

Lex joins her at the table. "Maybe he found a little local warmth."

Livia laughs. "Perhaps. He must know people here from his days as a runner. People he escorted to the Outpost."

"Or maybe someone new," says Lex with a shrug. "I get the sense that he moves pretty fast."

Livia tips her head, perplexed. "Really? Why do you say that?"

Lex shrugs. "Just an impression. Not like one of your senses about people."

"It was pretty obvious he and Martine had some history," Livia says. "That was hard to miss."

"I asked him about her. They were together for a while and she didn't like how he ended it."

"He told you that?" Livia asks, impressed. "When?"

"One of the nights in the tunnel," says Lex. "We talked a little, then I got annoyed with him and the conversation ended. But he's not here now. Let's enjoy that."

Livia looks over at Kane, who is sitting on his cot adjusting his breathing device. She asks, "How is your breathing, Kane? Have you been able to turn it down at all?"

"You two are so lucky you don't have to worry about the additive," says Kane. "I was doing fine turning it down slowly in the tunnel. Then after it was ripped off and I had that terrible reaction, I realized how vulnerable I am until I'm off the additive. I've been turning it down as fast as I can. I got a little dizzy last night, but I slept through it. I can't wait to be off this thing."

"What will happen if we go back to Indra?" asks Lex. "We'd be breathing air with the additive."

"That is a good point," says Livia. "You and I, even Del, we will mostly likely be fine, but what about Kane and Zavier?"

"They're going to have to do the breathing device thing again, I guess," says Lex.

"Blast!" barks Kane and punches the cot. "Why am I rushing to get off this thing if I'm going to have to start all over when we get back?"

Livia goes to Kane, sits next to him on the cot, and puts her arms around him. "I'm sorry."

"I just wanted to be done with this thing."

Quinn enters the cave carrying a tray of food and sets it on the table.

"Good to see you are all up," he says. "When you have all eaten and are ready, Del wants to take you on a tour of the colony. Meet some people."

"Yes, of course," says Livia. "That would be nice." Quinn turns to leave, and Livia hurriedly asks, "Quinn, before you go may I ask, how is Jules?"

"Not great," says Quinn.

Cautiously, Livia says, "If I can, I'd like to go see him."

"I can take you to Medical," says Quinn. "I'll wait outside. Let me know when you are ready."

"Thank you, Quinn," says Livia. "We won't be long."

Quinn nods and leaves the cave. Lex waits a beat and then in a low voice asks, "Livia, what are you doing? Do you really think it's a good idea to go see Jules? You practically took his leg off. Why would he want to see you?"

Livia says in an equally low voice, "I want to say I'm sorry in person. I have to do at least that. And I think we should all go."

"I don't think it's a bad idea," says Kane, putting a piece of something yellow from the tray in his mouth. "Oh, yes. That is sweet. Definitely fruit. Now what kind, I have no idea."

Lex glares at Kane. "Of course you agree with her. Fine. Let's go to Medical."

22

Lex, Livia, and Kane follow Quinn through the forest. He leads them along a well-worn path past several buildings tucked in the trees with narrow trails that branch off the main path. They reach a wood building with a low roof.

"This is it," says Quinn as he walks through the door. They enter a small room with a few chairs arranged against one wall. A heavyset woman with gray hair pulled back in a severe bun sits at a small table positioned in front of a door at the end of the room. She is reading a projection of scrolling text hovering above a battered holoscreen and looks up as they enter.

"Everyone, this is Evelyn," says Quinn. "They want to see Jules."

"Yes, I'll take you back," says Evelyn warmly, and stands.

"I'm going to go find Del and let her know where you are," says Quinn, and heads back out into the forest.

"All right, follow me," says Evelyn, and walks through the door at the back of the room. They follow her down a hall that leads farther back into the building, with small rooms off to each side, the doorways draped with rough fabric. "He is awake. It took over three hundred stitches to close the wound. The first layer was subcutaneous to knit the muscles back together. I gave him the heaviest boosters I have."

Livia grimaces. *Three hundred stitches because of my zinger. I'm so thankful I didn't kill him, my half brother. I never would have forgiven myself.*

"Did you work in the medical field before you came to the Outlands?" asks Kane.

"I did. But in Rock Bottom, medical care is nothing like in the Uppers. It is very primitive. I always had to make do with very little. That skill has been useful in the Outlands."

"When did you come to the Outlands?" asks Kane.

"After my son was killed in a PCF raid, I decided to leave and make the trek with a few others. That was ten years ago."

"I'm sorry," says Kane, embarrassed. "I didn't mean to pry."

"Most people out here have a similar story. Something pushed them to leave." She pulls back the curtain of one of the rooms. "Here we are."

Jules is lying in a cot propped up against a pillow, his face pale. His injured leg is wrapped in bandages and resting in a sling suspended above the cot by a metal frame. Enzo is standing over him, his hand on Jules's shoulder. They are talking in low voices. When the group enters the room, they go quiet and look up.

"Jules, you have visitors. Not too long, you need your rest." Evelyn smiles and walks back down the hall.

Enzo scowls. "What are you doing here?"

"We wanted to see how Jules was doing," says Livia, stepping farther into the room. Then addressing Jules, she says, "I'm glad to see you are awake."

Enzo swiftly moves across the small room and stands between Livia and Jules's cot. "You shouldn't be here!"

Livia says calmly, "I wanted to check on Jules and apologize."

"He's alive," snaps Enzo. "He doesn't need to talk to you. You should go!"

"No, Enzo," says Jules, his voice quiet and strained. "Let them in. I want to meet them." He tries to sit up a little more but grimaces and slumps back against the pillow.

Enzo turns to Jules. "You're too weak. You need to rest."

"We will go, if that's what you want," says Livia, looking at Jules.

With effort, Jules lifts his arm and beckons them over. "No, don't go.

Come in. Ignore Enzo." He says to Enzo, "Step out of the way, Enzo."

"My brother has a kinder heart than me," says Enzo as he moves out of the way.

Lex mutters to Enzo as she passes, "Oh, you have a heart?"

The group stands at the foot of the cot while Livia moves to Jules's side and crouches down so she is on the same level as him. She takes his hand.

In a quiet voice Livia says, "I'm Livia. I'm so sorry. I truly am."

Jules gives a small smile. "It's nice of you to say. We did attack you, though. I will say I wish you hadn't had a zinger. Our mother always told us that zingers are particularly dangerous in close combat. She was right."

"It's Del's zinger. She left it on Helix. I've trained with it since I was little."

"All right," Enzo interrupts. "You've said you're sorry. Time to go."

"Enzo, stop," says Jules. "We're just talking, and I haven't met Lex yet."

Lex steps forward, "Right. I'm Lex. So we're half siblings I guess. Roscoe is your dad."

Jules smiles. "Mother told you everything, I imagine. That sounds like her."

"That's enough," barks Enzo. "Who cares? You met. Now get out!"

Lex glares at Enzo, her voice fierce. "Enzo, you need to back off. Livia and Jules are talking. You and I can go outside if you want."

Enzo takes a step closer to Lex. "You want to fight? I can take you down."

"I doubt that," says Kane, one side of his mouth lifting into a smirk.

"Look, little brother," says Lex, stepping closer to Enzo, "we haven't gotten off to a great start, which I don't much care about. I have no problem beating you senseless. Just let Livia say what she came to say, and we'll go."

"Enzo!" yells Jules, and winces. He forces in a breath and his face calms. "Step back and cool off."

Enzo throws his hands up. "For you, Jules." He takes a few steps back from Lex and stands at the foot of the cot with Kane. "Everything has gotten off track," says Enzo, shaking his head. "You two don't even want to be part of this. If you weren't twins, you wouldn't be here."

Lex clarifies, "You mean if we weren't Del's twins, we wouldn't be here. She seems to think we are pretty important."

"Well, obviously you are not the only twins," grumbles Enzo. "Jules and I could be the prophesied twins."

Lex laughs. "You can't believe in this Prophecy garbage?"

"What if I do?" Enzo challenges.

"Enzo, stop!" yells Jules, pulling Enzo's attention away from Lex. Jules takes a deep breath, letting it out slowly. "Please, let it go."

"No," says Enzo, looking down at Jules. "It's in the Telling. A set of twins will set Indra free. It should be you and me. We could rally the people of Rock Bottom. We could be the spark of the revolution. We have gifts like the two of them." Enzo looks at Lex and Livia and continues, "You're not that special. Plus, we aren't that much younger than you. If it's just because you're seventeen, that isn't enough to take this away from us."

From the doorway Del interrupts, "Enzo."

Enzo turns to see Del. Evidently, she had been standing there for a little while and heard most of Enzo's rant.

Del says to Enzo, "We can't wait a year and a half for you and Jules to reach seventeen. The Independent High Council is ready now. We need to use every advantage we have to save the people in Rock Bottom."

"Yes, Mother," says Enzo, with a nod. "You've said that many times."

"Apparently not enough," says Del. "This is not about you and your brother losing the title of Twins of the Prophecy. It's about saving people. Your self-centered attitude disappoints me." Then, turning to the group, she says, "While we are in a holding pattern waiting on Roscoe, I thought I would take you around to meet some of the people here. Livia, you should bring my zinger."

23

With Del and Enzo leading the way, Lex, Livia, and Kane walk through the forest. Livia and Del both have zingers in sheaths strapped to their backs while Lex and Kane have blasters on their belts. They move down a narrow path cutting through the trees passing several colony buildings. As they leave the center of the colony behind, there are fewer buildings and the woods become more dense, the ground overgrown with a wide variety of plants and moss.

"I am still so amazed how beautiful it is here," says Livia, following right behind Del. Her head swiveling in all directions. "Indra could never replicate this no matter how hard it tries."

"It took centuries for the world to recover," says Del, "but it did. Indra's High Council has been very successful in keeping everyone ignorant of the situation outside the dome. The people of Indra should have the right to leave."

"What if they want to stay?" Lex challenges. "I bet most Islanders like Indra just the way it is, right Airess?" *I bet Livia never would have left her easy life in the Islands until I showed up and she had to jump off Helix.*

Livia objects, "Lex, you know I didn't want that life. But like you, I had no choice." *Why does she still act likes it's my fault she went to the Orphanage? I was a baby too when our destiny was decided for us.*

"Enough." Del stops, annoyed, and turns to face both Lex and Livia. "The choice was your father's and mine, and one that had to be made.

But the people of Rock Bottom have no choice. The High Council is going to kill them and destroy their home. They need to leave." She turns away from them and starts to walk again. The group follows in silence.

Del is right, thinks Livia as they walk. *Everyone should know they can live outside Indra if that is what they want. The Council has gone to a lot of trouble to make sure they don't know it is even a possibility. Lex is right that most of the Islanders would stay. I can't imagine they would leave their luxurious and pampered lives for the Outlands, but perhaps some in the Hub and maybe even Middlers would. They should have a choice.*

They move downhill. The forest is so thick with tall, mature trees that it lets very little light through, and the ground is covered with dead leaves. Occasionally, Outlanders pass them headed up the hill to the colony, some carrying tools and building supplies. Most say hello or nod a greeting as they pass.

Livia breaks the silence. "Excuse me, Del, where are we going?"

"I'm taking you to see the preparations we have been making for the people of Rock Bottom."

"They won't be part of the colony?" Livia asks, confused.

"No," says Del. "They'll be assessed, grouped, and assigned to the region where they will start their own colony."

"Their own colony?" asks Lex. "You're not going to let them stay here?"

"We can't," explains Del. "There will be thousands. They can't just move into the colony. They will just be passing through here. There are vast amounts of land beyond this colony. Everyone can spread out and reclaim the Earth."

They come through the forest to a low ridge that overlooks a valley cleared of trees and other plants. The closest part of the valley is dotted with several wood buildings followed by a sea of structures made of random fabrics and materials all set on a grid of straight paths that seem to go on forever. Beyond the buildings and tents, a huge area of land has been marked off into smaller squares with rope strung between wood pegs in the ground.

"What is that?" asks Lex.

"This is the encampment where they will be brought when they first come through the tunnel," she says as they climb down the path carved in the ridge. "This will be their temporary home while we prepare them to go out and form their own colonies. If everything goes according to our plans, people will be able to start coming through the tunnel in only a few days. In a week, this will be a hive of people, all who need shelter, food, and a plan for their survival."

When they reach the bottom, Zavier joins them.

Lex asks, "Where did you come from?"

"I have been exploring, if you have to know. I can't believe how huge this is." He turns to Del and asks, "How long did this take?"

"Several years. We started to make plans as soon as we learned the High Council was repairing the dam and intended to flood Rock Bottom. The preparations have been twofold. First, get the people out, and then this, prep for them to live in the Outlands."

They walk through the encampment, weaving through buildings and tents, Outlanders hustling all around.

"This is impressive," Kane observes.

"There are areas for habitation, medical needs, hunting and weapons training, farming skills, and food storage. In a way, most of this is a school. Our goal is to make everyone as self-sufficient as we can, as fast as we can."

"How did you stockpile all the food?" asks Lex, bewildered.

"We have had many breakthroughs in seed development thanks to a rebel still inside Indra. The results have been rapid and resilient growth. We will be able to feed the refugees until they set up their own food production."

"Do you think they will like the crops you have grown?" asks Kane.

"They will have to, or starve. Most of them have only had rations and the synth food they could scrounge from Upper Indra. It will take them some getting used to non-synth food. I'm sure you felt the difference after eating it for the first time."

"I sure did," says Zavier. "That's why I slept outside the first night. Didn't think it was a good idea to be in an enclosed space."

"Oh," says Lex, sounding somewhat relieved. "I thought you'd gone to find someone you knew from your time as a tunnel runner."

"No! I could have blown out the tunnel with the way I was feeling. It was best I was alone."

"Well, I'm happy you survived," says Del with a grin. "I want to take all of you to the planning center. Follow me."

Del leads them into one of the fabric structures. There are many tables covered with papers laid out with charts, diagrams, and maps.

Livia begins to look them over. "What is all this? Is it—"

"Please, don't touch anything!" A small, frazzled woman with short red hair comes rushing over. "I have a system. Don't touch anything!"

They all take a step back from the tables as the woman begins fastidiously checking the charts and diagrams, reassuring herself they are in the right place.

"Hello, Noreen," says Del, using a calming tone. "We won't touch anything. I just wanted to show them the plans for when the Rock Bottom refugees start to arrive."

Noreen seems to relax a little. "Ah, yes, yes, the plans. So many plans and now so little time. I wish we—"

"Noreen," Del interrupts curtly. "We are ready. We must be. By all accounts, the flood is imminent."

"Yes, yes. Imminent, correct, Del. Even if we stop the flood, the exodus is imminent. For their own safety, the exodus is imminent. You are right. The time for preparation is almost over. We have a system." Her words start to come faster, her tone touched with a hint of panic. "They will be assessed, grouped, and then assigned. I believe it will work, but we'll see, we'll see. Assessed, grouped, and then assigned."

Livia moves closer to Noreen. *She is so distressed. Perhaps I can calm her.* Livia puts a hand on her shoulder and says, "Noreen, take a deep breath and show us what will happen."

"All right, yes. Each person will be processed and assessed to see what, if any, useful skills they might have or could be taught. They will be placed in groups to form a colony. Families and friends can stay together, of course, but we will try to spread out those with skills that will help the colonies survive. Then we start to prepare them to leave. There will be training. These buildings here . . ." She smooths a map out on the table and points to an area marked with several rows of dark rectangles. "They are set up for training, all kinds of training. People have to learn the skills they'll need to survive out here. Basic structure building, farming, hunting, and food storage and preparation techniques. We'll tell each person what we think they should train to do, but we won't force anyone to take on a job they don't want. We're not Indra. Right, Del?"

"That is correct. People can choose, but every colony must have people who intend to farm, hunt, and build. And someone in each colony will have to take on medical training."

Noreen nods. "Most of the skills are not hard, but life in the Outlands will be very different from what they are used to in Rock Bottom."

"Noreen, you have done an excellent job," says Del with a small smile. "All of us Outlanders will be here to help support the plan." She turns and addresses the group. "Let's leave Noreen to her charts."

Livia steps forward. "Thank you, Noreen."

Noreen begins to stammer. "It has been my pleasure, my pleasure. Especially now that the time has come, The Time of the—"

"Noreen," Del cuts her off, "let me know if you need anything."

"Yes, Del. I will," says Noreen, nodding her head. "Thank you."

Del turns and walks out of the building. The group follows her out while Noreen starts straightening papers.

"This way," says Del as she leads them down a path between two rows of tents.

Livia asks, "Why did you cut Noreen off so abruptly?"

"Because she has a tendency to go on. Did you really want her to launch into a dramatic reciting of 'The Telling of the Twins?'"

"Still, it was rude," says Livia.

"We don't have time for proper etiquette," Del says dismissively.

"I don't believe that's true," says Livia. "My Etiquette Tutor says there is always time for niceties, particularly when someone is working hard and deserves our respect. I will admit I despised my Etiquette Tutor, but on this topic I do agree with her."

"Maybe you and your Etiquette Tutor should shut up," Lex says under her breath.

Del looks pointedly at Lex. "Now who's being rude?" She turns to Livia. "You make a fair point. I could have been less abrupt. I will keep that in mind."

Lex seethes as they follow Del, cutting across the encampment. *Of course Livia is proper and perfect with her perfect manners and "fair points," and I'm just gruff and rude. That's what happens to the one you dump at the Orphanage. We don't get etiquette training. We just get survival training.*

They pass areas where a large group of Outlanders, including children, are working at long tables. Lex spots Otto and Corah in the group hard at work carefully packing items into large rugged bags.

Kane asks, "What are they doing?"

"They are putting together the new colony kits. They will be taken by the refugees when they leave here."

"What's in them?" asks Kane.

"A map of where their assigned colony is, food and hydration for the journey, medical supplies, building instructions, tools, hunting gear, comm systems, and seeds to start their own farms. The first new colonies are already prepped for when they arrive."

"Where are they?" asks Zavier.

"They are in a twenty-mile perimeter spread out from this base, so we can offer support. Initially, there will only be twelve. Once they are established, we will start moving farther out and keep going."

They arrive at a building that has a few speeders outside. Del yells, "Patricia, are you in there? Patricia?"

A tall, imposing woman storms out, clearly irritated. "What?" she yells. She is wearing a pair of goggles on her head and her hands are covered in grime.

She stops abruptly. "Oh, hi, Del. I was trying to rebuild a speeder hover unit. They can be tricky. Jules would be able to fix it easy. It's hard with these old . . ." she stops herself and looks at Lex and Livia, stunned. "Are these your daughters? Are these The Twins?"

"Yes, these are Lex and Livia," says Del.

"Wow, I didn't know you would bring them down here." Flustered, Patricia wipes her palms on her coveralls and extends a hand. She heartily shakes both Lex and Livia's hands. "I never thought I would meet The Twins."

Enzo snaps, "You have met twins before. It's not that special."

"Of course, you and Jules, but these are The Twins, so it is pretty strato."

"Yeah, strato," says Enzo, his face in a fierce scowl.

Del puts her hand on Enzo's arm. "Patricia, can we borrow one of these speeders? Livia needs to learn how to ride one."

"I do?"

"Yes," says Del. "You'll need to ride one to Indra. It will slow us down to have you ride on the back as a passenger. You must be solo."

"Sure," says Patricia. "We only have a few down here at this substation, but take the last one in the row. The rest still have some tweaks I need to bang out. You don't want it stalling and throwing one of The Twins off without warning."

"Maybe you do," says Enzo.

"Enzo," Del says in a warning tone.

He looks off down the row of tents with an exaggerated sigh.

Patricia adds, "There are helmets on the ground too. Not sure of the sizes, but they'll do."

"Thank you very much for your hard work, Patricia. It is most appreciated," Del says.

Patricia looks surprised, her eyebrows shooting up. "Oh! Well, you're welcome, and thank you, Del." A huge smile crosses Patricia's face as she walks back into the building.

Del gives Livia a sideways glance. "I haven't forgotten everything I learned when I was in etiquette training. I can have manners too."

"You made her very happy," says Livia.

"I know," says Del. She turns to Enzo and orders, "Enzo, take that speeder out to the open field on the east side of the tents. We'll train Livia there."

He grabs a helmet, jumps on the speeder, and takes off. Del and the group follow him on foot. Enzo zips through the tents with ease. Lex and Kane walk together, with Livia, Del, and Zavier a few paces behind them.

Watching Enzo speed away, Kane says with admiration, "He's pretty good. He would have done well at the Academy."

Lex smirks. "I doubt he could be that disciplined."

Kane lets out a short laugh. "Like you were?"

"Point taken," Lex begrudgingly agrees.

Kane continues teasing her. "Maybe good speeder skills and a lack of proper respect for discipline is in the blood."

Lex laughs. "All right, too far. Don't remind me that we're related."

Livia walks up beside them. "What were you talking about?"

"About your half brother's speeder skills," answers Kane.

"Let's hold off on calling him our brother," says Lex. She tries not to look at Livia. *Why did she have to interrupt? Can't I have a moment with my best friend?*

"Why don't you want to call him our brother?" asks Livia. "He is, after all."

"This whole family thing is starting to be more than I can deal with. A sister. A mother. Now two brothers. It's a lot."

"I don't really think you have a choice," says Livia, with a small shrug.

"I can always choose. Just like our parents chose to leave us."

"You know they had no choice," Livia argues. "You can be so frustrating!"

They come to the end of the row of tents, and Livia stops abruptly. She lets out a gasp. They have arrived at a large, open field where Enzo is zipping around so fast on the speeder that he is almost a blur.

"I've never seen so much open space," says Livia. "It's breathtaking."

"Yeah," says Lex. "I would love to ride the speeder here. It will be a great place for you to learn."

Livia nervously asks, "Will it be difficult? Do I have to go as fast as Enzo?"

"No!" says Lex with a laugh. "He's good but an idiot. You'll be fine. It's similar to when we were trying to escape Helix from the PCF and you made me get on that wild beast of yours."

"She is a horse, and her name is Veda. How is it possibly similar?"

"Well, you're sitting on something that is moving fast, but you're in charge. Most of it is balance. Use your thighs and core to center yourself. You have a good sense of balance, and the speeder will react to you shifting your weight."

Zavier and Del walk up. "Are you ready, Livia?" asks Del.

"I suppose," says Livia, her voice unsure.

Del waves Enzo in. He approaches rapidly and makes an alarmingly short stop, coming within inches of Kane.

"Hey!" says Kane, annoyed. "Don't mess around. That speeder doesn't exactly look regulation."

Enzo jumps off. "I had it under control." He tosses the helmet to Livia. "Do you want me to show you how to do it?"

"No, I will," says Lex, pushing Enzo away. She grabs the helmet from Livia and quickly gets on the speeder. Enzo scowls at Lex and folds his arms over his chest as he steps back. Livia moves over to Lex and stands next to her.

Lex starts to point out its features. "Here is the accelerator. Take it slow at first. This is the brake. It will react very quickly, so be careful or you could go flying off. Also, this boost button. Don't touch it. You are not ready for it. I'll show you a few maneuvers first. Stand back."

Lex takes off across the huge valley. She quickly covers a great distance, turns around, and starts to come back, making sharp turns, pivoting the speeder to change directions, rapidly reversing, and making many quick stops.

"Whoa, I haven't seen that before," Enzo says, impressed, his anger starting to fade.

"Yeah, she was the best at the Academy," Kane says proudly. "No one could keep up with her."

"I think you are confusing skill with being reckless," says Zavier, not hiding his irritation.

Lex glides the speeder to a stop right in front of Livia. She pulls off the helmet. "That was amazing! Even on this outdated model, it was so different to have no obstacles and to just ride." She turns to Livia and hands her the helmet. "Your turn."

"You sure you don't want to show off some more?" asks Zavier.

Lex glares at him while Livia hesitantly gets on the speeder.

Lex instructs, "Lean forward a bit to compensate for your height, then you just grip the accelerator lightly. Take it slow but don't hesitate. You are in control."

Livia slowly starts to glide forward, then builds some speed and quickly stops. The whole speeder tilts forward severely, almost causing her to go over the front.

"Blast!" yells Kane, grimacing. "Are we sure this is a good idea?"

Livia waves her hand, indicating she is all right.

"Let's give her a chance," says Del.

Livia begins again, and the speeder moves across the valley without stopping. She then makes a few turns and controlled stops and starts.

"Look at her," says Lex with a smile. "She's got it. It was probably my excellent instruction."

"I'm sure that was it," says Kane. "I guess she won't need to ride on the back of my speeder," he adds with a hint of disappointment.

Del interjects, "Two on one speeder will not be as fast. We can't afford to be slowed down. Plus, Livia seems to be enjoying riding solo."

Livia rides the speeder back to the group. She smoothly brings it to a stop as if she has ridden one for years.

She pulls off the helmet. "That was fun!"

"You were really good," says Kane.

"Yeah, you were," says Lex. "I guess it is in the blood."

Del asks, "Zavier, would you take this speeder back to Patricia and meet us at the colony?"

"Sure, but first I'm going to take it for a ride too!" He hops on and races off without the helmet.

"If that speeder decides to malfunction, he'll be sorry he forgot this," says Lex as she picks up the helmet.

"I don't think he forgot it," says Kane.

"What? Zavier making a bad decision?" Lex says sarcastically. "That seems so unlike him."

"That was very impressive, Livia," says Del. "Good job."

"Thank you," says Livia. "I enjoyed it immensely."

"Now, if you will all follow me," says Del. "I want to show you something I know you have never seen before."

24

A light rain is falling, dripping through the canopy of leaves. Del leads the group through the forest. Lex, Livia, and Kane are walking together, while Enzo trails behind. Livia holds her hand out, catching a few droplets of water, and marvels, *Water from the clouds above. Amazing.*

Del says, "It's called rain. It happens quite often. You will get used to it."

"I don't see how that is possible," says Livia, watching the drops collect on her palm.

"Yeah, well, there is a lot to get used to," says Lex.

They break through the trees onto the sandy shoreline of a large lake. The light rain is subsiding, and as the clouds part, shafts of sunlight hit the water making it shimmer.

"Strato!" yells Kane, and breaks into a run headed toward the lake.

Lex smiles and picks up her pace to catch up with him. Livia and Del walk more slowly, while Enzo hangs back sulking near the edge of the forest and sits on a fallen tree trunk. Livia looks out at the water. *This reminds me of the ocean I saw once in the simulation with Marius, though this is so calm and not as big. But this is real. I didn't think anything like this existed. I believed the lie in* The Book of Indra, *that everything outside the dome was dead and poisonous. Was anything in the book true?*

Livia and Del stop, and Livia asks, "What is this called? It's not the ocean, is it?"

"No, not the ocean," says Del. "It's a lake. It is fed by the rivers and streams that make their way down from the mountains."

"But what about the ocean?" asks Livia. "Does it still exist?"

"It does," says Del with a nod. "I saw it years ago."

"I saw the ocean in a simulation once. It was so beautiful."

"There is a real ocean on the other side of Indra. It's more stunning than a simulation. There's another rebel colony on the other side that is much closer to the sea. Perhaps we can go there one day, when all this is over."

Farther down the sandy shore, Lex walks next to Kane. "I've never seen anything like this," she says, looking out at the lake. "I can't believe there is this much water."

"It's fantastic," says Kane. "Look at how the water catches the light. I wish I could capture it somehow. I can't sound paint here. I wish I had my equipment. But maybe there is something else I can do to capture it. The light and colors in the Outlands are so inspiring."

"I'm sure you'll figure something out," says Lex with a small grin.

He crouches down and runs his hand through the water. "I don't think I would have believed it if I hadn't seen this for myself."

"Yep. Pretty strato," says Lex. She leans down and picks up a rock and throws it out into the lake. It lands with a small splash. *I can't believe this. The Council has lied about so much. Look at this world. They keep everyone imprisoned under the dome. Why?*

Del says to Livia, "It is strange to think you were living on Helix all these years. It was a beautiful island, though I felt it was a cage."

"Yes," says Livia. "I felt I was trapped on Helix as well."

Even though Lex is far down the shore of the lake, she can hear Del and Livia talking. *So Livia felt like she was trapped on Helix. I was the one who was trapped in the Orphanage for twelve years. That was a cage.*

"I'm glad you found my zinger," says Del.

Livia pulls it off her back. "I found it hidden under your sleeper when I was little. I was able to convince Governess to allow me to train with it."

She hands it to Del, who swishes it through the air with such grace that the most beautiful notes sing out from the zinger. Lex and Kane turn and watch Del, the music coming from the zinger catching their ear.

Livia gasps, "That is wonderful. It sounds more beautiful than I've ever heard. Only once did I get it to do more than a few notes."

Del smiles, whipping the zinger over her head, the music getting louder. Livia studies Del's face. *This is the first time I've seen her really smile. Her eyes are so bright and alive. Her life out here must have been so hard.*

Del stops moving the zinger and the music fades. "A zinger is an amazing weapon. It taps into your emotions. The more passionate you feel and more connected to it you are, the more intricate the melody." With her free hand, Del pulls the zinger off her back. "Roscoe brought this one out to me years ago. He knew how much I loved training with a zinger. It's not as balanced as my old one, but still serviceable."

Del whips the two zingers gracefully through the air, weaving a complex pattern. The music coming from the two zingers combined is mournful and haunting, with long keening low notes and high notes that build and cascade. Lex and Kane walk down the shore, coming closer to watch Del with the zingers. Del moves as if she is dancing, spinning and gracefully jumping. The zingers cut through the air all around her, the melody stunning and heartbreaking.

Tears come to Livia's eyes. *Del's emotions are so strong. Sadness, determination, and a fierce anger, but there is a hint of happiness. I can feel all of it coming from her. I can hear all of it in the zinger's music. She doesn't show her emotions, but they are there.* Del stops swinging the zingers. The music fades.

She hands Livia's zinger back to her and says, "Spar with me."

In a quick, fluid move, Del positions herself, striking the swordsman pose. Her legs are set in a wide stance, one foot in front of the other, her knees slightly bent. She angles her body away from Livia and extends her arm with the zinger pointing at Livia's chest.

"Prepare," says Del.

Livia rushes to set herself. *Del's form is perfect. I feel so awkward.*

I must clear my mind as Master taught me. There is only now. Only this moment. This fight.

Livia raises her zinger. Both zingers hum a low note.

"Go!" says Del, and advances, her movements fast and confident. Her zinger clashes with Livia's and sings out with a high, clear melody. Livia stumbles back, her defense clumsy, her zinger letting out a strained, discordant note. She falls to the ground and is barely able to deflect Del's blow, knocking the blade away. Del steps back, allowing Livia to regain her footing.

Lex laughs. "So, Livia, not as easy when the other person has a zinger too."

"Show some respect," Del snaps at Lex. "We can spar next, and we'll see how you do."

"No, this musical sword is her thing," says Lex. "I prefer a blaster."

"Then hold your comments," says Del.

Lex shrugs and folds her arms. *Sure, I'll just stand here quietly while you two dance around. They have this in common, the zingers. And Helix. And Veda. I'm not surprised Del likes Livia more than me. Why should I care? Let them be a happy little mother-daughter pair. I don't need either of them.*

Livia stands brushing dirt off her leg. *That was pathetic. I've never sparred with anyone outside of a simulation except for Master, and he was always holding back. She wasn't holding back. She could have hurt me. In the simulation my opponents were mostly weak and predictable. She is not!*

"Who trained you?" asks Del.

"My Master," says Livia, as she gets into position.

"Forget everything your Master taught you," says Del. "He was training you to be a technician. That is not enough. To make the zinger sing, you have to be a warrior and an artist." Del sets herself. "Prepare."

Livia takes a deep breath.

"Go!" yells Del.

Livia advances, three quick steps. Her attack is fast, her zinger swift. She is slashing across, but Del is faster. Music rings out from her zinger as she smoothly spins out of the way, circling the zinger over her head.

Livia's zinger cuts through thin air, and the sound it makes is disquieting, loud, and awful. She staggers past Del but does not fall.

"No, Livia!" Del yells while Livia turns to face her. "Use your emotions. Your anger. Your pain. Your love. Your passion."

Livia's eyes dart over to Kane. He smiles encouragingly. Her eyes fall on Lex, who smirks. Livia looks back to Del.

"Put everything you feel into the zinger and let it sing," says Del, whipping her zinger through the air. A beautiful note rings out.

"Yes, I'll try," says Livia, rolling her shoulders and getting into position. *Is all her extra waving and spinning necessary? I can see she is better than me. Is she showing off? The only time I got my zinger to make anything resembling music was when I was fighting Lex. I was so angry in that moment I could have killed her. Now I don't want to kill her, but I would like to wipe that smirk off her face. And Kane. There is so much emotion there. Love, desire—*

Del yells, "Go!"

Del advances, her zinger coming up and across, ringing out a note that is low and beautiful. Livia meets it with her blade. They clash, and Livia's zinger makes a sound that is clear and bright. Del pulls her blade back and Livia quickly swishes up. As she hits Del's blade, more notes come from her zinger. Not quite music but closer. Del pulls her zinger back, whips it over her head, and brings it down toward Livia's shoulder. Livia spins and catches Del's zinger with her own. Now both zingers are making music.

Livia smiles. "Joy! I feel joy!"

"Well, it's working," says Del as she retreats.

In a heartbeat, Del is behind Livia. Livia spins and Del's zinger flashes in the sunlight, catching her eye, distracting her for a moment. Del drops low and slashes at Livia's legs. Livia jumps and the zinger whips under her feet. Del hops up and Livia advances on her. The zingers clash again and again. The music is loud and harmonious.

Finally, Del yells, "Hold!"

Livia stops midswing and lets her zinger drop to her side, her breath coming hard and ragged. The music of the zingers is already fading.

Kane runs to Livia. "That was strato!"

"That was exhilarating!" says Livia.

"Yes," says Del, her breath less strained than Livia's. "We should do this again. I've missed having a worthy opponent."

Lex walks over slowly. "That was pretty impressive. I might want to learn to use one of those things one day."

"Me too," says Kane. "But I would want some really thick body armor."

"You're so good," says Livia. "How long did you train with it?"

"Not long, actually," confesses Del. "Your father gave me that zinger when we first cohabited on Helix. My parents would never have let me have a zinger. It was not something a Proper Indrithian Lady would do. I started training and had a natural way with it. I could make it sing almost from the start. I think it was somehow connected to my years of playing the air harp."

Livia nods. "Everyone said you were quite good on your air harp. We saw you playing it in the Archive memories. You filled the room with color and music. It was beautiful."

"My parents insisted I play the harp. It was an appropriate pastime for a Proper Indrithian Lady. I did come to love the harp, but I found the physicality of the zinger training very satisfying."

"I know what you mean. I loved my zinger training. It made me feel strong and less vulnerable."

"And what happened to Veda?" asks Del.

Livia smiles. "Veda was my greatest joy. I rode her every day."

"When did she die?"

Livia stammers, "Oh, no, I'm sorry to confuse you. She is very much alive, but I fear I will never see her again. I had such a strong connection with her."

"I did too. Armand made it possible for Veda to go into the Archives with me. We spent many hours riding through simulations."

"I was able to bring her into the Archives as well," says Livia. "I felt like we could communicate."

Del gently touches Livia's cheek. "I felt that with her as well."

25

The group walks back to the colony. The setting sun is turning the clouds shades of purple and gray. The forest is getting dark quickly. Del is far ahead. Lex, Livia, and Kane walk together while Enzo trails behind.

Lex says, "Del is so cold and distant."

"We had a nice moment," says Livia.

"Yeah, I saw." Lex bats a low tree branch away. "Maybe 'cause you have a few things in common. I could hear you talking about Helix, your zinger, and Veda."

Kane interrupts, "No wonder you were so quiet. You were listening to them. We were really far away."

Lex grins at Kane. "Not too far for me." She turns back to Livia. "You and Del have some common ground. You grew up on her island. You knew things about her."

"I knew a little about her," Livia confesses. "Though truly it was not much. I couldn't get anyone to talk about her."

"Well, you know more than me. I know nothing about her, and we have nothing in common."

"That is not true," says Livia. "Out here, she has had to be tough, similar to you in the Orphanage and at the Academy. I'm just thinking about everything that she has been through. She raised Jules and Enzo out here in the wilderness, mostly by herself. She must have needed to be so tough and determined. I think she still is. She is the leader of these people. Respected. I don't think she is distant or cold on purpose. I think it is just her way."

"I'm sure it was hard," concedes Lex. "I still can't shake the feeling of being the twin who got tossed away. I grew up in fear and desperation, while you were pampered and protected."

"You have every right to be angry."

"I'm glad I have your approval to be angry," snaps Lex. She stops walking and turns to face Livia. "You will never know what it was like to belong to no one. I had no past. No one ever claimed me. I am an orphan, and part of me always will be!"

"But you're not an orphan anymore," Livia says with softness in her voice. "You have me, and Del. You have a family now."

"I know." Lex feels tears starting to come. *I will not cry. I am not sad. I am angry!* "I have a sister and a mother. Whatever that means. That doesn't change the fact that I was abandoned!"

"That's true, and it was unfair." Livia moves toward Lex, reaching her hand out to her shoulder.

"Don't." Lex blocks Livia's hand before it touches her. *If Livia tries to hug me right now, I might lose it.* "I can't just get over being an orphan because a few days ago you dropped into my life. Just as much as you will always be the Airess, I will always be a core-low orphan."

"Don't say that, Lex." Livia pushes past Lex's arm and embraces her.

"You have always been more than that," says Kane, putting a hand on her back.

Lex gives in to the hug and starts to cry. Her face buried in Livia's shoulder, Lex yells, "Why was I the one Del took from Helix?" She takes a breath, pushing the tears back. "You got to stay, live an easy life, while I had to fight for every scrap in the Orphanage."

"I'm sorry. I truly am. My life on Helix was a paradise compared to what you went through." Livia pulls slightly away from Lex. "But I don't think it's fair to blame Del. From what we saw in the Archive memories, it was our father who chose which one of us would stay and which would go. If we help Del and rescue Armand, we may get an answer to that question."

"I would like to know why he chose the way he did," says Lex, breaking away from Livia. "And we could ask him about the green marks in our eyes."

"I have always wondered about the mark in my eye. It must mean something that we both have one."

Enzo catches up to Lex, Livia, and Kane. Lex quickly turns her back to him and wipes the tears from her face.

Enzo eyes the blasters hanging from Lex and Kane's belts. "Why did you bring your blasters?"

Lex shrugs. "When Del told Livia to bring her zinger, I thought she meant there might be danger and we should all be armed."

"It's a good-looking weapon," says Enzo. "We only get old stuff. Jules is good at fixing things up so they work really well, but they never look good."

Lex pulls the blaster off her belt and hands it to Enzo. He inspects it and says, "This is really nice."

He sights the weapon on a small animal running past and shoots. He is a good shot and kills the animal. Livia instantly staggers and puts her hands to her head, letting out a strangled gasp. "Why did you do that?" she yells. "You didn't have to kill it." She grabs Kane's arm to steady herself.

"Are you all right?" asks Kane.

Livia closes her eyes. *It's dead. I could feel it die. The shock of pain. The end of its life. That was horrible.* "I don't know. I think so."

Del rushes back to Livia, Lex, Kane, and Enzo. She barks at Enzo, "Killing is not done for practice or fun. It's for survival." She snatches the weapon from Enzo and hands it back to Lex. "Go collect it. You will eat it tonight, so its death will serve a purpose."

Enzo drops his head. "Yes, Mother. Sorry." He runs off to retrieve his kill.

Calmly, Del puts her hand on Livia's back. "I can feel it too. You have to learn to block it out. You can't let yourself feel every living thing, or you will feel them die as well. You have to shut it out."

"Is that what you do?" Livia asks, opening her eyes and taking a deep breath. "Shut it out? Block everything?"

"Yes, I do," says Del, taking her hand away. "You have to. You can't block everything, but feeling too much can be crippling."

"I can see that," says Livia. *So she blocks most of her emotions. That is why she is so hard. She is protecting herself.*

Del asks, "Can you walk? It will be full dark soon."

Holding on to Kane, Livia stands a bit unsteadily. "Yes, let's go."

26

That night, Lex and Livia are alone in the cave. Lex is on her cot looking at the ceiling. *I can't believe Livia and Kane aren't together. I didn't think they could be separated. Wonder where he is?*

Livia comes over to sit at the foot of Lex's cot and asks, "Have you made a decision? Are you coming with us tomorrow?"

Lex sits up and looks at Livia. "So I guess that means you've already made your decision."

"I don't think there is much of a decision to be made," Livia argues. "We have to do what's right. It doesn't matter if there is a prophecy or not, people are going to die."

Lex sighs. "I didn't know having a sister would be this much work."

Livia glares at her. "Are you coming or not?"

"Yes. I'm coming," Lex says, resigned.

Livia smiles and wraps Lex in a hug. Lex instantly grimaces, "All right. All right. Let go!"

Reluctantly, Livia lets go and Lex scoots away from her on the cot. "I'm glad," says Livia. "We will do what we can."

Kane enters the cave full of energy, carrying a bundle of cloth and a cylinder. "Quinn introduced me to a whole group of artists."

"That sounds wonderful," says Livia as she goes to him.

Kane takes Livia's hand and leads her to the table and sits. He opens the bundle to reveal three crudely made paintbrushes and several small jars, each containing a different-colored liquid. "They make paint! And they gave me a canvas." He unrolls the cylinder. It is a square of finely woven cloth. "Their paintings are stunning, like the Outlands. I'll be able to paint here. Not sound painting, but this has exciting possibilities. I'm sure I could make sculptures too."

Livia hugs him. "I'm so happy for you."

"And I think I can finally take this off," says Kane, stepping back and removing his nose clip.

Livia is panicked. "Are you sure?"

"Yeah." Kane takes a deep breath. "I dropped it down to one a few hours ago." He extends his arms. "Look, not dying!"

Livia is too worried to be amused. "Are you dizzy or light-headed?"

Kane breathes in and out a few times. "No. I'm fine."

Livia hugs him. "Oh, good."

Lex pointedly stares at the ceiling. *These two. I can barely stomach all this hugging.* She looks at Zavier's empty cot. *Where is he? Zavier said he wasn't with anyone last night, but that seems unlikely. He could be with some Outlander girl right now. I shouldn't care, so why do I?* Lex looks at Livia and Kane still hugging. *I can't stay in here with them. I'm sure Livia and Kane want to be alone, and I could stand to be away from them.*

Lex clears her throat and says, "I'm going to see if I can find Zavier."

"Good luck," says Livia as Lex walks out.

After a moment, Livia says, "We were making her uncomfortable."

"You could sense that?" asks Kane.

"Yes, very clearly."

"I feel bad that she felt she had to leave, but I'm glad we are alone. You know, we have never really been alone."

"Really?" says Livia with a smile. "What about the night in the Outpost?"

"Well, yeah, but you just had your chip pulled out of your brain and I was barely holding it together, pumped up on every booster they had. It doesn't really count. Then all the time in the tunnel, and even here in the cave, there's always been someone with us."

Livia teases, “Do I need a chaperone?”

Kane pulls Livia into a tight embrace. “You might. I’ve wanted to be alone with you for a long time.”

Kane kisses Livia. There is passion and heat in their kiss. Livia catches herself thinking, *This is the man I want. He is perfect. Stop thinking! Just be here with him.*

Kane ends the kiss and says, “I love you, Livia.”

“I love you too.”

“We should try to sleep,” suggests Kane, holding her hand. He leads her over to her cot. They lie down together, Kane wrapping his arms around her in a way that has already become familiar. He snuggles closer to her and asks, “Are you cold? Should I get another blanket?”

She calmly says, “No. I don’t think I will ever be cold again.” She puts her hand on his cheek. “This is where I am supposed to be. With you by my side.”

Kane kisses her. “Always.”

27

Lex follows a path through the dark, chilly forest. The canopy of trees is blocking most of the light from the moon, and though it is almost pitch-black, Lex can see quite clearly. *This is stupid. Why am I looking for Zavier? I don't even want to see him. He's been gone since we saw him at the preparations encampment. It's been a relief. No badgering. No fighting. I don't really want to find him, I just couldn't stand feeling like I was in Livia and Kane's way. I hope they enjoy the privacy.*

She passes a few scattered buildings. The path goes deeper into the woods. Lex sees all the little creatures scurrying around in the night. *There is so much life out here.* Her ears are alert, primarily for her own protection. Then she hears him. *That is Zavier's breathing. He is close.* Lex focuses on the sound of Zavier's breathing and finds him in a clearing leaning against a rock, looking up at the sky. Lex notices Zavier is not wearing a breathing device.

Lex says as she steps into the clearing, "This is a nice spot."

Zavier doesn't look at Lex. "You missed me?"

Lex sits down next to him. "Just making sure you weren't dead. So you're all done with the additive?"

"Yep. Took it off earlier today. I was at a pretty low setting when we came out of the tunnel, just a few clicks left." He takes a deep breath. "It's nice to breathe clean air."

"It is," Lex agrees. "So, we head out in the morning."

"Is that your way of saying you're on board?"

"Livia wouldn't take no for an answer."

"Don't blame her. But I'm not surprised. I thought you would cave. You have too much integrity to let an injustice like this stand and do nothing."

They look up at the stars. Lex studies the sky. *The moon is amazing. Like a beamer with a full charge. And so many stars.*

They sit quietly for a long time. Then Zavier says, "Samantha would have loved it out here. I always told her that I would get her out of Rock Bottom. If I had, she would not have been killed that day. It is hard to see something so beautiful and not think of her."

"She was the kindest person I'd ever met. I'm sorry she's gone."

"You were lucky she was there for you in the Orphanage. She took care of you more than you know."

"If it wasn't for her, I don't think I would have made it. She saved my life."

"Probably. The rebels had other spies in the Orphanage, but in those early years, it was Samantha who was watching over you, protecting you. She made sure you didn't starve or bottom out. But Samantha couldn't stand by while other kids were in danger. She did little things, like switching the tags for the infants so the rejects could stay longer. When the caretakers at the Orphanage discovered what Samantha had been doing, the rebels had to get her out fast, before they could punish her."

"I was devastated when I found her sleeper was empty. I thought she had bottomed out and been taken by mutants. I believed she was dead."

"Well, she is now," Zavier says with venom in his voice.

Lex is stung and takes a deep breath. *He is hurt. He's lashing out, trying to hurt me. He wants me to fight. I won't. Not about Samantha.* After a pause, she says, "I wish I could have saved her."

"I wish I had saved her. So like her to get killed helping someone," Zavier says. They sit for a few minutes in silence, then he says, "It was hard on her when we had to pull her out of the Orphanage. She talked about you a lot. She loved you."

Lex can feel tears coming to her eyes but fights them back. "I loved her too."

Zavier pulls the blanket from behind his head and says, "You can sleep out here with me if you want. It's very peaceful."

"Just sleep," says Lex sternly.

"Yes, ma'am. Just sleep." They lie back-to-back. Zavier covers them both with the blanket.

Lex can feel Zavier's warm back against hers. *We are so alike. Both headstrong, stubborn, impulsive. Sometimes I am drawn to him, other times I want to kill him.*

Before long they are asleep under the stars.

28

Livia wakes and realizes she is alone in her cot. *Where is Kane?* She sits [illegible] and sees him sitting at the table painting. She lets out a [illegible]nd calming. *I'm so relieved. Why was I so panicked? Where* [illegible] *can count on him. He said he will be with me always, and I* [illegible]*n trust that.*

[illegible]p, walks to the table, and stands behind Kane. With her [illegible]k, she looks over his shoulder at the painting he is work- [illegible]painted the view of the lake they visited the day before, with orange and red clouds.

"It's breathtaking," says Livia.

Kane stops working, stands up, and hugs her. "I'm so happy. With you, with this place."

Livia smiles. "Yes, me too."

"I know this mission will be dangerous, but we have to do it. Just promise me we'll both make it through and come back here."

"I promise," she says and kisses him lightly. "We'll come back here and make a life together."

"I almost died before you and Lex saved me from High Security Detainment. Then again when my breathing device was ripped off."

"Yes, I'm quite tired of you almost dying. Let's have no more of that."

"Before you, I didn't have anything to fight for. Now, I do. I can see what I want my future to be and it's here with you."

Livia kisses Kane, his arms wrapped around her. Del pulls back the cloth door and enters the cave. Livia and Kane stop abruptly and, embarrassed, move apart a little. Del seems unconcerned that Livia and Kane were in the middle of an intimate moment.

Her manner is curt. "Where are Lex and Zavier?"

"I'm not sure, but I can find them," offers Livia.

"Yes, you'll need to," says Del. "It's time to leave. Change into your PCF uniforms. Quinn will be back to collect you in a few minutes."

Del turns and walks out of the cave as Livia says, "Yes, I'll find them."

"She is tough," says Kane.

"Yes, she is. I thought she had softened a bit toward me at the lake, but that must have passed. It's like she has emotional armor."

"You will break through. I know it."

"I better go find my sister and Zavier."

Kane kisses Livia on the forehead. "Good luck."

Livia smiles. "Thanks." She turns and briskly walks out of the cave.

Livia walks through the forest feeling how alive it is. *There are so many animals. I can even feel the plants, the life in them. I can feel people far and scattered.* Livia tries to focus on Lex. *Where are you, Lex? Where did you go?* Then like a dim light seen from far away, Livia senses the soft and distant shape of Lex in her mind. Livia can almost see Lex, not just feel her. *There she is. She must be half a mile away, yet I know exactly where she is. It's like there is a beamer globe shining right above her. I'm so connected to her it's like she is part of me. I feel I could find her anywhere.* Livia follows her sense through the forest directly to Lex. She easily finds her and Zavier asleep in a clearing just outside the colony center. They are sleeping back-to-back covered by a single blanket. *They look sweet. Almost like they don't hate each other.*

Livia wakes Lex with a loud "good morning."

Lex and Zavier stir awake. Livia continues, "Hope I'm not interrupting. You two have fun sleeping together?"

"We are not together!" snaps Lex.

Zavier smiles. "Just sleeping, as ordered."

"Well, it's time to break into Indra. Del's waiting. So let's go."

When Lex, Livia, and Zavier return to the cave, they find Quinn and Kane sitting at the table talking. Kane has changed into his PCF uniform and has shaved.

Quinn reacts quickly when they enter, standing and saying, "Oh, good, you're here. Get changed. Zavier, you'll have to shave. You look too scruffy for a PCF officer."

"Definitely not regulation," says Lex.

"Nothing about me is regulation," says Zavier.

"Then I'll take you to meet Del in the shop," says Quinn.

"The shop?" asks Livia.

Quinn says, "It's where Jules works on the speeders, comms, and other projects. Get changed and I'll take you."

29

Lex, Livia, Kane, and Zavier, all in PCF uniforms, follow Quinn through the woods. Both Kane and Zavier are freshly shaved. Lex quickly glances at Zavier's face as they walk behind Livia and Kane. *He looks different without any scruff on his face. Less like a rebel. Though I think I liked the beard better.*

They pass by Medical to another low, wood building some distance beyond it. The group enters the shop, a clean and organized space. There are several workbenches covered with electronic components. On the floor to one side, there are four speeders, each in different stages of being rebuilt. The walls are lined with shelves stacked neatly with equipment and speeder parts. Del and Enzo are standing by one of the tables, and next to them is a tall, rugged man with thinning hair and a bright-eyed teenage girl with short, curly, blond hair.

"Everyone meet Jacob and his daughter Iris," says Del. "They have prepped the speeders and our comm units."

Jacob says, "The speeders are around the back of the shop." He turns to his daughter. "Iris, give them their comms and packs."

Iris grabs the handheld holocomms off the table. "Wear these on your belt," she says as she passes them out. "They have a full charge." She gives them each a small pack. "Also, I packed rations, water, and beamers in your gear." They all put their packs on.

"Thank you, Iris," says Livia.

Lex adds a quick, "Yeah, thanks."

"We'll ride speeders for about six hours over the mountain ridge through the flatlands and most of the debris field," says Del. "We'll hide the speeders and conceal ourselves in an empty, unmanned refuse hauler to get into Indra. The haulers go in and out of one of the few gates in the dome. Once we are inside the dome, we'll be in a PCF compound. Roscoe's team will create a distraction, allowing us to slip out."

"Will we be in contact with Roscoe?" asks Zavier.

"We'll let him know when we are in position and ready to leave the compound," says Del.

"Too bad Jules isn't going with you," says Iris, giving Livia an accusing look.

"He should be going with us," says Enzo, glaring at Livia. "His skills would have come in handy, I'm sure."

"I wish he was able to come with us," says Livia, her tone sincere.

"That's enough," says Del. "It was the plan to have Jules come, but that is not possible. Dwelling on mistakes is a waste of time. During the mission, Jacob and Iris will be able to assist us over the comms as needed."

"Yes," says Jacob. "Iris and I will be on standby. Are all your weapons charged?"

Lex, Kane, and Zavier, who all have blasters on their belts, say yes almost simultaneously.

Jacob nods. "Iris packed extra power cells in your gear."

Del says to Livia, "You'll have to leave your zinger and carry a blaster. No PCF officer would have a zinger."

"She's right," says Lex.

"I feel so safe with it," says Livia.

Lex smiles. "Don't underestimate a good blaster."

Livia reluctantly pulls her zinger off her back and hands it to Del, who puts it on one of the shelves.

Del says to Jacob, "Take care of it for her."

Jacob nods. "Of course." He hands Livia a blaster. "It may not look like much, but it's been given the once-over by Jules. Probably works better than when it was new."

"Thank you," says Livia.

"Now, last," says Jacob. He pulls a box from the table. "You won't need these air filters until you are actually going into Indra."

"Air filters?" asks Lex.

"Yes," says Jacob, handing the box to Del. "You wear them when you go back into the city to filter out the additive. You just have to remember to breathe through your nose."

Kane blows out a relieved breath. "Thank goodness. I thought I was going to have to go through the whole getting-off-the-additive process again."

"With these, that won't be necessary," says Jacob. "They should work well. They were made by a scientist who lives inside Indra. He got off the additive years ago and uses them himself. They took years to develop. Ingenious."

"Let's go," says Del.

Jacob leads the group through the back exit of the shop. There are six speeders parked against the back wall of the shop, and beyond them are what appear to be several more speeders covered by tarps.

"Are those all functioning speeders too?" Lex asks, indicating the long row of speeders under the tarps.

"Yes," answers Iris. "Jules, my father, and I have restored more than twenty speeders, not including the four in the shop we are currently working on. Patricia has four more down in the encampment."

Zavier says with admiration, "Impressive."

"Thank you," says Jacob, with a nod.

"We should go," says Del as she mounts the closest speeder and puts on her helmet.

"Good luck," says Jacob.

"Thank you," says Livia as the rest of the group gets on speeders and puts on their helmets.

Del says over the helmet speaker, "Can everyone hear me?" A chorus of confirmations comes back.

"We'll ride single file," says Del. "I'm in the lead. Enzo at the tail. Let's go." She starts her speeder and heads into the woods. Lex, Livia, Kane, and Zavier follow her out, with Enzo at the end of the group.

30

On their speeders, the group whips through the trees and undergrowth. There is not much of a path, but Del knows where she is going.

Del says over the helmet speaker, "Everyone stay alert. This terrain is rough."

For several hours they wind their way through the forest, passing the tree line and cresting the ridge of the mountain. Looking down from the mountain they can see Indra in the distance, the dome an off-white, opaque semicircle reaching high into the sky. The flat land between the bottom of the mountain and the edge of the dome has four distinct areas. They can see the barren area of the flatlands that starts at the base of the mountains and stretches until it meets a bright band that looks almost white with light, beyond that is an area that looks uneven and discolored, and finally, closest to the dome, a ring that glows a dark yellow.

"Take a good look," says Del. "That's what we have to ride through."

"What are we looking at?" asks Livia.

As they ride down the mountain, Enzo explains, "The first area is the flatlands. Almost nothing grows there. It will take about an hour to ride through. Then the bright ring, those are the solar panels that supply power to Indra. We stole panels from that field and built our own solar plant. It is our main source of electricity for the colony. That was a Jules project. Then there are debris fields, the dumping ground outside Indra. Everything they don't need anymore gets loaded onto a refuse hauler and taken out of the city. The area closest to the dome is the irradiated zone. It is deadly."

Lex asks, "How do we get through, then?"

"Lucky for us, the unmanned refuse haulers go underground and pass below the irradiated perimeter," answers Del. "The PCF patrols use the same underground access to get out of the dome."

When they reach the base of the mountain, they ride out into the flatlands, dust kicking up behind their speeders. In the distance, the horizon is a line of bright light.

As they get close to the light, Del's voice comes in through the helmet. "We're entering the solar collection area. Switch your visor shields to 80 percent."

It takes almost an hour to ride through the huge sea of glaring solar panels. Once through the solar facility, they enter an endless wasteland of scraps and junk, passing rusted transporters, speeders, and patrollers. They weave around huge piles of plexi and giant sheets of metal discards from the constant maintenance and rebuilding of Indra. They pass mountains of furniture from the fine estates of the Islands, abandoned after they have served their purpose or fallen out of the ever-changing fashion, some of it unrecognizable as it disintegrates.

Livia looks at the piles of debris all around her. *I never thought about where the trash from Indra was going. Some was being pushed into Rock Bottom, but look at all of this. Such waste.*

Del says over the helmet speaker, "That's far enough on the speeders. We are on foot from here."

They pull to a stop and remove their helmets.

"So this is where all the old stuff goes," says Zavier. "It was always hard to get our hands on any tech. Most of it we had to steal. I'm sure they didn't want to dump anything in Rock Bottom that would be useful."

"Livia, you and I need to keep our senses open for any people around," says Del. "This trash dump is totally automated, so there should only be the unmanned refuse haulers. If you sense any people, they could be a PCF patrol. I wouldn't expect anyone out here, but we can't be too careful."

"All right," says Livia. "I only feel our group, but I will let you know if I sense anyone else."

"Good," says Del. "Now, let's get these speeders concealed."

They move the speeders into the mountains of trash. Once the speeders are hidden, Livia looks back and comments, "Wow. Those really blend in well."

Enzo says snidely, "This is where we got them in the first place."

They head off on foot through the dumping ground.

"We're looking for one of the unmanned refuse haulers that has just dumped its load," explains Del. "We will have a short window to get inside when the back hatch door is open. We will ride it back to the refilling station inside Indra."

As they walk, Livia is next to Enzo. *He is so angry. I can sense that he feels incomplete without his brother.*

"I'm truly sorry about Jules," says Livia. "He should be here with us."

"He would be if it wasn't for you."

"Are you serious?" Lex yells at Enzo. "Aren't we done with this? Your group attacked us. We didn't know who Jules was. What were we supposed to do? She is trying to be nice. What is wrong with you? She's said she's sorry more than once. This is getting old."

Enzo continues to attack Livia, "Jules could lose his leg because of you. I won't forget that."

"You're lucky it was Livia's zinger and not my blaster, or he would be dead," says Lex.

Livia steps in between Lex and Enzo. "Stop. We are all family. We have to work together, whether we like it or not."

Enzo barks, "I don't like it!"

Lex snaps back, "Neither do I!"

Del says from the front of the group. "This bickering is childish. It will get you nowhere. You all need to move forward. You're done arguing about how and why and by whom Jules was injured. This subject is closed. I don't want to hear about this again. That's an order."

"I don't take orders from you!" yells Lex.

Del's tone is calm. "I'm going to clarify something for you, Lex. When you agreed to come on this mission, you implicitly agreed to take orders from me. You know from your training there can be only one leader, and right now it's me. Now, everyone look for a hauler."

Lex walks silently. *She is so overbearing. When this mission is done, I'm done with her. If we weren't rescuing our father, I would leave right now. After this, she can rot in Core Low.*

Enzo quickly scales an unstable stack of old transporters that shifts and moves as he climbs, but he doesn't slow down.

"That looks like a bad idea," comments Kane.

Zavier adds, "That kid's got more balls than brains."

Standing on top of the unsteady junk heap, Enzo looks for a hauler. Livia walks up next to Lex and puts her hand on Lex's shoulder. It has an instant calming effect on Lex.

Livia whispers, "Take a deep breath."

Lex's voice is low. "She is infuriating."

Livia gives Lex's shoulder a reassuring squeeze.

Enzo yells, "There's one!" With a few well-placed steps, he hops down the shifting pile of junk and starts to run. The group follows him as he makes several twists and turns through the maze of garbage. They round a corner and see a hauler, a huge rectangular box, moving on revolving treads.

As they walk toward it, Enzo explains, "The front end of the hauler lifts up off the treads, tipping it backward, the entire back hatch opens, and the trash dumps out. Once everything is out, it'll sit for a minute while the front comes back down to level. Then the back hatch starts to close and it will start to move again. Jules and I have watched them a thousand times. It's surprisingly fast."

They stop walking and watch as the hauler stops and begins to go through its automated dumping process. The front tips up, the back opens, and a wall of junk starts to fall out.

"Go!" orders Del.

They break into a run following Del, who is quickly at the back of the hauler. She skillfully runs up the pile of junk the hauler just dumped and jumps in with Enzo and Zavier right behind her. Lex, Livia, and Kane are behind them, Lex and Kane flanking Livia, who is the slowest runner.

"Come on, Livia!" yells Lex.

When they reach the hauler, the front has tipped back down and the hatch is starting to close. Kane runs up the pile of junk holding Livia's hand, pulling her along, Lex pushing her from behind. When he reaches the hatch, Kane lets go of Livia's hand and jumps in. Once inside, he turns and reaches his arms out to Livia.

"Jump!" yells Kane.

Livia launches into the air and lands in Kane's arms. He quickly pulls her back and out of the way so Lex can jump in. The hatch is halfway down and the hauler starts to move forward. Lex leaps off the pile of junk and dives headfirst into the rapidly closing hatch, her legs hanging off the back. Zavier and Enzo each grab one of her arms and pull her in. Lex tucks her legs in just as the hatch closes.

31

As the hatch closes, the last bit of light coming in from outside disappears and the hauler becomes completely dark.

Del says, "You all have beamers in your packs."

Everyone starts rummaging through their packs trying to find the beamers by feel. Lex's eyes have adjusted and she can see. She is the first to pull out her beamer and switch it on. She sets it so the globe of light floats up at the ceiling so everyone can see.

"That was close," says Zavier to Lex while he pulls out his beamer. "You all right?"

"Yeah, thanks."

"You're welcome," says Zavier, the light of his beamer floating up to the ceiling. "So just remember, you needed my help."

"It wasn't just you. Enzo helped pull me in too."

"Right. So Enzo and I saved you."

"You helped me, and I'm sure you won't let me forget it," says Lex.

"Not a chance," says Zavier with a grin.

Lex scowls and turns to Enzo. "So we just ride this into Indra? How do we get out?"

Enzo finds his beamer, switches it on, adjusts the light so the globe floats just above the beamer, and mounts it on his shoulder. "I need to reroute this thing so when we get to the refuse processing plant it goes to the maintenance area instead of the refill dock." Enzo moves to the front of the hauler and uses a tool from his pack to open the cover on the electronic control panel.

"Is that difficult?" asks Livia.

"Well, Jules is really the expert at this kind of thing," says Enzo. "If he were here, it would be no sweat." He pushes a few buttons and looks at the display. "He told me what to do, but I think he skipped a step."

Lex asks, "Why do you say that?"

"Because I can't get into the routing menu," says Enzo.

Del looks at her wrist unit and says, "You have a little bit of time. If you can't get it, we can call Jacob and Iris for help."

Enzo continues to push buttons, occasionally making an exasperated noise. Finally he says, "This is no good. I'm just going in circles." He pulls his holocomm off his belt and switches it on. "Jacob? Iris? This is Enzo. You there?"

A projection of Jules flickers on above the comm. "Yeah, Enzo. I got you."

"Jules?" says Enzo, astonished. "What are you doing? Where are you?"

"I'm in the shop."

Confused, Enzo asks, "What do you mean? In the shop? How?"

"I had Iris and Jacob set up a cot for me over here. We are working on something to support my leg so I can stand up. Now, what's wrong?"

Enzo focuses on the control screen. "I'm in some kind of loop. I can't get to the menu where I route this thing to the maintenance holding area."

"How much time do you have?"

"Not much," says Enzo.

Livia quietly asks Del, "What will happen if they don't figure this out?"

"We'll end up at the refill station, the top will open, and a ton of junk and garbage will pour in. If we are still in here, it will be almost impossible to get out and not be crushed."

"It feels like we just started going downhill," says Lex.

Del says, "Enzo, we've entered the underground tunnel that travels under the irradiated zone. Are you and Jules going to be able to reroute us?"

"I don't know!" yells Enzo. "Nothing is working."

Lex moves up to the front of the hauler next to Enzo and grabs his comm. Enzo protests, "Hey! What are you doing?"

Lex ignores Enzo and says into the comm, "Jules, do these things have sensors? Can we break something so it will automatically go in for repair?"

"Yeah," Jules nods. "That could work. Do it! Good luck!"

"Thanks," says Lex. She hits a button and Jules's image flickers out. She tosses the comm back to Enzo and moves to the rear of the hauler.

"New plan," says Lex. "Let's break this thing."

Lex starts kicking the back hatch. Everyone joins in. After several random kicks, Lex says, "Wait." Everyone stops and looks at Lex. "Let's try to hit the hatch all at the same time. On my mark. Three, two, one. Go!"

They all hit the door at the same time, there is a terrible echoing crash, and the door shakes but does not but break.

"Again," says Lex.

Lex counts down and they kick the door with the same loud but ineffective result. Kane looks up at the top of the door, studying the mechanism that opens and closes the hatch.

"Maybe we can break that," says Kane, pointing up at the hatch mechanism.

Zavier pulls out his blaster and shoots it. The sound is almost deafening in the confined space.

"Whoa!" yells Lex. "A little warning next time."

Kane moves over to the door. Testing to see if it is still firmly closed, he gives it a kick. It pushes open easily. "Well, it's broken."

Enzo rushes back to look at the display, scrutinizing the red lights blinking on it. He pushes a few buttons. "Perfect. It is registering a lift arm malfunction. It is rerouting to maintenance."

Del orders, "Hold the hatch shut. We don't want anyone to see us in here. It's time to put in the air filters." Del pulls the case out of her pack and hands out the air filters, saying, "They fit snugly inside the nose. As Jacob said, just remember to breathe through your nose."

The group gets their air filters in place. Kane and Zavier take turns holding the hatch closed while the other puts in his air filters. The hauler continues to rumble forward and then starts to tilt up. At first the incline is slight, and only Lex notices.

"We're starting to move up," says Lex.

After a moment, the incline unexpectedly becomes extremely steep, causing everyone to slide back toward the rear of the hauler and crash into each other. Del slams into Zavier. He loses his grip on the hatch and it starts to swing open. Kane scrambles to grab the hatch, trying to pull it closed, but his weight is not enough to hold it down and he goes flying up as the hatch swings open. He is pulled out of the hauler and hangs out in midair holding on to the open hatch. Enzo quickly grabs the control panel to keep from falling and Lex clutches his waist. But she cannot catch Livia in time, who starts to slide to the rear of the hauler.

Del pulls herself off Zavier. He starts to sit up when he sees Livia sliding down the hauler feet first, headed right for the opening. He drops down to the floor and sticks his legs out to block her path.

Zavier yells, "Grab my leg!"

Livia paws at Zavier's legs as she slips past but cannot get a grip. Her legs fly through the open hatch just as she catches his foot, stopping herself halfway out of the opening, her legs dangling outside the hauler.

"I got you, Airess." Zavier leans forward, grabs her under her arms, pulls her back in, and places her behind him next to Del.

Livia screams, "Help Kane!"

Zavier gets to his feet, grabs Kane by the boot, and pulls him back inside, the hatch swinging down with him.

Kane, holding the door closed, looks at Zavier with relief and gratitude. "Thank you."

Zavier nods. "Sure. Saving you is becoming a habit."

"I hope to return the favor one day," says Kane.

"Yeah, we'll see," says Zavier.

Suddenly, the hauler levels off and everyone is thrown forward. Kane loses his hold on the hatch as he is jolted forward.

Enzo quickly gets to his feet, scrambles back, and manages to pull the hatch closed. The hauler resumes a steady pace, keeping level, and the group is able to right themselves. Lex untangles herself from Del and Kane. Livia pulls herself off Zavier and moves over to Kane.

"I think that's the worst of it," says Enzo. "We have leveled off, so we must have come out of the underground tunnel. We must be getting close to the refuse processing plant."

Kane says to Livia, "Are you okay? I looked away for a second and then I saw you sliding toward the open hatch."

"Me? You were hanging out in midair," says Livia.

Enzo snaps, "You're both fine now. It's over."

Del says, "Enzo, there's no need to be rude." She addresses the group. "I'm glad everyone is all right. You all handled yourselves well. I have no doubt we will face many more unexpected challenges as we continue. It is best to stay calm, keep a clear head, and act quickly. Most important, look out for each other. Zavier, thank you for your quick action. Good work."

Zavier says with a shrug, "Thanks."

Lex glares at Zavier. *I'm glad he was able to jump in and help Livia and Kane, but an ego boost from Del is the last thing Zavier needs. He already thinks so highly of himself, getting praise from her will only make it worse.*

The hauler makes a sharp turn, rolls along for a little while, then makes another turn. After a few minutes the hauler stops moving. Del raises her hands in a gesture that means *wait*. They all sit quietly, listening for activity outside the hauler.

After a few minutes, Del says to Enzo, "Slowly open the hatch."

Enzo lifts open the hatch and Del says, "Lex, you and Kane go take a look around. This maintenance area is off to the side of the processing plant. Check the immediate area for activity."

Lex jumps down, landing on the ground with almost no noise. Kane follows her. Enzo pulls the hatch closed behind them.

Lex looks around. They are in a building with a high ceiling, light coming in from windows set far up in the walls. The hauler is parked in a row of several haulers. There is no movement. She turns and says to Kane in a whisper, "Stay low." They run forward.

Livia asks Del, "Where exactly are we?"

Del pulls a battered holoscreen out of her pack and pushes a button on the side to bring it to life. She taps a few holokeys and a map of the compound pops up above the screen.

"We should be here," she indicates on the map projection. "This refuse processing facility is at the back of the PCF compound. The gate we came through is one of the few ways out of Indra."

Livia, Zavier, and Enzo look closely at the map. Zavier asks, "Is this whole thing the compound?" He points at a far corner of the map. "And we're way back here?"

"Correct," confirms Del. "And we need to get here," she says, pointing to a spot on the opposite side of the map.

"That's a lot of ground to cover," says Zavier.

Livia asks, "How are we getting across the compound?"

"Carefully," says Del.

Lex and Kane stop at the end of the row of haulers. From there they can see out of the building through the large open door. Several haulers crisscross the vast space moving back and forth, pulling up to one of the many refill stations, where garbage is dumped in, and then pulling away and heading into a tunnel. Lex scans the busy area for details. *There's a lot of activity but no people. Not close anyway.*

In a low voice, Lex says, "I've seen enough. Let's go back."

Kane nods. They run back down the row of haulers to rejoin the group.

Lex knocks on the hauler's back hatch, Zavier opens it, and she and Kane get inside. Lex reports, "Saw several unmanned haulers getting filled up and headed out, but no people. I believe we are secure for now. What's next?"

"We'll make our way across the compound to the base entrance gate, here." Del indicates it on the map. "We find somewhere to hide and wait for Roscoe and his team to cause a distraction."

"What kind of distraction?" asks Kane.

Zavier says with a smile, "I'm guessing we'll know it when we see it. Or hear it."

"It'll be obvious," says Del. "We'll leave the compound in the confusion."

"How do we get to the gate?" asks Lex.

"We walk," says Del. "We have no other option. We should be able to take a route that will allow us to stay away from most of the activity on the compound and as far from people as possible. The trick will be to look enough like PCF from a distance that no one looks too closely."

"Right," says Lex. "Now, where are we and where do we need to be?" Del shows her on the map. Lex studies the projection for a moment, then says, "All right. I got it. I know how to get there."

"Then you should take charge," says Del. "Everyone follow Lex's lead," says Del with authority. Enzo looks unhappy but keeps his mouth shut.

Surprised there are no objections from Enzo or Zavier, Lex nods and says, "All right."

Del orders, "Everyone out." They all climb out of the hauler.

"First," says Lex, "if we're going to look like PCF troops, you all need to straighten up and follow behind me in a tight group. We'll have to lose the packs. Bring whatever you can in your uniform pockets."

Del adds, "Power cells are the priority. We will have access to supplies when we are with Roscoe." Everyone pulls the extra power cells out of their packs and throws the packs into the open hauler.

"The blasters are fine," says Lex, "but the comms don't look like PCF issue. Keep them, but get them out of sight." Lex pulls her comm off her belt and shoves it in her boot. The group follows her example, with the exception of Zavier, who clips the comm on the inside of his belt at the small of his back. Lex gives him a smirk. He smiles back.

Lex continues, "Let's get in formation. Kane, up front with me. Then Livia and Del. Zavier and Enzo at the back." They move into position. Lex inspects them. "No matter what, face front and keep an arm's distance behind the person in front of you. Zavier, you need to stand up straight."

"Like I have a stick up my ass?" asks Zavier.

"Exactly," says Lex. "And don't talk."

Zavier says with a smile, "You're enjoying this."

Lex ignores Zavier's comment and orders, "Let's go."

32

They march down the row of haulers and out into the compound. With Lex and Kane in the lead, they weave their way through the first area, where dozens of refuse haulers dock at refill stations, then move off down the tunnel that leads out of Indra. They cross out of the processing area and emerge into the PCF area of the compound. There are uniformed troops everywhere marching in formation across the compound, with some entering and exiting various buildings.

Livia says, with dismay in her voice, "We're surrounded by PCF. Can't we get out of sight?"

While still looking forward and marching at a consistent pace, Lex says, "Keep your head up. No one is looking at us. They all have things to do. Don't panic."

Livia trips over her own feet and stumbles. Zavier catches her from behind before she can fall to the ground. Zavier puts Livia back on her feet, and in a few steps they are back in sync with the group.

Kane says to Livia without looking back, "Try not to think about it. Just look forward at the back of my head and walk."

A large group of officers marches toward them, headed in the opposite direction. Lex and Kane lead their group off to the side so they can pass and continue walking.

When the group is well behind them, Lex says under her breath, "Everyone has somewhere to be. And so do we."

A pair of officers comes out of a building and walks next to them for a little while, then they turn and head down an alley between two buildings.

Lex says, "We're almost there. Keep your heads up and backs straight."

They turn a corner and almost run into a group of six officers coming the other way.

"Hey! Watch where you're going!" says the taller of the two lead officers, his tone confrontational.

Lex snaps back, "You watch it!"

"Oh! Are we in your way?" asks the other lead officer, stepping closer to Lex.

The taller officer smiles. "See, I think you and your unit are in our way. None of you are up to code. What happened to your uniforms? You look like you've been dragged through Rock Bottom."

"Good guess," says Lex, with a smirk. "We've just come up from Rock Bottom. Been undercover, killing rebels and mutants. Look, I can think of a few fun ways to settle this. Most involve breaking bones. But I'd hate to have to explain to my commanding officer, Lieutenant Hauser, that we were detained by a bunch of core-low idiots who apparently had nothing better to do than waste time while on duty."

"Lieutenant Hauser isn't on this compound," says the tall officer.

"Not now," says Lex, her eyes locked on him. "That is why we're leaving. And what about your unit? Don't you have somewhere you should be? Maybe guarding some trash haulers? Or you want to come back down with us to Rock Bottom on a patrol? Maybe kill a few mutants?"

The group of officers looks uncomfortable. The tall officer looks away.

"I didn't think so," says Lex. "Now, we have to go."

Lex leads her group around the PCF officers. In less than a minute, the front gate comes into view. Lex cuts to the right, leading them past a tall building, ducks into a small alcove, where they are out of sight, and stops. From their position, they have a good view of the front entrance.

"This is a good spot," says Lex.

Relieved, Livia lets out a deep breath, and Kane puts his hand on her shoulder.

Del pulls her holocomm out of her boot and hails Roscoe. "Roscoe, this is Delphia. We are in position by the entrance gate."

Roscoe's face pops up over the comm. "Copy. Hold tight."

"That was good with those officers," says Zavier. "How did you know that would work?"

"I was assigned to the Rock Bottom Patrol. They are a well-respected unit, but most officers wouldn't want that assignment."

Livia asks, "Who is Lieutenant Hauser?"

"He gave a lecture when we were in our third year at the Academy," says Lex.

"A real hard-ass," says Kane.

"He is the highest-ranking person I could think of," says Lex. "I just saw him in Rock Bottom. He was dressed like he lived down there and had something over his face, like he was hiding it. I think he had been hurt, maybe burned, but he was definitely still with the PCF, on the hunt for rebels. He almost killed me."

"I didn't know that," says Kane.

"You were pretty out of it when we were going through Rock Bottom."

"Well, that's true. I barely remember anything from before the Last Outpost."

At the entrance, several opulent transporters pull up to the gate, surrounded by PCF security on speeders. The speeder in the lead position comes to a stop at the guard station. When the officer pulls off her helmet, Lex recognizes her immediately, the sharp features and almost white blond hair cut short at her jawline.

Under her breath, Lex says, "What is Cassina doing here? She was a nightmare at the Academy. I was hoping I would never see her again."

"Yeah, me too," says Kane.

Lex stares at Cassina as she gets off her speeder and stands at attention by the transporter door. She says to Kane, "You know, she is actually the reason I came to rescue you. She had an Archive recording of you getting beat up on Livia's island. In a way, she's the reason I met Livia. She obviously wanted to save you but didn't want to blast her career, so she got me to do it."

Several dignitaries disembark from the transporters.

"She must have a top-level security assignment," says Kane. "It looks like she's already in charge. How is she so connected?"

Del comments, "Those are High Council members."

An older PCF officer, his uniform heavily decorated with ribbons and medals, approaches the Council members. The gate is too far away for anyone but Lex to hear what is being said.

Lex focuses and can hear the PCF officer say to one of the Council members, "It is an honor to have you visit our facility today. We have followed all your new directives to tighten security. I am sure you will be pleased."

The Council member responds, "We will see. You may take us to the command center." The PCF officer leads the group away into the compound.

"Lex, could you hear them?" asks Del. "What did they say?"

"Apparently, the Council has new security procedures. That officer was assuring them that he has done a bang-up job of implementing them." Lex gestures to the group and says sarcastically, "Clearly, he's doing outstanding work."

A moment later, one of the dignitaries' transporters explodes. There is pandemonium at the gate.

Zavier quips, "That's our cue."

PCF troops from the compound rush in to help. On the other side of the gate, civilians crowd around to see what has happened.

"Get out to the entrance," says Del. "Try to look like you are helping. Move out into the crowd on the other side of the gate."

Lex says, "Project an attitude of command. Just keep barking orders. Tell people 'Move back,' 'Clear the area,' 'Disperse.' No one will question you if you are giving orders."

Kane agrees, "Very PCF."

"And don't stop moving forward," adds Lex.

Kane says to Livia, "Stay close to Lex and me."

The group moves out from behind the building and makes their way through the chaos to the entrance gate. They join the chorus of PCF officers saying, just as Lex predicted, "Move back, everyone!" and "Disperse!"

They move deeper into the crowd. Del and Zavier are quite convincing barking their PCF orders, getting a whole section of the crowd to back up. Soon they are moving down a side street away from the commotion.

From above, a large PCF transporter swoops down in front of the group, lights flashing and siren wailing.

The side door flies open, and the strong, lean frame of Roscoe is standing inside. He is flanked by two much younger rebels dressed in PCF uniforms. His wrinkled face breaks into a broad smile, his eyes bright.

Roscoe yells, "Get in!"

The group jumps into the transporter. Roscoe and the two rebels move toward the back to make room. There are ten more rebels dressed in PCF uniforms in the transporter, some sitting on the benches against the side walls, others standing holding metal handholds fixed to the ceiling.

When everyone is in, Roscoe pulls the door closed and shouts to the driver, "Becka, we're all clear. Go!"

"Yes, sir," yells the young female pilot as she flips levers on her console.

The transporter lifts off and starts weaving through the tall, gleaming airscrapers and skytowers of Indra. After a moment, Becka flips a lever on her control panel and the siren cuts out.

Roscoe turns and hugs Enzo, long and heartfelt. "Good to see you, son. I heard about Jules. I'm sorry he couldn't be here. We will all be together soon."

Lex watches Zavier's face during this father-son reunion. *He looks uncomfortable. Roscoe is like a father to Zavier, but he is actually Enzo's father. That must have been strange to watch.*

Roscoe turns to Del and hugs her. It is quick, obligatory.

Watching them, Livia thinks, *They were together. They have children together, but they seem awkward now. I wonder when they saw each other last. It could have been years ago.*

Zavier stands stiffly next to Roscoe. Roscoe offers his hand to Zavier, and his face opens into a smile. "Zavier, good to have you back at my side."

Zavier shakes it, saying, "Yes, sir. Surprised to be back."

"Yes, surprised by a few things I imagine," says Roscoe, his eyes quickly darting to Enzo and back again. "I couldn't tell you everything. Good job getting them through the tunnel."

"Thank you, sir."

Zavier turns to the two rebels and gives them each a quick handshake. "Chae. Luther. Good to see you."

Luther says, "I didn't know you were coming back."

"Neither did I," says Zavier.

Roscoe orders, "Everyone grab a seat." Some of the seated rebels make room on the benches, and they all find a spot to sit, Zavier in between his two friends, Roscoe and Enzo sitting next to them. Lex, Livia, Del, and Kane sit on the other side of the transporter.

Livia looks at the young, clean-shaven man with brown hair sitting across from her and recognizes him. *I don't remember his name, but when we escaped from the High Council Building with Kane, I rode on the back of his speeder. He had a beard then. That seems like so long ago, but it was only about a week. It feels impossible, so much has changed.*

Livia says, "I remember you from the speeder ride away from the High Council Building. I apologize, I've forgotten your name, and I never thanked you."

"No need, Airgirl. I'm Chae," he says with a grin. "You are surprisingly strong, though. You held on so tight I thought you were going to break my ribs."

"I'm sorry," says Livia, her face flushing.

A shadow crosses Chae's face. *He is remembering that day. They lost friends rescuing us.* With genuine compassion in her voice, Livia says, "I'm sorry for the losses you suffered that day."

"Thank you," says Chae. "They are missed."

"This endeavor has had its casualties," adds Roscoe. "It has been hard, but we hope it will save many more lives. We all fight knowing we could die for the greater good."

"Yes, sir," says Chae.

Enzo says to Roscoe, "That explosion was strato."

"You liked that?" asks Roscoe. "One of the new things we've been working on. The new explosive we used is very powerful. It's so concentrated it only took a piece the size of the nail on my little finger."

Zavier waves his hand, indicating the PCF transporter, and asks, "Where did you get this?"

Roscoe says with a wink, "Our benefactor secured it for us."

"Very authentic," says Zavier.

"We are headed to Rock Bottom," says Roscoe. "We have to spread the word that The Twins are coming. People are gathering to see for themselves the fulfillment of the Twin Prophecy."

"What do they expect us to do?" asks Livia.

Del reassures her, "You just have to stand in front of the people so they can see you. You don't have to do anything."

"That should be easy," says Lex sarcastically.

Del ignores Lex and continues, "Most people of Rock Bottom have been reciting 'The Telling of the Time of the Twins' all their lives. They believe so strongly in the Prophecy that they won't ever leave without proof that this is truly The Time of the Twins. Just seeing you will give them hope, and the strength they need to leave Indra. Your mere presence will convince them."

Livia says, "I hope you're right."

33

The transporter smoothly drops down from the sky and enters a tunnel that leads underground. It is congested with multiple levels of flying traffic, with hovers of all sizes and hundreds of people on speeders. Becka hits the lever on her console and the siren blares. Drivers hurriedly move to the side to make way for the PCF transporter.

"This is the way to get around," comments Zavier. "How many more can we get?"

"Not many," says Roscoe. "We have to be careful. We are trying to stay inconspicuous. It wouldn't work for our purposes if the Council realized we have counterfeit PCF vehicles. They have no idea we have this resource. Consequently, we are able to be invisible though in plain sight."

They quickly weave their way through the vehicles in the tunnel until the vertical swarm of traffic is forced down by the tunnel's sloping ceiling and slows to a standstill. Through the windows of the transporter, they can see a checkpoint ahead. The vehicles form several long lines and slowly inch toward PCF control booths in front of a metal gate. At each booth, vehicles come to a stop, and a swarm of PCF officers question drivers and passengers and inspect paperwork and cargo before signaling to the officer in the booth to lift the gate to let them pass.

"Is that Horizon Checkpoint Central ahead?" asks Zavier.

"Yes, it is," says Roscoe.

"I've never been through one of the checkpoints before," says Zavier.

"We've always come up and gone back down through tunnels."

"Not really an option with a full-size transporter," says Roscoe. "Lex and Kane, I'm sure you know it well. But for Livia and Enzo, who might not be familiar, Horizon Checkpoint is the barrier between Upper Indra and the Hub. Thousands of people pass through Checkpoint Central every day. The side of the checkpoint going up is more strict than this side going down into the Hub. Since we blew that transporter up top, they'll be on high alert. I'm sure security going down has been tightened, but not for PCF."

With the siren blaring, Becka maneuvers the transporter out of the densely packed traffic and approaches the gate to the side designated for PCF vehicles. All the other vehicles are being stopped and inspected, but not their PCF transporter. The gate lifts and the transporter speeds through. The man at the booth gives Becka a courteous nod as they pass.

"That was easy," Lex says.

Roscoe says with a nod, "There is no history of rebels using PCF vehicles, so it doesn't occur to them to be suspicious. Eventually, I'm sure some situation will arise where it will be unavoidable and we will have to expose this resource."

Through the Horizon Checkpoint, they enter the Hub level of Indra, an enormous hive of activity. From the windows of the transporter, they can see the steady stream of traffic pouring through the checkpoint, merging into the complex, well-regulated traffic moving down into the Hub. With their siren wailing, the traffic parts to let them through. The vast space below seems to go on for miles. Huge crowds of people in uniforms and coveralls, most of them blue and gray with the occasional spot of green or white, exit and board tube transporters. The transporters then roar off, some headed into the Hub and others into the city above. Thousands of people travel on foot in a steady stream up and down motorized walkways and in open lifts. All going to and from their jobs, engaged in their daily lives.

Livia is mesmerized by the sheer number of people. *There are so many who work to support Indra. What are their lives like? They must work in Upper*

Indra or on one of the Islands. I never really thought about where our staff went when they left Helix. They most likely came back down through here to the Hub.

They travel down through the Hub for several minutes, passing through various industrial districts, factory after factory, facilities making both the fine living items for the Upper Indrithians and those making the utilitarian, life-sustaining essentials for the people of the Middler and Hub levels. They pass through the Habitation Zone, a sea of buildings packed with cramped barracks and small habitation units for those with slightly more important jobs.

As they pass through one section, Roscoe says, "This is the sanitation facilities area. We can all be thankful this transporter is sealed. The stench will make your eyes water."

Finally, the transporter pulls to a stop. Roscoe says to Becka, "You and Luther take the transporter. Don't stay here. Keep moving. We won't be long. I'll contact you when we are on our way back up. The rest of you are with me." Roscoe opens the door and says, "Follow me. Stay close."

Lex stifles a gag. "It smells awful."

"Have you forgotten the smell of Rock Bottom?" asks Roscoe as he jumps out of the transporter. "This is tame by comparison."

The rest follow him out of the transporter, emerging into a deserted area behind a huge building. The ground is covered with rotting garbage, heaps of it piled everywhere. Luther pulls the door closed and the transporter takes off. With Roscoe in the lead and Zavier by his side, they head toward the building. Lex, Livia, Kane, Del, and Enzo walk in the center of the group, with rebels on all sides.

"The Hubber sanitation crews don't tend to this area," says Roscoe as they trudge through the trash. "It's too far down. The lowest areas of the Hub are practically in Rock Bottom. This is one of the old ration factories. The newer ones are farther up, near the Synth Food Zone."

Inside the building, Roscoe and his group switch on their beamers, the lights set to shine forward, and fix them to their shoulders. Roscoe and Zavier rush the group through the several empty rooms lit only by the crisscrossed lights of the beamers.

"The building has been stripped," says Roscoe. "Anything useful was taken out years ago and moved to other facilities. There is an old delivery elevator from back when Indra still supported Rock Bottom, before they sealed it off, hoping it would die. We got it working, but we've had to be careful using it. We don't want to call attention to this area with too much activity."

They move through a hallway and into a huge room that must have once been a warehouse. At the far end of the room, Roscoe and Zavier pull back a rusted metal grate and Chae pulls down a long lever that opens a large elevator, the two parts of its door splitting at the middle, one half retracting up, the other dropping down. They all file into the elevator. Its floor and walls are scarred and rusted metal, caked with dirt and chipped paint.

"The Hub used to send down pallets of rations to Rock Bottom," says Roscoe. "Now everything the Hub makes goes up unless we steal it."

The last rebel pulls down the strap hanging from the top section of the door, and it closes with a loud clang. Roscoe hits a black button and the elevator starts to move down with a horrible, grinding noise.

"Is this safe?" asks Livia, alarmed. Kane puts a reassuring hand on her shoulder.

"Safe enough, and fast," says Roscoe. "This will dump us out close to where we need to be."

When the elevator stops, Zavier pulls the door open, revealing a dirty tarp hanging over the opening. They are assaulted with the overwhelming noise and smell of Rock Bottom. Loud, pounding music, people yelling, the air hot and stuffy, thick with the smell of too many people too close together.

Lex steps back, covering her nose. *Blast, that is bad. Worse than when I was down here before. I can smell the decay.* She shakes her head. *I can handle it.* She puts her hand down and stands up straight, ready to move.

Roscoe says to Zavier, "Check with Phillips that we're clear to move out. He will have clothes for us."

"Yes, sir," says Zavier with a nod, and he ducks around the tarp.

"This is one of the indoor areas of the market," says Roscoe. "We'll make our way out of this building and into the center of the open market. We'll be passing through a huge crowd, and we can't walk out there looking like PCF. That would cause a riot. Zavier will bring us coverings to wear so we'll look like we belong down here. Our people have set up a place to speak and have been spreading the word that The Twins of Prophecy are coming."

"Well, twins, anyway," says Lex.

"You have a role to play, and you have agreed to play it," says Del with an icy stare. "I know how you feel about the Prophecy, but keep that to yourself."

"I have," says Lex, "and I will."

"Good," says Del, and looks away.

Lex looks at the filthy tarp. *I hope this is quick. I don't know what is expected of me or how long I can hold my tongue. I wish parading us out as The Twins of Prophecy garbage wasn't part of the plan. I just want to get to the mission.*

Livia reaches out to sense Lex. *I can feel that she is anxious but determined. I'm nervous too, but I will do whatever it takes to give these people a better chance to survive. I don't have to believe in the Prophecy to do that.*

A moment later, Zavier is back carrying a large bundle of dingy cloth. "We're clear. Put these on." Zavier hands out dark coverings. "Just pull them over your head. There's a hole in the top."

The coverings are made of a rough, black material with patches of metal and other scraps attached in strange and random places. Some have hoods, others do not, but all are long enough to hang past their knees, hiding their PCF uniforms.

"Let's go," says Roscoe.

Following him, the group slips out from behind the tarp and into the chaotic market. There are bright flashing lights and people everywhere. The blaring music is even louder, and the noxious smell is much stronger.

Roscoe's rebels form a protective circle around Lex, Livia, and Del. Kane, Zavier, and Enzo are right behind them. There is a constant stream of people yelling over the music.

"Blasters! Fully charged!"

"Water packs! Water packs here!"

"Rations and synth! Trade for rations and synth!"

They push their way through the unruly market, struggling to stay together.

Lex grabs Livia's hand and yells over the music and shouting traders, "Stay close to me!"

"I wish I had my zinger!" yells Livia.

Just outside the building, the crowd thins and they are met by several more of Roscoe's rebels, all in the strange dress of Rock Bottom, a patchwork of cloth and metal.

A younger rebel addresses Roscoe. "Sir, there's a big crowd in the middle of the open market. They're getting restless."

"We're ready. Take us there," says Roscoe.

Weaving through the dense but less frantic crowd, they reach the center of the market. A massive group is assembled in the open space. Roscoe leads Lex, Livia, and Del into the center of the crowd and up onto an elevated platform, as Kane, Zavier, and Enzo hang back at the base of the platform.

Roscoe speaks into a makeshift amplification system barely held together by loose wires. His deep voice rings out. "Fellow people of Rock Bottom. The Time of the Twins is here." The crowd cheers. Roscoe continues, "Lex and Livia, *The Twins*, stand before you as proof that the Prophecy has come true. The Time of the Twins is now!"

The crowd chants, "Lex! Livia! Lex! Livia!" Roscoe gestures for Del to come forward. Del steps up and stands next to Roscoe. The crowd quiets down.

"People of Rock Bottom," says Del, her clear voice loud over the speakers. "My daughters, Lex and Livia, twins in their seventeenth year, have come to set you free just as the Telling foretold. Your oppression by the City of Indra will end. Indra has cut you off, abandoned you, hoped that you would all rot away and die. But you have not. You are strong. But there is a great danger coming." A concerned hush moves through the crowd.

Del continues, "The Independent High Council of Indra has a new plan. They are no longer willing to wait for you to starve to death. The Council wants to get rid of Rock Bottom once and for all. With one terrible act, they plan to kill everyone in Rock Bottom, but we have a plan too. We have a way for you all to escape and be free." The crowd erupts with cheers. Del raises her hands and the crowd quiets. "You have been trapped, but no more. We do not ask that you fight with us, only that you believe and prepare to leave. You can escape this danger, but only if you follow The Twins out of Rock Bottom. Make yourselves ready for a great journey. A path has been prepared for you, and a new life awaits you. We know it will be difficult to leave your homes, your lives, but you must. When this is over, there will be no Rock Bottom. In only two days, your imprisonment in Rock Bottom will be over. The Time of the Twins has come!"

Del gestures for the girls to come forward and speak. Lex shakes her head and mutters under her breath, "I'm not saying anything."

Livia says quietly to Lex, "I think we have to say something."

Livia grabs Lex's hand and pulls her to the center of the platform.

Livia's voice carries over the crowd. "Do not be afraid. My sister and I vow to fight to protect you. When the time comes and you must leave Rock Bottom, know that you leave to be free." Livia then raises her and Lex's joined hands over their heads. The crowd erupts in cheers.

Lex says to Livia, "I think that did it."

Roscoe steps up to the girls and says, "Perfect. That is what the people needed to hear. We must get back up to the transporter. We have to get up to our benefactor's island."

Lex challenges, "Aren't we safer here?"

Roscoe responds, "Truly, the both of you are not safe anywhere."

Several of Roscoe's rebels surround them as they come down from the platform and into the crowd. They are escorted through the now enthusiastic believers, who are trying to touch them as they pass by calling their names, "Livia! Lex!"

A small girl with one shriveled arm, her clothes ragged and stained, limps in front of Lex and yells, "Thank you, Twins! Thank you!"

Lex pats the girl on the top of her head and says, "Sure, kid. You're welcome."

As Livia walks, an old woman reaches out and touches her arm. Livia looks at the woman. Her eyes are clouded, and there is a long scar down the side of her face.

"The Twins," says the woman, a smile showing her few remaining brown teeth. "I knew you would come one day. Bless you."

Livia says with a small smile, "Thank you. We will do our best, but it is time for all of you to leave Rock Bottom."

The old woman says, "Yes! Yes. We will leave. Finally, it is The Time of the Twins. You will save us."

As they walk away, Lex says to Livia, "This is ridiculous. What do they think we are going to do?"

"I think they expect some kind of miracle," says Livia. "I just hope they leave and get out of harm's way."

34

As the group, including ten rebels, comes out of the delivery elevator and runs through the abandoned warehouse, Roscoe hails the transporter on his comm. "We're back."

In minutes they are outside the warehouse. The transporter swoops down, and the door flies open. As they load in and sit down, Roscoe asks Luther, "Any trouble?"

"No, sir," answers Luther as he closes the door. "No one gave us a second look."

"Perfect," says Roscoe, then turns to Becka and says, "Let's go."

Becka maneuvers the transporter up into the air. As they make their way up through the various areas of the Hub, Roscoe tells the group, "We are going to the island of our most important ally, our benefactor. He is our primary source of capital and supplies and has prepped everything for these missions. A genius. He made the air filters you're wearing and formulated the new highly concentrated explosives I told you about. He also got us this transporter."

They quickly pass through Horizon Checkpoint Central and soon are in the air of Indra, once again soaring in between the airscrapers and skytowers. As they speed through the air, higher and higher, Enzo turns away from the windows. Livia can feel that he is starting to feel uncomfortable, disoriented, and agitated. *He is trying to look like it isn't bothering him, but he is quite distressed. I'm sure this is the highest he's ever been.*

Livia says in a low voice to Enzo, "It might help to take deep breaths and try to remind yourself it is not so different from riding a speeder."

Enzo scowls at Livia. "I'm fine."

Livia concedes, "My mistake."

"This is it," Roscoe says as they approach the ally's island. Kane's face changes as he looks at it through the window.

Lex sees the strange look on Kane's face and asks, "Kane, what is it?"

Kane is incredulous. "This is my family's island."

Lex is shocked. "Are you sure?"

Kane says, "It's been years, but yes. Absolutely sure." He turns to Roscoe and says, "This is Viridans, my family's island."

Roscoe's face is impassive. "Oh, is it? Interesting."

"This is not a joke!" Kane says, exasperated. "Why are we here? What does this mean?"

"Please hold your temper," Roscoe says calmly. "We will land, and then I can answer whatever questions you have."

Kane stares out the window as they approach the island. Even from a distance, they can see that the plants on the island are overgrown, with trees and vines everywhere. It looks more like the forest they have just left in the Outlands than the typical well-manicured Islands of Indra.

"It's gotten so much worse," says Kane. "When I was young, my father was never interested in maintenance. The appearance of the island was the last thing he cared about, but there were people who came and pruned the plants back. Not often, but they still came. It looks like no one has tended to the island in years."

It appears there is nowhere to land the transporter, but Becka deftly steers through a gap in the wall of vines, revealing a clear landing pad. She has obviously been here before and sets the transporter down smoothly. The transporter is completely camouflaged by the vegetation above and cannot be seen from the air.

Roscoe opens the door, and they can see from the landing pad there is a clear path to a huge house that is covered in vines. The group makes their way to the dilapidated house.

Kane shakes his head, confused. "The house looks terrible. It didn't look like this when I lived here."

They reach the door and it swings open. A small, wiry man with keen hazel eyes stands in the doorway.

"Dad?" Kane says, astonished.

Kane's father steps out of the house with tears in his eyes and hugs Kane. "Welcome home, son."

Kane's face is a mask of shock. He stammers into his father's shoulder, "What? How?"

His father breaks the hug, wiping tears from his face, and says to Kane, "I know. I know. Many questions. So many questions. I will answer them, I promise, but first . . ." He steps back from Kane, looks at the group, and says, "Good day, everyone. I'm Ephraim, Kane's father. Might be a bit of a shock, but there was no helping that. Couldn't just have everyone knowing. Too dangerous."

Kane stares at his father in disbelief. Livia puts a reassuring hand on Kane's back. *This must be so hard on him. A terrible shock. Be strong, Kane. Truly, this is good news. Your father is a rebel, a better man than you thought.*

Ephraim spots Del and says, "Oh, my dear Delphia."

Del gives him a rare smile and says, "Ephraim, it's good to see you."

Ephraim hugs Del, who seems genuinely pleased to return the embrace. "Too many years. Too many. I've missed you, sweet lady."

Lex watches Del hug Ephraim. *She is happy to see him. She didn't show Livia and me that kind of warmth. It's bizarre to think that Roscoe and our parents knew each other. Now it turns out they knew Kane's father too. I'm starting to think none of this is a coincidence.*

Ephraim steps back and holds Del at arm's length, inspecting her. "My goodness, you are so beautiful. Just like I remember you. You really have not changed at all. Remarkable. Oh, if the Council knew what Armand had accomplished. I shudder to think what they would do if they got their hands on you."

"Well, they don't know about me," says Del. "So let's keep it that way."

Ephraim nods. "Indeed." He turns his attention to Roscoe and says,

"Roscoe, old friend." The two men hug.

Roscoe ends the hug and says, "You know most of the team I've brought with me. They have all been here before, for one thing or another."

Ephraim nods. "Yes, yes. Good to see you all again."

The rebels greet Ephraim with a chorus of "Sir." Zavier turns and finds Livia's eyes.

Livia searches Zavier's face, looking for answers. *Did he know that we were coming to see Kane's father? He has known Ephraim this whole time, but did he realize his connection to Kane? Roscoe obviously did. That is why he wanted Zavier to get Kane safely to the Outlands. I can feel Zavier is ashamed.* Zavier looks away. *He didn't know who Kane was. Zavier has such respect and admiration for Ephraim, the rebels' truest supporter. He must feel guilty that he didn't treat Kane with more kindness.*

Roscoe says, "Now, you need to meet the girls." Roscoe extends a hand to Lex and Livia. "Ephraim, meet Lex and Livia."

Ephraim moves to the girls, his face glowing as he says to them, "Look at you two. We never met in person, but I hoped we would one day. That day is today! I can see your father, Armand, in you both."

Livia says with warmth in her voice, "Thank you for all you are doing for the people of Rock Bottom. It is an honor to meet you."

Lex adds, "Yeah. Nice to meet you."

Ephraim looks away from the girls and says to the group, "So much to tell all of you. So, welcome. Welcome. Please come in." He waves his arm toward the house and steps back inside. "Please follow me."

Kane is silent while the rest of the group looks around as they follow Ephraim into the grand entrance room of the house. The inside is clean and pristine, which is shocking given the neglected state of the island and the exterior of the house.

As they walk, Ephraim's words come out in a rush. "I have been involved with the rebels since Kane was a boy. I was a close friend of Armand and Roscoe. We were all scientists and worked closely together." He pats Roscoe on the shoulder.

They pass several huge rooms, all with high ceilings and beautiful furnishings. Enzo looks around, his eyes wide. He turns to Kane. "Is this where you grew up?"

"Yeah," says Kane, shaking his head.

Livia senses how hard this is for Kane. *This is so difficult for him. Painful and confusing. To see his father after years of being apart. He probably hasn't seen him since he left for the Academy when he was twelve. And now to realize he is a rebel supporter.* Livia reaches out and grasps Kane's hand. He squeezes it and looks at her. His face is filled with pain and confusion.

They pass another enormous room, but this one has no furniture. There are several strange sculptures dominating the space, and the walls are covered with explosions of vibrant colors.

Kane comes to an abrupt stop and exclaims, "Father! Those are my sculptures and sound paintings from when I was a boy." The group stops and looks at the intricate and stunning art in the room.

"Yes, son. I kept everything you made." He smiles. "I spend time in the gallery every day. It is difficult because it reminds me how much I missed you, but it helps me think and imagine new things. You are very gifted, Kane."

"You really are," says Livia, squeezing his hand. "I had no idea."

"I knew," says Lex smugly.

Ephraim continues, "I always thought you were destined to be an artist, maybe design simulations or make shows for the holoscreen. But the PCF took you, and there is no way around the PCF once they have recruited you."

"Well, I'm out of the PCF now," says Kane.

"That is true," says Ephraim. "Come along," he says and continues walking down the hall. "Now, I've been carefully maintaining this ruse that I am a recluse. It's a facade, of course. Well, I am a recluse, I suppose, but not because I'm afraid to see anyone. I just wanted to be left alone. It has worked very well. Once people got used to the idea that I didn't like to be out in public, everyone left me alone. Then it was much easier to do whatever I wanted. It's been years now. I'm sure people think I've gone mad, which I guess I have a little bit. It is quite lonely most of the time. But Roscoe comes to visit when he can. I can concentrate on my work and I can help the rebels, and no one has ever suspected a thing."

"How is this possible?" asks Kane. "How can you be a rebel supporter? What about your chip? Is it blocked like Armand's chip?"

"Well, back in the days when Armand was still here," explains Ephraim, "before he was taken and locked in the Archives . . ." Ephraim stops walking abruptly, and a look of anguish passes over his face.

He locks his eyes on Lex and Livia. "Your father. My dear girls, he was a wonderful man. Is a wonderful man. Truly the best of us. The smartest, the kindest. All these years in the Archives, I can't imagine. It breaks my heart, breaks my heart."

"We are going to get him out," says Lex.

"Oh, good!" Ephraim says, his face beaming. "Soon, I hope."

"As soon as we can," says Lex, then turns to look at Del.

Del gives a small nod and says, "Yes. As soon as we can."

"Good. Good," says Ephraim, and he starts walking, his quick stride taking him down the hall.

"Father," says Kane. "You were saying about your chip?"

"Oh, yes. My chip. It's not in here," Ephraim says, and taps the side of his head. "It's out. As I started to say, in the old days, when Armand was still here, my chip was blocked, but that was such a nuisance. I had to turn it off, then back on. I was afraid I would forget and do something while it was on and get myself thrown in the Archives. Bah! Too difficult to keep straight. Too dangerous. Roscoe helped me remove my chip years ago. It is in the other room being fed a memory loop of the same day over and over. If the Council ever bothered to check on me, which why would they check on poor, sad, harmless Ephraim? He's not bothering anyone, hiding on his overgrown island. The memory feeding to the Archives makes it look like I am always here, living my mundane life. My chip is transmitting the day of a quite convincing recluse." Ephraim smiles.

"I didn't know that was possible," says Livia.

Ephraim says with pride, "Well, as far as the Council knows, it's not." He leads them through a set of immense glass doors. "This is my lab."

35

The lab is a huge space teeming with activity. The center of the room is a large, open area with a dozen tables, some with beakers filled with bubbling liquids suspended over blue flames, others with colorful fluids slowly dripping into tubes that run into storage tanks. Several tables are covered with equipment in various states of being rebuilt. There are multiple screens projecting images, some of DNA sequences rotating and changing, while others show complicated equations, formulas running calculations, and streams of data. All around the room machines beep with lights blinking and flashing. There is a palpable energy, as if the room is alive.

Livia's eyes are bright with excitement. "This is incredible." She begins to walk around.

"Please do not touch, taste, or sniff anything," warns Ephraim, and Livia stops. "Almost everything is dangerous to some degree."

He points to an area along one wall and says, "Like over there."

There are several tables topped with plants in small planter beds under lights, all in different stages of growth. To the side of the tables is the entrance to a greenhouse with much bigger plants inside visible through the glass walls, which are speckled with moisture droplets. Most of the plants have brightly colored flowers. On the wall are several shelves lined with jars of every size labeled with long, complex names that are filled with seeds, dried leaves, and crushed plants.

"Like almost everything in nature," says Ephraim, "appearances can be misleading. There can be beauty, but that is usually just the face. Something dangerous can be hiding underneath. Please follow me."

Ephraim walks toward the center of the lab. They all walk behind him with their hands behind their backs, heeding his instruction.

"Ephraim, have you solved the wheat virus problem?" asks Del.

"Yes, it was seed-borne. So I eliminated the varieties that are highly susceptible." He stops at a table and hits some buttons on a console. A DNA strain appears and begins to rotate in front on them. "Then I sequenced the resistant genome so it can be identified and replicated for any crops being planted. Additionally, I'm engineering a new root vegetable that has an exceptionally high nutritional density. It is almost ready."

Kane interrupts, "Are you the rebel that helped with the crop development in the Outlands?"

"Yes, of course I am." He hits a key on the console and he starts walking again. "A rebel botanist. I like how that sounds. I made the air filters you are wearing too."

"Is there anything you can't do?" asks Livia.

"Sing," Ephraim says seriously. "I am completely tone deaf. Luckily, it has not been imperative for my work."

As they walk, Lex looks down to the back of the lab. There is a metal spiral staircase that leads up to a glass-encased room with a red symbol on the glass door. Behind it, Lex can just make out a second door, but the rest of the room is out of view.

Lex points to the room. "What's up there?"

"That is my hot room. It's where I do my most dangerous work . . . DNA mutations, viruses. It is triple sealed so nothing can get out."

"Why are you working with stuff that is so dangerous?" asks Kane.

"There are things I have to know, things I have to figure out for the people of Indra."

Suddenly, there is a loud crash. Everyone stops abruptly and looks back at Zavier.

As he picks something up off the ground, he says sheepishly, "Sorry, just bumped into an old . . ." He holds up a piece of metal and studies it. "I'm not sure what this is."

"Part of a shuttle pod," says Ephraim as Zavier places it back on the table. "Oh, Roscoe, how was the transporter?"

Roscoe smiles. "It worked beautifully, old friend."

Ephraim grins, his bright eyes gleaming with pride. "Not easy to get. It took a lot of 'get this from one person, get that from another.' I put it together myself. That was a chore. Speeders are much easier, but you can't put too many people on a speeder."

Roscoe pats Ephraim on the shoulder. "We could go anywhere in it."

Ephraim asks, "And the siren?"

"Good and loud," says Roscoe.

Ephraim claps his hands. "So glad."

"Ephraim, you should tell them what you've been working on," says Roscoe.

"Yes. Yes," says Ephraim as he leads them over to one of the worktables. Ephraim explains, "We have known about the plan to flood Rock Bottom almost from its inception. It has taken years for the Council to rebuild the dam and connect it to the old pipe system, so we have had years to work on a plan to get everyone out. As you know from your own experience, getting off the additive is critical. You can't just walk out of Indra. Making breathing devices and stockpiling enough additive for all the people in Rock Bottom proved impossible. I started working on a different approach. I thought, *What if I could just get the additive out of the air?*" Ephraim winks. "That is the key, remove the additive. I've made a device that will reduce the amount of the additive pumped into the air. We bring the additive down to zero, and then people will be able to breathe outside Indra. It must be installed at the air filtration plant. That is Roscoe's department. Your plan is ready to implement?"

"Yes," says Roscoe, with a nod. "We're ready to go."

"Good. Good," says Ephraim. "Once installed, this device will make it appear that there has been no change in the air's composition. All the system monitors will still read as normal."

Lex asks, "So the additive will be removed from the air throughout Indra?"

"Yes," answers Ephraim, "and the withdrawal symptoms will be noticeable. People will feel weak and light-headed because we must remove the additive quickly if there is any chance for the people in Rock Bottom to be free from it and make their way to the Outlands. With that in mind, I have designed a virus that will act as an accelerant that will allow people to purge the additive in half the time, and they shouldn't feel the withdrawal symptoms. The virus is highly communicable. I'll infect all of you with it so you can spread it to anyone you have contact with. A group of you will go back to Rock Bottom to spread the virus. Once exposed, the people of Rock Bottom will be able to breathe uncontaminated air within two days. I hope it works. I thought I needed a bit more time to perfect it."

"What will happen if it doesn't work?" asks Livia.

"If the virus doesn't work," says Ephraim, "everyone in Rock Bottom will be very weak from the side effects of removing the additive. They will be in no condition to make the trip out of Indra. If the Council was prepared to release the water right now, everyone in Rock Bottom would be trapped and they would die. The Council is not ready to do it just yet, but they are close."

Lex asks, "How much time do we have?"

"We should still have at least a week, perhaps a bit more," says Ephraim. "They are waiting for the dam to be at maximum capacity to ensure the most force and volume when they release the water. But if they released the water now, the loss of life would still be catastrophic. We must stop or significantly delay the release of the water from the dam. We will talk about that part of the plan in a moment." He opens a refrigerated cabinet and takes out a small vial filled with a clear liquid. Using a fresh syringe for each person, he administers an injection of the virus to all of them and explains, "Now that the virus is in your body, you are contagious, so anyone you come in contact with will become infected. And then they will spread the virus as well. Once you get down to Rock Bottom, you should be able to spread it quite quickly."

"You six go," Roscoe says, indicating which members of the team are to go to Rock Bottom. "You know where the speeders are. Make contact with as many people as you can, and tell them to do the same." Six of Roscoe's team leave the lab through the huge glass doors. Chae, Luther, Becka, and a few others stay behind.

Roscoe turns to Livia. "Now, Livia, this is going to be quite a shock for you, so take a moment to listen before you react."

Ephraim pushes a button on a household communication system and says, "You can come in now."

After an awkward silence, a tall man in a light gray suit with a high collar and white-blond hair slicked back from his hard, angular face enters Ephraim's lab.

36

Livia's eyes go wide, her mind racing. *It's Waslo! My guardian, my tormentor. He was the main reason I felt like a prisoner on Helix. I thought I would never see him again.* "Waslo!" She immediately goes into defense mode and draws her blaster. "Why is Waslo here? He is not to be trusted! He works with the Council." She demands, "Did you bring the PCF with you?"

Waslo holds his hands out in a gesture of peace. "Wait, Livia. Calm down. I came alone. I came to help you."

Livia is indignant. "I know those are not your intentions. I don't believe you."

Lex studies Waslo's face. *I've seen him before. He was in the Archive memory Cassina made me watch. The one where Kane had just tried to kill Livia. This is the man who was restraining Livia while Kane was being beaten on Helix.* Lex draws her blaster and points it at him. "You almost had Kane killed!"

Waslo quickly responds, "I never touched Kane. I intervened so you could save him."

Livia begins to charge at Waslo, saying, "You work for the Council. You are our enemy!"

Waslo says in a calm voice, "I do work for the Council, but I am not your enemy. I've always been on your side."

Ephraim steps in front of Waslo to protect him. His tone is surprisingly harsh. "Livia! Lex! Stop!" Ephraim takes a breath and says, "Please lower your blasters and take a moment to listen to Waslo. He is one of us. He works for the Council, yes, but he is our spy. Most of what we know of the Council's plans, we know because of Waslo. Livia, he has been protecting you all these years."

"That can't be true," Livia protests. "I have never been able to sense him, but I know from his actions he doesn't care about me."

Waslo calmly requests, "Livia, please wait. Let me explain." She lowers her blaster slightly. He continues, "You can't read me because I have been blocking you, for my protection and yours. When you were very young, I started to see little signs that you could sense people, know what they were feeling, perhaps even know what they were thinking. I talked to Roscoe about it and he informed me that Delphia had developed a similar skill. We knew that since you had this gift, I would have to prevent you from discovering my true allegiance, that I was working with the rebels. So to protect myself and you, Ephraim and I devised a way to block your gift of reading my emotions. I've always worn this device when I was with you."

Waslo reaches inside his mouth and removes a tooth implant and puts it down in front of Livia. Waslo says, "Livia, look at me. Sense me now, and you will know my true intentions. You can trust me."

Livia hesitantly hands her blaster to Kane. She takes a step back from Waslo and looks squarely at him. A wave of emotions crashes over her. *He is terribly concerned. Fiercely protective. Unwavering loyalty and love. Undeniable love.* She staggers backward. It is too much for her. She is overcome and almost faints. Quickly, Del steps behind Livia and catches her.

Del whispers to Livia, "I feel it too." Del helps her to a chair and she sits down. Kane rushes to her side.

Livia stammers, "It can't be. It's not true. All this time you cared so deeply for me? But you never showed me any warmth or kindness. I thought you hated me."

Waslo shakes his head and looks steadily at her. "I have always cared for you. I promised your father I would look after you. My loyalty was always to Armand. Protecting you and his work are my priority. I'm sorry I had to be so distant."

"Why did you do that to me?" asks Livia. "Why make me feel so alone?"

Waslo pulls a chair over and sits in front of Livia. "I had to block my feelings to protect you." He takes her hands in his, a tender gesture, and continues, "If the Council knew of your gift, you would be in grave danger."

"Why?"

"If the Council discovered that you had unusual abilities," Waslo explains, "they would know that Armand had achieved more with his genetic work than he had led them to believe. Armand convinced the Council for years that he had made very little progress, all the while making great advances. Because he was able to block our chips, the Council had no idea what he had achieved until the two of you were born. That changed everything. Somehow, despite all of Armand's efforts, the Council discovered Delphia had given birth to twins, so they knew that Armand had been hiding things from them."

Lex interrupts, "How did the Council know?"

Roscoe answers, "We believe one of the household staff on Armand's family island of Orona, where you were born, realized Delphia had twins. Someone may have seen her leave with an infant, Lex, and yet there was still an infant on the island, Livia. Whomever that was must have reported what they saw to the Council."

Livia turns to Del. "Why would someone report you? Weren't they loyal to you?"

"Loyalty is not possible in Indra," answers Del. "It would have been a crime if they hadn't reported what they saw. They had to turn us into the Council as a good Indrithian citizen."

Roscoe adds, "Or perhaps the Council found out some other way. Regardless, they knew that you were one of a set of twins. And more important, the Council knew that Armand had been able to override the chips and conceal this from the Archives."

Waslo continues, "The Council realized that he had been blocking his chip and working in secret. Armand was arrested, but he was able to convince them that I, his lowly lab assistant, knew nothing of what he had been doing. But the Council wanted your twin back, and Delphia as well. I was placed as guardian over you, and they left you out in the open on Helix, hoping to draw out Delphia."

"So I was bait?" asks Livia. "The Council was hoping Del would come back for me?"

"Yes," says Waslo. "And that she would lead them to your twin. It was a trap that was never sprung. I told Roscoe and Delphia that Armand had been arrested and what the Council was planning. That they would never stop watching and waiting, hoping to get their hands on Lex and Delphia. Delphia and Roscoe put Lex in the Orphanage in the Hub and left Indra. The Council didn't know that Delphia or you had developed special gifts. One of my responsibilities as your guardian was to report on you to the Council. They were interested to know how you developed. If you were different in any way. Brilliant like your father. I always told them you were intelligent but nothing special."

"You certainly did a good job of making me feel that I was not special," says Livia.

"I'm sorry I had to do that to you," says Waslo. "I was relieved that as you got older, you were very careful not to reveal your ability. Even those closest to you only saw that you were very sensitive and intuitive, not the true level of your gift."

"I knew it was something most people could not do. I did try to keep it secret and appear as normal as I could."

Waslo adds, "I was always afraid Marius would figure out you had a gift and report it to the Council."

"What do you mean?" Livia asks, shocked. "Marius is your cohabitant. Isn't she working with you to help the rebels?"

"No, she is not a rebel," says Waslo.

"I always trusted Marius," says Livia. "She was always kind to me. I loved her. She was the closest thing I had to a mother."

"I do think she cared for you," says Waslo. "But if she had ever suspected that you were gifted, she would have reported it to the Council.

And if Marius had ever discovered I was helping the rebels, she would not have hesitated to report it to the Council. She has her own agenda."

"What agenda?" Livia asks.

"Marius is concerned with her own power and prestige," says Waslo. "In Indra you must have a cohabitant and produce a child for your career to advance. I needed a partner who had her own interests and would not be paying close attention to what I was doing. She needed a well-placed cohabitant to give her access into the upper levels of Indrithian society."

"I always thought you two were a strange pair."

"We both knew our place in the arrangement," says Waslo. "I'm just glad she never suspected that you were special." He turns to Lex. "Now, as for you, Lex, even we didn't know about your abilities. You hid them well."

Lex shrugs. "It was a survival instinct."

"Well, it served you well," says Roscoe. "None of the rebels we had placed in the Orphanage ever suspected that you were different, just smart and tough."

Livia smiles at Lex. "Well, she is both of those and so much more."

With irritation in her voice, Lex says, "Yes, I'm strato."

"Indeed," says Waslo. "I was able to watch you both in the simulations."

"What do you mean?" asks Livia. "I never saw you in any simulations."

"Neither did I," says Lex. "And I was hardly ever in a sim before the Academy. In the Orphanage they only had one, 'The Girl Tied with Rope.' It was so boring. I used to chase the shadow people, those people trapped in there for some crime against Indra."

"Well, in your case, Lex," says Waslo, "that sim was donated to the Orphanage anonymously by me. I used it to check on you. Sometimes you were chasing people condemned to Shadow Status in the Archives, but sometimes the man in the dark cloak was me. It was harder to access the simulations used by the Academy, but I was able to break in occasionally. I have a friend who is very skilled when it comes to the Archives."

"I can't believe that was you," says Lex, incredulous.

"Only sometimes. You were quite smart and resourceful. You almost caught me once."

"I did glimpse a black-cloaked figure a few times," says Livia. "Was that you?"

Waslo nods. "Most likely. It was much easier for me to observe you, Livia. I had better access to the simulations you used and knew when you were using them. I watched you as a shadow, but I also posed as your opponent in sparring simulations."

"I remember sparring with a samurai who didn't feel like a simulation," says Livia. "He felt like a person."

"That was me," confirms Waslo.

"Waslo and I used to spar together," says Del. "He is a very good swordsman."

"What!" says Livia, looking at Waslo. "I never saw you pick up a zinger."

"I was trying to keep my distance, but I was instrumental in making sure you were able to learn swordsmanship. I never used a zinger, though. I don't like the music. I prefer a standard sword."

"All right, we get it," says Lex. "You were watching us, but what about the Council?"

"Yes, the Council," says Waslo. "They only knew that Armand had lied, but not to what extent. They demanded he make progress, but he did not, and they could never be sure if he was holding out on them or if he was legitimately stuck. When torture didn't work, and they had to be careful because they didn't want to go too far and kill him, they used you, Livia, as leverage. They threatened to hurt you to motivate Armand to continue his work."

Livia says, "Del told us how they tried to force him to work on the projects they wanted, but he wouldn't, and that is why he was banished to the Archives."

Waslo nods. "He said if they harmed you, he would never do what they wanted. The Council never gave up the hope that they could break him, so they trapped him in the Archives. Shadow Status, a living death. Bringing him out whenever it suited them, to prod him, to see if he would give in. Armand has been trapped in the Archives for a long time." Waslo's face turns grave. "They bring him out less and less often, and each time he is worse."

"Wait!" Lex interrupts. "You've seen him? When? How?"

"I am always there when they bring him out," says Waslo. "In the beginning it was to interrogate him. The Council knew I worked for him, so I was the logical choice. Every time he is brought out of the Archives, it takes him longer and longer to regain his footing. He is fading away. His mind is getting lost."

Panicked, Livia turns to Del. "We have to get him out of there!"

"We will," Del reassures her. "As soon as we can."

Lex says, her anger showing, "Yeah, but after we complete these missions!"

Waslo and Ephraim exchange a strange look. Ephraim nods, and Waslo says, "There is something you need to know. It may change your mind about trying to rescue him."

"I doubt that," says Lex sternly.

"We'll see," says Waslo. "It was not by sheer will that Armand was able to keep his achievements from the Council. He took a radical step to make sure he could never tell them anything useful."

"What does that mean?" asks Lex, her eyes narrowing.

Ephraim looks at Roscoe. "We never told you about this, Roscoe, because Waslo and I thought it was easier for you and Delphia to believe that he had withstood the Council's pressure on his own, but that would have been nearly impossible."

Ephraim taps a few keys on the console embedded in one of the worktables.

"Armand left a message for all of you," says Waslo. "He asked us only to share this if the girls were safe."

A projection flickers to life hovering over the worktable. The frozen image of Armand's face, very close, stares out at them, his unruly, dark hair framing his handsome face, his warm brown eyes clear and bright.

"This recording will be hard to watch," warns Ephraim. "Particularly for you, Delphia."

"Just play it," says Del, her tone hard.

37

Ephraim nods and pushes a key on the console. The recording begins to play. The close-up image of Armand blinks, and then he backs away so more of him can be seen.

He clears his throat and his voice comes through the household speaker system, clear and deep. "Delphia, Lexie, Livia, I'm not sure if any of you will ever see this recording, but I'm making it so you will know what I did and why. It's been only a few days since Delphia took our sweet baby Lexie and disappeared from Helix, leaving me here with Livia. I did not tell Delphia what I planned to do, because I knew she would have tried to stop me, but I believe it must be done. Lexie and Livia are in danger because they are twins. I cannot allow harm to come to either of you. I am doing this to protect you girls as well as all of Indra."

Armand rakes his fingers through his unruly hair. "For years the Council has been relentless in its pursuit of genetic manipulations that are unconscionable. In helping Delphia become pregnant, I made several amazing breakthroughs in my work. Operating in my own lab, I was able to hide those discoveries from the Council, but I fear that they are getting restless to see results the longer I try to stall them. They want to move me to the labs they have built in the High Council Building to keep me under closer observation. I fear they will only become more aggressive once they discover Delphia is no longer on Helix. I cannot let these discoveries be used by the Council. I have decided to impair myself so that the Council can never force me to reveal what I have learned about genetic manipulation. The goal of the procedure is to remove from my memory the existence of my twin girls and make it impossible for me to reveal any of the breakthroughs I made in my work to the Council."

Armand waves his hand and a young Ephraim steps into view and stands next to him. Armand turns to Ephraim and nods, then returns his focus to the recording and says, "My acutely concerned friend Ephraim wishes me to put on record that he does not fully support my decision. However, after much discussion and debate, he has agreed to assist me despite his strong apprehension."

From the projection, Ephraim explains, "We have created a procedure that will damage targeted areas of Armand's brain. I will administer precisely aimed electronic pulses into his cerebral cortex. The goal is to remove the memories of his genetic discoveries and damage his higher processing centers that led to those advancements so they will be incredibly difficult to re-create."

The message glitches and the image changes. Armand is reclined in a long, high-backed chair, straps across his chest, legs, and arms, his head constrained by a metal ring secured to the headrest of the chair. Suspended from the ceiling above the chair is a metal arm with a pointed probe on the end emitting a bright blue light that is slowly moving across Armand's face. Ephraim stands next to the chair intensely looking at a screen and entering commands into a console, remotely positioning the mechanical apparatus. The arm stops moving and the bright blue light constricts until it is a tiny focused dot at the top of Armand's forehead.

"Are you ready, Armand?" asks Ephraim.

Armand takes a deep breath. "Yes. Proceed."

Ephraim pushes a key on the console and the bright blue light turns a brilliant white for an instant. Armand goes rigid and his face contorts in pain.

Livia screams, "No! Stop! I can't watch this."

"Don't stop the message," says Del.

Ephraim nods at Del.

"Why?" shrieks Livia. "Why do we have to watch this? You told us what he did. Why do we need to see it?"

"We watch it to show our respect," says Del.

Livia begins to cry and buries her face in Kane's chest. He wraps his arms around her. Lex watches stoically standing next to Del and Roscoe while the message continues showing several more targeted pulses. With each light burst Armand's reaction is more extreme, his body becoming weak and sinking into the chair, though his head stays rigidly fixed in place, held tightly by the metal ring.

Finally, the message glitches again and Ephraim addresses them from the projection. "It took more pulses than I thought, but after questioning him I believe we have gone far enough."

The message glitches, and Armand sits in the chair, all the restraints removed. He looks gaunt and exhausted, with dark circles under his eyes.

Ephraim's voice in the projection asks, "What is your name?"

Armand looks at Ephraim for a long moment, blinks slowly several times, then says, "Armand Cosmo."

"What is the name of your cohabitant?"

Armand closes his eyes. Finally he answers, "Delphia."

"Did you and Delphia have a child?"

"I don't think so."

"What is the nature of your work?"

"Is it something with genetics?" answers Armand, a puzzled expression on his face.

Ephraim stops the message. "After the procedure, Armand had no memory of you girls. He remembered Delphia but not that she had been pregnant. His higher processing was severely affected, and he could not remember any of his work."

"He was the most brilliant man any one of us will ever know," says Del. "He destroyed his brain to protect everyone in Indra."

"It was insane," yells Lex. "Why did you help him?"

"If I hadn't helped him, he would have done it himself, and that could have been even worse," says Ephraim with a sigh. "He could have killed himself in the attempt. He was adamant that his work not to be used for evil, and he knew the Council would stop at nothing. I can't imagine what being trapped in the Archives for sixteen years has done to him. As Waslo said, every time he is brought out he is worse."

Waslo nods. "Over the years, he has been shown files of Livia to motivate him to continue his work, so he does know about her. The Council questioned him about Livia's twin, but he didn't remember your name, Lex, or what had become of you and Delphia. He knows you two exist, though not from his own memories."

Wiping her tears, Livia turns to Waslo and says, "I still want to rescue him."

"Yes," says Lex. "This changes nothing."

"He deserves it," says Del. "After all he's been through."

"If that is how you feel," says Waslo, "I will do whatever I can to make it possible."

"If you do rescue him," says Ephraim, pushing a few keys on his console, "I have some memory files and a recorded message he made for himself that he will want to see." A small metallic chip pops out of the side of the console and Ephraim hands it to Del. "These could help him remember Lex and Livia and perhaps some of his work."

"Why didn't you get him out long ago, if you're such a good friend?" Lex challenges Waslo.

"He wouldn't let me," says Waslo. "Armand insisted that my position as adviser to the Council was too important to jeopardize, and he was right. The information I've had access to because I am so close to the Council may save the lives of everyone in Rock Bottom. Everything I have learned I've been able to share with Roscoe. If I wasn't working with the Council, Livia would be dead."

"Me, dead?" Livia asks, stunned. "What do you mean?"

Waslo's gaze turns tender. "The Council was behind the attempt to assassinate you."

"What?" asks Livia. "Why would the Council want me dead? I

thought they were keeping me alive to have power over Armand."

"That was the case for many years," says Waslo. "But eventually the Council realized they couldn't use you to get Armand to do what they wanted, so they more or less just left you alone. Then a few months ago, the Council started hearing talk that there was a set of twins coming into their seventeenth year and they would fulfill The Time of the Twins Prophecy. The Council was aware of the twin lore that predicts, 'A set of twins in their seventeenth year will be discovered and bring freedom to Indra and all its people.' They had been told that the people believed the arrival of the prophesied Twin Saviors was imminent, and a revolution was soon to follow. The last thing the Council wanted was a set of twins who could give power to the old Twin Prophecy. The Council planned to make the fulfillment of the Prophecy impossible by killing one of The Twins, the one they had easy access to . . . you, Livia. Of course the Council believed the Prophecy was ludicrous, but they feared that if the existence of a set of twins was known, it would be self-fulfilling."

Lex is incredulous. "And you know all of this because you're on the Council?"

Waslo corrects her. "I'm not a member of the Council. I am not from a Founding Family. I am an adviser and work closely with the Council. That is how I know all of this."

"Who are these Founding Families?" asks Enzo. "Why are they on the Council?"

"Just as the term implies," says Del, "they are the families that founded Indra and are by blood and lineage the only members of the Council. They control the Council and the City of Indra because they created it. At least that is their excuse for holding Indra hostage."

"There is a section on the Founding Families in *The Book of Indra*," says Livia.

"We had to memorize it at the Academy," says Lex. "Basically it says that the Founding Families are responsible for the creation of Indra and that their descendants are responsible for keeping Indra running smoothly."

Excerpted from The Book of Indra, *Chapter III: "Indra: The Founders of Our Great City"*

OUR FOUNDERS, OUR LEADERS: THE FOUNDING FAMILIES

A thousand years ago, at the birth of our great city, the twenty Founding Families were selected to guide the development of Indra. They took on the great responsibility of creating a city more perfect than had ever existed before. The Founding Families were selected with great care for their expertise in every area that would ensure that Indra would flourish and prosper. Only the most intelligent and creative innovators, scientists, and industrialists were selected to serve as Indra's creators and protectors. The Founding Families established the Independent High Council as the chief leadership authority of Indra. Under the wise guidance of the Independent High Council and their descendants, Indra has grown and thrived. The Council has created and sustained the perfectly balanced, integrated City of Indra. The descendants of the direct bloodline of the Founding Families are by right and by blood members of the High Council with all the obligations that demands. It is the duty of those on the Independent High Council to support and foster Indra so it will continue to prosper. Just as each citizen of Indra has his or her job that supports Indra, the Independent High Council and the Founding Families continue to do their job of guiding Indra, which benefits all of its citizens.

Zavier asks, "Everyone on the Council is from one of those families?"

"Yes," says Del. "The Founding Families all have one member on the Council."

"So the Council wanted me dead, and they had to do it soon because I had just turned seventeen?" asks Livia.

"Correct," says Waslo. "And if Kane had just done what he had been ordered to do, everything would've gone smoothly."

"With what?" snaps Kane. "The plan to kill Livia?"

"That may have been the Council's plan," says Roscoe. "But we had a different one that would have worked until you two had to kiss and ruin it!"

"Livia kissing me didn't ruin your plan," says Kane. "I had already decided I couldn't go through with it."

"Well, the kiss was unfortunate," Waslo says to Kane. "That is when you took in the poison that was meant for Livia."

Livia asks, "So the plan was for me to be poisoned and die?"

"Well, not die, obviously," says Roscoe. "Only appear to be dead."

"Correct," says Waslo. "When the Council decided that you were to be assassinated, there was much discussion about how it was to be done, and when. I suggested to the Council that it should take place at your Emergence Ball."

"It's actually quite ironic that I was to be killed at my Emergence Ball," says Livia, "since there were moments when I thought I would rather die than go through with such a demoralizing spectacle, being put on display for the sole purpose of being judged and scrutinized. But I had no choice."

"Yes," says Waslo. "The Emergence Ball is a demeaning exhibition. I'm sorry that you were subjected to it, but it is required for all Proper Indrithian Ladies. I can't believe the tradition persists."

Lex interrupts, "Yes, it's barbaric. The fancy dresses, everyone looking at you. Emergence Balls are terrible. Can we get back to the part about Livia being assassinated by the Council?"

Waslo says, "I argued that the ball would be a well-attended event. Consequently, if Livia passed away there, the news of her death would spread quickly. If the rebels were planning on using Delphia's twins, they would soon know that Livia was dead and that there was no hope of reuniting The Twins to fulfill the Prophecy. The Council agreed to the time and place of the assassination, and then it was the question of how she was to be killed and by whom."

"How did I get involved in this plan?" asks Kane.

Waslo turns to Kane. "It was not random that you were selected to carry out the job. I worked very hard to make sure you were the one selected for the assassination assignment. I suggested that you were a good fit, a Proper Young Man from the Islands. You would know how to handle yourself at an Emergence Ball, and you had been trained to kill at the Academy."

Ephraim says, "But Waslo's true motivation for involving you was to get you released from your obligation to the PCF so you could return home. Waslo and I realized that an assignment like this could be your ticket out."

"After a high-profile assassination like that, you would be of no use to the PCF," says Waslo. "They would portray you as a lone rebel whose motives were unknown. The PCF would fake a manhunt for you and you would have to go into hiding."

"And Kane," Ephraim says with a sad smile, "I must say, though it caused huge problems, I'm so proud that you couldn't go through with it. You are not one of those who just follows orders. That is admirable."

"Problematic," says Roscoe, "but admirable."

"Now, the poison," says Ephraim. "That was tricky. Waslo knew what poison the Council planned to use. I just had to engineer an antidote that would stop Livia from dying, but she still needed to appear dead. That proved to be the difficult bit. Luckily, plant-derived poisons and antidotes are one of my specialties. I worked it all out and had everything ready in time for the ball. I designed the antidote that would protect Livia against the deadly effects of the poison but allow her to be incapacitated so she would appear dead."

"I placed Ephraim's clever antidote in your drink the night of the ball," says Waslo. "If all had gone according to plan, it would have gone as follows: Kane would deliver the poison, Livia would pass out, and

Kane would make a clean escape. Livia's body would be found, I would confirm that she was dead in front of many witnesses, and then take her unconscious body away to the rebels, who would get her to her mother. As Livia's guardian, I would have been responsible for her memorial and could have easily held a very public funeral without anyone realizing there was no body. Kane would be able to leave the PCF and come back here to his family's island."

"Son, you would've been able to safely escape Helix and return home," says Ephraim. "Livia would've gone into a perfectly benign, comatose state, and the security team would have been fooled into thinking she was dead. We could've gotten her off the island and then safely to the rebels. Our plan turned Livia's assassination into an extraction."

Kane protests, "Well, I didn't know any of that! Did I? I thought I was killing an innocent girl. Maybe you should have told me."

Ephraim sighs. "I wish we had."

"The best-laid plans of mice and men," says Roscoe.

Lex looks at Roscoe, her eyebrows pulled together. "What are you talking about?"

"It's from an old, old book," says Roscoe. "In short, it means that things often don't turn out the way you plan."

Lex snaps, "We don't need an old book to tells us things got messed up."

"Indeed," says Waslo. "Obviously, our plan did not go as we hoped. When I came into the stable and found that Livia was fine and that Kane was almost dead, there was nothing I could do. The PCF security team was right behind me, and they were on Kane in a flash, beating him, then taking him into custody. I could not attempt to stop the PCF. It would have been extremely suspicious."

"So your cover was more important than Kane's life?" accuses Lex.

Ephraim says calmly, with pain in his face, "Waslo's cover may mean that thousands of lives will be saved." He reaches out and squeezes Kane's shoulder, holding it to steady himself. "Waslo being close to the Council is more important than any one life. Even my son's life, I am sorry to say."

"I agree," says Kane.

"Still," says Waslo, "I regret I couldn't intervene. I put a rescue plan into action as soon as they took you from Helix."

"What are you talking about?" challenges Lex. "Livia and I rescued Kane."

"If you recall," says Zavier, "you had some help getting out of the High Council Building. If Roscoe and our team hadn't shown up when we did, all three of you would be in High Security Detainment."

Lex concedes, "Yes, you rebels helped, but not Waslo."

Waslo says to Lex, "That may be how it appears to you, but first ask yourself, how did Roscoe know to assist you? I contacted him. But even before that, how did you become aware of Kane's situation? Cassina showed you an Archive memory, correct?"

Lex thinks back. *I was supposed to meet Kane in the Archives, but he wasn't there. Cassina showed up and made me watch that terrible Archive memory of Kane being beaten by a security team. That was the first time I saw Livia. I rushed to Helix to confront Livia and find out what happened to Kane.*

"Yes," says Lex. "I remember how odd the Archive memory was. It was obviously incomplete. I wondered how Cassina had gotten hold of it, but at the time it hardly mattered. I instantly focused on helping Kane however I could."

"I gave the memory to Cassina," says Waslo. "Cassina is my daughter. The child I had with Marius."

"What?" Lex exclaims and turns to Livia. "Did you know he was Cassina's father?"

Livia says, "I did not know Cassina, so how could I know that Waslo was her father? He and Marius never talked about her. We saw her at the PCF compound entrance gate earlier today. You and Kane didn't seem happy to see her, but you didn't elaborate."

"She was at the Academy with us," says Kane.

"To be blunt," says Lex, "Waslo's daughter is vile."

"Lex! Don't be rude," Livia admonishes her and turns to Waslo. "I'm sorry, Waslo."

"Don't apologize for me!" snaps Lex. "You don't even know her. Cassina is untrustworthy and self-serving. She tried her best to get me kicked out of the Academy. In our final simulation she was in command and tried to fix the mission so I would fail. She really had it in for me."

"Honestly," says Waslo, "that doesn't surprise me. Cassina is not subtle. If she doesn't like someone, she's not going to hide it."

Livia asks Lex, "What did she have against you?"

"She hated me 'cause I was from the Orphanage," says Lex. "I was dirt. A mudgirl."

"No," says Kane. "She hated you because you were good, better than her at everything."

"Oh, yeah," Lex adds, "it may not have helped that she had a thing for Kane and was jealous that Kane and I were friends."

"I'm sorry I involved her," says Waslo, "but I needed some way to get you the information about Kane. I knew we needed to rescue him as soon as possible. Kane would be killed if he were left in the hands of the PCF. The Council would never let it be known that they had orchestrated the assassination attempt. Even though Kane had no information about who had ordered him to kill Livia, as far as the Council was concerned, he was a loose end. Also, I had to get Livia off of Helix without delay. The Council still wanted her dead."

Roscoe says, "Waslo contacted me, and together we devised the plan to extract Livia and Lex, plus rescue Kane, in one operation. As part of the plan, Waslo manipulated Cassina to involve Lex in Kane's rescue."

"Waslo, what about your chip?" asks Lex. "How can you do all of this with the Archives recording everything you do?"

Waslo explains, "Initially, I used the same chip-blocking technology Armand first developed years ago, but blocking your chip leaves gaps in the Archives. I needed something more undetectable. I couldn't remove my chip like Ephraim. He told you about his chip, that it's being fed an old memory?"

"Yes," says Livia.

"I use recorded memories as well. They are fed into my chip remotely.

This blocks the chip from seeing any of my current activities, allowing me freedom from observation. Of course, my memories are more complicated and varied than Ephraim's."

"We constantly have to record new memories and rotate the order so nothing looks suspicious," explains Ephraim.

"I couldn't be a recluse and work for the Council," says Waslo.

"I know, I know," says Ephraim. "I just hate that you still have that thing in your brain," he says, tapping the side of his head with a grimace.

"I wish it was out as well, but it is the only way," says Waslo. "Over the years, Ephraim and I have learned how to manipulate the chips much more precisely."

Ephraim says, "Oh, the chips. The chips are clever. Not as clever as me, but clever. Some of you from Rock Bottom never had a chip. Only Waslo still has his chip. I can't wait to take it out. Someday, someday."

"Yes," says Waslo. "Someday. In the meantime, we have learned how to block the location function. We are able to damp down the control on emotions while keeping a full connection to the Archives. I am responsible for blocking the chips of the rebel spies in the Hub, Middler, and Islands social levels so they can maintain covers. Ephraim and I created the kill switch Vippy used to break her connection with the Archives the day you all rescued Kane."

"We met her parents in the Outlands," says Lex.

Roscoe nods. "Otto and Corah. Such brave, strong people. Their daughter Vippy is impressive. She is posted at the High Council Building. That may be useful sooner rather than later."

"Now, Livia," says Waslo, "I've been wondering how you feel now that your chip has been removed. Can you feel the difference?"

"I do feel things much more strongly," says Livia. "I'm getting used to it, but it is an adjustment."

Del says, "I told her sometimes you have to block it out for you own protection. I suspect her gift is stronger than mine since she was born with it, and for me it was an alteration that was made later in life."

"Can you sense people more clearly?" Waslo asks.

"People's emotions are very clear. And other living things, animals and even plants, I can feel the life in them."

"Interesting," says Waslo.

"It doesn't sound interesting," says Zavier. "It sounds creepy. Don't be sensing me."

"I will do my best to refrain," says Livia.

"The day of the Emergence Ball," says Waslo, "in preparation for your extraction, I remotely adjusted your chip. If everything had gone according to plan, I was going to remove your chip, and adjusting it beforehand would make that procedure easier."

"They removed her chip at the Last Outpost," says Lex, "and it did seem like it wasn't as hard on her as when mine was taken out."

"Livia, I regret I couldn't do the procedure myself," says Waslo, "but there just wasn't an opportunity. Your chip had to be active during Kane's assassination attempt. I knew the Council would certainly review your Archive memories of the assassination. But immediately after, I would need to shut the chip down so it would appear that you were dead. Adjusting the chip beforehand would allow me to shut the chip down more quickly. I disabled the location tracker and turned down the emotional limiters. I believe when I adjusted your chip that day, it affected your emotions more than I anticipated, allowing you to feel more strongly than you would normally. You were more alert. Perhaps that is why you acted so impulsively and kissed Kane."

Kane smiles at Livia, and she smiles back.

"Perhaps," says Livia.

38

"I believe we have explained as much as is needed for now," says Roscoe. "We have got to get you all off to your respective missions. I will brief the team going to the dam on their mission."

Ephraim nods and smiles. "Waslo, since Livia and Del are not part of the group going to the dam, why don't you take them to see our special guest."

"Special guest?" asks Livia. "I'm not sure I can handle any more surprises. I've barely adjusted to Waslo being here."

"This guest you will be happy to see," says Waslo. "And she'll be happy to see you. Follow me."

He gently touches her elbow. She flinches. "Do not touch me."

"My apologies." He tucks his hands behind his back. "Livia, you don't have to be afraid of me."

"I'm not afraid of you. I can sense you mean me no harm, but for years you were unkind to me. This new version of you will take some getting used to."

He nods his understanding. Livia feels a gentle hand on her back as Del steps next to her.

"She likes the gardens," says Waslo. "Will you accompany me outside?"

Livia and Del share a puzzled look as Waslo leads them out of the lab through the huge glass doors.

Roscoe watches them leave, then turns and addresses the group.

"Your mission has one main objective, stop the flood. You have to get out to the dam to place the explosives, set the remote charges, get out of the way, and blow it."

"How do we get to the dam?" Lex asks.

"You will impersonate PCF troops," says Roscoe. "You'll exit Indra through the heavily guarded PCF exit gate on the north side of the city. Lex, you and Kane will be in the lead. Your PCF Academy training is essential, as I'm sure security is tighter than ever. You will be walking through the front entrance onto one of the most heavily guarded compounds. We can't afford a single mistake. You two know all the protocols, all the terminology. Your demeanor and attitude will be impeccable and beyond suspicion. None of my team could pass for PCF under close inspection. With you two in the lead, the whole team will appear legitimate. Four of my team will go with you." Four rebels step forward, including Chae. "You know Chae." Chae nods. Roscoe points to the others. "Plus Matson, Parker, and Amia. They are my best and fit the profile for PCF officers."

They all appear to be just a few years older than Lex and Livia. Matson has dark skin and black hair. Parker is pale, with light brown hair. Both are clean-shaven. Amia has warm skin and short, dark hair that frames her thin face with straight bangs cut just above her narrow eyes. Lex studies the rebels who are now part of her team. *They do look like PCF officers. Young and fit but older than recruits. I hope they can act like PCF officers. We'll be all right if these four follow our lead. Roscoe is right, they couldn't do this without someone who has been through the Academy.*

On a small handheld console, Ephraim pushes a few buttons and a three-dimensional, transparent projection of Indra pops up in the middle of the lab. The massive, detailed image of the city, constructed out of different shades of blue light, hovers in the air.

"We are here," says Ephraim. He taps the console and the map zooms in to show a close view of Viridans Island. "The gate is here." He taps the console and the map zooms out, showing the full view of the city, then it refocuses on the PCF compound on the edge of Indra.

Roscoe says, "You'll leave Indra through the gate in this PCF compound. It is dangerous, but it is the most direct and fastest route to the dam. There is no time to waste."

"We have new speeders ready for you," says Ephraim, "but it is still a long ride to the north edge of the city."

"There must be heavy security at that compound," says Kane. "It might be a bit of a problem that Lex and I are fugitives. Our faces are going to set off alarms before we get past the entrance gate."

"Indeed," says Ephraim. "Waslo has taken care of all your scans. He has a good friend who is assigned to Archive security who has altered your facial recognition images in the entire system. No scans will recognize you. You will all come up clean. He did the same for Livia as well. Lex, Livia, and Kane, the fugitives, are basically ghosts."

"You trust this person?" asks Lex. "If we're recognized, we're dead."

"Waslo trusts him with his secret and therefore his life," says Ephraim seriously.

"That is a good friend," says Lex.

"He is," says Roscoe. "I've met him and I trust him. Maybe you will all meet him one day."

"Also," adds Ephraim, "I have new uniforms for all of you. I've programmed their transponders with clean IDs and the proper clearances."

"Once you are through security," says Roscoe, "an underground transporter will take you directly to the dam. No one should be there. The Council has been monitoring the progress of the water in the reservoir remotely, but occasionally they have sent a PCF team out for an on-site inspection. You will pose as one of those teams."

Ephraim manipulates the projection so it flies through the compound, down a tunnel that passes under the dome, and ends at the dam and the connected reservoir. The projection shows the facility in remarkable detail, a seven-hundred-foot tall structure that gets wider as it reaches down to its base. The interior is crisscrossed with corridors and hallways, occasionally dotted with rooms. An elevator shaft runs right down the center, with a stairway that runs parallel to it.

Lex asks, "Where did you get these projections?"

"This is all through Waslo's access," says Roscoe. "As you can imagine, the Council has kept a tight lid on this project. Everyone who worked on it was threatened with being banished to the Archives if they talked about it, so no one talked about it. Plus, they were told it was being repaired as a power source for Indra. The workers have no idea what it will be used for. Though honestly, most people of the Hub and above wouldn't care if Rock Bottom and all the people down there just went away."

Ephraim puts his hand on Zavier's shoulder. "Not everyone thinks that way." He indicates the projection of the dam. "Once inside the dam, you will need to place the explosives very precisely so it floods the valley on the opposite side of the pipe system."

"Why can't we just blow the pipes?" asks Lex.

"If it were one pipe leaving the reservoir," says Ephraim with a sigh, "that would be much easier, but unfortunately there are many pipes. They are positioned at multiple points along the reservoir, each connecting to a section of the old pipe system. They can all be opened remotely at the same time. We would have to destroy them all at the same time, and that is a far riskier proposition."

"Too bad," says Lex.

"Indeed," says Ephraim. "Placement at the dam will be critical. Since the dam has been rebuilt, I've analyzed the structure, and the weakest points are on Level 10. You will each take a portion of the highly concentrated explosive I have created and the charges, which can be detonated remotely. Lex, you will have the detonator. You'll each place your explosives and get out of there. When you're clear, Lex detonates the charges and boom. The dam will be critically fractured and the pressure of the water in the reservoir will be too much. The dam will rupture and the water will rush out into the valley. After you've blown the dam, get to the north side of the reservoir. Del has a team camped there. They know you are coming and will get you back to her colony." He zooms in on the lower levels of the projection of the dam. "I'll show you where the charges need to go."

39

Livia and Del follow behind Waslo onto a large patio that wraps around the length of the estate. They stop and look out onto the expansive, overgrown grounds of Viridans.

Waslo looks around. "Please excuse me for a moment, I'll be right back."

Waslo walks off to the side. Livia watches as he moves around trees and dodges between bushes. Livia wonders, *He appears to be searching for something. What is he looking for?*

"Why did he bring us out here?" asks Livia.

"I'm not sure yet," says Del as she looks off at the plants. "It's nice to have a moment. Even if it's on one of Indra's floating Islands. I never thought I would be back here."

"Neither did I."

After a lingering silence, Livia continues, "It's so different than Helix." She steps off the stone patio into the garden. "I think its wildness is stunning."

"It truly is," Del agrees. "I tried so hard to undo the rigid, structured look of Helix. But I could never achieve this level of beauty."

Livia continues to walk around the grounds looking at all the vegetation. "Now that I have seen the Outlands, nothing in Indra compares."

"I completely agree. Just the air here is not air. It feels suffocating."

Waslo can be seen some distance away facing a vast and dense orchard amid huge, overhanging trees. He starts to whistle, the sound surprisingly loud and high.

"What is he doing?" asks Del, her eyes narrowed.

"I don't know," answers Livia.

Just then, in the distance, the sound of breaking branches and a loud neighing comes through the trees.

Livia visibly begins to shiver. "It can't be?" She begins to run toward where Waslo is standing.

"What is it, Livia?" Del yells after her.

Just then a large, impressive ivory horse comes through the trees.

"Veda!" Livia yells. "Veda!"

Livia and the horse meet at the edge of the trees where the grounds are covered by a low, deep green moss. She throws her arms around Veda's neck and the horse nuzzles her back, letting out a low, continuous nickering.

"I never thought I would see you again." Livia rests her chin on Veda's face and looks into her eyes. "I'm so sorry, Veda, that I left you on Helix." She continues to stroke her mane. "It is so good to see you, girl. Such a relief."

Del hesitantly calls, "Veda?"

Veda's ears prick forward. She starts to neigh and stamp her hooves in excitement.

Del takes a step forward. "My sweet girl." Veda trots to her, leaving Livia behind. Del reaches up and starts to scratch behind her ear. "It's been so long. I have so missed you." Del is speaking to Veda in a low voice, and with each neigh and snort it's clear Veda understands and is communicating back. With her head, Veda gives Del a hard push, and Del laughs. "I can't ride you now! I wish I could. My beautiful, brave Veda."

Livia watches as Del strokes Veda's mane. *I can't deny I feel a twinge of jealousy watching them reconnect. I know my father bred Veda as a special gift for my mother and they were very close, but they have been apart for seventeen years. Veda has been my closest friend for my whole life, and yet she was so quick to go to Del. It stings to see how much she cares for Del and how tender Del is with her. Del shows more affection to Veda than to Lex or me. Maybe it's easier for her.*

"How is this possible?" Livia asks Waslo.

Waslo clears his throat. "I arranged for Veda to be taken from Helix right after you so unceremoniously departed the island."

"Why?"

"Because without you, she wouldn't be safe. The High Council would most likely have taken her and performed experiments on her. She is one of your father's greatest genetic achievements. I knew she had to be removed quickly. Ephraim had the transporter, a vehicle big enough to move her, and a place where she could be concealed. We acted quickly and got her off Helix."

"Doesn't anyone wonder where she went?"

"I filed a report that she was gravely injured in your escape from Helix and had to be euthanized. According to my report, her body was destroyed."

"That was clever."

"As you can imagine, by necessity, I am quite a good liar."

"I don't have to imagine it," says Livia, giving Waslo a small grin. "Can Veda come to the Outlands?"

"I can't imagine how we could get her there. Moving her here was risky, but getting her down to Rock Bottom and out through the tunnel would be impossible."

Livia sighs. "I suppose that is true."

"At least she is safe. For now that is all we can do." Waslo starts to walk over to Del and Veda.

"Yes," says Livia, as she walks beside him. "Thank you for protecting her."

"Perhaps someday we will figure out a way to get her out of Indra."

"That would be wonderful. She would love the Outlands. There is so much space. We could ride for hours."

Ephraim's voice comes over the household communication system. "Waslo, Livia, Delphia, please meet us in the vehicle hangar. The team going to the dam is ready to leave."

"We need to go," says Waslo. "You'll have to say your good-byes."

Del spends one more moment looking into Veda's eyes, then Veda whinnies. Del nods sharply and steps back.

Veda turns to Livia and dips her head to nuzzle Livia's hand. With her other hand, Livia strokes Veda's muzzle.

"I will miss you, girl, but we will see each other again." Livia hugs Veda's strong, graceful neck and then releases her. Livia looks into Veda's eyes. "Soon, girl. Soon." Veda stamps a hoof once and then canters back into the green maze of trees.

"For now," says Waslo, "we must leave her safely shrouded in Ephraim's jungle."

Livia and Del follow Waslo into the vehicle hangar, a giant space with a high ceiling filled with rows of speeders and other hovercrafts, including two small PCF patrollers. Everyone has changed into new PCF uniforms, even those not going on the reservoir mission. Lex, Kane, and four rebels stand next to the six closest speeders, making their final checks.

Livia looks at Lex inspecting her speeder. *My sister is so strong. I can sense her determination. She will not fail. She is so important to me, nothing can happen to her.* Livia's eyes move to Kane, prepping his speeder. *And Kane. This is the man I love. He must come back to me. I wish I was not being separated from the two of them, but it must be this way. They have to be cautious. Are they capable of caution? I just want them both to be safe.*

Livia walks over to Lex and puts her hand on Lex's shoulder. "Please be careful. Don't be a hothead."

"That's when I do some of my best work," Lex says with a smile.

"Be serious," says Livia, her face sober. "You and Kane are the most important people in my life. Please keep each other safe. Promise me."

Lex nods. "I promise."

Livia hugs Lex. Reluctantly, Lex gives in to the hug. *Livia is so fierce. She's not some weak island Airess. She is surprisingly strong. How can she also be so tender?*

"Be safe," Livia says as she breaks the hug. "You promised."

"Yes, I will."

Livia walks over to Kane. "I'm nervous. I don't like you and Lex being away from me. I made her promise to be safe. Do I need to make you promise too?"

"I will do everything I can to complete this mission and come back to you. I'll try to keep Lex out of trouble, if I can. And I won't do anything rash."

"That is all I ask," says Livia.

Kane hugs her. "I'll miss you."

"I'll miss you more," says Livia, her face pressed into his neck.

Zavier saunters over to Lex and points to the still-embracing Livia and Kane and says, "Lex, do you need a hug?"

"You will regret taking one more step toward me."

"You sure you aren't going to miss me?" Zavier asks with a smirk.

"Oh, I'm sure."

Zavier shrugs and turns to Livia and Kane. "Time to break it up, you two."

Livia and Kane end their hug with a kiss.

Ephraim walks over to Kane. "I'm so sorry I had to keep this from you for all these years. It was too dangerous for you to know that I was a rebel when you were young. But I'm glad you know now."

"It was necessary. I can see that. It just meant that we were both alone."

Ephraim puts his hand on Kane's shoulder. "I'm very proud of you. Be safe."

Lex, Kane, and the four rebels mount their speeders and start them up. The speeders lift up off their stands, hovering about two feet above the floor. Ephraim pushes a few keys on a wall-mounted pad and a large door at the far end of the hangar retracts.

Del steps to Lex sitting on her speeder, getting ready to put on her helmet. Her tone matter-of-fact, Del says, "You, Kane, and this team are Rock Bottom's best hope."

"That's not much of a pep talk," says Lex.

"It is the truth," says Del. "I have no doubt that you will be successful. The plan is solid, but there are bound to be events that are unexpected. Just be smart, as I know you are. I wish I could have kept you with me and watched you grow. Though I have no right to be, I am proud of you."

"That was a little better," says Lex.

"Do what you must to destroy the dam."

"Yeah, I got it, or everybody dies."

"Precisely," says Del. "When you've blown the dam, my team will get you back to the colony. After our mission at the air filtration plant, we are going back to Rock Bottom and out through the tunnel. So we won't see you for a few days."

"Through the tunnel? Better you than me. That is a tough trek."

"I hope all goes well on both our missions. Good luck. Now, go."

Lex is the last of the team to put her helmet on.

Lex says over her helmet comm to the team, "Up and out."

She guns her speeder and takes off, racing through the open hangar door. The rest of the team follows behind her. They burst out of the canopy of trees on the island and into the open sky. As she pulls away from the island, Lex thinks, *I don't believe in destiny, but I will do whatever it takes to stop this flood. I just told Livia I would be safe, but I don't know if can keep that promise. I have to stop this from happening.*

Lex says over her comm, "We've got a long ride. Let's see what these things can do."

Kane responds, "We'll follow your lead. We're PCF. No one will mess with us. Let's have some fun."

"You read my mind," says Lex.

She accelerates to top speed, and the team follows close behind. They whip past huge, beautiful islands with manicured gardens and ornate sparkling houses. They weave around hideous maintenance rigs that hover close to islands doing various repairs. The rigs look like they are made of haphazard pieces of junk that could fall apart at any moment.

Lex looks at the city below, miles of tall, brilliant airscrapers and skytowers. *I used to think this was what I wanted. The PCF. The city. Now I can't wait to get back to the Outlands, the true open sky. Not this trap. This lie.*

As Lex's team streaks across the sky, she says over her comm, "These buildings are impressive, but I prefer the trees of the Outlands."

"Yeah," says Kane, "I'll take green over the steel and plexi. Now that I know more about the real Indra, it's pretty ugly."

Chae cuts in, "There is something wrong with my speeder. It's losing power."

Lex looks back and sees that Chae's speeder is starting to hitch and buck, then it stalls and starts to drop down. Chae is thrown off his speeder and is falling.

Lex yells, "I got him!"

She expertly maneuvers her speeder under Chae, and he grabs onto the back. The speeder is severely destabilized with Chae's weight and momentum pulling the back of the speeder sharply down. Lex wrenches the speeder into a dive to compensate. Chae holds tight, his body flung back and forth. Lex is able to bring the speeder back under control and levels off. Chae pulls himself up onto the seat behind Lex.

"Thank you," says Chae, just catching his breath.

Lex says, "I thought I lost you there."

"Same here," says Chae.

Kane pulls up beside them. "Are you both all right?"

"Yeah," says Chae, "I almost lost my rations!"

"To be safe, let's drop down," says Lex.

She leads the team down to street level, and they speed through the maze of gleaming buildings.

40

In the lab, Ephraim stands in front of the remaining group. "The mission at the air filtration plant is not as complicated as the mission at the dam, primarily because you don't have to get out of the city. It shouldn't take as long either." He pulls something small out of his shirt pocket. He holds up a thin silver square between his thumb and index finger and explains, "It is relatively simple. Delphia will install this at the regulator. It is programed to reduce the additive over the next forty-eight hours. I've already shown her how to attach it."

Livia asks, "Where is the air filtration plant?"

"There are actually many air filtration plants throughout the city," says Roscoe, "but there is only one control center. That's where we're going. It's in the Hub."

"Yes," says Ephraim, "you'll go to the control center and Delphia will patch this in at the primary air regulator. It will instruct all the plants to decrease the additive."

Roscoe adds, "We have an ally who works at the plant. He will get us in."

"So it's back down to the Hub," says Livia. "How many of us are going into the plant?"

"A team of four will go," says Roscoe. "It will be Del, Zavier, Enzo, and Livia. Luther and I will stay behind. Del, are you comfortable with that team?"

After a barely perceptible hesitation, Del says, "Yes."

"All right," says Roscoe. "We should head out."

Ephraim hands Del the thin silver square. "This is for you, my lady."

Del puts it in one of the side pockets of her PCF uniform.

"Thank you, Ephraim," says Del. "You have done outstanding work."

"Thank you for the compliment," says Ephraim, giving Del a wide smile. "One can accomplish quite a bit with unlimited funds and no distractions." He pats Del's hand and then says to the group, "Let's get you on your way."

Ephraim hurries out of the lab, leading everyone back through the house to the front entrance. Roscoe and Luther are up at the front of the group, right behind Ephraim. In the center of the group Zavier and Enzo walk with Becka, while Livia walks next to Del, trailing behind everyone. Livia can sense Del's concern and hesitation. *Is she worried about me? Maybe that I should not be going into the plant with them?* Livia looks at Del and sees that she is looking at Enzo walking a few paces ahead of them. *She is thinking about Enzo. She must be worried that he shouldn't go with us, perhaps because he is young and impulsive. Those concerns are warranted. He is immature and unpredictable.*

They make their way to the transporter. Roscoe opens the transporter door, then turns to Ephraim. "Thank you, Ephraim." The two men shake hands. "We have a real chance to stop this, but only because of you. As always, we owe you so much."

"I hope this all works," says Ephraim. "Good luck, my friend."

Roscoe breaks the handshake and climbs into the transporter. Both Becka and Luther say, "Thank you, sir," to Ephraim as they pass him and climb in behind Roscoe.

As Enzo steps up to the transporter, Ephraim says, "It was nice to finally meet you, Enzo. Roscoe talks of you and your brother every time he comes to Viridans. I was under the impression Jules would be with you and your mother."

"He would have been," says Enzo, glancing back at Livia, "but he was injured and had to stay behind."

“That is terrible news,” says Ephraim. “Will he be all right?”

“I think so,” says Enzo. “It was a nasty zinger slash. For a while, it looked like he would lose his leg. But I guess our good healing genes are pretty powerful. Neither of us had ever had such a serious injury before, so there was no way to know, but it seems he will be all right.”

“That is good to hear,” says Ephraim.

“With everything you’ve done,” says Enzo, “helping the rebels, inventing stuff, the virus. You’re pretty strato, sir.”

“Well, thank you,” says Ephraim as Enzo climbs into the transporter. “I’ve never been called strato before. I quite like it.”

Zavier steps to Ephraim and says, “I have to tell you, I did not know Kane was your son. I was charged with bringing him, along with Lex and Livia, to the Outlands, and I was really hard on him. I would have cut him some slack if I had known who he was, out of respect for you.”

Livia sees that Zavier and Ephraim need a moment and gingerly touches Del’s arm and says, “Let’s give them some space.” They stand a few paces away as Ephraim and Zavier talk.

“I suspect that was an extremely difficult trip,” says Ephraim. “From what I understand, he was very weak after being tortured in High Security Detainment.”

“Roscoe said he needed to be taken to the Outlands,” says Zavier. “It made no sense at the time. I understand now.”

“In retrospect, it might have made it easier if you had known who he was. I am grateful you helped him.”

“For you, I would have carried him to the Outlands on my back.”

Ephraim laughs. “I’m glad that was not necessary.”

Zavier gives Ephraim a respectful nod and climbs into the transporter while Livia and Del walk up to the transporter.

Ephraim says to Del, “It’s been so good to see you again, beautiful lady.” Ephraim hugs Del.

Del smiles. “Thank you for all you have done for the rebels. I know it has been difficult and lonely.”

"It has been hard but worth it. When Armand was taken, it fell to me to do what I could."

"He would be proud of you," says Del. "You were always one of his smartest, dearest friends."

Ephraim kisses Del on the cheek and says, "Until we see each other again."

"Until then," says Del, and steps into the transporter.

Ephraim says to Livia, "A pleasure, my dear Livia. I hoped I would meet you and your sister one day. I'm happy we've had this brief introduction."

Livia takes Ephraim's hands in hers. "It's been an honor to meet you, Ephraim."

"I hope to see you both again. Perhaps I will come join you and Kane in the Outlands, as soon as my usefulness here is exhausted."

"Everything you have done for the rebels is amazing. I'm still adjusting to the idea that you are Kane's father."

"I can see how you and my son feel about each other," says Ephraim with a smile.

Livia stammers, "I, or I should say we . . ."

"Don't be embarrassed," says Ephraim, patting her shoulder. "Love is beautiful. I'm glad he is happy. We are all entitled to some small amount of happiness, though it is not always possible."

With a smile, Livia says, "I hope we all find more than just a small amount of happiness." She gets into the transporter and sits next to Del.

"We're all in, Becka," says Roscoe, closing the transporter door. "Let's go."

The transporter lifts up into the air. In moments they have broken through the overgrown trees of Viridans and are in the bright, clear sky of Indra, leaving the island behind. Sitting next to Del, Livia can feel her tension, though it is subtle. *Is she masking her emotions? Maybe she is trying to hide her apprehension about Enzo.*

Del puts her hand on Livia's knee and says, "Pull back, Livia. You don't need to be in my head. What I am thinking about or feeling is not your concern."

"Yes. I'm sorry," says Livia, flushed and embarrassed. "I didn't mean to pry."

"I can feel you focus on me," says Del. "I'm sure it is a longstanding habit to sense, almost probe, those around you, but everyone needs their privacy. Probably no one but Jules and me will be able to feel you sensing them. His gift is quite strong, like yours, but as I told Jules when he was young, you have to work to keep it in check."

"I understand," says Livia.

"What you felt before," says Del, "when we were walking to the transporter, it is complicated. A mother can feel concern and confidence at the same time. I'm not trying to hide anything from you, but I am not open for you to judge. I will respect your privacy. Please extend me the same courtesy."

"Of course," says Livia.

Del pats Livia's knee and takes her hand away.

Livia sits quietly and ponders, *Del could feel me studying her emotions. She and Jules both have this heightened gift to sense people, but apparently Enzo doesn't. Like Lex, he doesn't feel people's emotions. She is right, I have always sensed everyone around me. It is an instinct. But before my chip was removed, it was weak by comparison.*

The transporter quickly drops down into the city and Becka weaves through the maze of buildings. Before long they speed through the PCF lane of Horizon Checkpoint with the siren blaring and enter the Hub. Becka navigates with confidence, driving the transporter through the complex traffic moving farther and farther down into the Hub, sporadically turning on the siren to encourage vehicles to get out of their way. She clearly knows where she is going.

They pass through the extensive Industrial Zone and enter the Habitation Zone, a sea of identical units stacked at least a hundred units deep that stretch out horizontally as far as the eye can see. Groups of people on foot travel along a system of open lifts and moving walkways to access their units. Speeders and small hovers buzz around, some pulling directly into units through sliding hatches, others attaching to docks outside their units.

Roscoe says to Becka, "The transporter can't stay here. I'll go in with them. Becka, you and Luther keep moving until I call you back."

As they get closer, Livia can see that the sliding doors of the units have an eight-digit code stenciled on them. Roscoe spots the unit he is looking for and calls out, "Right there, Becka."

"Got it," says Becka.

Roscoe says into his comm, "Aidan, we're outside your hab, lining up now."

Becka maneuvers the transporter parallel to the wall of units so the door of the transporter lines up with the door of the habitation unit and locks into place against the wall. Roscoe pulls open the transporter door, and the hab unit door opens a moment later. A short, middle-aged man with dark hair and a thin face wearing gray coveralls stands in the doorway of the unit.

"Your chip?" Roscoe asks.

"Interrupted," says the man. "I'm all clear."

Roscoe nods. "Everyone, this is Aidan. He works at the main air filtration plant and will get us in."

"Come in," says Aidan, as he moves back into the hab unit.

Del is the first out of her seat and through the open door of the hab unit, followed by Enzo, Zavier, and Livia.

"Luther, keep your comms open," says Roscoe as he leaves the transporter. "Contact me if anything comes up. Otherwise, I'll comm you when we need to be picked up."

"Yes, sir," confirms Luther, and pulls the transporter door closed as they start to pull away.

Roscoe closes the door of the hab unit, a small, narrow space. The six are forced to stand close together in single-file down the center of the hab unit. Roscoe and Zavier have to stoop to keep their heads from hitting the low ceiling. Livia looks around the room. The gray walls are lit by a single, round light attached to the ceiling near the door. A flickering glow comes from a screen embedded in the wall that seems to be malfunctioning. It flashes pages of text over changing images of Indra. The room is sparse, with almost no furniture, a retractable sleeper folded up against one wall, and a small utilitarian table and a single chair pushed against the other. There are no personal effects. *It is such a small space. This man can barely take two paces in this room. All the people in the Hub must live like this, or very similarly. There are so many who have so little while others have entire islands.*

Roscoe says, "I'll wait here, Aidan."

"Yes, all right," says Aidan. "Let's go. Keep some distance, so no one will know you are following me."

"I put the location of the plant in your comms," says Roscoe. "If you get separated, you can meet Aidan there."

"Yes, good," says Aidan. "Now, not too close."

Aidan leaves through a second door at the opposite end of the unit that opens into the interior of the hab complex.

Del turns to the group and says, "Remember, we are PCF. No one will question that. The uniforms and comms from Ephraim are all current issue. Just like when we crossed the compound with Lex and Kane, keep your heads up and faces forward. Try to look intimidating. No one down here is going to look at us too hard. I'm sure no Hubbers want to attract the attention of the PCF. Stay close together."

She heads out the door, and Enzo, Zavier, and Livia follow. They walk down a dingy corridor. It is empty except for Aidan, who is already surprisingly far ahead of them. At the end of the corridor, Aidan pushes through the door and merges into a steady flow of people dressed in various service uniforms, blue and gray uniforms and coveralls, a few scattered green coveralls, and the occasional white uniforms of household staff from the Islands. From a distance, they follow Aidan up a maze of moving walkways and escalators. As they walk, the crowd around them noticeably parts to let them pass. The Hubbers clearly want to be as far away from the PCF as possible, just as Del predicted.

The crowd becomes more dense, and Livia looks around at all the faces. *There are so many people, but their emotions are very low. Their chips must severely dampen their emotions. It is a terrible thing that the chips make people less of who they are. What right does Indra have to take people's very selves away from them?*

She looks forward and realizes that with so many people dressed in matching work coveralls, she has lost sight of Aidan. *Where is he? They are all in such similar clothes, I can't keep track of him.*

With a touch of panic in her voice, Livia says, "Zavier, I can't see Aidan."

"I can," says Zavier. "We're on track."

As they go up an escalator, they see two PCF officers coming down the opposite escalator. One of the PCF officers makes eye contact with Livia. She tells herself, *Project confidence. You are PCF. You are supposed to be here.* Livia gives the officer a curt nod and turns to look forward.

When the PCF patrol has passed, Del says to Livia, "Nicely done."

"Thank you," says Livia.

As they go farther up into the Hub, the crowds thin, and it is easier to see Aidan ahead.

Zavier looks at the screen of his comm. "It looks like we are almost there."

One escalator and two walkways later, Aidan walks down a side corridor and stops, waiting for them.

The group catches up to Aidan, and he tells them, "Follow me in. If the guard asks what you're doing here, let me answer."

Aidan leads them through the door of the plant and past a guard sitting at a desk just inside.

The guard on duty asks, "What's going on?"

Aidan answers, "They're here to inspect the pressure meters."

"Sure," says the guard, and lets them pass without much interest.

When the guard is out of earshot, Livia comments, "Security isn't very tight."

As they walk down the hallway, Aidan explains, "That guard's just there to make sure the workers come and go in an orderly manner. He's not there for the security of the plant, I guess since there has never been any attempt to sabotage an air filtration plant. I mean, why would someone? After all, everyone needs air." Aidan stops talking as two workers in blue coveralls walk down the hallway toward the group. Aidan nods at them as they pass, they nod back, then drop their eyes, trying to avoid making eye contact with the PCF. Aidan continues, "This plant has been in operation so long most people don't give it a second thought. People think it is for their protection. They don't realize it's part of their imprisonment."

Aidan pushes through a door and leads them down the center of a long, wide room with banks of monitoring equipment on both sides, lights blinking and text scrolling on all the displays, technicians in blue coveralls checking readouts. No one pays any attention to the group as they pass through.

Aidan indicates the rows of machines and says, "This is where we monitor the air quality, particulates, pollutants, and contaminants."

He pushes through another door and they enter a narrow empty corridor. As they walk, it becomes clear that the corridor is curved, like it is wrapped around a huge cylinder.

"The additive, PA127, is considered a fortification," says Aidan. "It has been in the air as long as anyone can remember. I think I'm the only one who even knows what it is. Pulmonary Accelerant 127. It's like fluoride or vitamin D in the water. Everyone just accepted years ago that it was necessary and good, and it has never changed. Most people in the Hub do their work assignments and never ask any questions."

"How are jobs assigned?" asks Livia.

"Mostly you are born into your assignment," says Aidan. "I could have been an *F* like my dad, but testing showed I was better suited for an *I* section assignment."

"I'm sorry," says Livia. "What do you mean an *F* and *I* section?"

"Right," says Aidan. "You are an Islander. You really don't know how things work down here, do you?"

"No, I don't, but I'd like to. And technically, I *was* an Islander. Now I am an Outlander and a rebel."

Aidan smiles. "I guess that's true. Well, everybody gets assigned a job with a section and rank. They all have color-coded uniforms. The letters stand for the section. *I* is *Industrial*, *F* is *Factory*. There's also *A*, *B*, *C*, *D*, *E*, *G*, *M*, *R*, and *S*'s."

Enzo says with a smirk, "Why don't you just say the whole alphabet?"

Del snaps, "Enzo, don't interrupt."

Aidan continues, "Hab units are assigned based on section and rank. I'm an I-4, so I qualify for a single hab unit. Below 4 and you are in the barracks. You have to be at least a Level 6 to qualify for access to the entertainment and sports feeds. I only get the Council feed on my hab unit screen. I wish I could just turn it off."

"What about cohabitants?" Livia asks.

"If your petition to cohabitate is granted," says Aidan, "you get the Level 2 hab unit. It's not much bigger than a Level 1 unit."

"And what about children?"

"If your procreation license is approved, and you actually have a kid, you get to move to a Level 3 unit. That's actually two rooms."

Livia asks, "Do you hope to cohabitate and have a child one day?"

"I hope to get out of Indra," says Aidan. "That's why I'm doing this. Then we'll see what happens."

"Yes," says Livia. *Their lives are so rigidly controlled. Such restrictions. They have almost no say over the way they live. I wonder if all the people of the Hub long to be free, as Aidan does.*

They walk for a while longer around the gently curving corridor, until finally they reach a door.

"The fan room is the only way to access the control panel," says Aidan. "I hope no one is scared of heights."

He opens the door into a vast circular room. They follow Aidan through the door and stand on a small platform built into the wall. The ceiling of the room has four giant fans encased in metal frames, the blades a blur as they spin. The floor a hundred feet below is a patchwork of smaller fans facing up to the ceiling, attached to ducts sucking the air out of the room and forcing it down into ducts that run out of the plant. The combined noise of the fans is deafening.

Aidan yells, "We have to get across to the control center." He points to a glass-encased space perched atop a pillar at the center of the fan room.

Livia yells, "How do we get across?"

"The shuttle," answers Aidan. "It runs on that track." Aidan points to the single, narrow beam that runs from the platform to the control center, suspended over the sea of spinning fans below.

Aidan points to the keypad mounted on the wall. "It's easy to operate once you're in it, but I don't have access to call the shuttle over."

"Yes. We know," yells Del. She pulls her communicator off her belt and a set of cables from one of the pockets in her jumpsuit. She links her comm to the keypad.

Del yells into her comm, "Ephraim, we are at the shuttle dock."

Ephraim's face pops up over the comm. "Give me a moment. It is antiquated. This may take longer than I thought."

Enzo moves to the edge of the platform, where the track is attached. He puts his foot on the track as if to inspect its strength. Livia watches as he steps out on to the narrow beam and starts walking across the track.

"Enzo!" Livia shouts. "What are you doing?"

Hearing Livia, Del looks up from the comm and sees Enzo calmly walking on the track, quickly closing the distance to the shuttle on the other side.

Del screams, "Enzo, come back!"

Enzo spins around on the beam to face them, waves his hand dismissively, and yells, "I'll just go get it."

Unexpectedly, Ephraim says, "Got it, you have access."

Immediately, the shuttle is activated on the opposite side and races across the beam headed right for Enzo.

"Enzo!" Livia screams, frantically pointing to the shuttle speeding toward him.

Zavier yells, "It's coming!"

Enzo spins back around to see the open-top shuttle coming at him. As it gets rapidly closer, Enzo takes a breath and starts to run toward it. When it is about to hit him, he leaps up and lands in the shuttle. He instantly hops up onto one of the seats inside and stands in the moving shuttle. He smiles as it pulls up to the docking platform, where the rest of the team is watching in stunned disbelief.

Zavier says to Livia, "That kid is crazy."

Livia nods but says nothing. *I don't need to sense Del to know she is furious.*

"What were you thinking?" screams Del. "That was not worth the risk!"

Enzo defends himself. "Ephraim was taking too long. I figured I could just go get it."

Del snaps, "Your impatience could have gotten you killed!"

Enzo jumps down from the seat and moves out of the way, and the group loads into the shuttle and sits down.

"And to point out the obvious," yells Aidan, "a mangled dead body in the fan room would be hard to hide."

Enzo smirks and yells, "Well, then, it's a good thing I'm not dead."

Aidan ignores Enzo, pushes a few buttons on a keypad in the shuttle, and it speeds away. They quickly reach the dock at the control center and the shuttle stops. Aidan steps out onto the small platform and pushes open the glass door. They all follow Aidan into the control center. As the door closes, the noise of the fans decreases significantly.

Zavier says under his breath to Enzo, "It was stupid, but it looked like a strato ride."

"It was," says Enzo, breaking into a broad smile.

"Enzo, your immaturity disappoints me," says Del, her voice cold. Enzo's smile disappears. "And, Zavier, I would appreciate it if you did not encourage his recklessness."

"Yes, ma'am," says Zavier. "Sorry."

Aidan points to the various screens. "These readouts are for all the different air filtration plants. Currently, they are all under local control. But since this is the main control center, from here we can send out new instructions to all the plants at the same time."

Del pulls the thin silver square out of her pocket and says, "Ephraim says this needs to go on the primary air regulator."

"Yes," says Aidan, pointing to one of the displays. "That's this one right here."

Del pries off the front display panel, revealing the internal circuit boards, a tangle of colored wires and tiny blinking lights. She pulls a thin cable out of a pocket. She plugs the connector on one end of the cable into the slim edge of the silver square and then deftly attaches the other end of the cable to the circuit board. Livia watches her. *She is so calm. So confident.*

Aidan asks, "If the displays all continue to read as normal, how do we know if it's working?"

Del puts up her hand and says, "Give it a minute." For a moment nothing happens, then, in soft green illuminated numbers, the figure 100 appears on the face of the silver square. "The percentage of additive will drop slowly over the next two days," says Del. Just then the display changes to 99. "There we go, it's working. We should go."

"Yes," says Aidan. He helps Del replace the front display panel of the regulator.

They ride the shuttle back to the docking platform. Everyone gets out and Aidan punches the button on the keypad to send the shuttle back over to the control center dock. As the shuttle speeds away, Aidan is yanked off his feet and pulled out onto the track, his sleeve caught in the door of the shuttle.

Aidan screams and flails as he is dragged almost twenty feet. His sleeve rips and he is released. He tumbles back, barely able to grab the beam before he falls. He frantically wraps his arms around the narrow beam, his legs swinging as he dangles. One of his shoes flies off and falls toward the spinning fans below.

Aidan shouts, "Help me!"

Without hesitating, Enzo yells, "Hold on!" and runs out onto the beam.

Zavier is only a second behind Enzo, running out to rescue Aidan. When Enzo reaches Aidan, he jumps over him, crouches down, and grabs one of Aidan's arms as Zavier grabs the other.

Panicking, Aidan yells, "I'm slipping!"

"We got you," reassures Enzo.

Aidan's shoe lands in one of the fans below and it grinds to a halt.

"Pull me up! Pull me up!" screams Aidan.

"On three," says Zavier. "One, two, three." Zavier and Enzo pull Aidan up onto the beam so he is draped across it, with the beam under his stomach.

Enzo pats Aidan's back. "You're all right."

They help Aidan up so he is straddling the beam. Zavier cautiously starts to walk back toward the docking platform. His eyes catch Livia's and he looks away, focusing on the door behind her. *He doesn't want to look down. I don't blame him. I can't believe they ran out there. Well, Enzo, I can believe he would, on impulse and full of adrenaline. But Zavier? There was resolve, obligation. He went because he knew Enzo couldn't pull Aidan up on his own. He was scared but went anyway. That was brave.*

"My shoe," yells Aidan as he inches along the beam in his sitting position, clearly afraid to stand up.

"Yeah, your shoe's gone," yells Enzo, who walks with confidence. He seems completely at ease.

Zavier reaches the platform and turns to help Aidan. Aidan lifts his arms. He is shaking. Zavier grabs his hands and pulls him up off the beam and onto the platform. Enzo jumps the last few feet onto the platform. Once on his feet, Aidan hurries through the door and starts walking down the curved corridor, his pace quick. Everyone follows close behind.

As the door behind them swings closed and the noise of the fans lessens, Aidan says, his words coming out in a rush, "My shoe. My shoe is a problem. The sensors are going to pick up that the fan has shut off. Someone is going to come investigate. We have to get out of here. What am I going to do about my shoe? Should we go get it?"

"No," says Del, "it will take too long."

"When they find it," says Aidan. "It won't take them long to figure out it is mine. They will know I was in the fan room, but they won't know what I was doing. I have to leave. Now."

As they approach the door at the end of the curved corridor, Del says, "Slow down. If we look like we are rushing, it will be suspicious."

"Yes," says Aidan.

"Well, him having only one shoe is already suspicious," says Enzo.

"It is," says Del. "Even more reason not to rush. We don't want to call attention to him."

Aidan slows his pace and pushes through the door that leads into the main monitoring room. There is a noticeable increase in activity. As they walk down the center of the room between the banks of monitoring equipment, a technician walks quickly past them to join a group clustered at one of the monitoring stations. One technician is pointing at the screen and says, "Yeah, number eleven. It's shut down. No warning, either. It just turned off."

Del says to Zavier under her breath, "Keep going. Get Aidan out of here."

"Affirmative," says Zavier with a nod.

"You're with me," Del says to Livia. "We're going to stall them a little."

Zavier and Enzo keep walking with Aidan as Del breaks off from the group and purposefully strides over to the cluster of technicians. Livia follows right behind her. In a piercing, authoritative voice, Del asks the group of technicians, "What's going on here? Is something wrong?"

The group of techs stops talking and turns to see the stern face of Del glaring at them. For a moment no one says anything, momentarily stunned to be facing two PCF officers.

Del points to the tech closest to her. "You. What's going on?"

"Oh, no, nothing," says the man, in a slightly nervous voice. "Just a small malfunction."

"What kind of malfunction?"

"A fan has shut off. It's not uncommon."

"Not uncommon?" barks Del. "So this is typical for this facility. Who is in charge of maintenance here? I'm going to need names."

"I'm sorry," the tech says, now quite flustered. "I misspoke. It is not common. It doesn't happen often. I just meant that it does happen, occasionally, very occasionally. It is not dangerous. We are taking care of it, Officer."

"See that you do, or this whole shift will have to be put up for review. I command you all to get back to your stations and review your work for the day. I'm going to be recommending this facility be put under a microscope. If anyone assigned here comes up short, it will reflect badly on all of you."

The group of techs scatter back to their posts as Del and Livia walk out of the room and into the next corridor.

In a low voice, Del says, "Well, that should give us a few more minutes before they get back on track and look into the fan. And they may be reluctant to report on Aidan if they think it will hurt them too."

"You were quite frightening," says Livia.

"Thank you. Now, the last obstacle, the security guard."

Del pushes through the door into the plant entrance area. The security guard is sitting at his post. He gives them a nod as they walk past.

Del returns the nod and says, "Keep up the good work."

They exit the plant, and Enzo, Zavier, and Aidan are nowhere around.

"They must have continued on to Aidan's," says Del calmly. She takes her comm off her belt and pulls up the location of Aidan's hab unit. "Got it. Let's go." Del strides off toward the walkway.

Livia matches her pace and stays by her side. As they move through the Hub, retracing the complicated route back to Aidan's hab unit, they pass hundreds of Hubbers on the walkways and escalators. Del meets the eyes of those who dare to look at them and the Hubbers quickly look away. *She is so impressive and intimidating. Can she ever be what I imagine a mother would be, or is this all I will ever know of her? I have seen a glimpse of her softer side. I just wish it wasn't so buried.*

41

Lex and her team speed through the buildings of the city, a tight group of five speeders, Chae riding on the back of Lex's speeder. *We've been riding through Indra for hours. I know the layout of the Middler level, but I never thought I would see it. Now I've passed through almost every zone. There were hardly any people on the streets in the Administrative Zone near the High Council Building, just a few people in gray suits like Waslo wears. A lot more people in the Education Zone, tutors and other instructors in their drab tan outfits. Lots of students clustered in groups dressed in the same color. I was lucky to get assigned to the PCF. Most all kids from the Orphanage ended up in a Hub factory. I was never going to be sent to Indra's School of Advanced Studies. That is only for Islanders and the Upper Indrithians.*

She looks at all the people milling about on the pristine walkways below. There are people in multicolored, finely made clothing, others in drab brown uniforms holding bags following behind them. *Those people in different colors must be Upper Indrithians. The ones in brown must work for them.* Lex watches a man in a brown uniform deferentially open the door of a luxurious transporter for a woman in a long dress of bright blue decorated with dark pink swirls. *This must be the Commercial Zone. The ones in brown must be the hover drivers, security guards, and other staff. The Uppers stroll along with the staff following behind them carrying whatever they bought with their overflowing debit accounts. They meet with their*

Upper friends for decadent meals and socializing. Their hover drivers standing by, ready to whisk them back to their islands.

Lex spots a man in blue coveralls picking up trash the Uppers have dropped on the walkway. She looks around and spots people in green coveralls tending to the beautiful trees and flowers that line the walkways and decorate the entrances of the buildings. *Sanitation and gardening crews keeping everything clean and beautiful. It's disgusting how these people live, blind to the people who work among them. And no thought to the people in the Hub who make it possible, much less Rock Bottom. I bet they wouldn't care if they knew what the Council was planning. In fact, I'm sure they would support it.*

Kane's voice comes over the helmet speaker. "Hey, Lex, on your right, that is the zip ball arena. Bet you would have been a dangerous player. You could have been recruited to play if you weren't already assigned to the PCF."

They pass the tall, circular building.

"My Recruiter was happy he found a kid in the Orphanage he could place in the PCF. I bet he got a debit bonus." Lex checks their location on her helmet display. "Finally, we're getting close," she announces over the helmet comm.

Kane says, "We can't approach the gate with two riders on one speeder. That would never be protocol."

"Right," says Lex. "Chae, I'm going to drop you off."

"Not a chance," says Chae, sitting on the back of Lex's speeder. "Matson, I outrank you. I'm taking your speeder. You know your way back to Rock Bottom."

"Yes, sir," says Matson.

Lex steers the speeder into an unpopulated alley in between two buildings. She stops the speeder, and the team pulls up behind her and stops. "You sure, Chae?"

"I'm one of Roscoe's top guys. I can't opt out of the mission. It's a matter of honor."

Chae jumps off the back of Lex's speeder and runs over to Matson's speeder, who has already gotten off. "Sorry, Matson. Roscoe would have my hide if I came back and hadn't seen this mission through."

"Yes, sir. That's true," says Matson. "I'm going to tell him you stole my speeder after an unfair battle of strength in which you cheated."

"He'll like that," says Chae with a grin barely visible through the dark visor of his helmet. "Roscoe loves a good story." Chae grabs the handles of Matson's speeder and hops on. "Ready."

"Matson, give Chae your explosives and remote charges," says Lex. "We don't want to be short." Matson pulls them out of a pocket and hands them over to Chae. "Now, Matson, the key to looking like a PCF officer is attitude. Think serious and impatient. Don't make eye contact, like you don't have time to worry about what the citizens around you are doing 'cause you have to get somewhere and can't stop to hassle them. People will probably try to avoid you. Good luck."

"Thanks," says Matson.

"And remove your helmet and leave it here," adds Lex. He nods and pulls off his helmet.

Lex hits the accelerator and speeds off, and the team follows, leaving Matson standing in the alley looking determined.

As the team of five approaches the entrance of the North PCF Compound, Lex says, "The guards at the entrance will remotely check our uniform transponders to make sure we have clearance."

The team rides up to the entrance gate and pulls to a stop. There are four PCF guards posted at the entrance in a booth with front and side windows. One of the officers looks up at them and then down at a screen. For a long moment, nothing happens.

Over the helmet speaker, Amia says, "I feel like this is taking too long."

"This is standard protocol," snaps Lex. "Stay off the comms."

Lex's mind races. *If these transponders don't check out, we are going to need to get out of here fast.*

They sit for another minute, then slowly the large gate rolls to the side and the PCF officer in the booth waves them through. They pass through the entrance and ride their speeders into the compound.

"Look for a parking facility for these speeders," says Kane.

"There's one up head on the right," says Lex. "I saw it on the map. Follow me." Lex leads them to an automated speeder parking facility.

"Ride straight into a stall," instructs Lex.

"And leave your helmet clipped on the handle," adds Kane.

They all park their speeders in empty stalls. When they step back, the speeders are automatically pulled away into a stacking hangar, housed with hundreds of other speeders.

"Stay in formation," says Lex. "It's all about attitude." She and Kane take the lead, as they go deeper into the compound.

They put on an air of confidence as they navigate through the base toward a huge building at the very back edge of the compound.

"The gate is in that building," says Lex. There is a pair of PCF officers standing sentry at the entrance, a set of double metal doors. "Let me do the talking."

As they approach the gate, Lex says under her breath, "We're going to stop in ten paces and stand at attention. One, two . . ." Lex's voice goes quiet. When they hit their tenth step, they all stop and stand rigid. *I can't believe that worked. Here we go.*

In a loud, clear voice, Lex says to the officer on the right, "Onsite inspection team reporting as ordered, sir."

The officer asks, "Ordered by who?"

"Lieutenant Hauser," says Lex.

The officer says, "You better hustle. He came through with his unit an hour ago," and pulls the door open.

"Yes, sir," says Lex. "Thank you, sir." Lex strides through the huge metal door with Kane at her side and Chae, Parker, and Amia following behind her. *Blast! Lieutenant Hauser is out at the dam. I only used his name because he is the highest ranking person I know, but he is actually there. We can't turn back. It would be too suspicious. Plus, Hauser will hear about us coming through this gate when he gets back whether we abort now or not. We'll never get another chance. We have to blow the dam before anyone knows what's going on. If we run into Hauser, we can't let him get word to the Council.*

Inside they see the building is a giant warehouse of construction equipment. They walk on the yellow line painted on the floor, passing massive machines that are covered in dust. *This must be the equipment they used to repair the reservoir. Some of it, anyway.*

Though it is several hundred feet away at the far end of the warehouse, Lex can see that the yellow line is leading them to a security station. There is a PCF officer posted in a booth identical to the one at the entrance. The booth is next to a reinforced metal door, guarded by two additional PCF officers with blasters drawn, one next to the booth, the second on the other side of the door.

Keeping her voice low, Lex says, "Our fugitive faces haven't set off any alarms. Waslo's friend must have done a good job of tricking Archive security. I hope the clearances your dad set up work, or this is going to get messy."

"They worked at the entrance," says Kane. "He seemed to know what he was doing."

"Well, one of his speeders did drop out of the sky," says Lex.

"Maybe he didn't expect us to push them to their limit in the first five minutes."

"Maybe," Lex says. "If the clearances are no good, we'll know soon enough."

Kane says with a smirk, "We can just shoot our way through if we have to."

"Yeah. Like I said, it could get messy. Let's hope it doesn't come to that."

When they are close to the security station, Lex quietly says to the team, "Stop in twenty paces."

On their twentieth step, the team stops and stands at attention a few feet from the booth.

Lex steps forward and says, "Security team reporting for duty."

The officer standing in the booth looks down, focusing on his display as their uniform transponders are scanned.

After a pause, the officer says, "They're cleared."

The officer on the opposite side of the door puts his blaster in its holster and opens the door.

Through the metal door, they enter a bright room with white walls. They follow the yellow line on the floor that now runs parallel to a long white counter to one side.

An officer behind the counter barks, "Halt." The team stops. The officer continues, "One at a time. Step forward onto the yellow square." He indicates to a yellow square on the floor. Lex steps forward. When she is in place, the officer pushes a few buttons on his console and looks at the display. A bright red light flashes on Lex's face.

Lex realizes, *This must be to deactivate the chip's perimeter defense function so our brains don't fry when we pass too far from the dome. Only I don't have a chip. None of us do. How am I going to explain that?*

The display the guard is looking at makes a shrill noise and his face takes on a puzzled expression. He looks up at Lex. "This is not standard protocol. I see your team just came through from the East Gate and you didn't go through full check-in procedures, but you are still clear to exit the dome."

She says with forced confidence, "Yes, sir." *Ephraim has us covered. I shouldn't be surprised.*

"East Gate should have checked you all back in properly," says the officer.

"Yes, sir," says Lex. "I believe they were trying to expedite things, knowing we were going right back out."

The officer turns to the group and says, "I still need to check you all through. Just in case." He turns back to Lex. "You're clear. Move down and get your breathing device."

Lex steps off the yellow square and Kane steps onto it. Lex moves down the counter to another officer, a female. The officer hands Lex a breathing device while the red light flashes on Kane.

"I'm sure you are familiar with the procedure," the officer says to Lex in a rehearsed monotone voice. "Switch on the breathing device before you exit the air lock or one of your team can do it for you while you convulse on the floor. Once the door on the other side of the air lock opens, you are no longer in the pure, protected air of the dome. You will be in the unfiltered, poisonous, polluted air of the outside. Do not remove your breathing device for any reason. The breathing device will filter the air you breathe, plus provide you with the essential air fortification you need. There is enough in the canister for you to breathe for six hours. Your team must return before that."

"Yes, ma'am," says Lex, taking the breathing device and putting it on over her nose and attaching the canister of additive to her belt. *She's obviously given that speech many, many times. I wonder how many times she said it today. How many men were in Hauser's unit? At least four. But that is a guess.*

"You can wait for your team in the air lock," the officer says, pointing to an open door at the end of the room. Lex nods and walks into the air lock as Kane steps up to the counter to get his breathing device.

The officer starts her speech over for Kane. "I'm sure you are familiar with the procedure. Switch on the breathing device before you exit the air lock . . ." The officer's voice gets quieter as Lex moves farther into the air lock, which is a large room with a thick glass door at the end. Lex moves all the way to the far door. She looks down at the canister of additive. In black stenciled paint, it reads PA127. *Essential fortification? So that's what they call the additive. Keeping up the lie. Though I'm sure these officers don't know any better. Only the Council knows it is safe outside. And the truth is no one living in Indra can breathe the air outside, so in a way it is true. It is not poisonous, but it might as well be.*

She looks closely at the breathing device. *It is exactly like the ones they gave us when we left the Last Outpost, only this doesn't have a regulator to turn down the amount of additive you're breathing. This only has two settings, on or off. The regulator must have been added. Probably something Ephraim designed.*

Kane walks into the air lock and stands next to Lex. He says, his voice low, "Almost there."

"Hauser's out there," says Lex, keeping her voice low as well. "He was in Rock Bottom last I knew. Do you think he knows what is really going on with the dam? What the Council is planning?"

"He must. Why else would he be out there?"

"I'm sure he thinks it's a great idea. He hates Rock Bottom."

"Maybe he's involved with the dam 'cause it's being used to rid Indra of Rock Bottom and the rebels, and that's his mission."

"Maybe," says Lex with a shrug. "Whatever he's doing out there, we can't run into him, but it is too late to turn back. I'm sure he knows all about me busting you out of High Security Detainment. We won't be able to bluff our way past him."

"Not a chance," says Kane. "I have a great idea, let's not run into him."

"Good plan. We have to blow the dam before he gets back here and realizes the dam has been compromised. We have to see this through."

Chae comes into the airlock and joins Lex and Kane by the far door.

"So Chae, you and the others need to switch on the breathing devices," says Lex. "Kane and I are already off the additive, so we are just going to leave ours off."

"I can't wait to be out of here," says Chae, "and off the additive."

When Amia and Parker are in the airlock, a glass door slides shut and a loud alarm starts to sound while a red light starts to flash. Over a speaker, the female PCF officer who gave them their breathing devices says, "Time to switch on your breathing devices. The door will open in ten seconds."

Amia, Parker, and Chae all switch on their devices while Lex and Kane mimic the same actions but do not switch theirs on. A few seconds later the far door slides open and there is a noticeable change in air pressure. Lex leads the team out to the dock where a low, rounded, high-speed transporter sits on a single track. Its cylindrical shape comes to a point at both ends to make it aerodynamic.

"Load up," says Lex.

They all climb into the transporter and sit down. Lex takes a spot by the door. Kane sits next to her.

He asks, "How many officers do you think Hauser will have out there with him?"

"No way to know," says Lex, and she hits the button by the door. The curved door hisses closed and the transporter hums to life and takes off, rapidly gaining speed. "I'd guess at least four, but let's hope we never find out."

The transporter heads down a steep grade, then levels off. *We came back to Indra and now we are leaving again. For good this time, I hope.*

"So who's this Hauser?" asks Chae.

"The highest-ranking officer I know," says Lex. "I threw his name out earlier and it worked, so I used it again, but I didn't expect him to be anywhere near here."

"There is no way he will believe we are PCF," says Kane. "We need to avoid him at all costs."

"Copy," says Chae with a nod. "If we do run into him, we can't hesitate to take him and whoever is with him down. We can't have the Council find out we know about the dam till we blow it and it's too late for them to stop us."

Lex and Kane nod.

After a moment, Lex can feel the transport angle up again. *We must have just passed under the dome and the irradiated zone around Indra.* "This thing is fast. I think we are already past the irradiated zone. That was a lot easier than our ride coming into Indra."

"You referring to me almost getting thrown out of the refuse hauler?" asks Kane. "Yeah, this is a lot easier."

After only a few minutes, the transporter slows as it pulls into the dock at the dam, the slight hum and vibration quieting.

Slipping out of her seat and down to the floor, Lex says, "We don't know what we're walking into, so everybody down." They all move to the floor. "I'll take a look around before we all head out." Kane readies himself to go with her. Lex puts up her hand. "Stay here. I won't go far. I'm just going to look." Lex taps her ear. Kane takes her meaning and settles back with the others. "Everyone sit tight and stay low." She hits the door release.

The door hisses open, Lex crouches, keeping low, and moves out of the transporter. The dock is a long, open space with pillars every twenty feet with a low ceiling. Lex can see far beyond the dock into the main machine room of the dam. She quickly moves across and ducks behind a pillar. She takes a moment and concentrates, listening. *I don't hear people, but this place is huge and the concrete walls of the dam are so thick. The water in the reservoir is absorbing the sounds from both inside and outside and bouncing them around. There are only muffled echoes. I can actually hear the water moving over everything else.* Lex focuses on her team in the transporter. *I can hear their breathing. The rustle of clothing. We will need to be careful. We need to place the explosives and get out of here without running into Hauser.*

Lex returns to the transporter and crouches down with the rest of the team. "It is really hard to hear very well in here. This place is huge, and the water is causing distortions. I can't hear anyone. No one close, anyway. Let's head down to Level 10, but once we're there, I don't think we should split up. It'll be safer if we stick together. It's too dangerous with Hauser here."

"Agreed," says Kane.

"Sure," says Parker as Amia nods.

"And don't forget I have Matson's set of explosives and charges," says Chae. "Only I don't know where he was supposed to set them."

"I do," says Lex. "Let's go." She heads out of the transporter, the team following behind.

42

Livia follows Del as she strides down the corridor toward Aidan's hab unit. When they reach his unit, Del gives two quick raps on the door and it flies open.

Aidan says, "Quickly, come in," as he steps out into the corridor and ushers Del and Livia into his unit, then steps back in himself and pulls the door closed.

From the other end of the hab unit, Roscoe says, "I'm glad you made it back safely. I've reprimanded Zavier for leaving the two of you behind."

"That was unnecessary," says Del, her eyes falling on Zavier, who looks uncomfortable. "I told him to get Aidan out of there, and he did. I didn't ask him to wait for us. If you are going to reprimand anyone, it should be me. I made the call."

"Regardless," says Roscoe, displeased, "I wish you had stayed together. Anything could have happened."

"Well, nothing did, so shall we go?" asks Del.

"There has been a development," says Roscoe. "Waslo sent word that the Council is bringing Armand out of the Archives. He said if we hope to rescue Armand, this may be the opportunity."

"Yes!" Livia exclaims. "Let's go get him."

"Wait," says Del. "I want to get him too, but what is the plan?"

"I have been working on one," says Roscoe. "Armand is in the Archive Detention Center in the High Council Building, the Spear. I have friends in place who will get us in. Once inside, we will meet up with Vippy. She is assigned there and will take us to Armand. Then we'll leave more or less the same way we got in."

"I will need more detail than that, but first I must say this seems like convenient timing," says Del. "Could it be a trap?"

"I don't see how," says Roscoe. "From what Waslo has said, the Council is unaware that we know about their plan to flood Rock Bottom and that it is imminent. They have no idea you are here or what we have been doing. They must be bringing him out so he can witness the extermination of Rock Bottom and Core Low."

"I don't know," says Del, her face placid.

Incredulous, Livia yells, "How can you be hesitating? We can save him!"

Del puts up her hand to quiet Livia. "I want to rescue Armand. More than you know. I'm just trying to be smart. We won't do him any good if we are impulsive and walk into a trap." Del asks Roscoe, "Could the Council have heard that The Twins were in Rock Bottom and that I was with them?"

Roscoe says, "Waslo said the Council doesn't know about The Twins in Rock Bottom or that you are in Indra."

"They don't know *yet*," corrects Del.

Roscoe nods. "You're right. The more time passes, the more likely it is the Council will hear about The Twins. Still, I don't think there will be a better opportunity to rescue him. At least we won't have to extract him from Archive stasis. If you think it is too risky, we can wait. We can return to Rock Bottom and head out the tunnel as planned. We can reassess in the Outlands."

"Wait? We can't wait!" Livia protests. "If we wait and the Council finds out about our big Time of the Twins rally in Rock Bottom, they will probably kill him. In fact, they probably brought him out of the Archives to kill him. They don't need him anymore. If he is no good to them as a geneticist and I'm beyond their grasp, why would they keep him alive?"

"That is my point," says Del. "I'm saying it feels like a trap. Why have they kept him alive all these years? If there was no hope he would work for them, then his only use is to draw us out."

"But Waslo says they don't know," argues Livia. "We can't leave him now. They will surely kill him."

"That does seem like the likeliest outcome," Del says matter-of-factly.

"What is wrong with you?" Livia screams. "Don't you have any feelings at all? You just admitted that they will kill him if we don't rescue him. We can't go back to the Outlands without him!"

"Please, keep your voice down," says Aidan anxiously. "These walls are quite thin. I don't have permits for visitors in my hab unit. I could be reported."

Roscoe says, "Aidan, you're not staying. You don't have much time before they come to question you about your shoe and the broken fan at the air filtration plant."

"Yes," says Aidan. "We should go."

Roscoe says, "Here is what I propose. Aidan and anyone who doesn't want to help rescue Armand, go with Luther on foot back to Rock Bottom. Whoever wants to risk it can come with me in the transporter to free Armand. We have a solid plan and two people on the inside, Waslo and Vippy, to help us pull it off. This may be our only chance because, as much as I hate to say it, I think the Council has no clear incentive to keep Armand alive. I would like to try to rescue him now rather than be cautious and let him be killed."

"Thank you, Roscoe," says Livia. "I'm going with you."

"I had no doubt," says Roscoe.

"I'm with you, sir," says Zavier.

Roscoe asks, "If you're sure?"

"Yes," says Zavier.

"I will come too," says Del. "But Enzo will go with Luther and Aidan."

"I will not," protests Enzo. "If there is a rescue mission, I'm on it."

Del does not look happy but nods her agreement.

"So it's settled," says Roscoe.

"It is," concedes Del.

"Let's go get my father," demands Livia.

Roscoe pulls out his comm. "Becka, we're ready to go."

Becka's slim face flickers over the comm. "On our way."

43

Lex and the rest of her team crouch in a concrete corridor around the corner from an elevator labeled Level 60. "I think we should take the stairs," says Lex.

"All the way down to Level 10?" asks Amia, shocked. "That's fifty levels."

"The elevator will be faster," says Parker. "Don't we want to get in and out as fast as possible?"

"Yes," says Lex. "The plan was to take the elevator, but with Hauser and who knows how many PCF officers here, we can't risk it. We don't want anyone coming to investigate why the elevators are moving. The stairs are our best option."

"I agree with Lex," says Kane. "We can't risk using the elevator."

"What if we parazip down the elevator shaft?" offers Chae.

"How?" asks Lex.

"We each have a single canister on our belt with five hundred feet of the microcord that Ephraim developed," says Chae, pulling a small cylinder off his belt. "The bottom fires a bolt that secures the cord to the wall. You open the release and the cord spools out so you rappel down at about half the speed of a free fall. Not really PCF standard issue, but he thought it might come in handy. I don't think that will be enough to get us all the way down to Level 10, but close."

Kane quickly calculates, "If the levels are eleven or twelve feet, five hundred feet should get us down to somewhere between Level 19 and Level 15. We can pry open the elevator on whatever floor we get to and take the stairs from there."

"I'll be able to hear if the elevators start moving below us. We should have enough warning to stop and get out of the way if we have to. Let's do it," says Lex.

Kane and Chae position themselves on either side of the elevator door and wedge their fingers into the seam between the two halves of the door.

"Ready?" asks Kane. Chae nods. "Go," says Kane, and they pull. The doors slowly slide open.

Lex and her team stand at the edge of the open elevator shaft and look down. There are small lights every few feet running down the side of the shaft, disappearing into the darkness below.

"That looks far," says Parker.

"Best not to think about it," says Lex.

"So shoot the bolt into the wall," says Chae. "Hook the canister back on your belt, then hit the release. It will automatically slow when it's getting close to the end."

Lex pulls her canister off her belt and with one hand holding onto the frame of the elevator, she positions the canister against the wall of the elevator shaft and fires the bolt. She pulls the canister back, and a thin cord spools out attached to the wall. She attaches the canister to her belt.

"You sure this will hold?" Lex asks, inspecting the incredibly thin cord.

"Ephraim made it," says Chae. "It will hold."

"Your dad is pretty amazing," says Lex.

"So I'm learning," says Kane.

Lex pushes the release on the canister and jumps into the elevator shaft. The air rushes past as Lex drops, the cord trailing out above her. The tight belt digging into her ribs. *Chae is right. This is not as fast as a true free fall, but still fast.*

Lex looks at the wall as she kicks off, rappelling down, watching the descending numbers painted over the elevator doors. *Already at 42, 41, 40. This is much faster than the stairs.* She looks down into the shaft. *It looks like it gets much darker. There are no running lights below. Are they off? No. Something is blocking the light. Something is in the shaft. It is the elevator!*

Quickly, Lex reaches down and closes the release on the canister. The cord stops and she is jerked violently. She hits the wall of the shaft with her shoulder and spins several times before she is able to stabilize herself, holding onto the cord and pressing her feet against the wall.

She looks down. "Blast!" *I almost crashed into it! I'm about twenty feet above the elevator.*

Lex hears one of her group coming and yells, "Stop! Close the release! Close the release!"

Kane zips past Lex fumbling with his canister. A few feet past her, he jerks to a stop and slams into the shaft wall. A moment later, Kane is still spinning when Chae and Amia zip down the shaft, one after the other. Both Lex and Kane yell as they approach, "Stop! Stop! Close the release!"

Chae closes his release immediately and jerks to a stop just above Lex. He bends his knees and pulls his legs up so he hits the wall with his feet. He spins away from the wall but is able to quickly stabilize himself. Amia speeds past Lex and Chae, groping for her release. She jerks to a stop right next to Kane. He deftly spins himself around and catches her before she hits the wall. His back slams into the wall with the impact, and he lets out a groan.

Catching her breath, Amia says, "Thanks. It's so dark, how did you know to stop?"

"The lights stopped," yells Lex. "Here comes Parker."

As Parker approaches, everyone yells, "Stop! Parker, close the release." Their voices blend together and Parker looks confused as he speeds past Chae and then Lex, yelling and waving their arms. Realization crosses his face and he reaches down to the canister on his belt as he passes Kane and Amia. He manages to close the release but only a foot above the elevator, and he slams into it. His body bounces hard on the roof of the elevator. Parker moans.

Chae yells, "Pulse the release, so you drop down a little at a time." He lets the release out on his cord and drops about five feet, then closes it again so he stops without jerking or spinning. Pulsing the release, they all lower themselves to the elevator roof.

Chae is the first to reach Parker. "How bad is it?"

"I don't think anything is broken," says Parker through clenched teeth. "But I slammed it core-low hard."

"We heard," says Kane, as he lands on the elevator roof followed by Lex and Amia.

"With all of you yelling," says Parker, pushing himself to a sitting position, "I couldn't hear what you were saying."

"Sorry," says Lex. "I should have realized all of us yelling at you would be too hard to understand."

"It was. If I'd hit with full force, I probably would have broken both my legs."

"Do you think you will be able to walk?" asks Chae, giving Parker a hand to get to his feet.

"My left is worse than my right, but I'll make it," says Parker, leaning on Chae for support.

"All right," says Lex. "So if the elevator is here, Hauser and his unit must be on this level. The only good thing about that is at least now we know where they are."

Lex crouches down and puts her ear to the hatch in the roof of the elevator. She listens for a long moment.

"Blast! This place is so noisy," says Lex, standing back up. "There is no one in the elevator or immediately near it, but that's all I can be sure of."

"Well, we can't stay here," says Kane. "I say we go. If we run into them, we all have blasters."

"Agreed," says Chae.

"Let's get this hatch open," says Lex. "I'll drop down first. Maybe I will be able to hear better from inside the elevator."

Lex and Kane pry open the hatch. She unhooks the canister from her belt and lowers herself down into the elevator. Suddenly she hears something. *It's muffled, but that is footsteps!*

Lex frantically motions to Kane and mouths "Hauser." She pulls herself back up. Kane and Amia slide the hatch into place just as Hauser and his team enter the elevator.

Kane motions to the group, points to the canister on his belt and unhooks it. The group follows his lead, pulling the canisters off their belts. Lex crouches down and puts her ear against the seam of the hatch.

"Water level in the reservoir is almost at the optimal level," says Hauser. "The Council will be pleased. I want to check one more reading. Take us down to fifteen."

Lex motions for the group to get down and hold on. Quickly, they all crouch as the elevator starts to move, rapidly gaining speed and dropping to Level 15, then coming to a smooth stop. Lex puts up her hand as she listens to Hauser and his unit leave the elevator. She waits for the sound of the elevator door closing.

"They're out," says Lex. "Let's go."

Lex and Kane remove the hatch and Lex lowers herself into the elevator, followed by Kane, Amia, and Chae. Parker comes down slowly, Chae practically catching him and placing him on his feet. Parker braces himself against the wall as he tries to stand on his own, wincing when he tentatively puts weight on his left leg. Chae ducks under Parker's arm to support him.

Lex listens at the elevator door for a moment. "Their footsteps have completely faded. If I can't hear them, they won't be able to hear us. The stairs are to the right."

Lex hits a button on the elevator panel and the door opens. Lex races out into the concrete corridor, followed by Amia, and ducks into the stairwell. Chae and Kane are on either side of Parker, his face contorted into a grimace as he limps between them. Their progress is painfully slow. Lex holds the door open. "Come on," she urges.

"I can't put any weight on my leg," says Parker as they slip past Lex into the stairwell. "Put me down," says Parker as Lex pulls the door closed. Kane and Chae carefully lower Parker to the floor, and he sits propped against the wall.

"Sorry, Parker," says Lex. "If you can't walk, you'll have to stay here."

"Yes, I'll only hold you all up," says Parker apologetically. "Take my explosives and remote charges," he says, fishing them out of his pockets and handing them to Lex. "I'm sure you know where they go."

"I do," says Lex. "Hold tight. We'll pick you up on our way back."

"Good luck," says Parker.

"Thanks," says Lex. She turns to the rest of the team. "Let's go."

They run down the stairs, their footsteps echoing up the massive stairwell. Lex's thoughts run as fast as her feet. *We lost Matson and now Parker. We're down to four. There are so many explosives to set, we're going to have to split up. Hauser is on 15, so he's out of the way for now. It sounded like they were going to leave, but I can't be sure he won't change his mind and stay. He could decide to inspect more levels. They could end up right on top of us on Level 10.*

They reach the door labeled Level 10 in black lettering.

Lex stops and puts her hand on the door. "I know I said we should stick together, but we need to get this done and get out of here. Hauser is on Level 15. I say we split up into teams of two so we can set the explosives as quickly as possible. Me and Kane. Chae and Amia. You two set your explosives, and Kane and I will set ours, plus Parker's and Matson's."

"We can take an extra set," says Chae. "Which are the farthest?"

"The ones Kane and I need to set are the farthest," says Lex. "We'll run right past the spots where Parker's and Matson's need to go. Yours are in the other direction. Just set yours and meet us back here."

"Got it," says Chae.

Lex opens the door and they run out of the stairwell. The ceiling on Level 10 is twenty feet high. Down the center of the enormous room are four huge antiquated generators, each fifteen feet high. Midway up the wall is a railed walkway supported by wide pillars. The walkway runs around the perimeter, with stairways at both ends descending to the floor.

Chae and Amia break off and run out of the room down a corridor while Lex and Kane run past the generators toward the far end of the room.

Lex points up at the walkway. "That's Level 11."

"Do you have a map of this whole place in your head?"

"Yeah. Don't you?" Lex teases.

"Nope."

"Lucky you're with me," says Lex, and smiles.

"I've always been lucky to be with you."

Lex picks up her pace. "Try to keep up," she says as she runs past the stairs and into the corridor that leads out of the generator room.

44

With Becka at the controls and Enzo in the copilot's seat, the PCF transporter streaks through the sky passing airscrapers and skytowers. Livia, Del, and Zavier sit in the back with Roscoe.

"Now," Roscoe says to Livia, "when you were last at the High Council Building, you and Lex were rescuing Kane. Lex crashed a stolen PCF patroller into the High Council Building and did a great deal of damage."

"Well," says Livia, "actually, *we* stole a PCF patroller. But Lex was the one who crash-landed it into the gardens and destroyed the fountain. It was impulsive, but it did work."

"It got you into the Spear," says Roscoe. "Although, if I recall, you had no exit plan. I'm just glad we came when we did and got you three out. That stunt raised concerns about security failures at the High Council Building. Since your breach, security around the Spear has been significantly increased. There is a wide no hover zone around the building. Only hovers with preauthorization can approach. They have a standing shoot-to-kill order on all unauthorized craft within fifty feet of the Spear."

"Do we have authorization?" asks Livia.

"No," says Roscoe. "We are getting in another way."

"Well, that's good," says Enzo from the front of the transporter. "Getting blasted out of the sky would be a bad plan."

"I agree," says Roscoe. "The rigs are our way in. More specifically, one of the building rig crews. With all of the damage Lex did to the gardens and the fountain, there are several rigs with full crews doing repairs on the Spear. There has been a crackdown on riggers because of the crew near Helix that went into a full-blooded rebellion to help you and Lex escape the PCF. All the rigs that work on the Spear were thoroughly vetted before they were allowed to get close. But one of the building crew rigs is manned by friendlies, and they are going to help us get in."

Becka maneuvers the transporter up to a building rig, one of many enormous haphazard looking structures floating close to the High Council Building.

Roscoe says into his comm, "Jo, this is Roscoe. We are on the west side of your rig."

The image of a dark woman with wild black hair says over the comm, "That was quick. You made good time."

"A PCF transporter has its advantages," says Roscoe. "Citizens just clear out of the way. Where should we dock?"

"We have a special spot just for visitors," says Jo. "Have your pilot pull that lovely transporter in between the red lines."

Roscoe asks, "The red lines?"

"Between the lines, it is not as it appears," Jo says mysteriously. "You know the trick."

Roscoe moves up to the front of the transporter and stands in the small space between Becka and Enzo.

"Red lines," says Becka. "I don't see any red lines."

They carefully study the jumbled patchwork of junk that makes up the rig, looking for the red lines, scrutinizing the hundreds of pieces of mismatched metal from dismantled hovers, deconstructed buildings, and leftover construction materials all welded together.

After a moment, Enzo says, "I got it. There." He points to two incredibly faint red lines near the lower third of the rig. The lines are horizontal with about twenty feet between them.

"Nicely spotted, son," says Roscoe.

Becka steers the transporter toward the lines and asks, "What does she mean 'It is not as it appears'? It looks like the rest of the rig."

"I think she means it is camouflaged," says Roscoe. "Like the overgrown plants of Ephraim's island, Viridans. It looks impenetrable, but it is just cover."

Livia, Del, and Zavier watch through the transporter windows as they get closer to the rig.

Zavier asks, "Is there an opening, or are we just going to crash into it?"

"You trust this woman?" Del asks.

"I do," says Roscoe.

Becka skillfully flies the transporter right up to the rig, aiming for the space in between the lines. It looks like they are going to crash into the rig, but when they reach it, the transporter passes through what appears to be solid metal.

"It's a projection," says Roscoe, a hint of relief in his voice.

Del asks, "Why didn't she just tell you that?"

"Jo likes to keep me on my toes," says Roscoe.

As they pass through the projected image, rays of light stream in through the windows of the transporter. On the other side of the projection, there is a hover dock. When the transporter has fully cleared the projection and is hidden inside the rig, Becka pulls to a stop at the dock. Roscoe pulls open the transporter door and a tall woman in blue coveralls with a warm smile is standing on the dock platform.

She laughs as Roscoe steps out of the transporter onto the platform, and attacks him with an aggressive hug. "You thought you were going to crash into my beautiful rig, didn't you?"

"Not for a moment," says Roscoe. "Everyone, this is Jo. We've known each other a long time."

"Too long," says Jo. The group follows Roscoe out of the transporter onto the platform. The inside of the rig is a huge, hollow space, hundreds of feet from top to bottom. The platform is affixed to the wall of the rig at about the halfway point. The vast open space in the center is crisscrossed by metal beams and flimsy bridges made of cables and pipes. Both above and below, a few people move around on the beams and bridges.

Livia looks around. *The last time I was on a rig, it was much different. I can't believe most of those riggers are dead. Hep, Durley. They helped Lex and me escape, and it cost them their lives. That rig was busy with people. This is quiet by comparison.*

"Doesn't the projection look good?" asks Jo. "I like to have a place for visitors to dock out of view. Nobody needs to know who all is coming and going from my rig."

Roscoe asks with a small grin, "Why, Jo, who's coming and going from your rig?"

"Never you mind," says Jo with a wink. "There may or may not be some unsanctioned trading going on here that the Council would not be happy about. Mostly, the PCF looks the other way if you don't make it too obvious. So I try to keep it out of direct view." Jo runs her fingers through Roscoe's hair. "A little more gray since I saw you last. You hardly ever visit."

Livia sees a flash of irritation pass over Del's face as Jo caresses Roscoe's hair then settles her arm casually around his shoulder. Roscoe looks a bit embarrassed. *Do Roscoe and this woman have a history? Del looks like she might kill her if she doesn't stop touching him.*

Roscoe says, "Thank you so much for helping us, but we need to get going. Our contact will be waiting."

"Yes," says Jo, and slaps Roscoe on the butt. "Enough chitchat. Let's get your team over to the Spear."

Roscoe turns to Becka. "Stay here. We shouldn't be too long, but keep your comms open just in case."

"Yes, sir," says Becka with a nod.

"Come on," says Jo. She starts walking, her pace fast. Roscoe and the team hustle to follow her. "My crew is all over at the Spear working, only a few underagers on the rig right now. We'll put you all in crew coveralls over those PCF uniforms and send you over in the shoot. Once you've done what you need to do, and I don't need to know what that is, you'll come back on the scrap conveyor."

Livia asks, "What is a scrap conveyor?"

"It's a conveyor belt that runs from the work site back to the rig," explains Jo, as she leads the group across a rickety bridge made of old cables and pipes.

The bridge wobbles and sways as they walk. Livia looks down through the widely spaced pipes of the bridge, holding tight to the cables that serve as handrails. *This doesn't seem safe at all. I could slip right through the pipes of this bridge.*

Jo continues, "Most jobs, there is a lot of scrap metal or other junk from the demolition. My crew loads it onto the conveyor and it comes back to the rig. It's good for trading or fixing up the rig."

"So we are coming back with the trash," says Enzo.

"Yep," says Jo. "We have a bit of a climb. If you don't like heights, don't look down."

Jo starts up a rusty ladder bolted to the wall. Enzo hops up on the ladder behind Jo.

"How far up are we going?" asks Livia.

Jo shouts back, "Five levels. We have to get to the launchpad."

Livia tries to hide her distress. *Five levels? How high is that? Enzo doesn't seem the least bit concerned.* She watches Roscoe mount the ladder behind Enzo. *Roscoe too. He looks like he does this every day.*

Del whispers to Livia, "Just put one hand in front of the other. We will be there before you know it."

Del mounts the ladder and starts climbing. Livia stands, not moving.

Zavier says, "I'll be right behind you. You won't fall, Airess."

"I hope not," says Livia, and steps onto the ladder.

They climb up almost a hundred feet, passing several bridges and beams that connect with the ladder and lead to other parts of the rig.

At the fifth bridge, Jo yells down to the group, "This is us," and steps off the ladder onto a platform with a wide-open hatch where a slight girl of about twelve with dark skin and black hair is waiting. "This is the launchpad."

One by one, they reach the platform and step off the ladder.

Jo explains, "At the start of a shift, the crew lines up and our launcher, Teddie," she gestures to the girl on the platform, who nods, "sends them out to the site."

Is Teddie Jo's daughter? Livia wonders. *Riggers must have children, and they would grow up on the rig. I'm sure the unstable bridges and dizzying heights don't worry her.*

"It's not hard," says Teddie, her young voice high and sweet. "You sit on a sling," she says, pulling over one of several slings dangling from a metal bar extending from the wall. The sling is made of a pipe suspended between two cables that come to a clasp at the top. Teddie attaches the clasp to a thick cable anchored on the inside of the rig that runs out of the open hatch and across to the Spear. The sling hangs right in front of the hatch. "I push the release and you zip right over."

Livia is alarmed. "We sit on a pipe and fly across the open air with nothing holding us in."

Teddie clarifies, "Well, you hold onto the cables."

"I can't do this," says Livia. "This is absurd."

"You don't have to come," says Del. "We can go get Armand and you can stay here."

Jo says, "Look, I know it seems dangerous, but it's not really. We move a crew of twenty-five over and back every day with no problems. Really, all you have to do is hold on."

Roscoe says, "I believe you can do this, and I think you will be happy you were a part of rescuing your father."

Livia takes a deep breath. "You are right. I can do this."

"All right," says Jo. "Let's get you all in coveralls."

Teddie hands out coveralls from a stack, and they all pull them on over their PCF uniforms.

"I need an extra coverall," Roscoe says to Teddie. "We're bringing back an old friend with us."

"Sure," says Teddie, and hands Roscoe another pair. He folds and tucks them into the front of his coveralls, then zips up.

"Who first?" asks Jo.

With no hesitation, Enzo steps forward and says with enthusiasm, "I'll go first."

"All right," says Jo.

Teddie grabs the sling hanging in front of the open hatch. "Come on," she says to Enzo, who practically leaps over to her. Teddie helps Enzo get into the sling. She holds it up so he can duck in between the cables, then lowers the pipe behind him. Enzo sits on the makeshift pipe seat and grabs hold of the cables. "There will be a bit of a jolt when you get to the end. Hang on and enjoy the ride."

"I plan to," says Enzo with a smile, his feet hanging out of the hatch.

Teddie hits a release and Enzo is propelled away from the rig.

Enzo lets out an energetic scream, "Wahoo!" that quickly becomes faint as he is whipped away from the rig toward the High Council Building.

Livia listens to Enzo's scream fading away. *Of course he loves it. This is fun for him. I wish I could just enjoy it like him. I do like speed. I relished riding Veda as fast as she could go, the wind in my face, my hair flying behind me. But this is not like the speed of riding Veda. This is different. On Veda I felt safe. There was ground under her, under us. I can't believe I jumped from Helix to a rig with Lex. That was frightening, and I was able to do it. I can do this.*

Teddie grabs another sling and slots it into place. Roscoe goes next, followed by Zavier, both casually shrugging into the sling and zipping off without a word.

Del asks, "Do you want to go next or last?"

"I think I would like to go last," says Livia with a tight smile.

"Or not at all?" teases Del.

"No," says Livia, "I want to be there when we rescue my father. I can do this for him. He has done much harder things for us."

"I think it will make him happy to see you," says Del, "but you don't have to prove anything to anyone. If you can't do it, don't."

There is a part of her that thinks I am weak. It is not unreasonable to be scared. I think it is unreasonable to act like this is perfectly normal and safe. I am not weak. "I will see you over there," says Livia, determined.

Del climbs into the sling. "See you over there."

Teddie hits the release and Del zips away.

While Teddie gets a sling in place for Livia, Jo says, "You are a skinny thing. You have nothing to worry about. I have guys three times your size that zip across twice a day. You will be fine. You can close your eyes if you want."

Livia ducks in between the cables and sits on the pipe. She grips the cables with all her strength. She can see straight out of the gaping open hatch. The High Council Building is at least two hundred feet away. *Oh, blast, this is so high. There is nothing holding me in, and just a thin cable stretching across the void. I will not look down, but I will not close my eyes, either. I am strong. I will hold on and I will not fall.*

Jo asks, "You ready?"

No, but I may never be. "Yes," says Livia.

Teddie hits the release and Livia speeds away from the rig. Instantly, the rushing air whips her hair back and stings her face. Livia reassures herself, *You will be there in less than a minute. Hold on and don't look down.*

In moments, Livia is yanked to a stop at the High Council Building. The sling jolts violently and Livia's grip slips and she flies forward out of the seat. Zavier is standing in the perfect position to catch her midair.

Putting Livia on her feet, Zavier says, "Jo sort of played down the landing. I hit the ground with my face. I caught Del too, so don't think you are getting special treatment, Airess."

"Thank you," says Livia, letting out a breath.

Del nods at Livia. "Glad you made it."

Livia looks around. They have landed near the edge of the demolished open-air garden, though not in the center of activity. There is a great deal of noise as several teams of workers are cleaning up debris and loading it onto conveyors that run to various rigs. Some of the conveyors are transporting only plant material while others take metal and other scrap. The fountain is drained and a team is inside the empty base working to repair the damage.

"You and Lex did quite a number on this place," says Del. "I remember it was extraordinarily beautiful."

"You've been here?" asks Livia.

"Yes," says Del, "many times. That was a different life. A life I didn't like."

Roscoe says, "Let's get closer to the building. Vippy will be looking for us." Just then, a door not too far from them opens, and Vippy pops her head out, her dark skin, short black hair, and black PCF uniform a stark contrast against the bright white building.

She waves. "Over here." The group rushes to the door, and Vippy ushers them inside.

Vippy pulls the door closed behind them and smiles, taps her head, and says, "Hi, my chip's interrupted. Follow me." She leads them down the corridor and makes a quick turn, then opens a maintenance closet door. "Get in."

When they are all in the small room, petite Vippy is just able to squeeze in and pull the door closed behind her.

"Good to see you, Vippy," says Roscoe, grasping Vippy's small shoulder and giving it a squeeze. "I know this was short notice. I'm glad you were able to help."

"Me too," says Vippy. "Waslo got me a message when I came on shift. Getting you all in and out of sight was the scariest part. Riggers are never in the building. Get those coveralls off." With hardly enough room to move, they all awkwardly start to peel off the rigger coveralls. "We'll leave them here," continues Vippy. "The Spear has its own maintenance and gardening crew. Their coveralls look a little different, not as beat-up. Your PCF uniforms will be much less conspicuous."

Roscoe nods to Livia. "You and Livia have met."

"Yes, briefly," Livia says with a smile. "Thank you for all you've done."

Vippy smiles. "Well, I am a rebel."

Roscoe says, "One of our best-placed operatives." Roscoe gestures toward the rest of the group. "This is Zavier, Delphia, and my son Enzo."

"Zavier, I've heard of you," says Vippy.

"So my reputation precedes me," says Zavier with a grin.

"Something like that," says Vippy. "And of course Delphia and Enzo, all the way from the Outlands. I didn't think I would meet you for years. Not until I came out to the Outlands."

"Enzo and I have heard a great deal about you from your parents," says Del. "They speak often of you. They are very proud. As they should be."

Enzo blurts out, "You're so tiny and young."

"A keen observation," says Vippy, a bit irritated.

Enzo scrambles, embarrassed. "Just from everything I've heard about you, so tough, brave, I thought you would look different."

"Well, I don't," snaps Vippy. "Coveralls," she demands and puts her arms out. Everyone hands over their coveralls and she crams them behind a shelf of cleaning supplies.

"Everyone ready?" asks Vippy, scanning the group.

Livia asks, "Where are we going? Where exactly is Armand?"

"He was pulled out of Archive stasis less than an hour ago," says Vippy. "A PCF squad, not mine, had orders to escort him to 87-43, that's room 43 on floor 87, one of the medical floors. This is 162, so we'll take a rapid-transport elevator down. There are PCF all over this building, so no one will give us a second look. Just remember, you're PCF. Head up, eyes forward."

Vippy opens the door a little and peeks out. Satisfied, she turns back to the group. "Behind me," she commands and strides out the door.

The group follows Vippy down the gleaming white corridor, the sound of her quick steps echoing off the hard, empty walls.

As they walk, Livia can sense Vippy. *She is focused and determined. This is the second time Vippy has put herself in danger to help the rebels that I know of. She works in the middle of the enemy. She would be dead in a heartbeat if they discovered her. Her parents were right, she is a strong, brave girl.*

Vippy leads them around a corner, where a group dressed in light gray suits with high collars stands discussing something in low voices. Vippy's pace does not falter and the team strides past the cluster of people in gray suits. When Vippy and the team are far down the corridor, she says, "All those people, they work for the High Council. We call them gray suits."

"Clever," says Zavier.

"Very," says Vippy. "They're advisers, administrators, and assistants. Their offices take up twenty-five floors. The High Council Chamber is actually only one floor up from here, I suppose so they can look out the huge windows down on the garden. Usually a beautiful view, which as you saw isn't very pretty right now, thanks to someone we know." Vippy turns and shoots Livia a smile without breaking her stride.

Livia smiles back. *This girl loves Lex. I can feel it. She is impressed by Lex, in awe of her. I think she feels the same way about me because I am Lex's sister. Vippy's feelings are strong, loyal.*

Vippy walks up to a bank of elevators and places her palm on one of the scanners. They stand for a moment, waiting. A group of gray suits approaches, some continue past, but several stop at the elevators, placing their palms on scanners and waiting. Livia keeps her eyes forward, not looking at the gray suits. *Why did they have to stop? We are in the middle of High Council territory. We will absolutely be caught. Why did I come? I should have just stayed on the rig. So I am a coward. It's too late. I am here. This is happening, and I can't panic at the first scary moment.*

Livia looks at the back of Vippy's head and reaches out to see what she is feeling. *Vippy is nervous, but she is hiding it well. Enzo and Zavier are nervous too, but not as good at masking it. Roscoe and Del are ready to pounce if they have to. No one but me is panicking. We are rescuing my father. All I have to do is focus on that and not do anything dumb.*

Vippy says to one of the gray suits, "Almost funny, waiting for a rapid-transport elevator."

"Almost," says the gray suit, cracking a smile.

The elevator door opens and a small group gets out. As the group files past, Waslo is the last person to step out of the elevator. For a brief moment, he and Livia lock eyes. *Waslo! I must not react! I can't believe we are running into him. I know he works here, but this is such a huge building*

I didn't think we would see him. I must keep my face calm. I sense that he is surprised but his face betrays nothing.

Waslo continues on without saying a word. They board the empty elevator and all turn to face front. Vippy puts up her hand to stop the group of gray suits from stepping aboard.

"Sorry, PCF only," Vippy says to the gray suits. "You'll have to take the next one."

"Of course," the gray suit in the front of the group says, nodding, and steps back. Vippy puts her palm on a scanner set into the wall by the door, then enters the floor number on the keypad below a small screen. The door slides closed with a faint hiss. The elevator starts to drop, the motion hardly detectable. The numbers on the screen count down so rapidly they blur together.

Livia turns to Vippy. "Was that wise, talking to the gray suits like that?"

"They are used to the PCF commandeering the elevators," says Vippy. "We do it all the time."

In moments, the screen displays 87 and the doors hiss open. Vippy steps out of the elevator and turns left. The group follows. They walk by doors, each with a scanner set above the handle showing a pale illuminated number. Livia looks at the numbers on the first doors they pass. *14, 15, 16 . . . He is in room 43! How far is that? We are close but still so far. Then we have to get him out of here.*

Livia looks away from the doors, down the long white corridor. A man with a white lab coat over a gray suit comes out of a door and is walking toward them. *Don't panic. Just look straight ahead. We are PCF. We are allowed to be here. I think! I don't know! Are there different rules for the medical floors? Breathe*, Livia commands herself.

The man's attention is fixed on the holoscreen he is carrying and he does not look up as they pass. At door 20, Vippy turns a corner and they enter a corridor with only one door on each side.

"There are four labs on each of the ten medical floors," explains Vippy, her voice low as they pass the doors reading Lab 87-C and Lab

87-D. "Most of the medical personnel work in the labs. The recovery rooms are full of test subjects. Some labs are dedicated to new rejuvenation procedures, others to combating mutated viruses and microbes. Some are working on life-extending projects."

The corridor ends at a wall of windows that stretches in both directions, running the length of the building. Floor-to-ceiling windows line one side of the hall, filling the space with diffused blue light. On the other side of the hall are more doors with illuminated numbers. Through the windows there is an expansive view of the airscrapers and skytowers of Indra interrupted by several ugly rigs hovering close to the High Council Building. Otherwise it is a stunning view.

Vippy turns and leads the group down the corridor. "The four labs on this floor and the ones on 88 focus exclusively on genetic research. The Council likes to keep a tight grip on all medical developments, so the only sanctioned labs are in this building."

The numbers on the doors start at 35. Halfway down the corridor three people dressed in white coats over gray suits stand talking. Livia quickly counts the doors.

In a whisper, Livia says, "They are in front of his door."

"Yes, I see," says Vippy, her voice low and calm. "Let me handle it."

When they reach Armand's room, Vippy says to the group, "You need to vacate the area. This is a restricted individual. We've been called down to transfer him."

A woman from the group protests, "Move him? You can't move him. He was just removed from stasis. He needs time to recover. An hour, at the very least. Do you know who's in this room?"

"No, ma'am," says Vippy. "That is not my concern. We have orders to move him, and that is what we are going to do."

"Where are you taking him?" asks another woman from the group.

"That is classified, ma'am," says Vippy.

"That is Armand Cosmo in there," says the man in the group. "The famous geneticist. We wanted to talk to him."

"That is out of the question," says Vippy. "This is the last time I am going to say this." Vippy moves her hand to her blaster. "You all need to vacate this area or you will be reported for impeding a PCF officer."

"Of course," says the man, with just a hint of irritation in his voice.

The three medical personnel turn and walk down the corridor. Vippy waits until they have turned the corner and are out of sight, then she puts her palm on the scanner. There is a muffled click.

"This is it," says Vippy, pushing the door open.

The room is large and furnished with two narrow sleepers and several screens alive with flickering lights, beeping softly. Sitting on one of the sleepers is a thin man in a loose gray gown. He turns to look at them as they enter, the door closing softly behind them. His wild, shoulder-length hair is streaked with gray. His gaunt face is covered with a scruffy beard, and there are dark shadows under his eyes. Round silver sensors are attached to his wrists and forehead with fine cables running to a set of monitors. Livia looks at the man's face. *It is Armand, my father, but he looks terrible. Only the shell of the man I saw in those Archive memories.*

Del rushes to Armand. "Oh, Armand, my sweet love." She kneels on the floor in front of him, taking his hands in hers, tears running down her face. "What have they done to you?" She kisses his hands.

"Hello, Delphia," says Armand, his voice sweet and untroubled. "You look lovely."

Livia senses the waves of emotions coming from Del. *She is shocked and devastated. She didn't expect him to be this bad. She still loves him. This is so hard for her. He is difficult to read. So vague and unclear. Like all his thoughts and emotions are blurred together. What he has been through is unthinkable.*

"We are going to take you out of here, Armand," says Del.

"Oh, yes," says Armand, his chapped, dry lips parting into a smile showing yellowed teeth. "That would be wonderful. Now, is this a memory or a dream? I can't be sure. A memory, I think."

"No, Armand," says Del. "This is not a memory or a dream. You are awake. We are going to take you away from here."

"All right," says Armand, still smiling. "Where shall we go? You do look quite well, Delphia. Beautiful. Always beautiful."

"We should get out of here," says Vippy.

Roscoe walks over to the sleeper and crouches next to Del.

"Armand," says Roscoe. Armand takes his unfocused eyes off Del and looks at Roscoe.

He blinks slowly several times and says, "Roscoe? Is that you?"

"Yes, friend," says Roscoe. "We have to go."

Armand studies Roscoe's face. "Roscoe? Hello. This is not a memory, is it?"

"No," says Roscoe. "Can you stand?"

"We can't walk him through the building like this," says Zavier.

"The sleeper has wheels," says Vippy. "We'll roll him out."

"All the way to the maintenance closet where we stashed the coveralls?" asks Zavier in disbelief.

"It is not that uncommon to see a test subject wheeled through the building," says Vippy.

"Who are they?" asks Armand, pointing to Livia, Zavier, Enzo, and Vippy.

"They are going to help get you out of here," says Del.

"Maybe I should stay," says Armand. "I'm quite tired. This dream is exhausting."

"Armand!" yells Del, releasing his hands and shaking him by his shoulders. His eyes go wide and he looks at Del. "This is not a dream. You are awake. We have to leave."

Armand seems to become more focused. Livia feels the change in him. *He is determined now. There is a strength in him that wasn't there a moment ago.*

Armand looks at Del. He studies her face. "Delphia?" His voice is clear and full of hope.

"Yes," says Del. "It's me. We are here to take you out of here."

"You are really here?" he asks. "This is not a dream?"

"Not a dream," says Del.

"Where are the girls?" he asks. "Are they safe?"

"One of them is here." Del motions for Livia to come closer. She walks over and kneels next to Del in front of Armand. "This is Livia."

"Oh, Livia," says Armand, his eyes filling with tears. "It is so good to see you in person."

Suddenly the door flies open and Cassina bursts into the room, followed by six PCF officers with weapons drawn.

"Disarm them!" orders Cassina. Vippy reaches for her blaster. Cassina grabs Vippy's hand and wrenches it behind her back. Vippy struggles, but Cassina quickly puts her in wrist restraints.

The six PCF officers descend on the group. Zavier elbows the officer closest to him in the face and breaks his nose, blood instantly gushing down his face. Then he attacks another officer, kicking him in the gut. Enzo head-butts the officer coming at him and tackles him to the ground. Del grabs Livia and pulls her to the floor. Roscoe pulls his blaster and gets off a shot, hitting one of the officers.

Cassina holds Vippy by her wrist restraints and pulls her blaster. Vippy stamps down on Cassina's foot just as she aims at Roscoe. Cassina shoots and hits Roscoe in the shoulder.

"Enough," yells Cassina, pointing her blaster at Vippy's head. "This rebel traitor will die right now if you don't stop."

Everyone stops moving. They look at Roscoe, who is pressing his hand to his shoulder, blood seeping through his fingers. Resigned, he inclines his head.

"Good choice," says Cassina. "You have a chance of surviving. A slim one but a chance."

In moments, the PCF officers have the group disarmed, with their wrists crossed in from of them in tight restraints. Roscoe's shoulder wound drips blood down the sleeve of his uniform.

Cassina inspects the group. "These PCF uniforms look like the real thing. Impressive. Of course, Vippy, yours is real. I knew you were rebel dirt. I could feel it. I've been watching you. Monitoring your movements. It seemed odd that you were scanning yourself in all over the building today, in places you shouldn't have been. And I was right. A core-low rebel spy. Now, who are all your companions?" Cassina looks at Livia. "I recognize this one. If I'm not mistaken, Kane tried to kill you. Too bad he didn't succeed. I'm sure the job will get done soon enough. The Council has no tolerance for rebels. So what are you doing here? You want this old man?" Cassina points to Armand sitting on the sleeper in restraints. "Why? Who is he? Hardly seems worth it, breaking in to try and get him out."

"I'm not telling you anything," says Vippy. "You caught me. Good job. Now can you just shut up?"

"Oh, you don't have to answer my questions," says Cassina with a grin. "I'm taking you to the High Council Chamber. They've been concerned a rebel infiltrated the building, and I found you. Let's go introduce you to the High Council."

45

Lex crouches behind a concrete support column while Kane stands on guard. She places a small amount of explosive and skillfully attaches the two wires of the remote charge, one on each side. "This is the last one," says Kane.

"Done," says Lex, standing up. "Let's get back to Chae and Amia." Lex takes off running down the corridor with Kane right behind. As they get close to the double-level room with generators, Lex hears muffled voices and skids to a stop, grabbing Kane's arm and pulling him to a stop.

She whispers, "I hear voices, and one of them is Hauser."

"Blast!" says Kane, keeping his voice low. "We were so close."

"Stay here," says Lex, and creeps to the end of the corridor that connects with the generator room. She concentrates on the voices.

"There are two of us," says Chae.

"Just the two of you?" scoffs Hauser. "That is a lie. We've already picked up your injured friend in the stairwell. But I know there are five in your group. You set off sensors all over this facility. So I checked with the gate and they confirmed that a unit of five came out here. So where are the other two of your group, and what are you doing here?"

"We're not answering your questions," says Amia.

"You rebels are so stubborn and stupid. Your friend from the stairwell didn't have a broken leg when we started talking, but he does now."

Lex quietly returns to Kane, backing down the corridor, and whispers,

"He's got Parker and is questioning Chae and Amia. This is getting bad really fast."

"What do we do?" asks Kane.

"We've got to get them out of there."

"Sure," says Kane. "How?"

"We're at a disadvantage if we both come at them head-on. It sounds like they're between this wall," Lex points at the wall to their left, "and the generators. You approach on the other side of the generators."

"What are you going to do?" asks Kane.

"I'm going to get in position right in front of them on the Level 11 walkway."

"They'll see you through the railing."

"No. If they are where I think they are, they're too close to the walkway overhead to see me coming, if I stay low and close to the wall."

"I heard a few ifs in that plan. I don't like it."

"The advantage of high ground is worth it," says Lex. "If I'm wrong, I'll come back down and we'll hit them together from behind the generators. But I'm not wrong."

"You never are," agrees Kane begrudgingly. "How will I know you're in position?"

"I'll take out whoever's closest to Amia. You take out whoever's closest to Chae."

"You're just going to start blasting?" asks Kane, surprised.

"You think Hauser is going to negotiate?"

"No."

Lex nods. "We don't have to shoot to kill, but they're not going to hold back."

"That's true."

"Let's go." Lex draws her blaster, turns, and runs to the end of the corridor. Kane does the same. Lex slows and quietly enters the generator room heading for the stairs while Kane heads toward the backside of the generators.

Lex starts to climb the stairs. *When we were on the other side of the room, the generators blocked the bottom half of the stairs, but I'll be completely exposed while I'm on the top half. I just hope Hauser and his troops are facing the other way. I'll go up enough to see if I'm clear.*

Lex reaches the midpoint of the stairs and pauses. *Beyond this point they will be able to see me. I just need to know which way they are facing.* She focuses on the sound of Hauser's voice.

"You're going to regret not telling me what I want to know," says Hauser.

"Maybe, but we still won't tell you," says Chae.

"Never," says Amia defiantly.

"We'll see," says Hauser, unimpressed. "We'll find your two friends and we'll all go back to High Security Detainment. Whatever you were doing here, we'll find out."

Hauser sounds like he's facing away from the stairs, and both Chae and Amia sound like they are facing this way. I just need to see them for a second to confirm.

Lex stays low and moves up another step. She looks out over the generators. At the far end of the room, past the four generators, Hauser and four officers are facing away from her. Chae and Amia are being held by two officers each and they are all facing in Lex's direction. Lex ducks down a step. *Blast! There are two facing this way. I'll never get up the rest of the stairs without anyone seeing. I should go meet up with Kane.*

"Soon," continues Hauser, "we won't have any of you Rock Bottom rebels to contend with."

Kane's voice echoes out into the huge room. "Hey, Hauser. Not all the rebels are in Rock Bottom." Followed by the sound of blaster fire.

Lex realizes, *Kane is distracting them. This is my chance.* While the sound of blaster fire fills the room, she runs up the stairs and sprints the short section of walkway between the stairs and the wall that runs the length of the room. She gets right up against the wall and crouches down. The blaster fire stops. *I have to get all the way down to the end of the room, but I have to take it slow. I'm only at the first generator. From the sound of his voice, Kane is between the third and fourth generators. A good position.*

He can easily stay back out of their range. Lex listens as she slowly creeps along the walkway. The voices are getting louder as she gets closer.

"Who are you?" yells Hauser. "Do I know you?"

"You wouldn't remember me," answers Kane, his loud voice full of defiance, "but I remember you. You came and spoke at the Academy. I respected you, but I don't agree with what you are doing now."

"You were a cadet? I order you to stand down."

"Not a chance." Kane fires off his blaster into the ceiling. Hauser and four of his men return fire, hitting the generators.

Lex steps out from the wall, just enough to see that everyone is facing away from her. *Nice work, Kane.* With blaster fire masking her footfalls, she runs down the walkway, passing the second generator, then catches a glimpse of Kane firing his blaster at the ceiling as she runs past.

Oh, please keep firing! I'm almost there. She passes the fourth generator and positions herself directly across from Hauser and his unit. Lex drops down to one knee and aims her blaster at Hauser. Hauser puts his hand up and his unit stops firing. Kane stops firing soon after.

"Only one blaster coming from back there, so there's still one member of your team unaccounted for," yells Hauser. "Not with you, so I'm guessing . . ." Hauser spins around and points his blaster at Lex up on the walkway. *He looks nothing like he did when I saw him in Rock Bottom just a week ago. He was dressed like he belonged there, dirty with a weird mask over his face. Now he is back to regulation, short hair, clean uniform. Without the mask I can see his face has been burned, scarred. How did that happen? He was handsome, not anymore.*

"I see you up there," says Hauser. "Tactically smart. How did you get up there? Your friend behind the generator was a good distraction. You should have taken the shot when you still had the element of surprise. Too late now. You can see you're outnumbered. You're not getting out of this, so I advise you to surrender."

"No!" yells Lex. "You and your team should leave before I have to kill all of you."

"Cadet Lex?" Hauser asks, astonished. "Is that you? I heard you were a rebel. I knew I should have killed you when I saw you in Rock Bottom. Right after you slipped away, I found out about you breaking out your rebel friend Cadet Kane from High Security Detainment. So let me guess. Cadet Kane? He must be the mystery cadet between the generators. You did a lot of damage at the High Council Building. We brought the PCF down to Rock Bottom looking for you, Kane, and the island girl with you. We didn't find you, but we did kill some rebels and some of those disgusting Unders who live there. Lex, you swore to me you weren't a rebel, and I believed you."

"I wasn't a rebel."

"But you are now? You were such a promising cadet on your way to doing very well in the PCF. This is disappointing. What a change of heart you have had, Lex. Do I have to remind you of all the damage your friends have done?"

Lex yells back, "The rebels are not my friends, but I can't stand by while the Council kills everyone in Rock Bottom."

"So you know the purpose of this facility," says Hauser. "That's interesting. Well, friends or not, you're going to die together. It will be such a relief for Indra to be free from the rebels and the putrid people of Rock Bottom." Hauser's body shifts slightly and Lex knows, *He is going to fire.* She shoots and hits Hauser in the hand holding his blaster. His blaster and most of his hand fly away and hit the floor.

Hauser spins, clutching his bloody hand to his chest, and roars, "Kill her!"

In the split second it takes the four men around Hauser to return fire on Lex, she gets off two more good shots, taking down the men holding Amia, then Lex is forced to roll back toward the wall to stay out of the shower of blaster fire. Amia jumps into action and grabs a blaster off one of the men Lex shot, now dead on the ground. She fires on the men around Hauser, taking down one officer, then takes cover behind one of the pillars that holds up the walkway.

Hauser bellows, "Get me out of here!" The three officers surround Hauser and start to retreat toward the elevator, two firing on Lex's position, one firing at Amia but only hitting the pillar.

Kane comes out from between the generators and fires on the men holding Chae, hitting one in the arm and the other in the side. Both men let go of Chae and are able to draw their blasters and fire on Kane. Kane drops back between the generators for cover and continues firing. Chae crawls across the floor and grabs Hauser's blaster. He fires at the two men Kane just hit, blasting the officer with the wound in his side, and he crumples to the floor. The other officer continues firing and ducks behind a pillar. Lex moves forward on the walkway, staying low, and fires at Hauser and his men as they retreat, hitting one in the leg. Amia fires at the remaining officers as they retreat, giving Chae cover as he scrambles back toward Kane. One of the men, retreating with Hauser, hits Chae in the back, and he collapses to the ground.

"No! Chae!" yells Amia, as she breaks from behind the pillar and runs to him. The officer hiding behind the pillar moves out to take a shot at Amia. Kane shoots him in the chest and he falls to the ground.

Lex continues to fire on Hauser and his remaining three men as they move to the elevator while Kane crawls to Chae.

"Quick!" says Kane. "Let's get him behind the generator."

"Yes," says Amia, "Hold on, Chae. We're going to move you."

"Now!" demands Kane. "While Lex has them tied up."

"Hurry!" yells Lex. "Get him out of there."

They each take one of Chae's arms and pull him across the floor. When Hauser and his men reach the elevator, they are out of range and Lex stops firing. Lex looks over and sees Kane, Chae, and Amia have made it in between the third and fourth generators.

Kane says to Amia, "Put pressure on the wound." Amia wraps her arms around Chae and puts both hands, one over the other, on Chae's back. Instantly, blood seeps through her fingers.

Hauser yells, "You never should have joined the rebels, Lex," and steps into the elevator.

Lex taunts, "You just going to run away, Hauser? I didn't know you were a coward."

"You and your friends won't leave here alive," Hauser yells to Lex.

Then orders his men, "Stay here and finish them."

In unison, his men answer, "Yes, sir."

As the elevator door closes, Hauser yells, "Good-bye, Lex."

The three PCF officers quickly take up a position behind a concrete pillar near the elevator, and Lex starts firing on them. They try to fire back, but from their position their shots are wild and ineffective.

Kane runs forward, stopping so he is still protected by the two generators.

"Lex!" yells Kane. Lex looks back at Kane but keeps firing at the two officers, keeping them pinned behind the pillar. Kane motions with his hand for her to come down. Lex nods. Kane crouches low and moves out, just past the edge of the fourth generator. As soon as Kane starts firing, Lex turns and runs down the walkway toward the stairs. It takes a moment for the officers to realize Lex is on the move. They redirect, and blaster fire starts hitting the walkway under Lex's feet. Kane sprays the pillar with blaster fire, and soon Lex is out of range, the officers unable to get a good shot at her without coming out from behind the pillar. Lex runs down the stairs and joins Kane, Chae, and Amia.

Amia holds Chae in her lap, his head resting on her chest. "I got you. You're going to be all right."

"It doesn't feel like it," says Chae. He coughs, the sound wet, his breath wheezing.

Lex looks at Amia holding Chae, her hands soaked in his blood. *Why did Hauser have to be here? We are trying to stop people from dying.*

Chae says, his voice weak, "Is Lex here?"

"Yes. I'm here." Lex moves closer to Chae.

"Do whatever it takes to stop this."

"I will."

"It's The Time of the Twins," says Chae, "and I was part of it."

Lex looks at Amia, and she nods. *She knows this is the end for him.*

"Thank you for your help, Chae," says Lex. "We will do whatever it takes to stop this. I promise."

46

Cassina marches down the long corridor toward the massive double doors of the High Council Chamber, holding Vippy by the elbow. A few paces behind her, Armand, still weak, is being escorted by a PCF officer on each side to help him walk. The rest of the group follow, surrounded by PCF officers. Livia walks between Del and Roscoe.

Livia focuses on Cassina. *I can sense Cassina's delight. She can hardly contain her feelings of triumph. I can't believe she is Waslo's daughter, and that she is the reason we were caught. If only Waslo had known Vippy was under suspicion. It wasn't a trap, just bad luck that Cassina was watching Vippy. What will the High Council do with us? Will they banish us to the Archives? Why would they bother? I'm sure they will just kill us. If I am going to die, I'm glad I met Kane and my father. We accomplished our part of the plan at the air filtration plant, so our main mission was a success. I hope Lex and Kane at the dam are luckier than we are. I wish there was something we could do. Even if we could get out of these restraints, how would we get out of here?*

They reach the tall doors of the Council Chamber, carved wood inlaid with metal. Cassina pushes them open and they walk into an enormous, magnificently decorated hall. The floor is highly polished metal, stamped with complicated patterns. The ceiling, thirty feet above, is paneled with intricately painted tiles. A spectacular crystal chandelier hangs in the center of the room. Across from the doors, a wall of enormous windows looks out onto the now-demolished garden under repair, the hideous floating rigs and the impressive skyline of Indra beyond. Just in front of the windows, the twenty members of the Independent High Council sit at a long table on a raised dais. The Council members are dressed in richly colored suits and gowns elaborately decorated with exquisite embroidery. There are several men and women in the gray suits of Council aids and advisers moving about the room, while others stand close to various seated members of the Council. Waslo stands between a man and a woman at the center of the table. He is leaning down and speaking to them in a hushed voice while indicating a projection hovering above a screen set into the table.

As the group enters, many of the Council members and the gray suits look up, including Waslo. He scans the group and briefly makes eye contact with Livia. *I can sense that Waslo is alarmed, but he is very good at masking his emotions. He appears to be quite calm, but I know that is not the case. What will he do? Can he help us?*

Cassina comes to a stop in front of the dais. "Praise the Council," she says, her head lowered.

Waslo straightens. "Cassina, this is highly improper." His loud voice carries across the large room. She looks up at him. "The High Council is in session, and they are not to be disrupted. Please take this group into the hall and I will be out to speak with you in a moment." Waslo turns and in a deferential tone addresses the Council member to his right, an old man in a bright green suit with a dark purple design on the collar. "Your Preeminence Head Council Edward, I apologize for my daughter's intrusion. This is most inappropriate. I will find out what this is regarding and report back." Waslo bows and steps back, preparing to leave, but Head Council Edward reaches out and gently touches Waslo's arm.

"No. No," says Edward, his face moving strangely when he speaks, as if his skin is too tight. "Let her speak." Waslo inclines his head, folds his hands calmly, and stands very still.

Livia looks at Head Council Edward closely. *His face is stretched over his sharp cheekbones. He can barely move. He's definitely had too many rejuvenation procedures.* She looks down the table at the other Council members. *They all look like they have had too many rejuvenation procedures. These are the most powerful people in Indra, all members of the Founding Families. These are the people who wanted me dead. They are the ones who sent Kane to kill me.*

All the members of the High Council look at the group. The gray suits in the room stand quietly while Head Council Edward continues, his voice low and relaxed, "What is the meaning of this, Cassina? Who are these people?"

"Your Preeminence Head Council Edward and honored High Council members," Cassina says with a bow of her head. "I've caught a rebel spy, working here in the building." She pulls Vippy forward. "She helped these rebels get into the building. They were attempting to remove this Archive prisoner."

The two guards holding Armand move him forward slightly. He looks around the room, confused.

Edward says, "Hello, Armand," his voice sweet.

Armand looks up at the Council table to see who is speaking. His eyes fall on Edward at the center of the table. "Oh, hello, Edward," he says, a sweet smile lighting up his thin, ashen face. "I'm being rescued."

Edward's mouth turns up in a small, tight grin. "Yes, I see."

"And this one," Cassina points to Livia, "she is one of the fugitives who broke the prisoner out of High Security Detainment and caused all the damage to the garden."

"Really?" asks Edward, his gaze moving to Livia. "One of the fugitives? Are you sure? Cassina, bring her closer."

"Yes, sir," says Cassina, roughly grabbing Livia from the group and pulling her forward to stand next to Vippy. "The other two fugitives are not with this group."

"Astonishing," says Edward, studying Livia.

This Head Council Edward makes me so uncomfortable. The only thing I sense from him is greed, like a simmering hunger.

"My goodness, Cassina, you are right," continues Edward. "This is the fugitive Livia Cosmo."

With a sweeping gesture, Edward beckons Waslo forward. "Waslo. Did you not recognize your charge?"

Waslo looks at Livia, an expression of disgust crossing his face. "No, Head Council Edward. I must admit I did not, perhaps because this is the last place I would expect to see her. And in that PCF uniform, she is virtually unrecognizable. Regardless, I apologize. I should have spotted her right away."

"Indeed, you should have. And Marius, dear, you didn't recognize Livia either?"

Livia scans the gray suits on the dais and spots Marius near the end. *Marius is here! I didn't realize she worked for the Council. I thought she was just my guardian.*

As Marius walks toward Edward, she says, "From where I was standing, Head Council Edward, she was blocked from view." She stops and stands next to Waslo and stares coldly at Livia. "It is most assuredly Livia, though she barely resembles the girl from Helix. She certainly doesn't appear to be the Proper Indrithian Young Lady I took such care to raise." Marius smiles at Livia. "It is quite a surprise to see you, Livia my dear."

Livia is incensed. "And I'm quite surprised to see you. You never said you worked for the Council. So were you spying on me? Was that your real job?"

"It breaks my heart to see what has become of you, Livia."

"I thought you cared about me!"

"Part of me does care about you," Marius replies, her voice sweet. Livia tries to sense Marius. *I sense affection from her, but it is a lie. Somehow she is forcing herself to feel it, but it is not genuine. I don't understand.* Livia notices that Cassina is looking at her with a strange expression on her face. *Cassina is staring at me. I sense a strange mix of jealousy and hatred coming from her. Of course she hates me. She thinks I'm rebel scum. But jealous of me? Why? Because her parents were often with me on Helix and not with her? She was in the Academy for most of her childhood, so she hardly knows them. I was with them a great deal, but it turns out I didn't know them at all.*

"So you came to rescue your father?" asks Edward. "Well, Livia, it is wonderful to have you here. And this little one is a spy. Good work, Cassina. We will deal with her in a moment." He points to Del. "Bring that one forward." The PCF officers closest to Del grab her and pull her out of the group.

"Let go of me!" yells Del, struggling to shake them off as they force her up to the front next to Livia and Vippy.

"Now, this is truly astonishing. Hello, Delphia. Your mother and I have been looking for you for a long time." He turns to the woman sitting next to him at the table, her gown the same green-and-purple design as his. "My dearest Sivette, isn't it nice to see Delphia after all these years?"

Sivette smiles, a terrible grimace that contorts her face. "A delightful surprise. Seventeen years is a long time, Delphia. And I am strangely pleased to see you, Livia. I didn't think I would ever meet one of my granddaughters."

"You could have gone to Helix and met Livia anytime you wanted," snaps Del. "Instead you tried to have her killed."

"We were quite vexed when Livia's Emergence Ball was such a catastrophe," says Sivette. "The night did not go as expected, and now here you are."

A man sitting at the Council table a few seats from Edward clears his throat. He is dressed in a rich crimson suit with intricate white embroidery on the collar and decorating one sleeve. "Head Council Edward, am I to infer that this is your long-lost daughter Delphia and your granddaughter Livia Cosmo?"

"That is correct, Council Vincent," says Edward, not taking his eyes off Del.

Livia spins to face Del. "These people, Edward and Sivette, are your parents! My grandparents! You didn't say anything about your parents being alive, much less one of the Founding Families on the High Council. The Council, they were the ones who gave the order to kill me. My grandparents want me dead! How could you keep this from me! I have a right to know who my family is."

"Livia!" says Del sternly. "This is not the time or place."

"They are going to kill us! There is no other time or place."

Edward smiles. "This is amusing. So Delphia, you didn't tell little Livia about us? About you? You can't run from blood, Delphia. We are your blood."

Livia's thoughts spin. *How could Del keep this from me, from Lex? If they weren't about to have us killed, I would strangle her!*

Sivette folds her hands on the table, rings glinting on every finger. "Yes, Livia, we are your grandparents, but you have been deemed unnecessary. We did try to have you removed. Though the events of your Emergence Ball were most unexpected, to say the least, it was what occurred next that was astounding. Soon after the ball, you inexplicably left Helix with a rogue female cadet and participated in the disastrous rescue of the prisoner Kane Williams. Of course, when we reviewed the three-dimensional projection our archivist assembled of the event, we discovered something entirely unexpected. The rogue cadet, a former ward of Orphanage 47 by the name Lex, bore an unmistakable resemblance to both you, Livia Cosmo, and our daughter Delphia."

Sivette's eyes lock on Del. "Imagine our surprise when we realized we were looking at your second daughter. Livia's twin. She finally has a name . . . Lex."

"Oh, Lex is Livia's twin sister's name," says Armand with a bright smile. "It is lovely. Lex and Livia, very lyrical."

"Yes, very nice," says Sivette. "However, Lex's chip is no longer functioning. She was last recorded in Rock Bottom, but despite our efforts to find her, she has managed to disappear. It is a shame you didn't bring her as well. I'm glad to have Livia back. It appears, for now, Lex will continue to elude us."

Livia is relieved. *So they know who Lex is, but they don't know where she is now.*

"It's so wonderfully ironic that you should come to us, Delphia, after all the years we looked for you," says Edward. "We dangled Livia on Helix to draw you out, and just when we had given up hope, believing that our patience had been in vain, Livia escapes and brings you to us. And why? To rescue Armand." Edward smooths back his unnaturally thick, dark hair. "You must know he is damaged. You put yourselves right in our hands to rescue a man who has been gone for years. Now that we have you here, the only one missing is Livia's twin, Lex. Perhaps hidden somewhere in Rock Bottom? We would love to meet her, though if she is in Rock Bottom that will soon not be possible."

"This is not a reunion," says Del defiantly. "We are taking Armand."

Edward says smugly, "Circumstances would indicate that is highly unlikely."

Council Vincent asks, "Head Council Edward, do we still feel the necessity to dispose of this twin?"

"Now that we have Livia here with us," Edward replies, "I believe The Time of the Twins Prophecy is of no consequence. They have already paraded them in front of the people of Rock Bottom. Yes, we heard about that. In a few days, it will not matter what the people believe. We will deal with Livia in due time. There is no rush."

He talks about me like I'm not even here. "I'm your granddaughter," says Livia, horrified. "Doesn't that mean anything to you?"

"Yes," says Edward. "It means that you, like Delphia, are a stain on our family name. You and your twin should not exist. You are prohibited. An abomination. *That* is who you are to me. Now, Delphia, I am intrigued. You look as if you haven't aged a day. As I suspected, Armand achieved some of the very genetic enhancements he refused to work on for us. I look forward to extracting those secrets from you. Our geneticists will be able to learn much from you, though I suspect the process will be quite unpleasant."

A gray suit rushes in and approaches the table. He bows low and says, "Praise the Council. I'm sorry to interrupt the most esteemed High Council, but we have received an urgent communication from Lieutenant Hauser."

"Continue," says Edward.

"Yes, Head Council." The gray suit straightens. "There is a group of rebels at the dam. He asks that you give him clearance to open the floodgate valves without delay."

Edward looks around the table and all the Council members nod their approval. "Send word immediately that the High Council gives the order to release the water," says Edward.

"No! Please!" pleads Livia. "Don't do this!"

47

At the reservoir, Lex crouches between the two generators firing her blaster toward the pillar. *Blast. I'll never hit them from here. We have to come at them from another position or they could keep us pinned here forever.* There is a burst of blaster fire from behind the pillar that shoots past Lex. *They have the same problem. Not a good angle.*

One of the PCF officers yells, "Let's get this over with. Come out and we'll make it quick."

Lex yells, "Yeah, sure. Be right out!"

Lex moves back to Kane, Chae, and Amia farther back between the huge generators. Lex looks at Chae draped across Amia's legs. She is no longer holding him tightly, putting pressure on his wound. His eyes are open and blank. Amia gently puts her hand to his face and closes his eyes, kisses him tenderly on the forehead, and moves out from under his heavy, lifeless body.

"How do we get out of here?" asks Amia, wiping a tear from her cheek.

"We have to get past those PCF officers and get to the elevator or the stairs," says Lex. "I think we have to split up. One of us takes the front position and distracts them while the other two go around the back of the generator and come up on them from the side."

"Better than waiting here," says Kane.

"Do you think they killed Parker?" asks Amia.

"I don't know," says Lex. *I would guess they killed him, but I didn't want to say that. There is nothing we can do about it right now.* "We need to do it now before they do the same thing and get a jump on us."

"Amia, you take the front position," says Kane. "Lex and I will come at them from the side."

"All right," says Amia.

Immediately, Amia moves into position and starts firing. Lex and Kane hurry around the back of the generator.

Keeping her voice low, Lex says, "We need to get as close as possible."

Kane nods. Suddenly, two officers come out from behind the pillar firing their blasters at Lex and Kane. Lex is hit in the leg and she falls to the ground. Kane returns fire, hitting both the officers and driving them back behind the pillar. Kane continues firing as Lex pulls herself around the back of the generator.

Kane yells, "Amia, keep them back! Lex is hit!"

"Kane, pull back," yells Lex. Kane continues to fire as he moves back to Lex.

He stops firing and looks at Lex's leg. "How bad is it?"

"Not good," says Lex with a grimace, pressing on her leg, blood turning her hand red.

Kane pulls off his belt. "Get this around your leg." He cinches the belt above the wound on Lex's leg.

"So much for our ambush," says Lex.

Suddenly, blaster fire comes from the elevator and the PCF officers can be heard screaming. A moment later all baster fire from behind the pillar stops and a voice yells, "Hold your fire. We're with Del."

Amia stops firing and six rough-looking men come out from behind the pillar. They are dressed in the mismatched clothes worn by the Outlanders at Del's colony, though theirs are all in shades of brown and tan, and are dirty and more tattered. Lex realizes, *These must be the men Del told us about. She said they were observing the dam and would get us back to the colony. I didn't expect them to come to our rescue.*

A tall man with dark red hair and a beard flecked with gray says, "I'm Travis. Those three are dead. Are there any more?"

"None down here," says Lex. "Their lieutenant was injured but alive. He left."

"Blast! We didn't see anyone on our way in," says Travis. "He could call for reinforcements. We should get out of here."

"Good timing," says Lex, pulling the belt on her leg tighter. "I don't know how much longer we would have lasted."

"I'm Kane, and this is Lex," Kane says as he helps Lex to her feet. She drapes her arm over Kane's shoulder, trying not to put weight on her leg.

Amia rushes over to the group. "We lost a man, a friend of mine, and I don't want to leave him here. Can a couple of you help me bring him out? He's back here." Amia turns and heads back to Chae.

Travis gestures to two of his men, both young with scruffy beards. "Dalton, Francisco, go help her." The two Outlanders run to catch up with Amia. Travis turns to another man in his group. "Markus, help get her to the elevator." Markus, a dark man shorter than Travis, ducks under Lex's arm opposite Kane.

"We had a fifth man in our team," says Lex as they all start toward the elevator. She leans heavily on Kane and Markus. "He was injured and we left him in the stairwell. I know the PCF found him, but I don't know what they did with him or where he is now."

"He is in the elevator," says Travis. "He's unconscious but alive."

"Parker's alive," Lex says, relieved. "I thought for sure Hauser and his men had killed him."

"He got worked over pretty bad," says Travis. "I wish we had gotten here sooner. Jules set up our comms so we could monitor the PCF comms. We heard a Lieutenant Hauser and his team arrive at the dam today. Bad timing. We hoped he would leave without realizing you were at the dam. We didn't want to rush in and make things worse, but when we heard him get confirmation that your team was here, we knew you were in trouble. We got here as quick as we could."

They step into the elevator and see Parker, a crumpled heap in the back corner. He has been beaten, his face bloody and swollen.

"Parker!" cries Lex, lurching toward him. Kane and Markus help Lex down to the floor close to him. She puts her hand tenderly on his shoulder. "Oh, Parker." He lifts his head slightly, then lets it drop back down. "I'm so sorry. We shouldn't have left you."

Amia steps into the elevator, followed by Dalton and Francisco, who are carrying Chae between them. "Amia, I'm sorry about Chae," says Lex while Kane and Markus help her up. "He was a good man."

"He was," says Amia. She looks down at Parker slumped on the floor. "And Parker too."

"Yes, but Parker is alive," says Lex.

Amia nods. "That's good."

"Let's get out of here," says Travis, hitting the button on the elevator.

As the doors close, Lex notices, *There is a new sound in the dam. The water sounds different, like it is moving. Hauser must have opened the floodgate valves connecting to the old pipes, and the water is rushing out!*

"The water is moving," says Lex, panic in her voice. "The valves are open. They're flooding Rock Bottom right now. We can't wait. I have to set off the explosives now." She awkwardly fumbles to get to the detonator.

Travis grabs her wrist, his grip firm. "Hold tight. This isn't a suicide mission. My men and I all have families to get back to. We'll be out of the dam in just a few minutes. Markus, take the detonator."

Lex glares at Travis while Markus pats her down and finds the detonator. "People are going to die if I don't detonate the explosives."

Markus hands the detonator to Travis. "Yes, but not us. Not today."

48

In the Council Chamber, as the water rushes into Rock Bottom and Core Low miles beneath the city, Livia is overwhelmed. *I can feel people dying. So many.*

"Stop this!" shouts Del. "It is unforgivable."

Livia crumples to the floor and whimpers, "They are dying. I can feel them. They're all dying." Vippy crouches to comfort Livia, putting her bound hands on her back.

"Marius, what does she mean? She can feel them?" asks Edward. "Is she saying she can sense the people in Rock Bottom dying?"

"That's what it sounds like, Head Council Edward," says Marius, "but I don't see how that would be possible."

In an accusing tone, Edward asks, "Is she just having some kind of hysterical fit, or can she sense people miles away? You must know if she has some special ability."

"I suspected Livia could sense people's emotions, but I was never sure," says Marius. "I never reported my suspicions because I didn't want to give the Council false information, but I never suspected anything like this. She could be faking."

Sivette addresses the High Council. "Regardless, I suggest that we put our genetics team to work on Delphia and Livia immediately and see what their genes are hiding. Obviously, Armand damaged his own mind to hide his achievements, but now we will discover them for ourselves. Take Delphia and Livia to the labs on 88."

Livia stands, swaying on her feet. "You are monsters!"

"We have no need for any of the others," Sivette says with a wave of her hand. "Dispose of them."

As the PCF officers move closer to the group, Roscoe, Zavier, Vippy, and Enzo all attack at once. Roscoe tackles the officer closest to him, ramming him with his good shoulder and wrestling him to the floor. Zavier kicks the guard next to him, knocking him back. The officer reaches for his blaster, but Zavier advances and kicks his hand away. The blaster goes flying. Vippy swings her bound hands at Cassina's face, hitting her with the hard wrist restraints. Cassina stumbles forward into Livia, while Vippy fumbles to grab Cassina's blaster.

Vippy yells to Livia, "Hit her again!"

Livia copies Vippy's arm swing and hits Cassina in the face. Being hit a second time with the restraints knocks Cassina out, and she falls to the floor, pinning Vippy underneath her.

At the same time, Enzo drops to the floor. He swipes his body across the legs of the officer behind him, knocking his feet out from under him, and the officer falls to the floor. Enzo grabs his blaster. From the floor, Enzo shoots up at the chandelier. His aim is impeccable, even in the restraints. With one blast, the massive chandelier detaches from the ceiling and starts to fall. Enzo fires on the PCF officers as they scramble to pull their weapons, killing three before they even draw their blasters. Del dives at the dazed Armand, taking him to the ground just as the chandelier hits the floor and explodes, shards of glass and crystal flying everywhere. Del covers Armand from the falling debris as the High Council members and gray suits run for cover, some ducking under the table. Waslo shields Edward and Sivette as they run from the High Council Chamber.

With the destroyed chandelier still raining down, Zavier drops and rolls to the blaster on the floor. Grabbing it, he fires at the PCF officers, hitting two as they retreat to the sides of the room.

Vippy awkwardly struggles under Cassina and yells to Livia, "Help me!"

"What do you want me to do?" offers Livia, as she crouches down.

"Pull her off me."

With Vippy pushing and Livia pulling, Vippy is able to wriggle out from under Cassina's limp body. "Put her thumb to the sensor on the back of the restraints," says Vippy, holding up her wrists. Livia grabs Cassina's drooping hand and puts her thumb to the sensor on Vippy's restraints. They pop open. Vippy puts her own thumb to the sensor on Livia's restraints and they pop open.

"I still have clearance," Vippy says with a smile. Vippy grabs Cassina's blaster and throws it to Livia. "Cover me!" Livia starts firing at PCF officers and Vippy rushes to Enzo.

"Give me the blaster," says Vippy to Enzo. "I'll cover us and get your restraints off."

"Great," Enzo says and hands over the blaster. Vippy continues firing as she opens Enzo's restraints.

"Give me the back the blaster," yells Enzo. "You go help Roscoe. I'll cover you."

Vippy runs to Roscoe who is still struggling with a PCF officer on the floor. She kicks the officer in the back and steps on the hand holding his blaster and wrenches it away. She hits the officer in the head with the butt of the blaster, knocking him out.

"Thanks," says Roscoe as he gets to his feet.

"We should go," says Vippy, putting her thumb to Roscoe's restraints. They pop open.

"Yes!" says Roscoe. Then he shouts, "Everyone get to the door and keep firing!"

They all head for the door. Livia, Enzo, Zavier, and Vippy fire blasters at the few PCF officers hiding behind the High Council table.

Del coaxes Armand, "Come on, let's go!"

Armand walks with Del, his steps shuffling. "This is quite an exciting rescue. Much more blaster fire than I expected."

49

Travis leads the group across the concrete road on top of the dam. On one side of the dam the low sun reflects off the rippling water in the huge reservoir, on the other is an expansive barren valley. Lex limps behind Travis, held up by Kane and Markus, her arms over their shoulders. Not far behind, two of Travis's men walk with Parker staggering between them. At the end of the group, Dalton and Francisco carry Chae, Amia walking alongside.

"Are you sure the water was released?" asks Kane. "It doesn't look like much is happening."

"I can hear it," says Lex. "The water is definitely rushing through the old pipe system."

When they reach the edge of the dam, Lex says, "That's far enough."

Travis hands Lex the detonator. "You can do the honors."

Lex grabs the detonator, quickly flips open the protective cover, and pushes the button. A split second later, there is a loud explosion and the dam shakes violently under their feet. With an earsplitting crash, several huge geysers of water burst out of the dam on the side of the valley, the sounds of cracking concrete and rushing water deafening. The dam continues to shake and starts to rupture, with giant pieces of the concrete structure tearing off, water erupting from every crack and fissure.

"It looks like this whole thing is going to go," yells Kane. "We should get farther back."

"Agreed," yells Travis, and they all get moving, making an effort to go as fast as possible for a few hundred feet until they are a safe distance from the disintegrating dam. The roar of the rushing water is slightly decreased, and they slow to a walk.

"Our camp is just over the ridge ahead," says Travis.

"I hope we were fast enough," says Lex as water rushes out of the reservoir into the valley. "Who knows how many people died because you forced me to wait."

"Well, however many die, that's on me," says Travis. "My first priority is to protect myself and my men. I'll make sure Del knows you would have blown the dam sooner and killed us all, but I stopped you. I'm sure she'll be impressed."

"I don't care what Del thinks. I care that people died and I could have stopped it."

"People you don't know," says Travis, unmoved. "Even with the delay, I'm sure this will save a lot of lives."

"How can you be so heartless?"

"I may be heartless, but we're all alive." Travis picks up his pace.

Lex watches Travis stride ahead of the group. *Travis is callous and self-serving. He came out here on Del's orders, but it sounds like he doesn't respect her. I don't like this guy.*

50

The group runs down a corridor in the High Council Building with Vippy and Enzo in the lead firing their blasters to clear a path. Shocked gray suits dodge out of the way of the blaster fire, ducking into doorways as the group runs past, while additional officers join those chasing them. Livia and Del help the shuffling Armand, followed by Roscoe. Zavier is at the end of the group, running backward and firing at the PCF officers pursuing them.

Roscoe pulls his comm off his belt. Over the blaster fire, he yells, "Becka! The garden! Now! You need to pull us out!"

They turn a corner and enter a stairwell. With blaster fire hitting the walls around them, they tear down the stairs and out into the corridor leading to the garden. They burst out the door into the open-roof garden as the transporter is dropping down, landing just beyond the empty fountain, teams of gardening and construction crews scrambling out of the way. The transporter door flies open. Vippy and Enzo run past the fountain and jump aboard, taking cover just inside the door. They immediately start firing at the approaching PCF officers.

As Livia and Del help Armand past the fountain, Roscoe yells, "Livia, give me your blaster. You and Delphia get Armand aboard. Zavier and I will cover you." She hands her blaster to Roscoe.

Roscoe ducks low behind the edge of the fountain and yells, "Zavier, with me." He crouches with Roscoe and they add to Enzo and Vippy's barrage of blaster fire holding back the increasing number of PCF officers bearing down on the transporter. Livia runs ahead and jumps on board. She reaches out and helps Del get Armand aboard and moves him to the back of the transporter.

Del yells, "Zavier! Roscoe! Come aboard!"

They start to move to the transporter. Roscoe takes a blaster hit to the chest and slumps to his knees.

Del screams, "Roscoe!"

"Enzo!" yells Zavier. He throws his blaster to Enzo, who catches it and starts firing both blasters. He hits several officers, forcing the rest to take cover. Zavier crouches next to Roscoe.

Enzo yells, "Help him!" as he continues to fire.

"We're close. I'll get you aboard," says Zavier, extending his hand.

Roscoe waves his arm weakly. "I'm not going to make it. Go. Get them out of here. Shoot out one of the relays in the dome like we talked about."

"Sir?" says Zavier, unsure.

"Father!" yells Enzo. "Come on!"

Roscoe tilts his head toward the transporter and locks eyes with Enzo. Roscoe shakes his head slightly and mouths, "I can't." Enzo nods, resolved. He focuses back on the PCF officers, firing with increased intensity.

Roscoe turns to Zavier. "Leave me! Now! That's an order."

"Yes, sir." Zavier jumps up and sprints the few feet to the transporter.

Del screams, "Roscoe! No!" and scrambles out the door. Zavier grabs Del around the waist as he boards the transporter, and pulls her back inside.

With his last bit of strength, Roscoe lifts his blaster and fires at the PCF officers. Enzo stops firing, slams the button, and the transporter door closes.

He yells to Becka, "We're clear. Go!" The transporter takes off, blaster fire hitting the door and windows but doing little damage.

"Blast this city!" yells Enzo, and punches the wall of the transporter. Then he hits his head against it.

Del pounds her fists on Zavier's back. "We can't leave him!"

Zavier turns and grabs Del's hands, forcing her to stop. Through the window, Livia sees Roscoe hit with more blaster fire, and he crumples to the ground.

"Why did you leave him?" Del wails, struggling to get her hands free.

"He was hit in the chest, Del," says Zavier, with tenderness in his voice.

"He wasn't going to make it, and he knew it," adds Enzo.

Zavier pulls Del into a hug and she collapses against him. "I'm sorry, Del." Livia rushes to Del, and with Enzo's help, they pull her off Zavier and help her to the bench.

"Oh, Del," says Livia, wrapping her arm around Del's back. "I'm so sorry." Del says nothing and buries her face in her hands. *Poor Del, she is devastated. And Enzo.* She looks at Enzo holding Del's hand, his face blank. *Roscoe was his father. He is in shock, trying to be strong. Roscoe died to make sure we all got away. He died saving Armand.* Livia looks over at Armand. He sits calmly, his eyes moving around the transporter. *He is here, but what he did to his mind was drastic. My father, that brilliant man, is he gone? Can he ever recover? I feel like somehow all of this is Del's fault. She knows so much more than she has told me, told us. She wants to use Lex and me as The Twins but keeps this huge secret from us. How can I be so mad at her and still want to comfort her?*

Becka yells back, "Jo said she would give us some cover." As the transporter pulls away from the High Council Building, they look back and see Jo's rig moving toward the Spear on a rapid collision course with the windows of the High Council Chamber. Jo and the others from her rig are racing away on speeders. The rig crashes into the High Council Building, plowing through the Council Chamber and tearing a huge hole in the building, causing catastrophic damage.

"Thank you, Jo," says Livia, her voice quiet.

"That won't distract them for long," yells Becka. "We're going to have PCF patrollers on us in a minute. What's the plan?"

Zavier moves up toward the front of the transporter. "Head straight up at the dome." He sits in the copilot's seat. "We'll shoot out one of the relays in the dome and we can fly through."

"What are the relays?" asks Livia.

"When we get close, you'll see. The dome isn't solid. It's a combination force field and projection. The relays are floating discs that create the force field and generate the projection. They work like a web, each relay sending out a signal to the ones around it. If we take out a relay, that section will fail and we can fly through. None of the PCF patrollers will follow us. They know it would kill them to leave the dome."

"We can't just fly out of Indra," says Livia, alarmed. "Vippy and Armand still have their chips. They can't go past the dome. And they need the additive."

"I don't have a chip," says Armand. "They took it out years ago."

"Yeah, well I do," says Vippy. "What will happen to me?"

"Your brain will get fried if you go much more than two miles past the dome," says Zavier.

"What? Is there a speeder aboard? I'll take my chances on my own."

Suddenly, Armand falls to the floor convulsing, his body shaking violently, one arm sticking out straight and his eyes rolling back in his head. Livia rushes to his side. Del is shaken from her sobs and jumps to Armand's other side.

"What's wrong with him?" yells Vippy, panicked. "Is it the chip?"

"He just said they took it out!" yells Livia as she and Del try to hold Armand as he shakes.

"It's something else," says Del. "Maybe from being in stasis for so long."

Becka yells, "Here they come. We've got PCF patrollers in pursuit. Taking evasive action. Hold on." The transporter swings sharply to the left and tilts up drastically. They climb much steeper. On the floor, Livia, Del, and Armand slide toward the back of the transporter while everyone else tightly grabs hold of their seats. "Zavier, start firing on them."

Zavier focuses his attention on the console controller for the blaster cannon mounted on the top of the transporter and fires off a few shots.

Armand's seizure slows. His body goes limp. Livia holds his hand while Del strokes his brow, tears running down her face.

"Zavier!" yells Vippy. "Is there a speeder?"

"Nope. No speeder," says Zavier, continuing to fire on the PCF patrollers, "but there's no need for that. Outside the dome, when we get past the irradiated zone, we'll leave you somewhere safe. I'll come back for you with equipment to remove the chip."

The transporter takes a blaster cannon hit and it pitches drastically forward. Everyone in the back is thrown from their seats and a loud wailing alarm starts to sound.

Becka is able to pull the transporter up and yells over the alarms, "Hold tight. This is going to be rough."

While Zavier continues to return fire on the PCF, he yells, "Vippy! The additive is less of a problem. Roscoe was prepared for us to leave Indra this way if we had too. Well, not exactly like this, but there are breathing devices on board. You, Armand, and Becka should probably put them on in case the transporter's air supply is breached. Everyone else is off the additive. Enzo, they're in the wall locker behind the pilot's seat."

Enzo jumps up and makes his way to the front, remarkably steady on his feet even though the transporter is bucking and weaving. The transporter takes another hit and lurches to the side, but Enzo is unfazed. One of the windows cracks. With a crackling noise, tiny fracture lines crawl across the window.

"Hurry, Enzo!" yells Zavier.

When Enzo reaches the locker, he pulls out two breathing devices and throws them back to Vippy, who catches them easily. "One for you and one for Armand."

Vippy hands one to Livia.

"The clip goes on your nose," says Livia. "Make sure to switch it on and dial the regulator all the way up."

Vippy puts on her device while Livia and Del put on Armand's. Enzo grabs a third device and awkwardly puts it on Becka just as the window blows out with a rush of air.

“We’re close to the top of the dome,” yells Becka, adjusting her nose clip. Zavier swings the cannon around and aims at a large white disc embedded in the dome. The cannon blaster fire hits the relay and nothing happens.

“It’s not working,” yells Becka. “The dome is still there!”

“I see!” Zavier blasts it again with the cannon and the disc sparks. The pale white dome around the relay flickers.

“We are going to hit it!” yells Becka.

“Don’t turn! This should do it!” Zavier blasts the sparking relay with a sustained burst of cannon fire and the relay explodes, small flaming pieces of metal and wires showering down toward Indra. A huge section of the dome disappears, revealing the sky beyond, bright blue and streaked with wispy clouds just turning purple in the setting sun.

“Whoa!” Becka gasps as she flies the transporter through the hole in the dome. A swarm of PCF patrollers slows and hovers at the edge of the dome as the transporter speeds away.

Vippy stands and stares out the window, her mouth open. “It’s beautiful.”

“It is,” says Enzo, standing next to her.

Armand’s eyelids flutter open, and he says dreamily, “I always wanted to go outside the dome.”

“Well, I’m glad that worked,” says Becka.

“Me too,” says Zavier, letting out a long breath.

“I didn’t think it would, and I was about to turn,” says Becka. “We wouldn’t have been able to fight off all those patrollers.”

“How far is it safe for me to go?” asks Vippy.

“To be safe, I don’t want to go more than a mile past the dome,” says Zavier. “We’ll find a spot with some shelter just beyond the irradiated zone. You’ll have to stay there until I can get the equipment I need to remove your chip. I’ll try to contact Chief Benton at the Outpost, but it will be several days at least.”

Del says, “When we get back to the colony, I’ll send someone with food and supplies.” She and Livia help Armand up off the floor and onto the bench.

"I'll stay with Vippy," volunteers Enzo.

"I don't need you to stay with me," says Vippy, indignant.

"No," says Zavier. "It will be better if you're not alone."

Vippy scowls. "Fine."

Livia looks at Del. *I shouldn't pry. I won't sense her feelings. She must be devastated about Roscoe, but she is holding it together. She is so strong.*

Livia says, "Roscoe's death is a terrible loss. He was a good man."

"Yes, he was," says Del.

"I felt so much death when the water rushed into Rock Bottom. I wish I had blocked it out like you told me to."

"You can't block out everything, and you shouldn't." Del takes Livia's hand. "We'll get a report on the damage when we get to the colony. We did everything we could. We'll just have to wait and see how many died."

"What do you think happened to Lex, Kane, and their team at the dam?" asks Livia. "Do you think they were captured or killed? I tried to sense them, but they are much too far away. The gray suit only said there was a breach at the dam. Perhaps they got away."

"I hope so."

"Vippy, there's a good spot ahead to leave you and Enzo," says Zavier. "Becka, take us down."

51

The Outlanders' camp beyond the dam is a cluster of small canvas structures surrounding a fire pit, well camouflaged in a group of trees. It is rapidly getting dark as the sun sets. The fire in the pit serves as the main source of light. Lex's jumpsuit is cut away to midthigh, Kane bandaging the blaster wound on her leg as she sits on the ground close to the fire. Travis's men are making quick work of breaking down the camp, disassembling the tents and loading gear in packs. Dalton lays a cloth over Chae's body.

"I hope you got the superhealing genes like your mother," says Kane. "This looks pretty bad."

"It doesn't feel too bad, unless I try to walk on it," says Lex.

Next to Lex and Kane, Amia hovers over Parker, carefully cleaning his beaten and damaged face. One of his eyes is swollen shut. Parker winces when Travis moves his broken leg, positioning it in a splint made out of two slim tree branches and a few lengths of cloth.

"That Lieutenant Hauser is vicious," says Parker. "He smiled when he heard the bone in my leg snap. He was not happy that I wouldn't tell him what we were doing at the dam."

"It must have been him that opened the floodgate valves and sent the water into the pipes," says Lex. "I wish I had killed him when I had the chance. If he hadn't gotten away, we could have blown the dam before any water got released."

"Well, at least you shot his hand off," says Kane, pulling the bandage tight and tying it in a knot.

Lex asks Travis, "How long have you been out here?"

"Del had us watching the dam and the reservoir for the last few months," says Travis, wrapping cloth around Parker's splint. "I'll be glad to get back to the colony." Then he orders, "Markus, prep the speeders."

"Yes, sir," says Markus, and darts off toward the back of the camp. He clears away a pile of branches, revealing six beat-up speeders.

"You four will ride on the back of our speeders," says Travis. "We can bury your friend here or secure him to a speeder and take him back to the colony."

"I'd like to take him back with us," says Amia.

"All right," says Travis. "We'll make sure he gets a proper burial."

"How long will it take to get to Del's colony?" asks Lex.

"A long time," says Travis. "The better part of the night. It's far. And it's not *Del's* colony. It doesn't belong to her."

"Sure. Got it," says Lex. *I thought Del was in charge at the colony, but it seems like not everyone feels that way. Travis said he and his men came out here on her orders, or that's what it sounded like. If Del isn't the leader of the Outlanders' colony, who is?*

"Amia," says Lex, "when we get to the six-hour mark from the start of this mission, you and Parker can swap out your breathing devices for mine and Kane's. That should get you there."

"Right, the additive," says Travis. "Del sent extra additive in preparation for this mission. She thought there would be six of you who would need it, so there will be plenty. That's as good as we can do for now," Travis says to Parker, then turns to Kane. "You done with Lex's leg?"

"Yeah," says Kane, handing Lex the leg of her cutoff jumpsuit. She pulls it on over her foot and up so it covers her bandage, the silitex clinging tightly to her leg.

"Time to head out," says Travis.

52

Becka is looking at the sky as she flies the transporter. With the sun just below the distant mountains, the clouds have turned a dark gray against the fading blue.

Becka asks, "Does the sky always look so strato?"

"Yep," says Zavier. "This is a sunset. That's why it's changing color. Even when it's not changing color, just big and blue with white clouds, it's still incredible. You can put us down at the edge of those trees."

"Those are all trees? They go on forever."

Zavier chuckles. "It's called a forest. I already forgot what it's like to see this for the first time."

Becka lands the transporter in a clearing on the outskirts of the Outlanders' colony. They all disembark, Livia and Del helping Armand, followed by Zavier and Becka, her eyes wide.

Zavier slaps her on the back. "Good flying today. Welcome to the Outlands, friend. You'll want to start dialing down the regulator on the breathing device so you can get off the additive as soon as possible."

"Yeah, all right," says Becka, her voice distracted.

Quinn runs up to the group with Jules limping a few paces behind him, his leg in a mechanical brace.

"We weren't expecting you back for days," says Quinn, alarmed. "What happened?"

"There were changes and complications," says Del.

"Mother," says Jules, just reaching them, "we heard from the team at the dam. Is it true the water was released?"

"Yes. We don't know the extent of the damage."

"We'll try to reach out to our contacts in Rock Bottom and check on the Last Outpost," says Jules.

"Yes, good," says Del.

"I hope Aidan and Luther are all right," says Livia. "They were headed back to Rock Bottom."

"We will find out as soon as we can," says Jules, looking around at everyone. "Where's Enzo? And father?"

"Enzo is fine," says Del, and pauses, looking at Jules. "But Roscoe didn't make it."

"What do you mean? He didn't come back with you?"

"No, Jules." Del's voice is thick with emotion. "I'm sorry. Your father is dead." Del pulls Jules into a hug.

"I can't believe it," says Jules, pulling out of the hug, his eyes filling with tears. "He was going to stay this time, be in the Outlands for good. We were all going to be together, finally."

"I know. I'm sorry."

"What happened?" asks Jules, wiping his face with his sleeve.

"I'll tell you the long version later, but the short version is, he was being Roscoe, selfless, brave, and honorable. It was because of Roscoe that we rescued Armand." Del indicates Armand, and Jules's mouth drops open.

"You're Armand?" he asks Del, shocked. "Lex and Livia's father?"

"Yes, I'm Livia's father," says Armand. "Only Livia is in this dream. I just learned her twin's name is Lex, but perhaps that name is part of my dream."

Jules whispers, "What's wrong with him?"

"Nothing wrong with my hearing," says Armand, with a smile.

"He's been in the Archives for almost sixteen years," says Del. "He thinks he is still there now."

"I could be dreaming, or remembering," says Armand. "But too many new faces for remembering, so dreaming I think."

"Where is Enzo?" asks Jules.

"He stayed back with Vippy, Corah and Otto's daughter. She helped us rescue Armand but still has her chip. Until it can be removed, she has to stay close to the dome. We have to get supplies out to them. Quinn, take care of that. They will be there for several days."

"Yes, ma'am," says Quinn.

Zavier looks at Jules. "When you contact the Last Outpost, if they're all right, tell them to send a team out here with the equipment to remove her chip."

"Yes, I'll comm them right away," says Jules. "Corah and Otto will be surprised she's out of Indra. It wasn't part of the plan for Vippy to leave her post at the Council Building."

"No, it wasn't," agrees Del.

"The team from the dam commed us a little while ago," says Jules. "They have Lex and most of her team."

"Most of her team!" Livia says, alarmed.

"Travis, the team leader, said there were five, but one is dead."

"Dead!" yells Livia. "Who is dead?"

"He says that a rebel named Chae was killed."

"Blast!" barks Zavier.

"I'm sorry, Zavier," says Livia, gently touching his arm.

Zavier nods. "Go on, Jules. What else?"

"And one of their team had to head back to Rock Bottom before they made it out to the dam. They were going to head out soon after we spoke. Travis thought they should be here sometime before sunrise."

"I need to get Armand to Medical so he can rest," says Del. She turns to Armand. "We're going to take you where you can lie down."

"Oh, yes." A smile lights up his face. "That would be lovely."

Quinn takes the lead position and switches on his beamer. Its light floats above him as they head into the woods, Del and Livia steadying Armand with Jules following close behind them. Zavier and Becka both switch on their beamers and walk at the back of the group.

"There are so many trees here," says Armand. "I like it very much."

"I do too," says Livia.

They walk quietly for a while, then Del says, "I know you are angry I didn't tell you and Lex about my parents. I left them. I left that life. Even when I was young, I never wanted to be part of a Founding Family or be on the Council. Edward and Sivette are terrible people. Like all the Founding Families, everything they do is to protect their power and position. I wanted nothing to do with them or the Council. I considered that part of my life dead. The truth is, I never planned on telling you who they were, who I am."

"That was not your decision to make," says Livia. "They are not just your family, they're ours too. It's our history. Lex and I had a right to know. You can't expect us to just do what you ask if we can't trust you."

"Your parents are terrible people, Delphia," says Armand quietly. "Scary. They are always in the nightmares. I never liked them."

"It would have been better if you didn't know," says Del. "Knowing you share the blood of such vile people is a burden. I didn't want you to feel any connection to them."

"They were going to kill me. I feel no connection to them. Is there anything else we should know? Are there any other secrets you're keeping?"

"No."

"I don't know if I believe that."

"Believe what you want," says Del. "I did what I thought was right. I won't apologize. I'm only sorry you found out about them."

"I see," says Livia. *She is infuriating! She thinks she is justified. She won't hesitate to keep things from Lex and me if she thinks it is for the best. She is so sure she is right. Now I know why she wrote "I belong to no one" on the wall at the Last Outpost. She meant her parents and the Council. I don't know if I will ever trust her.*

They enter Medical, and Evelyn gets up from the small table in the entrance room.

"Who is this?" she asks as she comes over to inspect Armand.

"He's a dear friend," says Del. "We need to get him to a cot."

"Of course," says Evelyn, and leads them down the hall.

"He's just come out of stasis," says Del. "He was in the Archives for sixteen years."

"Oh, my!" exclaims Evelyn, alarmed. "I've never dealt with anything like this before."

Livia asks, "Do you have the supplies needed to treat Armand here?"

"We have some boosters and some natural herbs that might help," says Evelyn.

They enter a room, and Livia and Del settle Armand into a cot.

"Mainly, we should let him rest," says Del. "Hopefully, he will be much more aware in a few hours. Livia, you should go rest too. Quinn will get you back to your cave."

"Yes, ma'am," says Quinn.

Livia crouches next to Armand. "I'm glad you're here, Father."

"Me too," says Armand. He smiles and closes his eyes. Livia kisses him on the forehead and he mutters, "This is a beautiful dream. Such a beautiful dream."

Livia stands and walks to Del. "Please let me know how he's doing. If he becomes alert."

"Yes. Of course," says Del, then turns to Becka. "Quinn will find a place for you to stay. Go with them."

"Yes, ma'am," says Becka. Quinn heads out of Medical, Livia and Becka behind him.

53

With the noise of the six speeders echoing through the quiet forest, Lex looks at the sky from the back of Dalton's speeder. *I love how the moon moves across the sky so slowly you barely notice. And the stars, thousands of tiny specks of light on a dark blue blanket, beautiful. It's been hours. I can feel Dalton slumping forward. He must be exhausted from this long ride, piloting around the dome of Indra and through the wilderness.* She looks ahead and spots Kane on the back of Francisco's speeder. *Everyone must be exhausted. There are more trees now. I think we are getting close. The smell has changed. It's not just the dirt and the trees and the animals. I smell the Outlanders' colony, the people, the food, the fires. We are close. Finally.*

A short time later, Travis's voice comes over the helmet comm. "Welcome home."

Slowly, they weave the speeders through the colony, passing familiar buildings until they reach the back of the shop. They pull in and park along the wall with the other speeders and all pull off their helmets.

Travis orders, "Dalton. Francisco. Get Parker to Medical. That leg needs to be properly set."

They both respond, "Yes, sir," and jump off, leaving Lex and Kane on the backs of their speeders.

Amia gets off the back of one of the speeders and goes to Markus's, where Chae's body has been tied down. Markus hops off and helps her untie his body. Kane dismounts and goes over to help Lex.

"That was a long ride," says Kane. "How does your leg feel?"

"Stiff." She carefully swings her leg over the side of the speeder. A few speeders down, Parker groans as Dalton and Francisco help him off. "Parker must feel terrible. I hope they have some boosters in Medical they can give him."

Kane helps Lex to her feet just as Livia rushes up. "Lex! Kane!" She attacks them, hugging them so fiercely Lex stumbles back.

"Whoa! Careful," says Lex, grabbing Livia's shoulder to steady herself.

Livia looks down. "Oh! Your leg? I'm sorry. Are you all right?"

"It's not bad," Lex says dismissively and sits back down on the speeder.

"I'm so glad you're here." Livia hugs Kane tightly and kisses him. "When they released the water, I feared you both might be captured or dead."

"Almost," says Kane. "Del's team at the dam showed up, but we lost Chae."

"Jules told us. That's terrible," says Livia.

"The leader of their group, Travis, made me delay setting off the explosives," says Lex.

"Which is why we are alive," says Kane.

"Well, I'm glad you are," Livia says, relieved. "I can't even let myself think about losing either of you." She can see that Kane is banged up and asks, "Are you hurt too?"

"Not badly," says Kane. "It all went wrong 'cause the PCF had a unit at the dam. We had to—"

"Wait," interrupts Lex. "What are you doing here? I thought you were going back to Rock Bottom and out through the tunnel. How did you get out of Indra so fast?"

"Zavier shot a hole in the dome and we flew out."

"How was that even possible?" asks Lex.

"The dome is not as it appears," says Livia. "It's a projection and a force field. It only looks solid. There are relays that make the whole thing. We shot one out and a section of the dome disappeared."

"Like so many other things in Indra, the dome is just another lie," says Lex, shaking her head.

"Still, that was a lot faster than going through the tunnel!" says Kane. "And no mud."

"How did your mission at the air filtration plant go?" asks Lex.

"That went fairly well, then we rescued our father."

Lex blurts out, "What? Really? From the Archives? How is he? Have you spoken to him? What did he say?"

"Slow down," says Livia. "He's here. We took him to Medical, but he's still recovering. He's very confused. I'm not sure how much of it is from the procedure he and Ephraim did to his brain and how much of it is from being in the Archives for so long. He needs time to rest and recover, and then we'll see. Del stayed with him in Medical. She said she would let me know when he was awake. But there is so much I have to tell you. The rescue did not go smoothly. We were caught in the High Council Building by Cassina."

"Cassina? I hate her," says Lex.

"Yes. I do too. I hit her in the face and knocked her out."

"I wish I had been there to see it," says Lex, smiling. "Now who's the hothead?"

"Lex, I met our grandparents."

"What?"

"Del's parents," clarifies Livia. "They are on the High Council. Del is from one of the Founding Families, and that means we are too."

"We're from a Founding Family? Why didn't Del tell us about this? About them?"

"She thought it would be better if we didn't know. She wasn't planning on telling us."

"Not tell us, ever?" Lex yells, her face a fierce scowl. "She can't keep something like that from us! She has no right."

"I agree with you. She should have told us. She said it would be better if we didn't know who they were because they are such awful people."

"I don't care if they are core-low mutants, she should have told us!

She's got us running around like we work for her and she's keeping things from us. Big things! I barely trusted her before. Now I don't trust her at all."

"I talked to her about it and she is only sorry that I found out," says Livia. "She feels she was right to keep it from us. She is right about one thing, though. They are truly horrible people. They wanted to keep Del and me so they could do genetic experiments on us."

"Our grandparents sound delightful," Lex says with a smirk. "Really sorry I missed it. Do we have any more family that is going to surprise us and appear out of nowhere or come back from the dead? So far, you are the only one I even halfway like."

"Thanks," says Livia, smiling. "I halfway like you too."

Zavier walks up and sees Amia helping Markus pull the body off the back of the speeder.

"Is that Chae?" he asks.

"Yes," says Lex. "I'm sorry. I know he was a friend."

"He was. A good friend. I see Amia. What about Parker and Matson? I heard one of the team had to go back to Rock Bottom."

"That was Matson," says Kane. "We lost a speeder and he headed back to Rock Bottom before we even got out of Indra. Parker is on his way to Medical. He's pretty beat-up."

"I'll have to go check on him," says Zavier, his face tight. "I hope Matson is all right. We still don't know how bad it was in Rock Bottom. That was a rough mission." He looks at Lex. "I'm glad you made it through. Did Livia tell you about Roscoe?"

"I was about to," says Livia. "While we were escaping, Roscoe was killed."

Kane's eyes go wide. "Killed? When?"

Lex's eyes lock on Zavier's, searching his face. *He must be hurting. Roscoe was his mentor, his hero. This is terrible.*

"When we were escaping," says Zavier. "Just before he got to the transporter."

"Del must be devastated," says Kane. "And Enzo and Jules, they lost their father. This is awful."

“I’m sorry,” Lex says to Zavier. “He was like a father to you.”

Zavier nods. “Roscoe was the strongest, most principled man I’ve ever known. I would have done anything for him.”

“This has been a dreadful day,” says Livia as Kane wraps his arms around her. She takes a deep breath. “After the Council released the water, I could feel it when the people started dying. We still don’t know how many people were killed.”

“At least we did something,” says Lex, dejected. “Hopefully it wasn’t too late. The sun will be up in an hour or so. We should all try to sleep a little. You two can have the cave. I’m going to sleep outside. I could use the fresh air.”

“No!” protests Livia. “Come back to the cave with us.”

Lex shakes her head and limps away. Zavier runs after her and ducks under her arm, helping her walk. He points to her leg, “What happened there?”

Lex says, “Just a scratch.”

“It must have been rough. I’m glad you’re all right.”

“Me too. I heard you blasted the dome. Wish I could have seen that.”

As they head into the woods, Zavier says, “So you think Livia and Kane will want the cave to themselves tonight?” He smirks. “Very selfless, volunteering to sleep outside. You’re welcome to join me in our spot.”

“It’s not our spot.”

“It could be.” Zavier smiles. “I’ll keep my hands to myself like a Proper Indrithian Young Man.”

“Zavier, there’s nothing proper about you.”

“True, but there is nothing proper about you, either. Just let me know if you get cold.”

54

With the morning sun breaking through the trees, Lex wakes in the same clearing she and Zavier slept in before, the cool ground beneath her and Zavier's warm body tucked up against her. The two of them lie closely on their sides, his arm wrapped around her waist. *I can hear Livia and Kane stomping through the woods. This is not how I want them to find me. Though I shouldn't care. He's not the most terrible person in the world.* She gingerly lifts Zavier's arm and rolls away from him. Just as Lex is moving away from Zavier and sitting up, Livia and Kane walk up, holding hands.

Livia raises an eyebrow. "So you did get cold last night?"

"Maybe," says Lex. "How was the cave?"

"I was quite warm," Livia says with a smile, and squeezes Kane's hand.

Lex groans, "Oh, stop."

"You asked," says Livia. "Don't ask if you don't want to know."

"That's a fair point," says Zavier with a yawn, stretching his arms and sitting up.

"We came to find you because Quinn said Del wants us to meet her in her cave," says Livia. "Apparently our father is awake and remarkably alert."

"Let's go!" says Lex, jumping up.

"Zavier, you're welcome to come too," says Livia.

"No. He doesn't need to," Lex says and strides into the woods, Livia and Kane following behind her.

"Don't speak for me," says Zavier, hurrying to catch up with the group. "I was part of the rescue that got him here. I'd like to see how he's doing."

"Fine," says Lex with a sigh, and stalks ahead. *So we're back to him wanting to do the opposite of whatever I say. I thought we were past that. He's such a stubborn rebel. I guess that will never change. He is going to drive me crazy.*

When the group enters Del's cave, Quinn and Jules are sitting at the table.

"Come sit," says Jules. "Mother will be here shortly," he continues as they all take seats around the large table. "She's bringing Armand. He is doing much better."

"That is amazing news," says Livia.

"I still can't believe he's here," says Lex.

"Apparently he is anxious to meet both of you," says Jules. "Though technically, he's already met you, Livia. But from what Mother said, he doesn't remember much of yesterday. Now that his head is clear, he says that the rescue and meeting you feels like a hallucination."

"I'm glad we got him out," says Zavier, "but we paid a heavy price. We lost Roscoe, Del's evil parents know that she and Livia have crazy genetic enhancements, they know who Lex is, and worst of all, they know we're out here in the Outlands."

"No one asked you to give your opinion," snaps Lex.

"Rescuing Armand was the right thing to do," says Livia defensively.

"Yeah, I'm not arguing with you about that," says Zavier. "I'm saying there was a price. You can't deny that."

"There was no way to know it would turn out the way it did," says Jules. "But it's done. And there is no changing it." He looks at Lex and Livia. "My father lost his life saving yours. I know he always regretted that he was not able to protect Armand. I'm sure he saw this as his one chance to finally save his oldest friend. We need to look at the good that came out of the last few days. We have gotten a report that Core Low was flooded, and parts of Rock Bottom, but the water lost momentum and many people did survive. Most of the mutants drowned, but those who didn't fled the water and came into Rock Bottom. Some people were killed in the chaos."

"When the Council released the water all I could feel was death," says Livia. "Whether it was mutants or people, it was horrible."

Jules nods. "I can imagine how terrible that would be. Still it could have been much worse. So many people lived that would not have if we had done nothing. I've reached the Outpost and it was untouched. They will send a team of runners out with the machine to remove Vippy's chip."

"The sooner the better," says Livia.

"Yeah," says Zavier. "We don't want Vippy and Enzo out there too long. I'm sure the PCF will start patrols looking for us."

Del enters the cave with Armand, walking slowly as he leans his frail body against hers, the tube from the breathing device clipped to his nose. His face is now clean-shaven and his wild hair is smoothed back. His eyes, alert and bright, scan the room and fall on Lex and Livia, who immediately stand and walk to him. He puts a hand on each of their cheeks.

With tears in his eyes, he says, "My girls. My sweet girls. You're so grown-up. I've missed so much. Though truly, I never thought I would meet you. I've watched the memory files and the message I recorded for myself. My mind is more clear. I can actually remember some things now that could have been lost forever." Armand says to Livia, "My sensitive one. I'm sorry they took me away from you. I made Waslo promise to look after you."

Livia smiles. "He did, in his way."

Armand turns to Lex. "You were the strong one. I could see it in your eyes. I knew you could survive anything."

"I did," nods Lex. "It was awful, but I survived."

"I'm so sorry," says Armand. "Both of you. I'm so sorry."

Livia says, "Father, come sit," taking his arm.

As they all take seats around the table, Armand says, "On those rare occasions when the Council brought me out of the Archives, Waslo was able to tell me about you two. At first I was quite confused because I had no memory of you girls. But since the Council had discovered you were twins they had questioned me about you many times, and I accepted it to be true. I was very grateful that Waslo was watching you both, though he kept Lex's name and location from me so I could never share it with the Council. At least I knew you were both alive. And look, now we are all here together. I never thought this would happen. I thought the Council would kill me. There were times I wished they would. Being trapped in the Archives is a terrible punishment."

"I'm so glad we got you out," says Livia. "I'm sorry it took so long."

"That was the way it had to be," says Armand with a sad smile.

"What happens now?" asks Lex. "Will the PCF come after us?"

"I'm sure they will try," answers Del. "Now that they know what Armand accomplished with Livia and me, the Council will want us back, and they know we are in the Outlands. I imagine they would want Lex as well, now that they know she exists. Plus, they will find out that we have used the Twin Prophecy to free Rock Bottom, and this will truly worry the Council because they know your true lineage. That you are not only twins but the direct descendants of Andru and Atros, the twin founders of Indra. That has even more power."

"So you're not only from a Founding Family, you are a descendant of Atros!" yells Lex. "What else are you hiding?"

"I'm not hiding anything," says Del. "I just thought there were things you didn't need to know."

"I disagree," says Livia. "We need to know everything."

"Well, we know the Council will come for you," says Del. "If for no other reason than to destroy you and the Twin Prophecy, but they don't know the Outlands. We have resources we can utilize to fight them. We can defend ourselves. Though not perfect, our missions were successful. In a day or so, all those we have saved will leave Rock Bottom and come through the tunnel. We will help them adjust, though some are very weak and have disabling genetic flaws."

“I believe I can help repair their corrupted genes,” says Armand. “Now that I have my research back.”

“What do you mean?” asks Livia.

Armand smiles. “I couldn’t risk the Council using my work for their own ends. I stripped it from my mind, but I didn’t want to destroy it. I preserved all my work and hid it. I promised myself I would only access my research again if both you girls were safe. So I split the research in two. You each have only half. The small green marks in your eyes are micro data chips. With both of you, I can reassemble my work. Though I don’t remember any of it, I believe I will be able to retrace my steps and help so many people. Future generations will have a better chance.”

“So the twin lore is true,” Livia says. “We are The Twins who will ‘bring freedom to Indra and all its people.’”

Lex adds, “Whether we believe it or not, The Time of the Twins has come.”

ACKNOWLEDGMENTS

Kendall & Kylie's Acknowledgments

We want to thank our mom and dad who have always supported us and told us every day that nothing is impossible. To our Momager, the fabulous Kris Jenner, you help us achieve our dreams, and we are eternally grateful. Thank you to the incredible Jenner-Kardashian family and our fantastic friends for your encouragement, which has never wavered. To all our beautiful sisters, thank you for your support. You are the inspiration for this story about the power of sisterhood. To Liz, we love that our story that started as a conversation in 2012 continues to grow. Thank you for being our partner in this amazing journey.

Elizabeth Killmond-Roman and Katherine Killmond's Acknowledgments

Thank you Kendall and Kylie for continuing this extraordinary literary adventure with us. It is thrilling to build the world of Lex and Livia with you. To the remarkable and inspiring Kris Jenner, thank you for your friendship and for always being an enthusiastic champion for this project. We are so grateful for our wonderful and patient husbands, Mark Roman and Eric Cannady, and our family who are a constant source of support, particularly during the many long nights and weekends we spent in front of the computer. Special thanks to our amazing brother John Killmond and the insightful Sarah Cannady for all their help.

Everyone's Acknowledgments

There are so many brilliant and creative people who have been involved in this project. The phenomenal Judith Regan and her terrific team at Regan Arts: Lynne Ciccaglione, Kathryn Huck, Richard Ljoenes, Nancy Singer, Kathryn Santora, Gregory Henry, and Clarke Bowling. Charles Suitt, who brought us together with Regan Arts, thank you for always believing in Lex and Livia. Our cowriter of Book 1 *Rebels: City of Indra*, the talented Maya Sloan. Everyone at Simon & Schuster: Brigitte Smith, Jennifer Long, Carolyn Reidy, and Dennis Elau. The incredible agents at WME: Mel Berger, Lance Klein, and their teams. Mel, your advice and guidance were instrumental in helping us navigate this project. The social media guru Jennifer Cohan, your advice has been truly invaluable! The sensational group at Whalerock, the creators of lexandlivia.com: Jen Garcia Allen, Evelyn Crowley, Kathleen Perricone, Brenna Egan, Adam Maffei, Kelly Kaufman, Eliza Gold, Micah Miller, Kim Hogan, Ashley Dana, Stephanie Hankins, Kristina Carucci, and Abby Varinsky. Our marvelous publicists Carrie Gordon and Katie Greenthal from 42West, and Ina Treciokas and Megan Senior from Slate PR. Our tirelessly supportive team at Boulevard Management and Todd Wilson, Esq. for always having our backs. The cover artist Louise Mertens, photographer Easton Schirra for Studio64, and Josh Heller. And to all our family and friends especially Ethan Roman, Mary Killmond, Virginia Dooley, Rosemary Fogg, Jack Fogg, Ed Killmond, Teresa Killmond, Kathleen Driscoll, Danielle Roman, Jan Roman, and Hal Roman for being an outstanding sounding board. Thank you all for helping us get *Time of the Twins* out to the world!

ABOUT THE AUTHORS

Kendall Jenner is one of the world's top ranked supermodels. Kendall is a popular television personality, starring with her family on *Keeping Up with the Kardashians*, which is seen in over 160 countries. With a combined social media following of over 100 million users, Kendall is the most-followed model in the world. Kendall is a cowriter of *Rebels: City of Indra* and lives in Los Angeles.

Kylie Jenner is a successful entrepreneur and creator of the cosmetics brand and online phenomenon Kylie Cosmetics. Kylie is a popular television personality, starring with her family on *Keeping Up with the Kardashians*, and is one of the world's most-followed people on social media with a combined fan base of over 100 million users. Kylie is a cowriter of *Rebels: City of Indra* and lives in Los Angeles.

Elizabeth Killmond-Roman is a cowriter of *Rebels: City of Indra* and is Creative Director for Kendall and Kylie Jenner. She lives in Los Angeles with her husband and their son.

Katherine Killmond studied film and television production at Loyola Marymount University and is an award-winning television editor. She lives in Los Angeles with her husband and two children.